Yesterdays

A Collection of
Short Stories

J. Robert Whittle
and Joyce Sandilands

By J. Robert Whittle
and Joyce Sandilands

Whispers Across Time [1]
Race For a Treasure
Yesterdays - A Collection of Short Stories

The Lizzie Series by J. Robert Whittle
Lizzie: Lethal Innocence [2]
Lizzie Lethal Innocence - *Audio Book (CD, MP3)*
Narrated by J. Robert Whittle
Lizzie's Secret Angels
Streets of Hope
Lizzie's Legacy

Victoria Chronicles by J. Robert Whittle
Bound by Loyalty [2][3]
Loyalty's Reward [2][3]
Loyalty's Haven [1][3]

Laughing Through Life: Tales of a Yorkshireman (CD)
Autobiographical - *Narrated by* J. Robert Whittle

Moonbeam Series
Leprechaun Magic
by J Robert Whittle and Joyce Sandilands
Leprechaun Magic - *Audio Book (CD)*
Narrated by Joyce Sandilands

3 On A Moonbeam
by Joyce Sandilands
3 On A Moonbeam - *Audio Book (CD)*
Narrated by Joyce Sandilands

[1] Independent Publisher Gold Medal
[2] Canadian Bestseller
[3] Paperback and Hardcover Editions

Yesterdays

A Collection of
Short Stories

J. Robert Whittle
and Joyce Sandilands

To purchase any of the authors' books, contact them directly or through:

Whitlands Publishing Ltd.
4444 Tremblay Drive
Victoria, BC Canada V8N 4W5
Tel: 250-477-0192
www.jrobertwhittle.com
whitlands@shaw.ca

Cover photograph © 2002 Joyce Sandilands
Cover design, text and layout by Jim Bisakowski, Desktop Publishing
Illustrations by Simone Padur
Back cover photo by Ocean Photography

Library and Archives Canada Cataloguing in Publication

Whittle, J. Robert (John Robert), 1933-
        Yesterdays : a collection of short stories / J. Robert
Whittle, Joyce Sandilands.

 ISBN 978-0-9809834-1-8

I. Sandilands, Joyce, 1945- II. Title.

PS8595.H4985Y47 2010   C813'.54   C2010-900743-3

Printed in Canada on environmentally friendly paper by Friesens, Altona, MB

To our amazing fans
who make this a delightful adventure.

Acknowledgements

What can we say that hasn't been said innumerable times over the past 12 years, and the past 9 novels, without you this would not have been possible.

Another year has come and gone and we love seeing you all pass by and wave to us at our displays at summer markets and Christmas Shows, and especially at Bastion Square where Robert has spent almost half of his life for the past nine years!

We think you're going to enjoy this change of genre as Joyce has said for a long time that we had enough selection to produce a book of short stories and this is certainly a diverse collection.

Many of you have been asking for Robert to write his autobiography, well here you have some of it. The biographical stories are all completely true and give an interesting picture of rural Yorkshire life some 70 years ago. Alternatively, *Introduction to Reality* will give you a taste of his experience as a mining engineer, something many of you have been curious about. If you like these stories and, you enjoy hearing his unique voice, you will find many more autobiographical stories on Robert's CD, *Laughing Through Life*.

On the other hand, the Janion stories began as a diversion for Robert many years ago and we liked the concept so much, he often found himself adding to them. Our first western—A Debt to Pay—is another change of genre. Knowing Robert is an old cowboy fan, and once a rider and a horse trainer from as far back as his Yorkshire days, it's not surprising that he rose to the challenge when a reader dared him to write a western. It was such fun recreating some of that old western atmosphere and cowboy jargon. In others, you'll see his different interests and always his love of history. We hope you enjoy the mixture and I'm sure you'll be as eager as always to tell us how much you approve!

This year, in addition to the usual accolades given to our team—Jim Bisakowski (cover design), Deborah Wright (proofreading), Tara Poilievre (Joyce's Office Assistant), Friesen's Printing, and the many friends and readers who support us in so many ways—we also thank a returning Simone Padur, our illustrator on *3 On A Moonbeam*.

We'd also like to give a special 'thank you' to the local area bookstores and shops who continue to carry our books, and especially ... Bolen Books, Munro's Books, Tanner's Books and Falconer Bookstore (Nanaimo). These stores have been there for us since our first book in 1998 and we are very grateful that you've hung in with us. We try to send them as much business as possible but limited space prevents them from keeping a complete and large selection of our books. Don't forget you can always ask them to order what they are missing or you can contact us directly (see below).

Please note that we have been further simplifying our websites, blogs and email addresses. This is important to note as some of our old contact information is no longer in existence. Always check a more recent book or bookmark, phone us, or simply put one of our names or book titles in Google and you'll find us very easily. If you write to us, Joyce tries to reply within 48 hours. If you don't hear from us quickly, we may not have received it.

So, this brings us to the beginning of 2010, a new decade and an exciting new year for us. Please continue to tell us your thoughts on our books; it keeps us on our toes and helps us to decide what to bring you next time.

And always, thank you for spreading the word about our books, people-power is amazing … you are the best!

Kindest regards,

J. Robert Whittle and Joyce Sandilands
whitlands@shaw.ca
250-477-0192 PST (Victoria, BC)
www.jrobertwhittle.com

TABLE OF CONTENTS

ENVIRONMENTAL BENEFITS STATEMENT

Whitlands Publishing saved the following resources by printing the pages of this book on chlorine free paper made with 100% post-consumer waste.

TREES	WATER	SOLID WASTE	GREENHOUSE GASES
16	**7,547**	**458**	**1,567**
FULLY GROWN	GALLONS	POUNDS	POUNDS

Calculations based on research by Environmental Defense and the Paper Task Force. Manufactured at Friesens Corporation

Part 1: Bobby's Story

Bless your heart—I wish the cat had it! ~ Bobby's granddad

Rubber Leg Disease

Being a man of his time, my grandfather was a heavy drinker as were most men in our village. The pub was the local social club's meeting place, always the centre of any community activities. Inside its friendly walls, property deals were made, stock changed hands, and many a husband and wife fought wild battles over the demon drink.

From being a small boy and granddad's constant companion, I had often frequented those places. With his high-stepping pony and shiny buggy, we would meander through the lanes, always calling at some ale house for refreshment.

Known far and wide, publicans got to know granddad's order off by heart. "Pop for the lad, mild for me pony and bitter for me," he would say as we entered.

We could hear the pony stamping impatiently as it waited for its beer. I think on reflection the pony was an alcoholic too; they made a great pair though the pony never became drunk.

Two pints of mild ale in a leather bucket were the pony's limit. The bucket hung beneath the shafts was standard equipment and part of my job was to stand and watch until it drank the last drop, while granddad went inside.

I would wander through the farmyard attached to every country pub, checking the sheep, pigs and chickens, or playing with the landlord's children as I waited for the call that granddad was ready to go.

As he wobbled outside grasping my tiny arm, he'd grin foolishly at me and say, "Ah think 'av got the rubber leg disease again lad."

As I helped him into the buggy, his eyes would begin to droop and soon he would slip onto the floor snoring loudly. There was no panic; the pony knew its way home and I was in charge. I would take care of him.

Nearing home, I would try to stir granddad into life. Jumping on him sometimes had the desired effect. Other times, I would pull on his nose or tweak his cheeks in desperation, knowing my eagle-eyed grandmother would be watching for us and her temper would be boiling over.

Sometimes, if he was awake, he'd tell me to throw his cap into the house ahead of us, warning ... "If your grandmother throws it back, we're not welcome!"

I tried my best to protect him from the harsh ranting, standing between the brush my granny swung impatiently, and my pal.

"Don't hurt him!" I would yell. "He's just tired out."

Once when my mum was there, she scooped me up into her arms and whispered, "It's all right love, we won't hurt him; we love him too."

It's grand to see the back of yer lad! ~ Bobby's granddad

First Day of School

It was the first day of school for the small boy who stood by the farm gate, his eyes pleading with the mother he loved so dearly, as she reluctantly pushed him away toward the village school. He longed to feel the big calloused hand of his granddad, a hand he'd never been denied before. Peeking through the farm gate at the old man shuffling despondently across the yard to lean on a gate post, the boy had no way of knowing that tears were splashing on the old man's shirt front.

Kicking rocks as he walked down the lane, the curly-haired youngster felt betrayed. School! Why did he need school? At five-years-of-age, and smart as a whip, he could read and write his name, and numbers were no problem at all. And, anyway, who needed school when his granddad knew everything.

The schoolmaster believed in a harsh discipline. Scaring the youngsters into terrified submission was his favourite pastime. He stood for no nonsense and was eager to show it to this bright-eyed little cherub. Alas, this man was in for the surprise of his life. He was about to meet the type of rambunctious courage only small boys with a wily old grandfather would attempt.

Moustache bristling, he bent over to stare the boy in the eye.

"Lad!" he hissed fiercely, expecting young Bobby to start quaking in fear. "If you're the slightest bit noisy or naughty, I shall beat you to within an inch of your life."

Then it happened … as if in slow motion.

The cherub's eyes glinted with fire. In his mind, he heard his granddad's words. "Don't ever be bullied son, a bully never expects his victim to fight."

The boy swung his lunch box … hard.

2

Crack! The big red nose on the schoolmaster's face got even redder when the lunch box came in contact with it, sitting him down with a bang onto the floor of the schoolroom.

As the class gasped in surprise, Bobby ran for the door and out across the schoolyard. Looking back, as he raced down the fields for home, he realized the schoolmaster was in hot pursuit.

It was an uneven race and the lad beat him easily.

Bobby's grandfather and mother met him as he tore into the farmyard. Here, the lad found sanctuary and protection in the giant arms of the old man, but the schoolmaster raced in after him.

"Give that boy to me. I'll deal with him!" he snapped, holding a bloodied handkerchief to his nose as he reached for the lad.

"Now just you wait a minute," his mother said softly, trying to hide her smile as she watched the blood trickle from the intruder's red nose and into his moustache. "What have you done to our Bobby?" she asked, now glaring at the schoolmaster.

"Done to him? He burst my nose, the brat!" the man bawled reaching for the boy.

"Oh no, you don't," granddad growled. "You won't lay a finger on this lad."

"Tell me sir," mother asked, smiling disarmingly, "what caused this upset?"

"I was only giving him a lecture on behaviour, scaring him a little. It's the way I deal with all new starters."

"Damnit man, you were being nasty without reason, admit it," granddad growled. "Well, you picked on the wrong lad, didn't you? This little man don't scare too easy, does he? Now be off with you!"

The old man's arms tightened protectively around the boy as he glowered at the deflated schoolmaster who turned reluctantly and walked away.

So ended the cherub's first day at school.

You're as welcome as the flowers in May! ~ Bobby's granddad

The Race

Granddad was a great horseman and always ran his trotting horse in the Sunday morning village races. These were a local affair where wagers were made between the valley farmers. Standard equipment was a flat, shandy cart with a high seat for two and six-year-old Bobby always rode right beside him strapped into the seat from where he could yell encouragement at both horse and driver. There were even times when his grandfather let him drive, or hold the reins.

Bobby's dad was the person who made the wagers, after a long conference with grandfather, of course, and rarely did they lose a bet.

This week, the two men had been offered a race on a road that had a big hill, against a horse that loved hills. The old man's horse could run like the wind on level ground but was lazy and refused to go if it came to a hill.

Now, this was a well-known fact amongst the farmers and, despite this, Bobby's dad still made several large wagers that granddad's horse could beat the local champion. So, the money was laid and the farmers were chuckling that they were on a winner. Would this Sunday be any different?

Nobody noticed that over the wall next to the starting position lived Farmer Briggs who, as usual, was boiling potatoes to feed his pigs. Just before the race started, Bobby's dad came over to the shandy and handed Bobby his folded cap.

"Hold that tight lad, until your granddad needs it," he muttered, stepping away as the flag dropped.

The horses were off.

Bobby's granddad was a tremendously crafty old man who had already been responsible for teaching the young lad many simple things that gave him an advantage over the other lads of his age. Most of all, he taught him to do what he was told without question. The questions could come later when they were alone, if there were any.

When his dad handed him the cap, young Bobby felt some warmth radiating from it but was so busy yelling encouragement at the horse, he didn't give it a second thought. His grandfather was grinning from ear to ear as the horse galloped on wildly, pulling slightly ahead of his opponent as the big hills drew closer and closer.

Just before the first rise in the ground, the old man called over to his grandson, "Open the cap lad!"

4

Granddad's big fist grabbed the still-hot potato and placed it quickly under the horse's tail. Down came the tail and on went the acceleration! They went so fast they left the other horse like it was standing still.

That was a lesson in craft that Bobby never forgot.

Luck is a matter of preparation meeting opportunity. ~ Bobby's granddad

The Jam Jar

In 1940, war was raging throughout Europe as well as in England, and rationing was a fact of life. For Bobby, an astute eight-year-old business kid, it spelt opportunity ... opportunity to increase his growing fortune. Rationed to two ounces of candy a week, each child would closely guard his own small bag of goodies, usually eating it long before the week was up. Three pennies would buy a whole week's ration at the local store.

Bobby's plan was simple and gained his granddad's immediate approval. He asked his mother to buy him candies that were wrapped from now on. When they came, he hid them in his drawer. Then, by mid-week, he would take them to school and sell them to his eager friends for much more than their original value. He was always careful to put the money away in his private bank—the row of jam jars lining the shelf in his bedroom.

No one except his grandfather knew just how much money this small boy was amassing. Occasionally, the old man would even change the small coins for silver, or pound notes, leaving more room in the jars.

Bobby's skill, at recognizing an opportunity to make a penny or two, was growing in leaps and bounds. Thanks to his granddad, he quickly learned that beer and pop bottles, as well as empty jam jars, all had a value no matter how small it was. As he got older, he often remembered his granddad's words—"It's pennies that makes pounds lad, and every little bit helps."

You can buy flattery, but you have to earn respect. ~ Bobby's granddad

The Bicycle Ride

Every Saturday morning Bobby and his dad, a small moorland farmer, took their bicycles and travelled to the local feed merchants. They rode down the lanes, walked up big Botany Hill, and then rode again on the flatland to the store. This part of Yorkshire was a windy place with plenty of rain, so it was quite natural for them to wear raincoats and caps for this weekly trek.

One particularly memorable trip unfolded as they finished their shopping and turned toward home. Heading down Botany Hill, George, Bobby's dad, noticed that even though his son had his head down to cut the wind resistance, his coat-tails were flying, and he was using his boot sole on the front wheel as a brake. Arriving home, he gave the lad an ultimatum.

"Better have some brakes on that bike next Saturday lad, or you will be in big trouble, believe me."

"Yes dad," the boy answered obligingly.

Well, the next week passed like all the others. Bobby tried his best to please, but didn't get too upset when his dad blew his stack. The lad was inventive, had an excuse for everything and could get under his father's skin in no time flat. It was a good job the kid moved fast or he would have been permanently bruised. Initiative was something Bobby had plenty of.

"Have you got some brakes on that bike lad?"

"Yes dad!" Bobby yelled back, as his father began to move even faster.

"Where did you get them from?" his father yelled.

"From your bike!" screamed Bobby at his fast-disappearing father.

As he careened down Botany Hill, George did not at first notice the horse and cart approaching the bottom of the hill, coming directly into his path. When they collided there was an ominous dull thud as bicycle and man separated.

Fortunately, the cart carried a full load of hay, and he was not seriously hurt, but his bicycle needed far more attention than new brakes!

Needless to say, the kid wore his bruises proudly and for a while his mother couldn't hold back her laughter each time she thought about the near tragic incident.

You're like a bucket without a handle lad—next door to useless!
~ Bobby's granddad

Introduction to Reality

Darkness was falling in the colliery yard as he made his way from the shaft cage to the lamp room, a smile of tired satisfaction playing around his coal-dust-blackened lips. It had been a long day. He had stayed late to complete a job and was now looking forward to a hot shower.

"Bobby, I want to see you in my office as soon as you're washed," a familiar voice cracked from out of the shadows.

Grinning to himself, he nodded silently, slipping his lamp battery from his belt as he walked on.

"Have ya seen yer Uncle Arnold lad?" the lampman spluttered through his chew of tobacco.

"No, but I heard him, what's he want?"

"How the hell would I know, he's been pacing up and down the yard for the last two hours. You must have done something!"

"He can go to hell for all I care," Bob said tiredly.

Shaking his head, lampman Fred Ellis glanced up from his workbench as the young miner made for the showers. He had known the lad since the day he was born. He also knew the man he called Uncle Arnold was really his godfather, manager and member of the executive council of the government coal board. Their relationship was abrasive at best and downright violent in an argument. No man would dare venture to interfere when a difference of opinion was under discussion between those two. It was a strange sort of love-hate relationship yet, when apart, they would defend each other to the death.

Recently built mine head showers made washing easy and the young man was soon standing at the canteen counter ordering tea and cookies, water still dripping from the curl on his forehead.

"Your Uncle Arnold was looking for you son," the lady attendant warned, trying to look serious as she smiled at the handsome young man.

"I know."

Sitting down at a table, he wondered why his godfather was looking for him. If it was so important, why hadn't he told him when he saw him? *It's probably another blasting for some perceived misdemeanor*, he thought.

Fifteen minutes later, as he walked toward the manager's office, he saw the glow of a cigarette outside the dark doorway.

"What are you doing stood out here," Bob asked, "are you trying to get pneumonia?"

"I told you I wanted to see you, but you took your own damned sweet time coming."

"You never said it was urgent."

"They want you at a meeting tomorrow, so come to work at nine in a suit."

"Who's they and what the hell have you volunteered me for this time?"

"That's an order lad and, just for once, do as you're told," the older man grunted as he stormed off toward his car.

Arnold Piece was a distant relative of Bob's father as well as the young man's godfather, and he had seen the potential in the boy when he was still a schoolboy. Knowing he would never be allowed to go to grammar school due to family finances, Arnold had arranged for him to work at the mine. Registering him in a free education course at the mining college—three days a week at work and two days at college for the first year, meant lots of work and study but, as expected, the boy thrived on the work.

He had left school as a 14-year-old and, being a farmer's son, had already worked every day of his young life. Not yet full grown, with a mop of curly hair and a penchant for laughter, he had a deceivingly innocent look in his twinkling hazel-coloured eyes. Those who knew him, however, recognized that these eyes hid a scheming, brilliant mind. Coupled with a pair of fists that could strike like lightning when the need arose, he was a man you didn't want to aggravate.

His manners were impeccable and his smile disarming. He quickly became a firm favourite with everyone who met him, though his godfather and mentor could always find something to grumble about.

Older workers often told him that when his godfather reprimanded him severely in public it would scare the other young men at the mine.

"If he'll shout and yell at you lad, his own godson, then what would he do to them?" It worked and no one stepped out of line when Arnold was around.

This was the foundation of their animosity and, as the years went by, other things were added to the list—like every dirty job imaginable—under the guise of learning each facet of the mining industry. After Bob qualified as a mining engineer, the torment still didn't stop—there was always more to learn and experience in the deep, dark bowels of a coal mine. It was time, experience and frustration that made him the complete mining man. He learned well, understanding the heart and soul of that violent underground world and soon had the reputation of being the best.

He was 24-years-old that fateful day he sauntered into the mine offices, a man with a purpose. The clock on the office wall showed 8:55. There were five minutes to spare before he was expected in the boardroom. It was just enough time to draw a bright red blush of colour to the attractive receptionist's face when he smiled his boyish smile and, with that devilish twinkle in his eye, whispered 'you're so beautiful' and carried on his way.

Moving on quickly as the clock stuck the hour, he stepped into the room, punctual to the minute. Three faces followed his progress to the table; these were the men who controlled the mining industry, powerful men who made the important decisions.

"Sit down son," the chairman invited him with a smile. "Have you been told why you're here?"

"No sir."

"Then let me explain. We are here to offer you a chance to lead a first response team; we think you're the right man for the job."

"And just what would you expect from me?" Bob asked, flashing his ever-ready smile. "Do you have a contract already written?"

"Yes, we have a provisional contract written, it's not the final word though. We expect you'll want a few changes."

"Do you want me to take it home and read this lot?" Bob chuckled as he picked up the documents pushed across the table toward him.

"No son," his godfather replied, frowning, "we want a decision now, today."

"Then why don't you give me a quick synopsis, you know what it says in here," he put the papers back down on the table.

"Basically you'll lead a team of experts. It could be here in England or anywhere in the world where they need you. It won't always be rescue work, but it'll always be a problem or dangerous."

A cold thrill ran through Bob's brain, knowing the uncertain challenges he would be called on to face. They were asking him to risk his life and take the responsibility for others. His decisions could mean life or death for his team or the men needing their rescue effort. Several quick questions sprang into his mind.

"I can pick my own men?"

"Yes."

"We all get a salary that reflects the job."

"Say yes and we'll start negotiating right now."

"I have complete control of the job site?"

"Yes."

"Then I'll do it. I can give you a list of the men I want in about five minutes, and the salary will be …?"

"Hold it lad," Arnold interrupted with a frown. "Before you start talking about money, hadn't you better take a look at what we've offered?"

"Why don't you tell me?"

"Read it, it's on Page 5."

"It's very generous Bob," the third man at the table stated coldly with a hint of disapproval in his voice.

Bob quickly found the relevant page and quietly studied the numbers for a moment, frowning at the paper though chuckling inwardly when he realized it was more than he was going to ask for. "It's not enough for what you want and there's no mention of a bonus," he muttered without lifting his eyes from the papers.

"Don't get greedy lad, we're offering you twice as much as an area manager, and you're not the only one who is being considered."

A smile played around Bob's lips as he lifted his gaze to focus his twinkling eyes on the speaker. Slowly straightening the papers before him, he rose purposefully from his chair, "Then go talk to them, because my life ain't on sale for peanuts!"

"Damn ya, sit down!" his godfather's voice thundered through the room. "And you Mr. Emery," he addressed the third official, "keep your blasted opinions to yourself. He's the one we need, and I know better than anyone what he's capable of. I arranged every phase of his training."

"You're also his godfather."

10

Leaping to his feet, his chair went tumbling noisily to the floor. Arnold Peace was obviously angry now. The thinly veiled accusation that he was unjustly favouring his godson was like waving a red cape at a bull and Bob sat back down to enjoy the continuing confrontation. Office staff outside the room chuckled as the noise reverberated through to them. Typewriters stopped their rhythmic chatter as everyone listened to the thundering row.

"He's done it again," an old gentleman clerk laughed. "Bob's got them fighting among themselves. It's like lighting a fuse when those two get together."

"It's not Bob who Mr. Peace is shouting at," a typist whispered nervously, "it's Mr. Emery."

"I know lass, but you can bet yer last penny it's Bob that caused it. You watch, he'll come out of there all smiles and with a nice contract tucked in his pocket. He'll get everything he wants now that he's got them upset with each other!"

Inside the room, Bob struggled to control his urge to laugh, as the chairman banged the table in an effort to control the men. Shaking his head as the noise subsided, he watched calmly as Arnold picked up his overturned chair, irritably banging it on the floor before setting it back down.

"Can we get on with it now, gentlemen?" the chairman snapped sarcastically. "Bob, we want you to lead the team. Yes, you can pick your own men subject to our approval, and yes, there will be a generous guaranteed fixed salary which will be paid irrespective of whether you're working or not. There will be times when someone gets hurt, it's a very dangerous job son, and we all understand that. In any event, your salary will still be paid in full. Bonus within reason we'll consider, especially if it's outside your normal duties. Now would you like me to assign a lawyer to talk to you?"

"Yes sir, and when am I supposed to start this job?"

"You're already doing it. We transferred all your papers last Friday. One of the girls will show you your office and any messages will be left there. Now, you'd better get us a list of those men you want."

Quickly writing four names on a sheet of paper, Bob slid it in front of his godfather. Eyebrows raised, the fierce old man looked it over and nodded his approval, signing his name across the bottom before passing it to the chairman.

The chairman smiled as he also signed the paper, stating, "Oh, I think we forgot to mention, you'll be on call 24 hours a day, 7 days a week, and we may send you abroad if the need arises. Right son, I think

11

that concludes our business. You'd better start contacting your men and the chief safety officer wants to talk to you."

Rising at the gentle dismissal, Bob brushed the stray curl that had flopped down over his eye back into place and smiled boyishly at his godfather.

The older man looked up at him and whispered emotionally, "Be careful son."

Bob winked and walked toward the door. Stepping out of the boardroom, he noticed the dead silence in the outer office and grinned at the expectant faces.

"All right you lot, back to work now, they didn't hang me yet!"

"I'll show you your office if you like," a senior lady clerk murmured.

"Only if you turn the light off Ann!" Bob replied with a chuckle. "I'm feeling quite amorous."

"Will you behave yourself," she snapped, "and act like a man with responsibility now you've accepted this new job."

"How'd ya know I've accepted?" he asked.

"Oh everybody knows, it went through the offices like wildfire this morning. I think Janice told me. She was very upset; she said you were trying to kill yourself."

"But I hadn't taken the job yet. I wasn't quite sure what they wanted me for until I came here this morning."

"Well everybody else knew," she stressed adamantly. "The production manager said they were going to offer you the moon to coax you to take the job. He said you were the most competent miner that had ever been born."

"How the hell would he know? He's never been down a mine."

Over the next few days, Bob contacted the men he wanted, explaining why he needed them and what the job would entail. Agreement was quickly reached with each one of them and transfers implemented. During the next few months, he met the doctor, who was also going to be part of the team—a soft-looking 28-year-old who had volunteered for the job.

"Have you ever been down a mine?" Bob asked.

"Yes, they gave me a tour last week to the bottom of a mine shaft."

"Are you sure you want to go with us; this ain't no tour. When we go in, it'll scare the hell out of you!"

"They told me at the meeting it would be hard. How old are you? I thought you would be much older."

"I'm 24 and, if you come with us, you'll do exactly what I tell you. We'll train you to go where a rat wouldn't dare venture, and you'd better learn to keep your questions until later."

"They said you were hard, but you're asking for blind obedience and that doesn't sit well with me."

"There'll be times mister, when your life will depend on how quick you do what you're told and, if you don't like it, the door is right behind you. Go now and there won't be any hard feelings, but if you go with us and cause me a problem, I'll personally break your bloody neck!"

A touch of colour rose in Dr. David John's face, and he realized they were no longer alone. Glancing over his shoulder, he watched Joe Dyson step into the office and stand with his back to the door grinning impishly. Having recovered from Bob's harsh words, the doctor turned back to face the young, curly-headed man across the desk.

"Are you always so rude?" he asked.

"Always," the man at the door laughed, "and sometimes he's worse!"

"Shut up, Joe," Bob snapped. "I'm trying to tell this man it won't be no walk in the park where we're going, and he needs to be prepared to handle it."

The phone rang and Bob's hand flashed out to lift the receiver. His expression changed to one of intense concentration as he first listened, then muttered, "We're coming."

"Get the boys Joe, there's been a coal face collapse at Moorside Colliery. Two men are buried at the tail end."

Joe sprang into action, disappearing at a run without offering a single comment.

"Can I come too?" Dr. John asked.

Bob nodded and picked up the phone again dialing a number.

"I want a perimeter gas check, guards posted, and we'll be there within the hour," he snapped.

David John felt a thrill of excitement run through his body. He could feel the powerful surge of energy from the man behind the desk. This young man they called Bob had instantly assessed the situation, cracking his orders out with a confident ring in his voice. He was in charge and David had no doubt of that. Going outside, the team piled into a dark blue van and changed into dusty work clothes as they tore through the country roads. Staring in wonder out of the window, David watched as police cars blocked intersections giving them unrestricted access to the mine. Pulse racing, the doctor stood beside a group of men as they watched the shaft cage disappear with a whooshing sound. Bob and his men were inside. As it shot down into the bowels of the earth a man in a white hard hat came toward him.

"Who are you?" the official asked with a scowl.

"Dr. John, I came with the rescue team."

"Then find a hard hat, this is a restricted area!"

It was almost four hours before word came to the waiting officials that the rescue had been successful and men were returning to the surface. He saw the stretchers arrive and the bloody, bandaged miners being whisked away in the waiting ambulance. David gasped at the scene as the rescue team stepped out of the mine cage and that curly-headed young man, who had been so rude to him, turned to face the waiting officials. Blackened all over by coal dust, Bob's shirt was stained red with blood as it hung in shreds on his slim, muscular frame. He slipped off his belt and lamp, handing them to waiting hands.

"Keep the air flow at maximum and nobody goes in there until I come back tomorrow," he yelled at the jostling officials before hurrying away.

Their eyes met through the crowd—David saw the flashing smile as he turned to go—then felt a hand on his arm and the voice of Arnold Piece.

"He's gone to the bathhouse lad, why don't you go talk to him?" he murmured.

"Won't he be busy?" the doctor asked.

"Yes, they'll be getting washed, then a doctor will need to stitch them up and there's no guarantee he'll talk to ya, but you could try if you still want to work with them."

David John walked slowly toward the bathhouse, unsure of his feelings for the job he'd been so eager to volunteer for. Hesitating, as he stepped through the bathhouse door, he heard noisy laughter coming from the shower stalls. Turning to look into the first aid room, he watched for a moment as a doctor and nurse readied their medical equipment, then he walked on through the steamy atmosphere.

Looking into the open cubicles of the shower stalls as he walked by, he gasped when he saw the naked bodies of the team—blood and coal dust running down their backs. He moved quickly back to the first aid room before they saw him, shaking his head in shocked wonder. He now understood a little better that these men were a special breed of miner and, the realization hit him, it was going to take a super-human effort to become part of this team.

Minutes later, one by one the team walked into the first aid room wrapped in their blood-stained towels and laughing at stupid comments

14

being passed as their torn flesh was stitched and repaired. His eyes met those of the curly-headed one who had waited until the last.

"Still want to come with us Doc?" Bob asked with a grin, sliding onto the table and mischievously reaching out a bleeding hand to pat the nurse on the rear end.

Later, while riding back to their home base, David listened to the men's conversation. Surprisingly, not one word was spoken of the job they had just risked their lives to do. No moans or gripes passed their lips. The worst thing he heard was from the Irishman, Michael, who cursed a broken shoelace.

Upon arrival, the men quickly dispersed and Dr. John followed Bob across the yard to his office. Lights were flicked on as he moved down the dark corridor until they found the right door. Slipping into the chair behind his desk, Bob glanced up with that disarming, boyish grin that gave the impression he was little more than a teenager.

"Well, what do you think Doc?" he asked.

It was quite a few years later when Dr. John wrote his observations of the rescue team for a medical journal. Stressing the danger faced by the team at every call and, the dynamic leadership and courage of the curly-headed young man who led them, he proudly proclaimed he was a fully fledged member of the team.

Everything looks impossible to those who never try anything.
~ Bobby's granddad

Part 2: A Bit of History

Janion Ring: Meeting Grandfather

Twelve-year-old cousins David Web and Nathan Dawes were visiting Victoria, BC, from their home in Port Angeles in the summer of 2002. They had made many trips to this Vancouver Island city, so they were quite familiar with the place, especially liking the harbour area with all its different boats.

As boys often do, to kill time while they waited for the tourist train that would take them to the top of Malahat Mountain, unbeknownst to their mothers, they had gone off exploring. They ran across the track to the back of the nearby Janion Hotel, a derelict building for many years, sitting boarded up on the waterfront next to the train station. Here they had virtually stumbled upon the ring in the dirt. Thin with age, the dirty

15

circle of gold had no doubt been lost by its owner but would provide a magical adventure beyond imagination for these unsuspecting boys.

Sunlight, shining on the tiny object disturbed from the soil by Nathan's running feet, drew David's eyes like a magnet. Hurrying, he scooped the ring into his pocket, urged on by the incoming train. Blowing its whistle as if to warn them, it slowed as it crossed the Johnson Street Bridge, and then with brakes screeching like alley cats, it slipped into the station.

Their mothers' urgent calls brought the boys racing back, panting for breath. "Where have you two been?" Nathan's mother demanded, pushing them ahead of her onto the train. "We were getting worried."

"We were treasure hunting by that old building." David pointed through the train window at the old hotel's brick wall. "We found something ... a ring. See!" Searching in his pocket amongst some candies, he located the ring and dropped it into his mother's outstretched hand.

"Brass, not worth a dime," Mary Web chuckled, handing the dirty little object to her sister Grace, Nathan's mother.

"It's very dirty," Nathan's mother commented, making a face. "If you're going to keep it, then at least wash it before you handle it."

Eyes sparkling with excitement, the boys went to find a washroom while the great iron monster clanked and jerked into motion.

"And don't you boys get out of our sight!" Mary called after them.

"It's gold, I know it is," David whispered over his shoulder to his cousin.

Finding the washroom at the end of their car, they ran water from an antiquated tap, watching in silent fascination as the dirt peeled off. When finished, they dried their hands and the ring on paper towels.

"Use your shirt," Nathan urged his cousin. "That will shine it up."

"Come on lads, get out of there!" an old gentleman coaxed from the doorway. "It's my turn."

"Sorry sir," they mumbled, quickly leaving the tiny washroom.

The boys found a pair of empty seats beside an open window and sat down, allowing the cool breeze to wash over them. The train tooted as it passed through Esquimalt with its unused station and tiny old houses lining the track. Brief flashes of water and interesting views could be seen as the swaying carriage moved along, but the boys were not paying attention to any of it.

"Have you finished with it yet? Let me see!" Nathan demanded nudging David.

"No!" David insisted, continuing to stare at the ring as he polished it on his shirttail. "Be careful, you'll make me drop it."

"Well, hurry up then, it doesn't take all day to clean a little ring!"

David's eyes and attention were focused squarely on the ring as it slowly gained lustre between his fingers.

Their mothers chatted as they relaxed and enjoyed the conductor's commentary giving details of landmarks and points of interest as they rattled on through the western communities of Colwood and Langford. Seeing where the boys had sat down, they seemed content in the knowledge that their boys were quiet and trapped within the confines of the train where they couldn't get into any mischief.

"Let me rub it for a while," Nathan insisted, peering over his cousin's shoulder ... and that was when it happened.

A tingle ran through David's hand and he expelled his breath as the ring began to move, turning in his fingers and shining even brighter.

"Oh my gosh!" he whispered, alerting Nathan as he involuntarily loosened his grasp and they watched in disbelief as the ring floated away. Mouths open, they watched it float toward a diminutive, strangely-costumed lady standing in the aisle. She held out her hand and the ring slipped onto her finger.

"Who are you?" Nathan gasped, shrinking into his seat.

"Why bless you my boy," she said with a smile. "I'm the Janion Lady, a spirit from 1914. I grant wishes to those who find my ring."

"Y-you're a r-real g-ghost?" David slowly stammered, staring at her.

"Holy cow, she's a ghost," his cousin exclaimed.

"You need not be worried boys, I'll not harm you," the Janion Lady whispered. "Let me explain."

Gawking at her, they both realized she looked like the ladies in some of the movies their mothers watched—her long black dress was fashioned out of shiny fabric and lace, looking quite regal. High puffy sleeves narrowed to fit tightly on her arms and her greying hair was

17

swept into a bun on the top of her head. Beneath, shiny black pointed toes peeked out from under her dress.

"My name is Miss Dolly Walker," she explained, smiling. "I was once the Manager at the Janion Hotel. I knew everyone in town, I did, and they all called me 'The Janion Lady'!"

"You can't grant wishes," Nathan snickered. "That's fairy story stuff for kids."

"Yeah," David joined in, "if you're magic, make us invisible!"

Dolly smiled patiently, this was nothing new to her. Over the years finders of her ring had often been hard to convince especially as she had no power to grant riches or treasure. Her power had been limited to fun things and giving knowledge to inquisitive minds.

"It's done," she whispered, "but I must warn you … I can only stay with you for three days, then the ring disappears again. So use the time wisely boys. Now come, let's take a little walk through the carriage."

Moving slowly down the walkway, no one seemed to notice them. A small child ran up the isle, as if they weren't even there, passing clean through David.

"She's done it, we're invisible!" Nathan yelped excitedly. "This is great, let's find our moms."

Their mothers were sisters born in Everett and had always visited Victoria on their holidays. Now, living just across the strait in Port Angeles made it even easier, especially if they didn't want to bring a car which they had done this trip. Intensely interested in early Pacific Northwest history, they had formed a historic discussion group much like the one they had belonged to in Everett. They were at present studying prohibition using their three-day holiday to search for answers to some puzzling questions. Their 12-year-old sons, born within months of each other, were great pals and travelling companions who had an unquenchable thirst for adventure, historic or otherwise.

"This is really great," Mary murmured, watching the scenery pass by the window. "I hope the boys are enjoying it."

"We are," David shouted, frowning when his mother took no notice of him.

"She can't see or hear you deary," Dolly commented, "but you can see and hear them."

Nathan sat down beside his mother as the women continued to talk. There was no feeling of closeness, no warmth from her body and she was totally unaware of his presence. He reached for her arm but his fingers passed through her flesh as if she wasn't there. A soft whimper escaped his lips and dismay showed on his face, flinching when Dolly's cold fingers touched his own arm.

"You don't like being invisible do you?" she whispered. "Do you want to cancel your wish?"

"No, no," David exclaimed, "let's play a trick on them first." Glancing at the seat beside his mother, he saw her notebook lying open. "We'll write something in it and she won't know how it happened," David giggled. He reached for the book and surprised himself when he felt it in his fingers. "I thought I wouldn't be able to feel it," he commented.

"Quickly," Dolly urged, "hide it under your jacket, then it'll be invisible like you are."

"Get the pen Nathan," David told his cousin.

Running through the carriage and back to their seats, the boys soon realized the Janion ghost was still with them. David opened the book and read his mother's comments. She had written two questions. *What was the date of prohibition in Victoria?* and *How long did it last?*

"Cripes Nathan, I don't know the answer to these questions!"

"Let me see," Dolly asked, taking the book from David. "Oh that's easy, I was there," she chuckled. "Prohibition began October the 1st, 1917 and was repealled in 1921 by Premier John Oliver," she took the pen and began to write, glancing suspiciously at the ballpoint pen.

A lady passing in the aisle stopped to watch dumbfounded, as a pen floated through the air then wrote in what appeared to be a floating book.

"That's not possible!" she muttered. "That is, unless this train's haunted!" The thought of ghosts sent the lady scurrying on her way calling weakly for the conductor.

"What is it ma'am?" the conductor inquired as the invisible boys and the Janion ghost slipped by them.

"There's a ghost in that seat," she insisted weakly, pointing.

Overheard, their conversation sent a buzz of interest through the carriage as braver passengers pushed forward in an effort to see the apparition.

"And what was this ghost doing ma'am?" the conductor asked with a chuckle, "eating an ice cream?"

"Don't be ridiculous!" she snorted, her voice growing louder. "It was writing in a floating book."

"A floating book!" A whisper rippled through the carriage.

As the boys hurried back to where their mothers were sitting, more people got out of their seats and went to look. David managed to return the book to the seat beside his mother just as she heard the commotion and looked around for the boys who hurried back to their seats.

"Grace, I don't see the boys. I have a bad feeling that they're up to their tricks again."

"Oh no, cancel that wish!" David gasped. "Make us visible in our seats Miss Dolly or we'll be in big trouble."

In an instant the boys were back in their seats innocently looking out of the window. David held the ring in his hand as the trees of Goldstream Provincial Park flashed by.

Nathan whispered, "They've seen us!"

When the train arrived back in Victoria that afternoon, the boys pulled their mothers toward the old Store Street building.

"Come on, we'll show you the old hotel," they urged.

"Look, you can still see the name," Grace murmured, "but it's all boarded up, nobody's been in there for years."

"Hang on a minute," her sister chuckled. "It's a place of interest; I'd better make a note of it." Mary rummaged in her bag and took out her notebook and pen, turning to the page she'd been writing on. She blinked in surprise, staring at the page. "W-who wrote these answers to my questions?" she stammered, looking at her son. "This isn't your writing!"

"It wasn't me mom, honest, it wasn't me," David tried to assure her, making Mary even more suspicious.

Grace took a look at the book, reading the answers before speaking. "Well, it certainly sounds right."

"Yes, I'm sure she was right," Nathan interrupted, his eagerness to be helpful causing David to scowl at him. "Whoops!"

Mary looked from one boy to the other, making them squirm under her scrutiny. "I think it's time to go back to the hotel. We're going to get to the bottom of this before we do anything else."

They returned to their car and Grace groaned when she saw the parking ticket trapped under the wiper blade.

"Blast it, just what we need," she grumbled, angrily releasing the paper.

David's fingers felt the gold ring in his pocket. Trying not to be noticed, he rubbed the tiny trinket and under his breath made a wish.

"Please, Miss Dolly, can you fix Aunt Grace's ticket."

"Excuse me ladies!" A well-dressed man startled the women as he stopped beside them. "Are you visitors to our fair city?"

"Yes we are," Grace replied, frowning as she waved the parking ticket at the man, "and we've already received your official welcome!"

Smiling broadly, he asked. "Would you like me to take care of this for you?"

"Are you serious?" Mary laughed. "Who are you?"

"I certainly am serious. I'm Alan Lowe, the Mayor of Victoria," he chuckled, watching the look of surprise on their faces. "I would personally like to welcome you and show you how pleased we are that you visited us ... please allow me to deal with this inconvenience."

The Mayor's reputation for friendliness was legendary in Victoria—his oriental ancestors would be proud of his many achievements.

"Please," he insisted with a smile, reaching for the ticket.

Timidly, Grace placed the parking ticket in the Mayor's hand and, still smiling, he waved and walked away. She felt her sister's fingers on her arm.

"Was that really the mayor?"

"I think it must have been," Grace replied. "Now that's a story to tell the group."

"Thank you Miss Dolly," David muttered as Nathan's arm draped over his shoulder, forgetting his mother could hear a pin drop at forty paces.

"And just who is Miss Dolly, young man?" Mary asked.

Desperately trying to find a believable answer, David's fingers fiddled with the Janion ring in his pocket. *I wish me and Nathan were invisible*, he thought to himself, *then I wouldn't have to think up an answer*.

The women blinked as their sons vanished right before their eyes.

"Where have they gone?" Mary asked frantically.

"We're here mom," David shouted. "I'm standing right next to you."

"No need to shout David. Remember, they can't see or hear you," Dolly chuckled, materializing beside them. "Now what are you going to do?"

"I need some chalk so we can write a message on the sidewalk."

"No David," Nathan groaned, "we're in enough trouble already. Let's go back."

"Oh all right," David pouted, "but I wish Miss Dolly would come with us so she could meet them."

In the blink of an eye the two boys were back on the sidewalk of Store Street. Their mothers gasped, stepping back in surprise and then staring in disbelief.

"W-Who are you?" Mary stammered, looking at the strange lady standing beside David, at the same time, realizing that everything around them had suddenly changed. The noise level had also increased

21

substantially as an old-fashioned black steam engine rumbled by. The parking meters had disappeared as had their car.

"Hey, get outa the way!" a man yelled, interrupting their thoughts as he drove a wagon and two big horses out of the building beside them.

The women jumped back in surprise.

"What on earth is happening?" Grace sputtered, reaching for her son.

"Wow, this is great Miss Dolly!" David laughed.

"Mrs. Dawes, my name is Dolly Walker and you've now travelled back to my time in 1914. May I be presumptuous and call you Grace?" the ghost murmured, before turning to Mary. "I realize you are sisters and your name is Mary."

"This is ridiculous," Mary said hesitantly. "You're as real as I am but this can't be 1914 and how do you know us? What on earth is going on?"

"Let me assure you that this is indeed 1914 and your surroundings are very real deary," Dolly acknowledged. "Come, let's eat dinner at my hotel while you adjust to … the situation!"

"Let's do it mom," David pleaded. "It was Miss Dolly who wrote those answers in your book."

Mary's mind held back her eagerness to ask what he was talking about, shaking her head in confusion as the strange lady tapped her parasol on the uneven curb.

"Follow me," Dolly announced, "and please be careful of the train tracks."

"Look down at the street David," his cousin whispered. "It's made of blocks of wood!"

Hearing Nathan's comment, their mothers also looked down at the hard wooden blocks that made up the road's surface. But their attention was quickly turned to some approaching horses pulling a large dray, their steel-shod feet made a loud, but dull, clumping sound as they moved past. As they followed the Janion Lady, their gaze strayed to the harbour where several ships with tall masts unloaded cargo at the dockside.

As they entered the hotel, the women were immediately aware of an odd musty smell and asked Dolly what it was. She said one word, 'beer' as she led them past a group of rough sailor types who were calling back and forth to each other across the long, shiny mahogany bar. They went through a door and down a wide hallway to what appeared to be the dining room. Tables were set with white linen and silver cutlery. She indicated a table beside a window.

"Take a seat please. I'll join you in a moment." Dolly smiled before swishing away.

"Are we dreaming Mary?" Grace whispered looking all around, "or is this really happening?"

"I'm not sure of anything anymore," her sister replied as if in a daze.

Grace frowned, taking a seat which gave her an unobstructed view of the hotel dock and waterfront. They were barely aware of the boys chatter until Nathan exclaimed excitedly.

"Look, the Blue Bridge has changed."

"Yes, you're right dear," his mother replied. "It's quite a bit smaller now and made of wood. The new, colourful townhouses across the inlet have also vanished." The rocky headland was now littered with the shanty homes of natives and squatters. "It was pretty rough in 1914!"

Various shipyards, small by modern standards, stretched along the opposite shoreline and the boys gawked as they watched the activity.

Dolly returned in a few minutes and stopped to talk quietly to a waitress who was dressed in a black floor-length dress with a little white apron and a cute hat, before joining them.

"I've ordered roast beef dinners; I thought you would be hungry as you missed lunch," she announced with a smile. "Do you mind if I join you?" Watching the ladies nod their consent, she withdrew the chair at the end of the table and primly sat down. Mary's eyes followed every movement of the lady in the long black dress. She wasn't as old as she had initially guessed, noting her tightly strapped waistline and that her dark hair contained only a hint of grey.

"Please," Grace begged, "we need an explanation Miss Walker."

"That's easy deary," Dolly smiled as the waitress returned, setting two covered dishes in the middle of the table and giving them each a dinner plate. "First off, please call me Dolly. Back in 1914, I lost my favourite ring when I was boating on that fateful day. In my eagerness to catch it before it fell into the water, I too went over the side and drowned. Like a fool, I refused to go to heaven because I dearly wanted to find my ring. So the angels decided to make me immortal and left me here as a wish mistress."

The waitress interrupted by placing two more dishes on the table and removing the lids of the steaming food. The smells wafted around them causing the women to smile. Dolly indicated that they should begin.

Grace helped herself to potatoes and passed the dish to Mary. They both turned puzzled faces to Dolly.

"A wish mistress?" they asked in unison.

"Yes, I'm a spirit suspended in time searching for my ring. When somebody finds it, if they rub it, I can enter their world and grant their wishes."

"Like a genie in Aladdin's lamp."

"Not quite." Dolly took a bite of food and made them wait for her answer. "Angels have unlimited power, but I can only grant small wishes and give out information."

"But you made us invisible," David interrupted, talking with his mouth full and gaining a disapproving glance from his mother. He finished chewing and continued, "You wrote in mom's book too."

"Yes, I most certainly did. There's one other thing you should know about my ring," the Janion Lady added. "As I told you before boys, you may only have possession of it for three days, after that it disappears to a new hiding place near the hotel."

"And what happens to you then?" Mary asked.

"I wait," Dolly sighed. "It could be years before I'm freed again."

"You said this was your hotel," commented Grace.

"Well, it seems like it is. I was the Manager for many years."

Reaching for her notebook, Mary made a quick decision. In her heart, she felt sympathy for the ghost who had passed up the chance to be an angel in her quest to get her ring back.

"You could help us immensely by answering all our questions on Victoria's history," she said eagerly. "Would you be our guide tomorrow and show us the city ... how it used to be?"

"Yes, I can certainly do that," Dolly replied, "but your son found my ring and he must be the one who makes the wishes unless he orders me otherwise."

"That's okay mom; I'll wish for it for you," David said eagerly.

"Wait, wait," Grace interrupted. "You guys don't really believe all this do you?"

"Yes I do, so be quiet for a minute little sister," Mary stated, using a term she liked to use on her younger sister when she was about to take control of a situation. "So you can send us back to the year 2002 whenever David wishes?" Mary asked, watching the Janion Lady nod in agreement. "And then he can call you back whenever he wants in the next three days?"

"Yes, he's called me many times already so he knows the rules," Dolly assured her. "Don't forget, one day is almost over."

"Right, we'll pay the bill then and my son will wish that we're back at our car."

"There's no bill to pay," Dolly replied. "You're my guests."

The women got up and thanked Dolly then David broke into their conversation. "Thanks for dinner Miss Dolly. Is everyone ready?"

"Ready!" his mother replied as the boys moved closer to them.

24

"Then send us back to our car please Miss Dolly," he whispered.

In the blink of an eye they were standing by their car in Store Street. The meter was as it had been, but no ticket protruded from the wiper blade this time, and familiar modern day sounds filled their ears.

A sigh of relief escaped Grace's lips as she stared at the derelict Janion Hotel, flinching when she caught sight of Dolly standing nearby.

"We didn't dream it Mary," Grace stammered. "Sh-she's still here."

"You can go now," Mary ordered the ghost.

"No I can't deary, not until Master David tells me to go."

"You can go now and thank you Miss Dolly," the boy whispered.

"My pleasure David," she replied as she faded away.

Hardly a word passed between the two sisters as Mary drove away, turning up Fisgard Street in the busy late afternoon traffic. The boys commented on the many Chinese stores with their produce and other wares spilling out onto the sidewalk.

"Turn right onto Government at the fancy Chinese arch," Grace directed, "then first right again onto Pandora."

"Look," Nathan shouted, after a few minutes of driving, "we're back at the railway station!"

"It sure makes a big difference to the way we view things," said Mary as she watched a steady stream of traffic move across the Blue Bridge as people made their way to View Royal and Esquimalt.

"Left, turn left on Wharf Street and keep going," Grace continued, her finger following the city map on her knee. "There's the Empress, you need to turn right at the next corner."

"There's the Wax Museum mom!" shouted Nathan.

"Oh, there they are!" exclaimed Mary. "Huntingdon Manor and The Gatsby—this old house was once a mansion belonging …."

"What's the Gatsby mom?" David interrupted in a puzzled tone, staring at the well-kept character house but wondering what all the fuss was about.

"Does it have a ghost?" his cousin asked and David gave him a thumbs up.

"Don't you dare suggest that," his mother snapped. "I don't even feel comfortable with your Miss Dolly, let alone any other ghosts. The Gatsby was owned by the Pendray Family. He was quite a Victoria businessman, one of his businesses was a soap factory near here."

Once the car was parked safely and their suitcases unloaded, they checked in at the desk and were taken upstairs to a room overlooking the harbour. A connecting door led to a smaller room with two single beds.

"Perfect," Grace chuckled, "and I love the view!"

"Agreed and isn't it wonderful," her sister added, flopping down on the bed, "we have those two trapped! We'll go out for a nice harmless walk later; I think I've had enough excitement for one day!"

They took their time unpacking, then changed their shoes and decided to go for a ride on one of the little harbour ferries.

"It should amuse the boys and keep them busy for a while," Mary commented.

On the way down to the ferry's landing spot below the Causeway, they stopped to watch one of the portrait artists drawing a hilarious caricature of a bald-headed man. Another artisan was making unique jewellery.

After the ferry ride, they returned to the same dock and began walking in the direction of the Gatsby. Hearing music coming from a group of lively musicians, they stopped to listen but the boys soon tired of it. Exchanging sly nods and giggles, luckily unnoticed by their mothers who now turned to follow them, they set out for the Wax Museum. The steps they went up were in front of the location of the old CP terminal building which had originally been built in 1924 for its ocean-going ships. Now, it was the home of many famous wax figures. David ran over to the open museum door and then back to his mother.

"Hey mom, we've still got an hour before closing. Can we go in, please, please!" he pleaded, with the plea being repeated by Nathan.

Looking at each other, their mothers raised their eyebrows.

"Well, I guess we did promise them," said Mary, getting out her wallet. "It will be one less item on our agenda for tomorrow."

Inside the doorway, a young man was standing like a statue portraying a wax London Bobby, shocking visitors when he suddenly winked at them. The boys glanced at each other and Nathan pulled a pin out of his baseball cap.

"Don't you even think about it!" his mother hissed, grabbing his hand and removing the pin he was about to stick in the Bobby's behind.

Darting away, the boys stopped to stare wide-eyed at the lifelike figures of English monarchs, American presidents, film stars and sportsmen. David's fingers itched to touch the ring in his pocket—his thoughts wandering over the possibility of Dolly bringing the wax figures to life.

"Not a good idea!" Nathan didn't need to read his thoughts; they always thought the same things. "Madmen and murderers live here."

There were fascinating moments for the young Americans as they stood in reverence before the wax figure of the Queen of England and felt the cold unblinking eyes of Sir James Douglas staring at them from his pedestal.

"Seen enough boys?" the voice of an elderly volunteer croaked hoarsely from nearby. Leaping with fright, David and Nathan raced away to find their mothers.

"I wasn't scared back there," David boasted quietly to his cousin as they walked along Belleville toward the Gatsby.

"Not much you weren't," Nathan giggled.

Grace pointed to the outside tables of a hotel cafe across the street. "Feel like a coffee and a sandwich sis?" she asked.

"Good idea, I don't think that early dinner is going to last me much longer!" She looked across the harbour and spoke her thoughts out loud as the last of the day's sunshine sent its brilliant rays of light dancing across the water. "It's hard to imagine what this harbour would have looked like in 1914."

Later, in their room, the boys lay on their beds watching TV as darkness crept slowly over the city. David looked up at the window briefly and took the ring from his pocket. He clutched it tightly in his hand as they patiently waited for their mothers to retire—he and Nathan had made some plans and were most eager to carry them out. When their TV show finished, they went over to the window. At 11 o'clock there were only a few people walking along the street and lights in nearby hotel rooms were scarce. The boys held their breath as they listened to the eerie silence. Their moms' TV had been turned off.

"Right, let's do it," David whispered.

They turned off their TV and the light, then forgetting they were wearing their pyjamas, jumped off their beds and looked at each other.

"Are you ready?" David asked. Hearing Nathan whisper that he was ready, he rubbed on the ring.

"I'm here boys," Dolly's voice murmured beside them.

"Can you show us something special from a long time ago?" David whispered bravely.

"Sorry boys, I can't make suggestions," she replied, "but you can ask me questions and that may make your wish easier to make."

"When was the Empress Hotel built?" asked David.

"It was started in 1904 and opened in 1908," she instantly replied.

"Can we see it?" he asked.

"What year would you like to see?"

"1904, before it was built," Nathan's voice was filled with excitement.

"That's good, take us to 1904 please," David agreed.

27

Suddenly, they were walking on air in the hot midday sunshine, looking down at the dirty water and empty swampland where Dolly told them the majestic Empress Hotel would be built. A wooden bridge spanned the inlet from one muddy bank to the other connecting Government Street to the homes and businesses of James Bay and the Legislative Building.

Seeing some men working with a great pile of stones at the other end of the harbour, Nathan asked what they were doing.

"They're building the new stone bridge that will become known as the Causeway," Dolly chuckled. "Next, they'll dredge the bottom of the harbour and pile all the mud in behind it."

"You mean the Empress is built on mud?" David scoffed.

"Yes that's right, it's actually a swamp, but piles were driven 125 feet down into the mud to help support the structure. It's actually sinking at a very tiny rate each year."

"I'd like to see what Government Street looked like," Nathan whispered to his cousin.

"What year?" asked the apparition.

"Show it to us when something important happened."

"David?" she asked.

"I remember mom telling me about a really bad fire, can you show us?"

Immediately, they found themselves floating over the dark city. Below them Government Street was ablaze as fire swept from building to building.

"It's on fire!" David yelled in panic. "Quick, call the fire engines."

"That won't happen David," their ghostly guide explained. "You're watching history in 1910. There are no fire engines as you know them in your time. We can't alter the facts, I'm afraid."

They floated closer to the crackling flames feeling none of the heat but the noise was deafening as showers of sparks burst upwards toward them. Despite the noise, strangely, they could still hear each other speak.

"W-wow does the whole street b-burn up?" Nathan's voice trembled.

"No," Dolly whispered, "but what you're watching is the most dramatic thing that ever happened to Government Street."

"It's too scary," David mumbled. "Please take us back to the hotel Miss Dolly."

In the blink of an eye they were back in their room, standing in the darkness and gazing out of the window at the eerie glow of the moon bouncing off the water of the harbour.

"Wow, imagine no fire engines. That's awful!" David whispered. "I'm glad we didn't live back in those days."

The boys crawled wearily into bed but lay awake for a long time, each in their own thoughts, as the 1910 fire filled their minds.

They awakened to the sound of David's mother knocking on their door and calling their names as sunlight streamed in through the open curtains. "Come on you two, we have things to do."

Dressing quickly, the boys were soon ready and they all made their way downstairs and across the street to check out the Coho dock where rows of cars waited for the ship to Port Angeles.

"Breakfast first," Grace advised. "Afterwards, the boys can go to the BC Museum while we check out the archives. We'll have to get here early tomorrow to get the car in the line-up."

The boys weren't paying attention and Nathan asked, "Can we find a McDonald's mom?"

"No, we cannot!" she replied sharply. "We all need something more nutritious to start the day."

"Why are you going to the archives?" David asked as they made their way to a restaurant with tables set out in the sun, his fingers finding the Janion ring deep in his pocket.

"Maybe Miss Dolly can help you mom," he said aloud. "I bet she knows the answers to your questions."

"Now there's an idea," Mary chuckled, "but I don't want whisking back to 1914, do you Gracie?"

Unsmiling, Grace shook her head. "It would give us more time to find out about granddad though," she said. "Or maybe Miss Dolly even knows about him and grandma."

Seated and served by a smiling, efficient server, they quickly tucked into their food and the two sisters conversed quietly across the table on questions to ask Dolly.

"Do you realize what's happening?" Mary whispered. "We're talking about a ghost like she's a real person."

"She is real," David interrupted, his fingers subconsciously rubbing the gold ring.

Grace blinked when Dolly Walker suddenly materialized behind David's chair.

"You need me sir?" she purred, her voice sending a chill through Grace's body.

"Are you joining these people ma'am?" the server directed her question at Dolly, looking at her curiously although it wasn't uncommon to see women walk the streets in Victorian costume here in summertime. "Shall I get you a chair?"

"No, we're leaving, could you get our bill please. Will $30 American money cover it?" Mary interrupted, opening her purse and offering the bill to the young lady.

"That's plenty ma'am, I'll get your change."

"Keep it," Mary replied, moving quickly away from the table. "Take us somewhere quiet, Dolly, to a place where we can talk."

The apparition shook her head, staying close to David and whispering as they left the restaurant. "Sorry Mary, your son found ...."

"Oh for heaven's sake, I keep forgetting ... ask her David!" his mother urged. "This is a ridiculous situation."

"Miss Dolly," the boy giggled, "would you do what mom asks please."

His voice was still echoing in the air as their surroundings changed. Those who noticed them stopped and stared not believing what they were seeing as the three ladies and two boys just disappeared.

A lady tourist stopped suddenly, her face displaying her dismay as she grasped her husband's arm. "Honey," she murmured, "did you see those people? They just disappeared ... I think!"

"Pretend you didn't notice Anne," he whispered. "This is Victoria, maybe ghosts wander around like tourists here!"

Meanwhile, Dolly had transported the visitors into the quaint area surrounded by old buildings known as Market Square. Setting them down on a bench, they found they were overlooking the lower floor.

"Would you like a drink ladies?" she asked.

"Yes I would, thank you," Grace sighed, "but I still don't believe this is really happening."

"I would please." Nathan bounced off the seat. "I'd like a cola."

Dolly snapped her fingers and two glasses of whisky appeared in her hand, which she handed to Mary and Grace. Snapping her fingers again, mugs of brown frothy liquid appeared in the boy's hands.

Mary sniffed suspiciously at the strong smelling amber liquid in her own glass. "We meant coffee not liquor, Dolly, and what is that brown stuff you've given to our sons?"

"Root Beer ma'am, highly medicinal," the apparition snapped haughtily, "and I would have you know, your drink is the finest Scotch whisky on the Island." She paused for a moment, frowning at the two sisters. "Coffee, you say. Yuck! That's poison!"

David giggled as Dolly wriggled her fingers and the glasses of whisky changed instantly into two cups of steaming coffee that appeared to have milk in it.

"There," she hissed, "are you satisfied now?"

"You mean you even know what we take in it? Amazing!" said Mary. She smiled to herself and glanced over at her happy son and nephew—their visit to Victoria had certainly turned into an unbelievable adventure. Things had happened this weekend that could never be explained or told to their friends. She was actually talking to a ghost like a friend, a ghost that obeyed her 12-year-old son! Sipping on her coffee, which was perfect to her liking, she took out her notebook and prepared to ask the apparition some questions but Grace asked one first.

"Apparently you know something about prohibition Miss Dolly, can you give us some more details?"

Dolly smiled but gave no answer, staring blankly up at the rafters.

"She doesn't know," Grace whispered.

The boys were not paying attention and they began to fidget, bored with grown up chatter. They were eager to be off exploring one of the nearby old buildings that made up the market complex.

"Sit still you two," Mary scolded the boys. "Do you know Miss Dolly?"

"Of course I know, but Master David is the keeper of my ring and he's not given me permission to answer your questions!"

Mary glanced at her sister and shook her head. "David!"

"Oh sure mom, you can answer both my mom's and my aunt's questions now Miss Dolly."

"Certainly my boy," she replied. "It all began on October 1st, 1917 and continued until 1921. We had to close the bar at the Janion."

"And all drinking stopped?"

Grace's question sent the ghost into fits of laughter and her parasol tapped excitedly on the wooden floor. "Oh my!" she gasped. "That was just the start of some very interesting and exciting years in Victoria."

"Rum running from the states?" Mary whispered.

"Heavens no," Dolly giggled. "We trucked it in from Alberta to a warehouse in Chatham Street."

"But why not from Washington?" Grace interrupted. "It's closer."

"Washington was having its own problems."

"We didn't have prohibition though," Mary added, "not until 1921."

"Don't you believe it," Dolly exclaimed. "Washington had the wet or dry referendums going on—some municipalities prohibited liquor while others allowed it.. Ridiculous, I called it!"

Writing furiously in her notebook, Mary noted everything the ghost had told them then glancing over at the boys she realized they had stood up and were trying to sneak away.

"Come back here!" she ordered. "Where are you going?"

"Let them go Mary," Dolly intervened. "I'll seal up the exits and they won't be able to leave the area. Over there," she pointed her parasol at the Johnson Street entrance, "is the fountain from Humber Green, a small part of Victoria's history."

"You mean they can't get away?" Grace asked.

"What is Humber Green?" asked Mary

"Humber Green became known as the Roundabout, I'm sure you recognize that name," said Dolly.

"Yes, I do," the women chorused.

Mary's eyes began to sparkle and a grin pulled at the corners of her mouth. Grace knew the signs, her sister was about to drop a bombshell.

"Did you ever hear of a man named Tom Duncan?" Mary asked.

The sisters waited with baited breath—Tom Duncan was their grandfather. Born in Victoria on October 1st, 1908, he had lost his memory from war wounds. Clues dragged from their mother's early childhood recollections were scant but all pointed to Victoria.

"Yes, I knew Thomas; he was an E&N Railway worker."

Mary and Grace sat bolt upright, their faces suddenly flushed with excitement. The Janion ghost did know about their grandfather.

"Will you tell us about him?" Grace asked softly.

Dolly Walker's shoulders sagged a little, her hands resting firmly on the parasol handle, as memories flooded into her mind.

"Thomas was a widower," she began, "a drinking man and a customer and friend of mine." She paused to sigh. "Your two boys remind me of his son, young Tom, or Tommy as he was known."

Both David and Nathan now returned and, seeing their mother's interest in Dolly's conversation, sat down and listened.

"He wanted to join the army in 1914, but Tommy was only five, so I offered to take care of the lad." A long pause from Dolly had the sisters on the edge of their seats. "Somehow Thomas got mixed up with the trouble in town when the Lusitania was sunk in May of 1915 and, he spent a month in jail, then he joined the army."

David's arm crept over his cousin's shoulder. Their moms had often talked about their grandfather and he wished he had been able to meet him.

"Thomas had changed when he came home after the war," Dolly continued. "He'd lost his job in the early days of the depression so I loaned him money for a boat."

The pen hovered in Mary's hand as she turned the page in her notebook.

"But who took care of the child while Thomas was away?" Grace murmured.

"I did."

"And while he was off fishing?"

"Who said anything about fishing?" Dolly chuckled. "We shipped liquor into Seattle but Thomas took the boy with him on those trips."

"A rum runner!" Mary exclaimed. "Wow, what a story."

"The lad was only sixteen when his father died," Dolly added.

"What year was that?" Mary's pen paused waiting for the answer.

"1926."

"And that was the end of their rum running?"

"Gracious no!" a cackle of laughter erupted from the ghost. "That lad went right on running until 1930 and never got caught I might add. Then he dropped clear out of sight, never came back again."

Mary's pen was shaking with excitement as she asked, "Do you remember when that was Dolly?"

"He was 20," the ghost mused. "Winter of 1930, I'd say."

"He married grandma on New Year's Day 1931," Grace squealed, "our mystery is solved Mary! Thank you Dolly." She turned to the ghost and realized she had left as they walked from Market Square into the sunshine on Johnson Street. The sisters gazed up at the old buildings lining the sidewalk, their faded signs telling their own tale of a street that had seen a more prosperous time in days gone by.

"1914," Mary chuckled. "Listen boys, wouldn't you like to explore this street in that long ago time when your grandfather and great grandfather lived here?"

"Sure Aunt Mary," Nathan agreed none too enthusiastically, "but can we eat first? I'm starving."

His mother, however, now totally convinced of the Janion Lady's powers, made an interesting suggestion. "Nathan, you just ate! We're going to visit 1914."

"Should I ask Miss Dolly to take us to 1914, mom?" David asked. As he waited for his mother's reply, Nathan changed his mind.

"Do it Davie!" his cousin encouraged, grinning.

The moment David's fingers grasped the ring, Dolly appeared. She smiled broadly when she heard him say, "I wish we were back in 1914."

33

Suddenly the street changed and old cars and trucks, all black coloured, lined the sidewalk. Curtains flapped from the open windows of the Jubilee Hotel across the street and next door a soldier and his sweetheart hugged as they stared in the window of Henry Greensfelder, the jeweller. Nathan tugged on David's arm and pointed next door to the Bijou Theatre. A notice on the wall said, *Hear the wonderful voice of Susan White at intermission singing your favourite songs*. Then the boys noticed a tobacconist shop a few doors away and nearby a sign that said, *Eat lunch at the Rainier Cafe* reminding them they were hungry.

"Mom, mom," David called. "Let's eat down there."

Mary dragged her eyes away from the entrance to Oriental Alley where Chinese people were bustling about doing their shopping and visiting and looked to where her son was pointing.

"All right we'll go there if you want," she said, her voice lost in the noise of a locomotive, releasing a fierce blast of steam as it turned onto the bridge from Store Street. Following behind the boys, they entered a spacious restaurant which had a thickly carpeted floor and neatly set tables. The sisters gazed around in wonder at the surprisingly luxurious interior. Walls were covered in a large floral wallpaper pattern and classic English pictures were liberally displayed. The high ceiling was quite decorative with gold chains supporting the large, glass chandelier.

"Table for four ma'am?" a uniformed waitress asked.

"Five please," Mary replied, forgetting to look for Dolly.

"You'll be joined by one more?" she asked looking around, but it was the look on her face as she peered with interest at the women's clothes that took Grace's attention.

Mary turned, realizing Dolly had disappeared again. Composing herself, she corrected herself. "F-four will be fine dear."

"What's wrong mom?" David whispered as they followed the waitress to a table. "You're as white as a ghost."

"Don't say that word," she snapped. "My nerves are edgy enough."

"It is rather unusual," her sister agreed, scanning the menu which the girl had left, "in fact, it's impossible. But here we are in 1914 and these prices are certainly from long ago—$1.60 for a roast beef dinner and tea or coffee only five cents extra—this is positively depressing!"

The waitress returned about five minutes later, interrupting their conversation when she asked if they were ready to order. Again, her attention was drawn to their clothes particularly staring at Mary's outfit of green capri pants and colourful, layered T-shirts.

"Your clothes ma'am," she whispered, blushing a little as she looked from one to the other, "are they a new London fashion?"

34

Mary's mind began to race even before Grace's foot nudged hers in warning. *"Darn, we should have asked Dolly to change our clothes!"* she thought. Then, a sigh of relief escaped her lips as her sister jumped up and quickly did a pirouette in front of the boggle-eyed girl—her knee-length dress in a colourful floral print, flared slightly as she turned.

The waitress gasped, her eyes fixed firmly on Grace's legs.

"What's wrong?" Grace asked. "Is my dress too short?"

"It is a bit daring ma'am," the waitress replied, again looking embarrassed, "but it's your legs, ma'am. They're so smooth and shiny!"

"Can we eat now mom?" Nathan interrupted.

"You can bring us two of your chicken sandwiches and two ham sandwiches," Mary told the waitress, "then come back and talk to us."

The girl thanked them and scurried away.

"You be careful what you tell her," Mary warned her sister when they saw the waitress hurrying toward them.

"You were telling me about your legs ma'am," the girl whispered eagerly.

"They're silk stockings," Grace chuckled, remembering that nylon stockings didn't come into existence until near the end of WW2. The girl had no doubt never seen anything like this before.

Stooping to look more closely at Grace's legs, she giggled and backed away looking embarrassed at first and then she suddenly raised her long dress to reveal her own heavy woollen stockings. Before they had time to comment, a bell summoned her away. It wasn't long before she returned with their plates of sandwiches and Mary instructed her who was having which sort. After asking if they needed anything else, she politely left them.

"Such a nice normal sandwich!" Mary whispered staring at her plate which had neither salad nor French fries, as they were used to.

They all dug in gratefully and soon the clothes were forgotten. Later, their hunger satisfied, the boys begged to be excused.

"Go on then," Mary replied before calling for the bill. "Don't you boys go away."

Once outside the door, the boys conveniently forgot her instructions and wandered across the street to check out Oriental Alley which they had passed earlier. Its dim, narrow walkway was alive with strange little men in odd-shaped garments, but the scene had changed now as there seemed to be a lot of smoke about. Going closer, they discovered it wasn't smoke from a fire … it was actually caused by something the men were smoking. A heavy, odd-smelling tobacco smoke hung in the air as men stood smoking in the many doorways that made up the alley.

"Shall we take a look?" David whispered.

Before Nathan could answer, men were shouting back and forth in Chinese and others were running about. The boys saw the flash of a knife and that was all that was needed to quickly change their minds. Hurrying back to the road, they dodged a horse-drawn vehicle and a couple of slow-moving old vehicles as they ran back to the safety of the cafe and their mothers.

Soon after, as they all left the cafe, Mary gazed up the street and a smile tugged at the corners of her mouth. "Let's just walk up to Government Street," she chuckled. "Look boys, there's an old bicycle shop."

The boys glanced one more time across at Oriental Alley, still inquisitive, but glad they were leaving the area of that sinister place.

"Hey Dave, come have a look at this," his cousin yelled.

Nathan was standing in front of the building with the address 574 and the sign said *Marconi Brothers Bicycle Shop.* He pointed at the odd-looking cycles and laughed.

Ed Clancy, the shop's ever-eager young salesman appeared in the doorway. "Like to try one young sir?" he grinned. "They're easy to ride and very fast machines."

Nodding, both the boys hid their amusement. Mountain riding was their favourite hobby back home and they were good at it.

"Could you handle one of these super bicycles Nathan?" Grace asked sarcastically.

"Can I try too?" David begged his mother.

Eager for a sale, Ed stressed the safety instructions, pointing to the brake levers and giving them a demonstration of how to mount and dismount correctly. "Now young sirs," he began confidently, "would you like to try?"

Mischievous glances passed between the two boys who were now the centre of attention. Ed Clancy had seen these looks before from young men eager to show off their skills, so he waited patiently.

On the other hand, knowing what to expect, Mary rolled her eyes at her sister and the boys leapt into action, racing for the Government Street corner. They reared up their cycles, spun a full circle balancing on the back wheel and headed back to their audience. A gasp left Ed Clancy's lips as he watched dumbfounded, jumping out of the way by grabbing a lamp standard when the boys moved perilously close.

"Oh no," he whined, clamping his eyes shut as he waited for the inevitable crash. A shopper leaving the store screamed, dropping her parcel and dashing back into the store; and two horses tied to the hitching rail pulled violently on their restraints.

"All right you two show-offs," Grace shouted, feeling a bit embarrassed by now. "Give this poor man his bicycles back before you damage them."

Speechless, Ed accepted the cycles, his hands still shaking as he eagerly put them away.

"Now then," a deep authoritative voice shouted from behind them. "I want a word with you people."

Mary groaned inwardly as the uniformed policeman strode purposefully toward them. Book in hand, the sergeant licked at the lead of his pencil and seemed prepared to write out a fine, when he noticed the odd way they were dressed.

"You folks foreigners?" he growled, raking the women with his eyes.

David's fingers rubbed the ring in his pocket. *I wish I was in front of Rogers' Chocolate Shop.* The next instant he was staring in the store's window with its giant chocolates elegantly displayed in the window. The image reflected in the glass sent a whimper of horror from his lips and he turned toward the street.

"Mom!" he whispered, glancing around at the many strange faces as a loaded streetcar went rattling by on Government. He was suddenly panic-stricken and unable to think clearly.

Back in Johnson Street, the policeman blinked in surprise as David seemed to vanish into thin air.

"Where's he gone?" he muttered. "He can't just disappear."

"David!" his mother yelped, "you come back here right now."

Removing his tall hat, the policeman scratched his head and cocked an eyebrow at Mary. "Look here lady," he said nervously, "we don't allow children to just disappear in Victoria."

"How will we find him?" Grace whispered, holding tightly to Nathan.

"Co-ee!" A parasol-waving figure yelled from the tobacconist's doorway across the street. Ignoring the traffic of horses and automobiles, Dolly Walker marched boldly toward them, her parasol swinging wildly in front of her to clear a path.

"Dolly!" the policeman gasped. "I've warned you before about …."

"I'm sorry officer but this is important," Dolly snapped, poking the constable with her parasol. "What's happening deary?" she asked the women turning her attention to Mary.

"He's gone," Mary moaned.

"Who has gone?"

"David, he just disappeared."

"He's over on Government Street at Candy Rogers' shop," Dolly replied. "That's what he wished for!"

Just then, David's fingers touched the ring in his pocket as he wished he could be back with his mother. The Janion Lady smiled and instantly brought David back.

"Give *me* that ring," Mary snapped angrily, grabbing her son's arm, "before we lose you permanently."

Constable Jackson jumped backwards in surprise dropping his pencil and pad when David reappeared. "Hey you can't do that here in Victoria," he muttered nervously. "You tell 'em Miss Dolly. It's illegal to just disappear."

"Quick David," his mother urged, "take us to Rogers' Chocolate Shop in our time."

"I can't mom," the boy giggled. "You have the ring!"

"Take us to the chocolate shop," Mary ordered sharply, rubbing the ring between her fingers.

"Sorry my dear," Dolly replied. "You know the rules!"

"Here," Mary snapped, pushing the ring at her son, "you do it!"

Before they knew it, they were standing outside the chocolate shop in the year 2002.

"Thank goodness we're back," Grace sighed, going over to a bench and sitting down. "That was getting quite scary."

"I wonder what that policeman thinks now?" Nathan giggled.

"Oh, you ruined his day, that's for sure," Dolly chuckled, appearing on the curb beside them. "I'm going to have some explaining to do and, Ed Clancy at the bicycle shop, he almost killed himself trying to copy your fancy bicycle riding!"

"But this isn't the shop I was looking in," David said with a puzzled frown. "It was over there." He turned and pointed across the street.

"No, you're wrong dear," his mother murmured. "I think the brochure said they had been here forever."

"Why don't you ask Dolly?" Grace chuckled. "Dolly, who's right?" she called glancing around. "Darn it, she's gone again."

Mischievously, David's finger rubbed the ring in his pocket, bringing Dolly back.

"You have more questions my boy?" she asked, still smiling.

"Yes," Mary sighed tolerantly, "just tell him Rogers' Chocolate shop has always been right here."

"It wasn't, it was over there," David insisted, pointing stubbornly across Government Street.

"He's right you know," the apparition said softly, "and as you are interested, I'll tell you that right next door was the Empress Drug Store."

"Then what was here?" Grace asked, pointing to a nearby doorway.

"Oh this was a jewellers and a big furniture store was on the corner. Me and little Tommy often walked through there."

"grandfather," Mary murmured, her interest being renewed in their family history. "Tell us more about him."

"Not here love. Come, let's walk back to the hotel and I'll tell you."

"But that means we would have to go back to 1914 again," Grace interjected, "and that scares me Mary, we might get stuck there."

"I'll look after you mom," Nathan whispered reaching for her hand.

"We could find out so much more about granddad if we went there," Mary added, struggling with her thoughts.

"Let me put your mind at rest," Dolly chuckled. "Neither you nor the boys can get lost in the past. When David has used my ring for three days his time will be up, the ring will disappear and your life will return to the way it was. I will wait for the next finder, hoping they are as nice as you folks." She paused as the two sisters glanced at each other and nodded.

"All right," his mother said firmly. "David, wish us all back to 1914."

In the blink of an eye, Government Street changed back to the now familiar and quaint-looking street with old cars and costumed inhabitants. Dolly had disappeared again and a streetcar came rattling up the hill to stop for passengers at the corner where Broughton Street met Government.

"Look Grace." Mary pointed across the street. "David was right, the chocolate shop is over there. Dolly said we can't get trapped here in 1914 so I think we should make the most of this opportunity. We'll never get another chance to come back here."

"You're right mom," David agreed eagerly. "Where shall we go first?"

"I know," Grace chuckled, warming to the adventure, "let's try to find granddad. Dolly said he was staying with her."

"Mom," Nathan whined, pulling on her hand. "You and Aunt Mary go find him. I want to go down to the harbour; it'll be full of old ships!"

"All right, you two can go down to the Wax Museum and wait there for us. We want to check out some of these old buildings, then we'll get Dolly to help us find granddad."

Racing off, the boys headed down Government toward the Inner Harbour. They were eager to check for any old boats or sailing ships that might be in town.

"The harbour sure looks different and the Empress must be quite new. The garden doesn't have trees and there's no ivy growing on it," Nathan commented.

"This isn't even a road yet," David added as they looked over the area. "It's more like a bridge. I guess they built the road later."

"Look ... some soldiers," shouted Nathan, pointing to a group of uniformed men marching back and forth in front of the Legislative Buildings. Their uniforms are sure funny-looking in 1914!"

"Yeah and the Wax Museum building isn't there either," his cousin exclaimed. "I guess they haven't built it either and we were in there yesterday!"

Meanwhile, their mothers were causing quite a stir amongst passing residents—from the headband Mary often used to hold back her long hair, to their colourful and unusual summer outfits, people were giving them some strange glances.

"I feel like an oddity," Mary whispered when a stern-faced lady pointed at them with a walking stick and cackled with humourless laughter.

"But we are oddities," her sister giggled. "They have no idea we're just visiting from another time and, as we'll never see them again, I am going to enjoy it!" She grabbed Mary to cross the street in front of a horse and cart and they both had a good laugh when they saw the driver's startled reaction.

"Look at those delicious-looking chocolates," Mary gasped, looking in a candy store window. "We're back at Rogers' and look at that price. They're only five cents each, come on!" They hurried into the store and waited patiently behind two soldiers and a small boy.

"Hello Tommy." The clerk smiled warmly at the boy. "Is Aunt Dolly buying you chocolates again?"

Grace's ears perked up and she jabbed Mary, but her sister wasn't paying attention. Grace watched the boy go toward the door and tried to get Mary's attention again, as Tommy turned back to shout over his shoulder.

"Bye Mrs. Rogers."

"Are you the owner," Mary asked, "the one who makes the chocolates?"

"Yes and no dear. My husband makes them and I sell them."

Suddenly a thought flashed through Mary's head. *Autograph! That would be the perfect way to prove to the club that we'd been here and that we had met Mr. and Mrs. Rogers. How could anyone dispute an authentic autograph?*

40

"Would you please give me your autograph?" she asked. "And your husband too, if he would."

"Oh no, I don't think so," Mrs. Rogers politely refused, blushing a little as she handed the bag of sweets across the counter, "it's not the sort of thing we normally do."

"Please," Mary pleaded, "I am collecting autographs, to show friends back in Port Angeles."

"What was that you said?" a man's voice asked as he appeared in the basement doorway. "It would be darned good advertising Mary. Yes, yes, we should do that for you young lady."

Thanking them profusely, a few minutes later, Mary and Grace stepped out onto Government Street and turned to look back at the front of the building. Mary was elated with her success of acquiring the original owners' autographs.

"That was a brilliant idea sis," Grace congratulated her. "Nobody can doubt us now but I hate to tell you that you missed something else in there."

"What did I miss?" Mary asked.

"Well, I think that boy was our grandfather!" Grace replied with a grin.

"What!" Mary exclaimed loudly, turning on her. "Why didn't you stop me talking?"

Because you were busy and I know how you hate to be interrupted. Dolly is going to take us to him anyway, so it's all right," she sighed. "Forget about it for now and take a picture of this building; it no longer exists as that Harbour Mall was built here."

"I guess you're right. We'll have to get the boys first anyway. Go stand in the doorway," Mary ordered, reaching into her bag for her digital camera. "I'll go across the street so I can get it all in."

Waiting patiently for a streetcar and a brewery dray to pass, Mary hurried across the street and got into position. People stopped and stared as she raised the small blue box to her eye.

"Cripes!" she squealed. "Quick Gracie, come look at this."

Scooting across the street to join her sister, Grace stared over her shoulder as Mary replayed the pictures, gasping at what she saw. In the viewfinder was a perfect picture of Grace standing in front of the Harbour Mall, exactly as they had seen it yesterday.

"This is weird," Grace whispered. "The camera's seeing it in 2002, as it really is now. Point it at that grocery store on the corner."

Slowly turning, Mary's hands shook as she stared at the camera's display. "It's a real estate office!" she muttered, letting the camera sag in her hands.

"Ooh, this gives me the creeps," her sister shuddered, "but now we know we can't take any pictures of this visit to 1914. It's a good thing you thought of getting autographs."

They continued down Government Street to the corner, looking in the windows of various stores and drinking establishments. They stopped at the corner of Courtney Street and stared up at the large Dominion Building.

"What is this place?" Grace murmured. "You should take a look through the camera."

Her sister pointed the camera at the building. "It's almost the same!" she gasped. "All that's changed is an addition on top. Take a look."

"Gracie turn around," her sister interrupted, "and look at the Windsor Hotel."

Across the street, a group of soldiers were staggering through the batwing doors of the bar and onto the sidewalk, talking noisily and shouting as they made their way toward the cigar shop next door.

Mary trained the camera onto the hotel and saw that the verandah was gone and a gift shop was now housed in the old brick hotel. The men weren't even visible in the picture and the cigar shop, in modern times, had windows full of china. Interest now captured Mary's attention and she eagerly pointed the camera up the street to the jeweller's where Rogers' Chocolates would later be situated.

"You take a look," she said excitedly, handing the camera to Grace. "This is a chance to look at today and yesterday, both at the same time. I bet nobody else has ever been able to do that and, nobody will believe us, but who cares."

"Let's find the boys." Grace suggested, and Mary noted that she had a touch of anxiety in her voice. Her sister was such a worry-wart.

Watching a streetcar rumble by, Mary looked over toward the harbour and found the boys—leaning precariously over the harbour wall with another youngster. "There are the boys. It looks like they've found a friend."

"How old are you kid?" David was asking the boy beside him.

"Almost six."

"What's your name?"

"Tommy. I saw you in the chocolate shop," the younger boy exclaimed, his face lighting up with recognition.

"Yeh, we saw you too ... Tommy who?" asked Nathan.

"Tommy Duncan."

Their attention was suddenly drawn toward a boat chugging slowly around the end of the jetty. The nearby sign said, *Evans Coleman*.

"Hey Tommy!" the man on board yelled.

Leaping to his feet, Tommy stood on the wall and waved vigorously.

"Who's that?" Nathan asked. "Can we go down there?"

"It's Johnny, he takes me with 'im sometimes. Come on."

Racing around the end of the bridge, Tommy led them down the rough gravel slope to the Empress jetty.

Unmarried and alone in the world, Johnny Schnarr, manager of the Empress Boathouse, had befriended young Thomas Duncan and often took him on trips up the harbour. Knowing his father well as a drinking companion at the Janion, Johnny held a soft spot for the motherless lad with the twinkling green eyes and happy, bubbling laughter.

Nervously standing back as the rough, unshaven boatman scooped Tommy into his arms and hugged him, David and Nathan cast their eyes longingly over the boat.

"New friends lad?" Johnny chuckled.

"Yup, but I don't know ther names. Can we go with ya Johnny?"

"Of course ya can son, but we'd better find out who these two fancy-dressed gents are first!"

"I'm David Web and he's my cousin Nathan Dawes. We're from Everett but live in Port Angeles now."

"Worked nearby in Marysville for a summer," the boatman growled. "Mill town—dirty place! Come on then, jump aboard. I'm just going up to the rice mill."

"Rice mill?" David asked, a frown creasing his brow.

"Aye lad, the rice mill on Store Street."

"It's just past the Janion where Aunt Dolly lives," Tommy volunteered. "On by the railway sheds."

Looking at each other and frowning, David and Nathan knew their mothers would soon be looking for them. Adventure loomed, however, and forgetting the warning they'd received, they eagerly scrambled aboard.

Luckily, Mary had been keeping an eye on the boys as they disappeared down the ramp to the dock.

"Come on Grace, those little brats are up to no good, I can feel it!" she yelled at her sister breaking into a run.

Hearts pounding with worry, they were just in time to see the boat disappear. Frantically yelling and waving their arms, they drew the

43

attention of a man and a red-haired young woman coming up the harbour in a smart-looking blue boat.

"What's wrong?" the man asked leaping onto the dock beside them.

"Our sons," Mary gasped, "someone's taken them in a boat!"

"Jump in," the redhead commanded, giving Grace a hand as the men assisted Mary. "We'll catch them. Which way did they go?"

Grace pointed up the harbour, grabbing tightly to the side of the boat as the woman expertly swung the blue boat around and opened the throttle. The boat hurled forward with a tremendous burst of power.

"There they are!" Mary screamed, pointing to a boat just going under the west side of the railway bridge.

"That's Johnny Schnarr and young Tommy," the redhead laughed. "He won't hurt your boys."

They soon caught up and followed the boat to the rice mill dock.

"David!" his mother shouted angrily. "Come here this minute!"

"Oh ho, lads," Johnny chuckled, "it sounds like yer in trouble now!"

Standing on the dock at the rice mill, Tommy Duncan immediately showed his courage.

"Please missus, it were my fault. I asked 'em to come," the little boy explained. "Don't be cross with 'em."

"And who are you young man?" Grace asked gently, realizing by now that he was the same boy she had seen in Rogers'.

"Thomas William Duncan and I'm almost six!" he said, standing straighter and proclaiming proudly. "My dad's Thomas Duncan too!"

"Oh my gosh!" Mary gasped, turning white as she sat down hard on a stack of rice sacks. "Gracie it's him!"

"What's wrong?" the redhead asked, moving quickly to Mary's side.

"Oh, it's nothing ... really," Mary said evasively.

"What's the matter mom?" David whispered.

"Be quiet for a minute David," his mother sighed. "I want to find out who these people are."

"Sis, your autograph book," Grace reminded her. "Get some signatures."

"I'm Dan Brown and this is my sister Nancy," the young man interrupted Mary's thoughts and, she couldn't help but think what a charming couple these young people were, unusual for siblings.

Dan flashed her one of his disarming grins, taking all thoughts out of Mary's head. "We own the dock near the harbour master's office and that chap who brought your sons over here is Johnny Schnarr, the boatman who runs the Empress Boathouse."

Pushing in front of Dan, Tommy looked up at the young man with an expression that could only be described as pure adoration. Dan scooped the boy up into his arms and Tommy dropped his head affectionately onto Dan's shoulder as if this was second nature.

"This is my friend Tommy Duncan, the smartest kid in Victoria."

A tear trickled down Mary's cheek as her fumbling fingers searched her purse for the notebook. Her damp eyes never wavered from the face of the boy in Dan Brown's arms. Then, suddenly kicking himself free of Dan, Tommy went over to stand in front of Mary. He put his arms out to hug her legs, but instead, Mary bent down on one knee—it was as if time stopped while they embraced. Grace gasped and grabbed Nathan's shoulder, holding him so tight he tried to squirm away. This was more than they could ever have dreamed of.

"That boy's related to you, isn't he?" Nancy murmured, feeling Dan's arm encircle her waist as she spoke to Grace. "We're orphans and I can feel there is a connection between you and Tommy. Who are you?"

Sniffling, Grace reached into her pocket for a tissue, which Nancy looked at curiously. Grace took a deep breath and turned to face the young couple. "It's rather complicated to explain, but believe me when I say you're watching the impossible happen."

"Then don't distress yourself," Nancy murmured. "Is there anything we can do to help you?"

"I'm Grace and this is my sister Mary. The boys are our sons," Grace whispered. "We're from Port Angeles and we're searching for information on a relative."

"Oh, now I can see it," Nancy chuckled. "Tommy looks the spitting image of your boys."

"And so he should, would you please give us your autographs?"

"Of course, but why? We're not important or famous." Nancy was tempted to ask more about Tommy but she didn't want to be nosey.

"Oh, it's sort of our way of proving to our friends back home that we were actually here," Grace replied, picking her words carefully as the young couple signed her sister's book. When Nancy turned to Tommy and told him to print his name, the sisters watched with bated breath as their grandfather printed his crude signature in Mary's book.

"Would you like us to take you back to our dock on Wharf Street?" asked Nancy.

"We would appreciate that, but what about the man who brought the boys over here?"

"Do you want his autograph too?" Nancy laughed. "Give Dan your book, he'll find him."

Tommy called the boys over to the boat and they climbed aboard, laughing and talking in whispers as they waited. No one, even the boys, could have guessed that the adventure they were planning was an exciting night out with their own great-grandfather!

David and Nathan really liked little Tommy and they'd discovered that he was a bright boy who appeared to be allowed to freely wander the waterfront. He knew all of the Wharf Street residents and was liked by everyone. They all seemed to watch over him. When questioned, he told them he was born on Cook Street but his mother had gotten sick and died while he was little. So he was raised by his father with the help of neighbours. He was certainly a happy boy and Nathan and David found themselves quite in awe of this young boy's independence and confident nature. He obviously wandered the streets of Victoria alone and he had absolutely no fear.

Tommy had been instantly aware that he felt strangely drawn to these people and couldn't understand why. He had never experienced this before. Mary's embrace also gave him an odd sensation of warmth, not felt when Dolly or the other ladies at the Janion gave him hugs. The boys especially, gave him an unusual longing for more of their company.

Talking with Nancy while they waited for Dan, the women were impressed by the girl's friendly nature and eagerly accepted her offer for a tour of the harbour. As they went to join the boys, Grace asked her a question.

"You said your name was Nancy Wilson, didn't you?"

Seeing Nancy nod, her mind suddenly realized why the name was so familiar ... it was in a book she'd used while researching Victoria! It was a book that had listed Nancy Wilson as the American Forces sweetheart of song during the First World War. Her husband was Dan Brown. But how could that be? This girl was a Canadian and her brother was Dan Brown, not her husband. She had also seen a list of the most successful rum runners of the prohibition era and Nancy, Dan and Johnny Schnarr had headed the list. A smile crossed Grace's lips when she remembered the text, it had said they were all under suspicion but never caught. Her thoughts were interrupted when Dan returned.

"Here's your book Grace," he announced, holding up the notebook as he strode toward them. "It's six o'clock Nan, Aunt Meg will be waiting dinner for us."

"Did you get his autograph?" Grace asked eagerly.

"Yep sure did. We need to be leaving Nan."

"We're going to take a quick spin around the harbour, so hold on tight everyone!" Nancy shouted, turning on the engine and waiting for her passengers to get settled. She winked at Dan and pushed on the lever sending the craft shooting backwards. The boys squealed as she swung out into the channel, their bow dipping low in the water. A train was just passing over the railway bridge as the blue boat passed underneath and headed down the inlet in a shower of spray. She skirted a Hudson Bay freighter before pulling back on the throttle. Slowing, they circled in a wide arc, then passed the rice mill again on their way toward the harbour entrance. Swinging back around, she eased up on the throttle again and moved slowly into the Brown and Wilson dock.

Grace looked up at the name and made a mental note to do some more research when she got home.

"Could you point us toward a nice restaurant?" Mary was asking.

"Go over to Yates Street and turn at the blacksmith's shop," Nancy replied, pointing up the street.

"I'll take 'em!" shouted Tommy, leading the way as they all shouted their thanks to Nancy and Dan.

Tommy ran along Wharf Street with David and Nathan, waving at people as he passed several warehouses and docks. They waited for the boys' mothers in front of the ship's chandlers of Peter McQuade.

"Don't go up Yates missus," Tommy advised. "Go up Johnson, ther's lots of places up there."

"My word Tommy, you're just a fountain of information," Mary commented. "Tell me, when do you go home? Won't your father be worried about you?"

"No," the boy sighed. "My dad's at the Janion right now. He goes there after work. I eat in their kitchen, Miss Dolly's my friend."

"You can come eat with us if you like," Mary offered.

"I'd better go see my dad," Tommy softly insisted.

"Let's all go see your dad," Grace suggested glancing at her sister. "Then you can come back and eat with us."

"Yeah!" Tommy squealed excitedly. "Come on!"

"You be careful around those trains David," his mother called as the three boys scampered off along Wharf Street. "Are you ready for this?" she asked her sister. "The man we're going to see is our great-grandfather."

"I know, but to be honest sis, I'm actually beginning to enjoy this strange experience," Grace replied, shivering slightly.

"Me too! Tommy fascinates me. No wonder he was an independent old cuss. He'd grown to live life on his own terms. Fancy our relatives being gangsters."

"Don't be silly. They weren't gangsters, they were rum runners."

"Same thing, isn't it?" Mary replied, looking at her curiously.

"No it's not … a wild adventure and, maybe a little shady, but wouldn't you have liked to be there? Think of it, living one day of our lives with great-granddad and his son."

"It might be dangerous," Grace said with a worried frown, "and the boys would have to go with us." Further conversation was suddenly disrupted when a railway engine driver blew his whistle releasing several thundering blasts of steam into the air and the huge iron monster rattled and squealed into motion just ahead of them. Taking refuge in front of the Occidental Hotel, their eyes met and the wild adventurous blood of their grandfather came rushing to the surface.

"Let's ask Miss Dolly if it's possible," Mary shouted over the noise as the train pulled slowly away.

The three boys, having already arrived at the Janion, now moved between the tables following Tommy. They went right up to the bar and stopped in front of a big man with a pint of beer in his hand.

"Dad … dad!" Tommy laughed pulling on his father's arm. "This is David and Nathan. Can I go have dinner with them and their mothers?"

"Steady boy," his father smiled, setting his beer down on the bar. "Who are these rascals you want to go off with?"

"We're from Port Angeles," Nathan whispered, feeling a tremendous longing to touch this man with the stubbly whiskers and oil-stained coveralls.

"Let him go Thomas," Dolly chuckled from behind the bar. "You never know, they could be kinfolk."

At the door, Mary and Grace peered through the smoky atmosphere filled with noisy railway workers and grimaced as they saw the collection of rough patrons inside. They found Tommy at the end of the bar sitting in the lap of man with a short beard.

"That must be him," Grace whispered, grabbing her sister's hand in nervous anticipation. "It's hard to tell with that beard."

"Hold on girl," Mary said firmly, tugging her sister along with her as she moved toward the drinkers. "We aren't turning back now."

"So you're the folks from Port Angeles?" Tommy's father asked. "You're two darned good-lookin' gals!" he added cheekily.

Colour draining from her face, Mary impulsively brushed the outstretched hand aside and stepped into his arms, a tear springing from her eyes as she felt a tingle of excitement run through her body. Grace followed when her sister stepped away, but not without feeling an unexplainable warmth and contentment.

Dampness clouded Tom Duncan's eyes too. He released Grace, but curiously held onto her hand. "Damnit ladies, you take my breath away," he mumbled. "Is that the usual way you greet a man?"

"Would you come to dinner with us?" Mary blurted out.

"Yes he will!" Dolly's voice interrupted their conversation, as she leaned toward them over the bar.

"I need to get cleaned up," Thomas growled, glancing up at Dolly.

"Then go upstairs and do it, you dope. This is no time for indecision. I'll entertain the ladies for a while."

Reaching for his beer, Thomas Duncan shook his head and walked slowly toward the stairs, wondering to himself why he was doing this. Why had those folks tugged so hard on his heart strings and why did he feel such a desperate need to accept their invitation?

Sipping tea in the Janion Dining Room while Dolly savoured her good Scotch whisky, the women watched the harbour traffic from the windows and saw the boys out by the dock with Tommy. A high-masted sailing ship moved through the open swing bridge and Grace commented how thrilled the boy's must be.

"We don't see many ships like that anymore," Dolly said wistfully then she leaned toward them. "You should get all your questions answered tonight ladies," she said softly. "Thomas isn't a talkative man but I saw the effect you two had on him. You must be mindful of the fact you're guests in our time. I'll not allow you to hurt him."

"By all means Mrs. Walker," Mary whispered back looking over at her sister. "He's our great-grandfather and, through you, we've been privileged to meet him. We assure you that we will be most cautious of what we say." A silent tear rolled down her cheek as she reached for her sister's hand, but she quickly wiped it away just as the boys entered.

"Thomas is here," Dolly whispered. "I'll leave you now but Mary, I should tell you, I'm a Miss not a Mrs. We could easily have been relatives too! Thomas is much more than a customer you see."

"My goodness," Mary exclaimed, coughing slightly. "I think that's far too much information Dolly. We're learning more than we really wanted to know!"

"Right ladies," Thomas greeted them cheerily as he arrived at the table with the boys. "Let's find us a place to eat and feed these rascals."

"Pick a nice place Thomas," Grace instructed as they left the table. "You know them far better than we do."

Thomas led them across the train lines to the other side of the street. "There's 9 or 10 hotels between here and Government Street. Every one of 'em has good food, so I think ya can pick yer own place to eat," he chuckled, gazing up the street. "Let's take this side first and I'll tell ya what they have. Here, by yer elbow, is the Queens, then the Grand Pacific, Panama, Empire up there, and the Rainier Hotel. Now over that side you've got the Gordon, California, Grand Central and the Jubilee. Then, there's a couple of restaurants, the White Lunch Cafe and the Rainier Cafe, so we ain't short of any choice are we?"

"Tell me," Grace laughed, "do they all sell liquor and beer?"

"Of course they do!"

"Make a choice Mary," her sister sighed, "it doesn't matter to me."

"All right, I pick the Grand Pacific Hotel."

"Oh good," young Tommy yelped, "Mrs. Anderson makes good apple pie."

"Well there, someone's satisfied with your choice Mary," Grace chuckled as the three boys tore off up the street again. "Do you go there often Thomas?"

"Never, but that little devil knows everybody and has probably eaten at most of them over the years," he paused as they set out after the boys. "His mother's gone you know and I'm the only one he has. I don't put any restrictions on him. He goes where he pleases and does what he wants. He knows I'm there when he needs me. Apart from that, he's a law unto himself."

"You didn't have to tell us all that," Mary purred, slipping her hand through his arm, "but it certainly is interesting. Young Tommy's a nice boy and quite a character, I might add. Our boys are having a wonderful time with him and they're actually behaving themselves."

Arriving at the Grand Pacific, they were quickly shown to a table as Tommy chattered with the waitress.

"See what I mean, he knows everyone!" his father laughed.

"Can we have a hamburger please mom?" Nathan bleated.

"What did the lad want?" Thomas asked, appearing to be puzzled.

"A hamburger."

"What the devil's a hamburger?"

"We could get fish and chips on Broad Street," young Tommy suggested eagerly, "and eat 'em out of a paper."

"Yeah mom, can we?" David pleaded.

"Best let 'em go missus," Thomas muttered reaching into his pocket for money.

"Let me pay," Mary insisted, reaching into her purse. "Will $20 be enough?"

"Hell woman, 20 cents will be enough!" Thomas snapped, tossing his son two coins.

50

"David, Nathan," Mary raised a threatening finger, "I want you back here in one hour."

Ordering the most expensive meal on the menu at $2.55, they asked for coffee and a pint of local brew for Thomas as he murmured humorously, "You ain't never been in a place like this before, have ya?"

"We ate lunch at the Rainier Cafe," Grace replied, her eyes darting around her, "but this is much grander. Are all the hotels like this?"

"It's all show," Thomas replied with a grin. "The back alleys are full of rat-infested drains and garbage."

"Stop that!" Mary ordered, making a face. "We want to know all about you, not the rats."

"Why?"

"I'm writing a book," she said quickly.

Bringing her notebook out, she caught the approving wink of her sister as the waitress arrived with their drinks.

"First," said Mary, "I need your signature." Sliding her notebook in front of the man who was totally unaware he was their great-grandfather, her fingers found her sister's hand under the table. They watched him sign the page, then slowly add the words, "Always yours."

"Why did you add that?" Mary gasped.

"I don't know. I can't explain it but somehow I feel close to both of you," he said frowning. "Maybe you're both ghosts from the past."

"Or the future," Grace chuckled nervously.

"No, no, not the future," Thomas sighed. "If that were true, you would know the date the war will finish and if I'm lucky enough to get into it."

"November the 11th, 1918 and yes, you will."

Blood drained from Thomas Duncan's face when he heard Grace's statement. She had taken a wild chance and told him the truth, but would he believe her. There was no way he could understand.

"Hell, you gave me quite a turn there girl," Thomas whispered. "I almost believed ya."

"What's your birthdate Thomas?" Mary quickly changed the subject.

"March 4, 1888. I was born up on Spring Ridge. Dad worked for Judge Begbie."

"And your mother?"

"My mother was Isa, a full-blood native Indian. I don't remember her, she died when I were very young."

Furtive glances passed quickly between the sisters. Here in Victoria to trace the roots of a grandfather, they'd stumbled upon a revelation unknown to their family, a secret well hidden in the annals of time. The dark sparkling eyes of the family had finally been explained.

"Is your father still alive?" Mary continued frantically scribbling notes into her book.

"No, he was lost at sea in 1900."

"I thought you said he worked for the Judge?"

"He did," Thomas sighed. "That was his first trip as a whaler."

They could feel the terrible sadness Thomas was feeling as his mind disturbed old memories and his thoughts took him back to when he had become an orphan.

"I was only twelve," he whispered, "and just started my first job at the railway sheds on Store Street."

"Who looked after you?" Grace asked, concern in her voice.

"Oh I managed. I moved into town."

At that point, questions became inappropriate and they were rescued by the waitress bringing their meals.

"I wish we'd never come," Grace snivelled quietly into Mary's ear as Thomas ordered another pint.

"Don't be silly Gracie." Mary wiped her tears away quickly with her fingers. "We've learned more in the last hour than we could ever have found out in the archives or the library. Now I wonder what those boys of ours are up to."

Mary's cause for concern was well-founded. The boys had started out for the British Fish and Chip Shop on Broad, but Tommy's chatter of tunnels running under the city sparked the imaginations of both his new friends. When they saw that the line-up of customers stretched out of the store and into Broad Street, they stood looking helplessly at each other.

"Wait here, I'll go to the back door and get 'em," Tommy announced with a grin, tearing off down the alley.

"This kid's older than five," David muttered, "more like nine or ten."

"He's fun," Nathan smiled, "and I like him. It's weird, but I feel like I know him."

"What I was thinking too. I wonder why."

Wild shouts from the Hotel Canada Bar on the corner drew their attention as two fighting drunks went flying outside and into the street, screaming and punching at each other. Curious patrons followed and the crowd soon swelled out onto the street until two policemen with tall hats arrived and took the rowdies away.

"Wow, that was exciting," Nathan chuckled, "and did you see those cool-looking hats the policemen had!"

"Hey David, come on," Tommy yelled, coming around the corner of the building holding a newspaper-wrapped parcel. "Follow me."

Running down Johnson and darting across Government Street, young Tommy led them over to Yates then onto Langley Street, turning quickly into Bastion and skidding to a stop in front of the courthouse.

"We eat here," he proudly announced, sitting down on the steps.

"What is this place?" Nathan asked.

"The courthouse," the youngster laughed. "Nobody's gonna bother us here!" He was opening the parcel as a stern-faced lawyer appeared.

"Hello Tommy, looks like you have a good meal there."

"Yes sir," the instant reply brought a quick smile to the lawyer's face. "He's my friend," the boy explained nonchalantly as the man continued on his way.

"Where are we going next?" David asked, picking out two hot chips, blowing on them and stuffing them into his mouth.

"The tunnels." Tommy struggled to answer through his own mouthful. "You wait, I'll show you."

"It's almost 7:30 Davie," Nathan muttered, "shouldn't we be getting back to the restaurant?"

"Not yet, I want to see this tunnel."

"It's all right," Tommy assured them, "my dad will take your mothers back to the Janion. He knows we'll come back there. He always waits for me."

"He never gets mad when you're late?" David asked.

"No, he says life's too short. All he wants me to do is keep out of trouble and love him, and I do."

The boy's simple, frank statement caused a puzzled look on his companions' faces as Nathan giggled, "I love my mom but she sure gets mad sometimes."

"Mine too," David grimaced.

Their concern was soon forgotten as they finished eating. Then Tommy folded the greasy fish and chip paper, stood up, and carefully put it in his pocket.

"Are we going now?" Nathan asked eagerly, also standing.

Nodding, Tommy's eyes flashed with excited anticipation as he led them out of Bastion Street, dodging around the noisy delivery vehicle that chugged up dusty Wharf Street leaving a lingering trail of smoky fumes in the air. Glancing around to check that no one was watching, Tommy darted down the rough, litter-strewn alley beside the Hudson Bay liquor store, twisting around and down the rickety stairs to the dock.

Following at a run, David and Nathan noted the craggy rock foundations of the buildings and the heavy wood planking of the dock.

"Where are we Tommy?" Nathan muttered apprehensively.

"Down below Wharf Street," the muffled reply came from the darkness under the stairs. "Come here."

Nervously the cousins shuffled slowly forward and, as their eyes grew accustomed to the dim light, they saw the shape of a stone archway. Moving cautiously closer, David's fingers touched the icy cold rusted door and goose bumps were raised on his arms in excited fear.

Suddenly they heard a scraping noise and Tommy whispered fiercely, "Somebody's comin' ... hide!"

Scared into action, their blood pumping wildly through their veins, they jumped behind some barrels. Nathan's shaking hand found David's arm in the dark. He could feel the tension in his cousin's body as the door creaked open. They almost stopped breathing even though their hearts were racing. The footsteps came closer and closer. Ducking low and not daring to look, they held their breath as the men passed by. Finally the voices faded away.

"Come on," Tommy's voice whispered, "they've gone!"

Hands groping to find the hidden obstructions, Nathan and David followed the sound of Tommy's voice into the dark mouth of the tunnel. Water splashed under their feet, cold air brushed their faces and an awful smell crept into their nostrils.

"Where are you guys?" David bleated as the big iron door squeaked shut behind them. As he reached out all around him, finally finding Nathan, Tommy's voice came out of the darkness.

"Here, behind you," he hissed. Nathan and David jumped in surprise, clinging to each other until Tommy struck a match. He pulled out the fish and chip paper he had so carefully folded and kept; lighting it, the boys sighed in relief.

Eerie shadows played tricks on their minds as Tommy lit a lantern and the tunnel became dimly visible. Over six feet high, like the inside of a pipe and lined with brick, the two boys shuddered as the water dripped steadily from the roof. A low murmur of unintelligible voices could be heard and David panicked, spinning around to run for the door. At that moment, the door began to creak as if someone was opening it.

"Run," Tommy whispered calmly, "and follow me."

Splashing through the water, they ran like rabbits following Tommy and his flickering lantern into a much smaller side tunnel.

"Stop," the boy snapped as he snuffed out the lantern.

The noise of the door crashing shut, multiplied in the enclosed tunnel, sent a rippling echo rushing past them. Their teeth chattering, the boys held their breath; suddenly David felt the Janion ring in his pocket.

"Quick," he whispered, "all hold hands."

"They're somewhere around here," a rough voice growled. "It's that kid again. He won't get away this time."

"I wish we were all back with my mom," David whispered, as a lantern shone into their faces.

In the blink of an eye, they found themselves standing in front of a table at the Janion Hotel. Tommy's father burst out laughing at the sight of the wet and muddy boys.

"Where in heaven's name have you been?" Mary gasped, the urge to be cross with her son disappearing as she also joined in the laughter.

"Bathtime my lad," Dolly announced, gently grasping Tommy's shoulder. "Say goodbye to your friends now."

The three boys turned to each other and vowed their friendship forever. As they hugged, David and Nathan had tears in their eyes, realizing they would never meet again. They waved one last goodbye as Tommy disappeared up the stairs.

"David," Dolly whispered gently, "it's time you took your folks back to your own time. In your absence, your mothers have had a nice dinner and got to know our time a little better."

"Just one moment," Grace whispered. "We need to hug this man."

"This has been the most wonderful day of my life, meeting you two," Thomas murmured. "I shall keep it as a treasured memory."

"And so will we," said Mary with tears in her eyes. "Let's go boys."

Dolly walked them to the door. She waved them goodbye, dabbing at a tear as she obeyed David's command, sending them whizzing back to the year 2002.

They crossed the street at Pandora, then Johnson and scampered across the Wharf Street crosswalk to the front of Chandler's restaurant.

"We were down there mom," David explained, pointing over the wall to the parking lot below.

"When?"

"Tommy took us there," Nathan bubbled. "There's a tunnel goes under the road."

All the way along Wharf Street, the boys excitedly pointed to places they knew where buildings had been long ago.

Standing at the corner of Wharf and Government, Mary and Grace stared up at the Federal Building and smiled at each other.

"It's hard to believe," said Mary, "that we actually know that was the Post Office at the beginning of the war because we saw it!"

"But which war?" Grace asked.

"Mom, mom," David yelled. "Johnny's boat dock was down there, and the Empress is built on a swamp."

"I thought you said history was boring," Mary teased her son. "Well, now what do you think?"

"This is a great place and history is a lot more interesting than we thought. Can we stay another day?" David asked eagerly.

"No son, we can't stay. We have to catch the ferry home tomorrow. Now, let me tell you something. Most of the time finding out things from the past is hard work and dedication. There will never be another Miss Dolly to help us."

Darkness had fallen and the Legislative Buildings were now illuminated, glowing brightly as the group made their way wearily back to the Gatsby.

"Are you hungry boys?" Grace asked. "You both missed dinner."

"No we didn't, we had fish and chips with Tommy."

"But that's not a proper meal."

"Yes it is Aunt Grace. We're full," David interrupted, sniffing at his cousin, "but he sure stinks! I think we both need a shower."

"Agreed and clean clothes!" his mother laughed. "Off you go. Your Aunt Grace and I are going to have a cup of tea before we come up."

Selecting a quiet table with a view in the dining room, they looked out at the harbour lights as they shone with a peaceful serenity on the calm water.

"I don't believe what's happened Gracie," Mary sighed contentedly. "We found all the answers to our questions."

"We found more than that Mary." Grace bit into her lip in a struggle to control her emotions. "We met him ... and his father. We held them in our arms." Choking back tears, she added, "Darn it sis, they're our flesh and blood and I feel so helpless."

"I know." Mary reached over to grasp her sister's hand. "But think of the memories we'll have. They're not names on a piece of paper anymore. They're real people and we met them."

"Coming to Victoria will never be quite the same again. This place now holds very special memories for us; part of us belongs here."

Finishing their tea, they dragged themselves upstairs and quietly prepared for bed, checking on the boys who appeared to be sleeping soundly, before turning out the light.

"Are you ready?" David whispered awhile later.

"Wait," Nathan whispered back, "I'll listen at the door."

With his ear to the door, David heard the door brush the heavy carpet as his cousin silently opened it and knew he was creeping out to check their mothers' bedroom door.

"They're asleep," Nathan's whisper made David jump as he spoke in his ear. "I could hear my mom snoring."

Dressing quickly, the boys stood in front of their bedroom window and Nathan held up his arm to show that the time on the illuminated face of his watch showed midnight. David rubbed the ring in his pocket. Making no wish, he stood silently and waited.

"Yes David, you called for me?" Dolly asked from behind them.

"Can you make sure my mom and Aunt Grace don't wake up until morning?" David begged her.

"Consider it done sir."

"We want you to take us to visit Tommy in 1926 … after his dad died," said David. "I'm not even sure why we want this though."

Suddenly, it was daylight and they were standing on the tiny dock behind the Janion Hotel. A boatman returning to the dock in an old battered-looking craft waved to them as he pulled up to the landing.

"Hi David! How ya doing Nathan?" he greeted them cheerily. "Haven't seen you boys in a long time."

"You remember us?" David asked. Tommy had been so young when they met him and he had changed a great deal. If Dolly hadn't taken them directly to him, David wasn't sure he would have recognized him.

"Sure do," he said eagerly. "You're the boys from Port Angeles. We almost got caught in the tunnel that day didn't we? That was a long time ago. How come you've come back … and you look just the same?"

"Are you running rum tonight?" Nathan whispered, ignoring his question.

"Yes, but what're ya whispering for?" Tommy asked with a laugh. "It's not illegal until we cross the line."

"But isn't it dangerous?"

"Not the way I do it, wanna come?"

"W-when are you going?" David asked hesitantly, not daring to look at Nathan.

"Right now, as soon as I get the stuff loaded." Producing a key, he unlocked the basement door of the hotel and disappeared into the darkness. "Hey, can you give me a hand?"

With no thought of hiding the liquor, they piled 10 cases of what Tommy called 'the best Irish whisky,' next to the boat.

"Aren't you afraid somebody will see you?" Nathan asked.

57

"Who cares, are you coming or not?"

"Yes," the boys chorused.

"Then get aboard and pull that tarp over the stuff," Tommy ordered.

With the liquor hidden, they pushed off and Tommy started the little motor that pushed them slowly toward the bridge.

"I thought you'd need a speedboat to outrun the cops," David asked. "I could walk faster than this thing goes."

"You'll see," Tommy laughed. "Just wait."

Under Johnson Street Bridge they chugged and down the harbour until they had a wonderful view of the Legislative Buildings, then came the Empress Hotel and, swinging around, they passed the Bapco Paint store and Pendray's soap factory. On they went out into the open sea, never varying their speed. The wind suddenly whipped across the waves, sending Tommy scrambling for his sail. Soon they were feeling the thrill of hurtling along as showers of sea spray splashed across them.

"Wow," David shouted, as Tommy fiddled with the ropes tied to the sail, and calmly held the rudder arm under his leg.

On and on they sailed with breathtaking views of coastal mountains and killer whales for company.

"That's Port Townsend," Tommy pointed, "but we're going over there." He moved his arm to point in the opposite direction. "This lot's for Jack at Keystone."

A grey customs vessel sat in the harbour at Keystone watching Puget Sound from an almost hidden position. A sailor waved as Tommy lowered his sail and started the motor, chugging slowly into the harbour.

"Are you running booze again Tommy?" the sailor yelled. "Damn, that's an awful fast boat you've got there."

Cheekily, Tommy waved as he eased past the customs vessel and chugged into the harbour tucking in between two local fishing boats.

"Wow, you almost got caught that time," David chuckled nervously.

"Don't be silly," Tommy laughed. "Who would believe I run booze in a crazy old boat like this. Why I couldn't outrun a row boat!"

"But they'll see you unload."

"No, they won't," he said confidently, "because I leave it in this fish locker right here." He jumped onto the dock and snapped the side of the locker open. Tommy chuckled to himself as he pulled three big salmon out onto the dock and stacked the 10 cases of liquor inside before closing it again. Heaving the salmon into his boat, he covered them over with the tarp, winking mischievously at David and Nathan. Then, he put the gears of the old motor into reverse and sent it chugging backwards. Sailors watched them closely from the coastguard vessel's deck, grinning at the odd little craft and its youthful occupants.

"What you got under that tarp boy?" an officer asked.

"Show him Nathan," Tommy laughed.

Nathan pulled back the tarp and the men laughed, nonchalantly waving them on. David and Nathan let out a big sigh of relief realizing this was an experience they would never forget … ever!

A stiff breeze filled the boat's lone sail as they moved up Puget Sound for home. Settled contentedly in the stern, the boys held the rudder arm between them and grinned.

Dawn's first rays of sunshine were sending their streaks of gold into the eastern sky as David and Nathan made their way back up Wharf Street. They were joined by a smiling Dolly Walker when David's fingers gently rubbed the Janion ring in his pocket.

"You have need of me sir?" she inquired.

"Can you please take us back to our beds at the Gatsby," he asked quietly, "and make us both sleep like we've slept all night? We're awful tired Miss Dolly."

The next morning their mothers got up early, making a pot of coffee as they got ready.

"It's awfully quiet in there, I guess we'll have to go wake up those sleepy heads," Grace commented awhile later, but before Mary could reply, the door of the boy's room opened.

"Hi mom," Nathan yawned. "What time is it?"

"Almost 8 o'clock, is your cousin awake? We have to get packed and get the car into the ferry line-up."

"Yes, he's getting dressed, but I'm hungry mom."

"We'll eat in a little while, now hurry up you two," called Mary.

With an eye on the clock, Mary and Grace hurried their sons along and got the suitcases loaded into the car. The plan was simple and, as the receptionist had advised, they should get their car into the ferry line-up before having breakfast, to be sure of getting onto the ferry.

"You check out Grace," Mary advised, "we'll go get the car into the line-up." Driving down to the Coho embarkation area, Mary braked in surprise when she saw the long line of cars ahead of them and a sign that said, *Ferry Full*. "I don't believe this, where are all these cars going?"

"Must be Seattle," David laughed, "there's a Mariners' game today."

"But we have to get home," his mother objected, as Grace came tearing across the road. "Looks like we'll have to go from Swartz Bay or try for the Anacortes ferry."

"No we don't mom," David chuckled as he gently rubbed the ring.

"You have a wish Master David?" Dolly asked from the front seat.

Grace squealed at Dolly's sudden appearance, drawing strange looks from a passing couple.

"Don't worry, they can't see me," the ghost assured them.

"Darn it David, I wish you wouldn't do that," Grace snapped at her nephew. "It scares the living daylights out of me."

"Sorry Aunt Grace. I still have some time left to make wishes and just wanted to wish we were at the front of the line-up," David mumbled.

Grace blinked her eyes and stared at the empty space where the car had been. Shivering involuntarily, she dared not look around to see if anyone else had noticed the car's sudden disappearance. Rubbing the beads of sweat from her forehead, she looked over at the dock area and there, at the head of the line, was her sister's car.

"Oh my goodness, I have to get over there and quickly!" she murmured under her breath, racing for the car.

"How did that get there?" a ferry worker stammered, pointing at Mary's car. "That car changed colour!"

"David," his mother snapped, "use that ring and get us out of here."

Nathan was looking out of the back window and yelled, "No! We have to wait for my mom!"

Mary looked at the other seat. "Yikes, I've forgotten about Grace!"

"What's going on here?" another ferry worker demanded knocking on the car window.

"Where is your mother Nathan?" Mary asked frantically trying to ignore the man now rapping harshly on her window.

"Here she comes, open the door mom, quick!" David exclaimed.

Mary pushed the door button and Grace jumped into the car, so breathless she could only say, "Oh, am I glad to see you!"

"Now where to mom?"

"Anywhere! Just get us out of here!" Mary replied.

"1926 Miss Dolly. Quick!" David wished.

"Hey," another male voice shouted, "you can't be in here."

Mary rolled down her window and in an obviously confused voice asked, "Where are we?"

"This is the C.P.R. commercial dock lady."

Suddenly noticing the old vehicles, Mary sighed and rolled up her window. "What are we doing here David? What year is this?"

"1926 …," David replied.

Dolly's voice interrupted him. "You're in exactly the same place you were in before. It's just the year that's changed as David requested."

"Look mom!" Nathan yelled. "That's Tommy's boat, he's seen us."

"Hi fellas!" An even older-looking Tommy was waving and shouting at them, looking strangely at their car as he ran toward them. "What're you doing here? Want to come with me tonight?"

"No, sorry Tommy, we have to go."

"Goodbye Tommy," they all called sadly, as David began his wish.

"Please take us back to the ... the beginning of the ferry line-up, Miss Dolly!" He remembered just in time to be specific.

"Loading cars in 10 minutes," a voice called over the loudspeaker.

Mary looked around and it was as if no one had noticed them this time. She let out her breath waiting impatiently for the cars to move.

Meanwhile, David glanced down at his watch. It was almost exactly the same time three days before when he'd found Dolly Walker's ring. *Thank goodness we got Aunt Grace back in time*, he thought. Then another concern popped into his head. "How will we send the ring back to Miss Dolly," he asked aloud, concern in his voice.

"You won't need to David," Dolly's voice whispered. "I've already taken it from your pocket. It's been a pleasure, goodbye deary."

He felt her ghostly lips kiss his cheek as his fingers instinctively reached into his empty pocket.

Janion Ring: Lost in History

It was an unusually hot day in June 1935 when newlyweds Tim and Linda McCray left their new home in Regina, Saskatchewan and began a journey to spend a honeymoon of six days visiting Linda's cousin and her family in Victoria, British Columbia. Born in Newfoundland, Linda's mother and Harriet Joyce were cousins who had never met. Linda had written to Harriet and they were now expected at their home on Saturday.

Putting the prairies behind them on a long and monotonous bus ride, they began the first scenic leg of their journey in Calgary aboard the CN Rocky Mountain Railway Train. It was here that they discovered for the first time that the Rocky Mountains formed the border between the western Provinces of Alberta and British Columbia. They were taken aback by the beautiful scenery so foreign to them from the usual prairie monotony. As the train snaked its way through mountain passes and down to the lush green valleys of Canada's Pacific-bordered province and the large coastal city of Vancouver, they marvelled at each wonder of nature. The depth of the Fraser Canyon took Linda's breath away as they moved across eight majestic, yet seemingly fragile-looking, railway trestles.

In Vancouver, they boarded the overnight Canadian Pacific ferry to Victoria. The colours of the ocean combined with coastal scenery, again took their breath away, as they slowly cruised down the strait to the southern tip of Vancouver Island. When a passing deckhand pointed out several black and white killer whales surfacing among the white-capped waves their joy seemed complete. Wind blew cold spray on their faces as they clung to the deck railing, determined to catch every moment of daylight, not wanting to miss anything. Unknown lights blinked mysteriously on darkened shorelines, adding a sense of adventure to the journey. Unused to the vessel's rolling motion as the chill of damp night air descended, they reluctantly returned inside.

Nestled together in their seats, having refused to pay for sleeping berths, they slept fitfully, although warmly, until the first rays of dawn slipped through the ship's window. Looking outside, they were surprised to see houses on the nearby shore and realized they were almost at their destination. Quickly drinking a cup of tea and sharing toast, they hurried outside to watch as the ferry slowed for its turn past the long expanse of the Ogden Point breakwater. A tall, familiar-looking, grain elevator stood on a nearby dock. They looked southward and Linda smiled at the sight of snow-capped mountains rising majestically on the United States side of the Straits of Juan de Fuca.

"What a glorious sight!" Linda whispered.

"Hmm, sounds like you're wishing this was our home darling!" Tim teased, pulling her closer and kissing her forehead.

Linda smiled. The thought had crossed her mind. She had seen pictures of Victoria and was already very sure that none of them had done it justice.

On shore, they searched the luggage trolleys for their bags then asked directions to a streetcar stop. Struggling with their load, they decided to walk around the harbour getting their first glimpse of the large and very regal Empress Hotel.

"Oh Tim, isn't it simply marvellous and this harbour ... we're going to love Victoria!" she exclaimed.

Tim just knowingly smiled as they caught their breath and watched the activity in the busy harbour, then they crossed the street to wait for the streetcar which would take them into town.

"Here we go," Tim murmured as a streetcar pulled alongside, squealing to a stop. "Do you go to Hillside and Quadra?" he shouted to the conductor.

"Sure do lad. It's a seven-cent fare."

Tim stashed their bags as indicated by the conductor, paid the fare and quickly grabbed for support as the streetcar wobbled on its way up Government Street toward the centre of town. It was only a few minutes before they knew they were in the business centre of BC's capital. Although Victoria is a much smaller city than Vancouver and, quieter today as it was Sunday, Linda's inquisitive interest kept her turning in her seat as she attempted to take it all in.

Clanking and grinding, the ungainly iron monster screeched around the corner into Yates and stopped in front of a sign that proclaimed "Dentist" at the corner of Broad Street. The driver checked his watch against a large clock atop a sidewalk pole, then jerked the streetcar into motion again.

"I think I can smell the sea Tim," Linda giggled.

"No ma'am, that's the foundry you can smell," the conductor informed her as they rattled around a corner and turned north onto Douglas. "It's on the left up ahead, after we pass the Hudson's Bay store—that's the big white building up on the right."

As they looked in the direction he indicated, they noticed a yellow vapour-like cloud suspended in the hollow between Douglas and Government Streets.

"Sulphur, stinks like hell," he stated with a grin, covering his nose and mouth with his hand until they were clear.

Every block or so they stopped, picking up passengers; it wasn't long before the conductor told them they would soon be turning right onto Hillside Avenue and their stop would be next.

"What's that place over there?" Linda asked, pointing across the street to a high-fenced area.

"That's the prison, poor devils," the conductor muttered. "Until a few years ago, chain gangs were a common sight in this area. He suddenly turned to face the passengers and called, "Next stop, Quadra!"

As they got off, they bade farewell to the amiable conductor and stood on the curb watching as the streetcar moved off toward a distant hill. Linda looked around while Tim fumbled in his suit pocket.

"I have their address here somewhere," he assured her. "That has to be their house." He pointed at the two-storey house with the wide verandah near the corner. "The stop is almost in front of it just as Hattie described!"

Fifteen-year-old Dorothy Joyce was peering through the curtains and squealed, "I think they're here!" She made a dash for the door without waiting for instructions. Outside, she waved madly at the young couple standing on the curb with their luggage.

Enthusiastically, she ran down the steps to welcome their guests. "Hello, I'm Dorothy. You must be Tim and Linda," she bubbled as they smiled in acknowledgement. "Ma and Pa are looking forward to hearing all your news. Here, let me help with your bags."

Chattering all the way, Dorothy led them over to the house and up the steps where they were met by her smiling parents. Nelson and Hattie Joyce welcomed the visitors with hugs inviting them inside.

"Tea will be ready in a jiffy, I'm sure you're both tired," Hattie flung over her shoulder as she went toward the kitchen. "Dorothy, help our guests take their bags to their room dear, then I'll have tea ready."

Within 20 minutes they were all sitting around the large kitchen table chatting about their visitors' journey and bringing Harriet up-to-date on her family over a nice cup of tea. When they got onto the subject of Victoria, Tim mentioned that he had noticed their streetcar was going toward a hill when it left them and his curiosity now came to the forefront.

"Where does the streetcar go from here Nelson?" he asked. "You certainly have more hills than we do on the prairies. It reminds Linda a bit of Newfoundland."

"But you have a lot more trees; we find that the hills tend to make us dizzy!" she quipped and everyone laughed. "Sadly, I haven't been back home for too many years."

"We have many flat areas here as well and a great deal of good farmland beyond the city limits Tim. I gather you're a prairie boy," Nelson added watching the young man nod. "To answer your question, the streetcar continues eastward, and beyond that hill the road changes its name to Lansdowne and goes about two miles almost to the sea."

"It does a circle up in the posh area known as The Uplands," interrupted Dorothy, "then it turns around and comes back."

"That would be a nice ride for you if you have the time while you're here," added Hattie, bringing a plate of hot scones and jam to the table. "You'll meet our three boys tonight at dinner; they're out playing baseball."

After tea, Linda said she could hardly keep her eyes open and she and Tim went upstairs to unpack. Tim returned awhile later and said Linda had fallen asleep. He was chatting with Nelson when loud footsteps sounded on the steps outside and three young men entered from the kitchen; Nelson introduced them as their sons, Don, Stan and Jim. The men's clothes were unusually dusty, from playing baseball they explained. Seeing them, their mother made a quick clucking noise with her tongue and chased them back outside to brush themselves off. Hattie was obviously used to this routine having raised five sons before Dorothy came along.

"Then go get yourselves decent for dinner!" she ordered.

"Ah Ma! A little dirt never hurt anyone!" Stan teased.

"Git!" she laughed, flicking a wet dishcloth at him.

Linda came downstairs soon afterwards and found the house abuzz with light-hearted conversation. She helped in the kitchen and promptly at six o'clock, dinner was on the table.

Afterwards, the boys went out again and it gave the visitors a chance to talk about the places they should see while in the city. The next morning, Linda decided to go to church with Harriet and Dorothy, walking to Pandora Street and finding it a good stretch of the legs. Later, Dorothy would explain that they never used the car on the Lord's Day, although she suspected it may have been her ma's way of keeping her pa away from the car … he had such big feet he was prone to accidents!

"On Monday, I'll show you around the city, if you like," Dorothy offered when they were eating dinner that night.

"Dorothy knows all the interesting nooks and crannies," explained her mother.

When Monday arrived, Nelson and his sons left the house early and the others then had their own breakfast. Dorothy seemed keen to tell them what she had planned and, by the time they left the house at 9:30, Linda was impatient to start their first day of sight-seeing.

"If you don't mind walking," Dorothy said as they walked out onto the sidewalk, "we'll cut across the brickworks and I'll show you the roller rink. We can catch a streetcar over on Douglas if you like."

No strangers to walking, Tim and Linda followed Dorothy up the street in the direction they had come from town the day they arrived. A couple of streetcars loaded with passengers rumbled by.

"Why is everyone so unhappy-looking?" Linda asked.

"Pa says it's the recession, lots of men are out of work," Dorothy said solemnly. "My brothers are helping Pa build a house but not many people can afford houses right now they say." She looked very solemn as she said this and it was plain to Tim and Linda that things at the Joyce house were not as good as they had been led to believe.

"Your pa's right," Tim muttered, "it's the same in Manitoba. Most of the farmers, and my father is one of them, are having trouble selling their produce. Wheat is rotting in the fields and many are out of work. It's very sad. We would never have come here if your folks hadn't kindly offered to put us up."

65

"We don't see many visitors so it's awfully nice to have you. This is the end of Blanshard Street. The railway used to run along here and go into the brickyards," Dorothy told them. "Pa says there was a railway station near here on Hillside but it disappeared a long time ago while we lived in Everett." They were past the prison now and cutting across a field with a few grazing cattle when Tim asked Dorothy about living in Everett.

"Did you live in Everett for long?"

"Not really, a few years, but we all went to school there. Two of my brothers stayed there and married their girlfriends. I really miss them."

"Why did you move to Everett?" Tim continued, hoping he wasn't being too nosey as Linda was giving him the eye.

Dorothy didn't seem concerned with the question and explained that when she was about three-years-old, the depression hit the family so hard her father couldn't build houses anymore or find other work, so all six kids packed into their big Nash car with Harriet and Nelson and set out to follow the crops through BC and Washington State. They picked hops, berries and fruit wherever they could find work.

"It was really hard for ma though. She had to cook on a tiny little coal stove and we lived in a tent with a wooden floor. Every few days, we moved to a different place because the crops ran out. Pa worried a lot about having enough money to buy food but I was too young to understand. The boys explained it all when I got older. Finally, we stopped in Everett and we lived on a chicken farm."

Dorothy was obviously a bright girl with a huge love for her family and an interest in everyone and everything. She continued to chatter and answer their questions as they walked toward Douglas Street, proving to be a mine of information.

"See, that's the brickworks. There used to be a railway bridge over the clay pit, but they took it down when the railway stopped coming here."

"My goodness," Linda exclaimed with a frown, "what a messy place to work!"

"I know, but it's a great place to get clay so you can make flowerpots. Last year I made a whole bunch of them for ma and painted them too. They sure brightened up our porch last summer! Look, that's Douglas Street with all the cars on it," Dorothy announced pointing. "That's the way you came from town. I go roller skating up there at the rink on Tolmie Street." She now pointed in the opposite direction, then added, "You can't really see it from here, it's too far away." They followed the direction of her finger and saw four streetcars coming toward them, one after the other.

"There must be the depot over there," said Tim, then he chuckled, "and no, we don't want to see it. We want you to take us downtown now, please Dorothy."

"Yes, they're coming from the streetcar barn on Cloverdale. It's not very far from here."

"Oh no, young lady, take us to the nearest streetcar stop. It's time to ride into town!" he laughed.

They reached the corner of Hillside and Douglas and for the first time were aware of the complicated traffic pattern as cars seemed to be driving every which way in this area. Getting safely across the street seemed to be an exercise in agility as they darted between two streetcars going in different directions and cars honked their horns.

"Why is this corner so dangerous?" Linda asked breathlessly when they reached the other side of the road.

"It has too many streets running into each other and pa says they better fix it soon before someone gets killed!" Dorothy explained, walking quickly to a tram stop on Douglas Street. They were gasping for breath as a tram squealed to a halt just in front of them.

"James Bay and the docks via Government Street," the conductor shouted.

Linda paid their seven-cent fares and, holding tightly to handrails in the violently wobbling conveyance, they found window seats. Wheels grinding, they turned into Government Street and moved on down the hill almost running down a horse and cart that lumbered across Bay Street in front of them. Sharp words were exchanged between drivers through the open doors and repeated gestures from the drayman caused ripples of laughter to run through the small group of passengers.

"Look, look!" Dorothy squealed. "There's the gas works." Switching sides with youthful agility, she pointed out the iron works, a brewery and Chinatown. "We'll get off here at Yates," she called to the others before jumping up again and moving to the door.

"Careful lass!" the conductor growled a protective warning in his thick Scottish brogue as they all trooped off with a group of other riders.

"We'll go down Yates Street toward the water," Dorothy announced, stopping in front of an interesting-looking building and pointing to the sign that said, Majestic Theatre. "I think my ma said that some of the first moving pictures in the city were played here."

They walked a bit farther and she pointed out the San Francisco Hotel, saying it had been there since the early boom days. It looked sadly uncared for, a remnant of days gone by.

"Show us the railway that goes up the mountain," Tim suggested. "Did you call it the Malahat? Linda loves trains."

"Oh sure, that's easy," their young guide replied running to the end of the street. "It's there!" She pointed across the street to a tiny station building at the entrance to the Johnson Street Bridge. They crossed the street and Linda went inside, eagerly looking for a timetable, but when she returned disappointment was written on her face. She sat down on the bench beside them and stared at the railway tracks.

"We'll come back later dear," Tim consoled her. "I wonder if that's part of the old railway. He was looking next door at a three-storey redbrick building just across the tracks. Curiosity getting the better of him, he got up and started walking toward the front of the boarded-up building. The girls followed him. Dorothy read the sign engraved into the top of the facade.

"The Janion 1891. I remember ... I heard my brothers talking about it only recently." Turning thoughtful she continued, "Apparently, it was used as a hotel for only a few years then the E&N Railway used it for offices."

"Oh!" Linda perked up with interest. "Too bad we can't go inside."

Looking at the dirty front of the old hotel with inquisitive interest, Tim frowned. "Looks like nobody loves the old place," he muttered. "Let's go take a look around the back."

Dorothy led the way down the side of the old building toward the water. It was steep and rough and she quickly found herself sitting in the dirt.

"My goodness, are you all right Linda?" her husband asked, rushing to her assistance.

"No, just my pride is dented a little, but what's this?" she said in surprise, her fingers scraping at something in the dirt.

"It's a ring," Dorothy whispered as Linda held up the small object. "I wonder if it's valuable."

"Well it's dirty, that is for sure," Linda chuckled, as Tim offered a hand and pulled her up.

"Look, there's water over there, we can clean it," he suggested. She gave the ring to him and he went to the edge of the waterway as the others followed. As he held it under the water, the dirt fell away and its dull yellow surface shone through the water. "I think it's gold and there's a small stone that may be a diamond," he announced. "Let me polish it."

68

Suddenly the ring disappeared from Tim's fingers and a voice spoke from behind them making them all jump.

"Who are *you*?" Tim asked abruptly, being the first to see the diminutive lady dressed in the clothes of an earlier era standing behind them. She was holding out her hand and the ring was floating through the air toward it. The girls turned around to see who Tim was talking to and was just in time to see the ring slide onto her finger all by itself. Dorothy gasped and Linda let out a little scream and moved farther away.

"I'm Dolly Walker, the Manager of the Janion Hotel."

"But how can that be?" Tim asked doubtfully. "It's a derelict."

"I don't need to answer your questions young man; you were not the finder of my ring!"

"I found it," Linda whispered, finally finding her tongue.

"Yes dear," Dolly smiled, "and you shall have your every wish fulfilled for the next three days."

"Wishes for three days?" Dorothy giggled suspiciously. "Are you a ghost or something?"

"Be quiet girl, of course I'm a ghost. Come back to the front of the hotel and I'll show you."

Turning abruptly, her long black skirt swirling about her ankles, the fancy-bonneted lady swiftly walked back up the path the way they had come.

"Come on Tim," his wife chuckled. "Let's see what she's up to."

Dolly waited in front of the hotel entrance, her foot tapping impatiently as she adjusted her bonnet. "Are you ready Linda? Am I to take all three of you?"

"Hold on a minute lady," Tim retorted, "just where do you think you're taking us?"

"I'm taking you back to the glory days when the Janion stood proudly here on Store Street and the railway ran right past the door."

"Is she going to hypnotize us?" Dorothy whispered, grasping Linda's arm.

"All right, this has gone far enough," Linda snapped. "Do whatever you're going to do then buzz off and let us enjoy our holiday."

The Janion Lady smiled then snapped her fingers.

Linda and Dorothy screamed, clutching at Tim as all three staggered back a step. Everything around them had changed, even the walls of the Janion were clean, the windows were no longer boarded, and people walked past them into the hotel as if they didn't even see them. A steam engine was moving down the street clanking and blowing black smoke as it strained on its load. Linda and Tim stared in fascination unable to comprehend what had happened. Dorothy was unusually silent.

"Now do you understand?" the Janion Lady chuckled. "This is 1916 and yes, I am a ghost, but I won't hurt you. The reward for finding my ring is that I will answer all your questions and grant your wishes for the next three days. I can't give you riches or treasure but you will have an interesting time and can end up with a wealth of information. Now, I am going to leave you."

"But how do we call you back?" Tim muttered.

"*You* don't. Linda is the one who found the ring, she is the one who will be rewarded with my attention when she rubs the ring."

"My goodness! She's gone!" Dorothy gasped. "Where on earth did she go? Oh my gosh ... look, everything's gone back to normal."

Glancing around, they shook their heads in amazement as they stood rooted to the sidewalk.

"Did that really happen or am I dreaming?" Linda asked.

"I'm not dreaming," Dorothy giggled, "that was exciting, let's do it again!"

"Where's the ring?" Tim muttered. "I bet that woman took it with her."

"No, she didn't," Linda replied. "It's right here in my pocket."

"This is crazy," Tim growled. "It's impossible to just jump back and forth in time."

The conversation turned to laughter as they walked away from the bridge through Pennington Alley, across Johnson, and over to Bastion Street where Dorothy pointed out the old courthouse, now empty and disused.

"Maybe you should try the ring and ask that lady to show us what it looked like when it was new," she suggested.

"Don't you even try it," Tim insisted sharply, "that's foolish talk young lady."

A streetcar rumbled by as they reached the end of Bastion Street at Government and Dorothy pointed to the Arcade and Spencer's Department Store across the street. Turning right, they wandered down to the front of Woolworth's Five and Dime Department Store.

"We just have to go in here Tim," Linda exclaimed, tugging on his arm. "I love this store. Maybe they have different things here in Victoria."

Looking around at the nearby buildings and storefronts, Tim gazed up at the Royal Bank Building next door with its grand columned entranceway then over to Morris's smoke shop next to the restaurant they had passed at the corner of Bastion Street.

"These buildings are so amazing, I don't think they will ever change," he said. "Nobody will ever convince me that Victoria would pull down these grand old buildings."

"You could ask the lady in the ring," Dorothy eagerly urged.

"It could never happen," he laughed, throwing his hands up in frustration. "Oh all right Linda, try it just to satisfy her."

"Ask her to take us to 2005," said Dorothy.

Linda smiled at Dorothy's request. *Why 2005?* she silently wondered.

"Let me call that silly woman," Tim demanded holding out his hand for the ring. "I'll bet you nothing happens."

Hesitantly, Linda handed him the ring and watched as he rubbed its surface. As he wanted, nothing happened and he looked delighted.

"There I told you, it was all just a trick."

"Can I try?" Dorothy held out her hand and rubbed on the ring, but again nothing happened. "Darn it," she muttered. "I really wanted it to work for me, although don't you remember that she did say it was only you who could make the wishes Linda?"

Doubt suddenly filled Linda's mind, but she held out her hand and accepted the ring from Dorothy. *Has this whole episode been imagined?* she thought. *Maybe I was merely dreaming and none of this is really happening at all.* Staring down at the tiny gold ring, she picked it up and tentatively rubbed her thumb across the gold surface.

"You have a request my dear?" The voice of the Janion Lady startled them as she suddenly appeared beside Linda.

"I-I thought I might be dreaming," Linda stammered, inching closer to her husband.

"This is ridiculous," Tim snapped, "where did you really come from lady?"

"Young man," Dolly purred, "you're only party to this exercise because your wife wants you along, but if you continue to annoy me, I shall sit you on that windowsill up there for the next three days!" She pointed up to the top of a boarded-up building.

Dorothy giggled. "I think that would make him believe you're real!"

"Shall we girl?" the Janion Lady's eyes sparkled with excitement. "Shall we?"

"No, you shall not!" Linda declared, stamping her foot to assure herself she was in control. "You said you would obey *my* wishes."

71

"And I will, but try to keep him quiet, if that's possible," Dolly whispered sarcastically. "Now my dear, what is it your desire?"

"We want to go to the year 2005," Dorothy said eagerly.

"Yes that's right," Linda agreed, "please take us to 2005."

Tim blinked in surprise as the whole street once again took on a completely different look. Instead of F.W. Woolworth's Five and Dime, they were standing in front of a hotel with a huge window. Speechless, Tim pointed to the smoke shop, still just as it had been in 1935, except the restaurant at the corner of Bastion Street was now a ladies' clothing shop. Glancing southward, Linda saw that the classic structure of the Royal Bank now housed a bookstore and, farther down the street, the Bank of Commerce building on the corner of Fort had become The Christmas Store.

"What the dickens is a Christmas store?" she whispered to Dorothy, but received only a shrug of her shoulders in reply.

"There aren't any streetcar tracks," said Tim, obviously puzzled.

"Gosh, look at the clothes people are wearing in 2005," Dorothy giggled. "Ma would kill me if I showed even my knees in public!"

"Good gracious," Linda muttered in disgust, glancing at her husband as his eyes followed the short-skirted girls, "whatever has the world come to!"

"It's 2005," he muttered sheepishly. "Fashion seems to have gone through some changes!"

"Well you don't have to stare at them Tim McCray."

"Sorry love," Tim grinned through his apology, "but it is kind of startling."

"Let's go look at the harbour," Dorothy suggested, "the ferry might be in. I wonder if it's changed."

Walking toward the harbour, the prairie couple stared in amazement through shop windows and winced at the prices on the displays.

"Two for $50! Wow, everything is so expensive in 2005," Linda moaned. "We can't afford those prices!"

Shaking their heads, they continued down Government until Linda spotted Rogers' chocolate shop and, seeing no cars, made a dash across the street. She gazed in wonder through the window at the huge selection of delectable-looking morsels.

"Can we try one Tim?" she pleaded.

Tim frowned as his eyes saw the price. "$2.50 each," he growled, "why that's the price of a bale of hay!"

"All we need is one to share," his wife pleaded. "We've heard so much about them and they're so big!"

Looking longingly through the glass, Linda's fingers absentmindedly fiddled with the Janion ring in her pocket.

"You called me?" Dolly's voice startled them.

"Where on earth did you come from?" Tim gasped.

"I was called," Dolly replied testily, "and you, country boy, had better mind your manners. You've already annoyed me once too often today!"

Dorothy giggled. "Can you pop up anytime you want?"

"Only when I'm called."

"I must have rubbed the ring in my pocket, Dorothy. Why is everything so expensive?" Linda asked. "We can't afford these prices."

Dolly smiled at the visitor and tapped her parasol on the sidewalk to get everyone's attention. "You're forgetting this is 2005 not 1935. Prices have changed, but if you check your money you will find I have made the necessary adjustment."

Opening her purse, Linda took out her wallet and emptied the change into her hand.

"This isn't Canadian money," she squealed, pointing to a large gold-coloured coin and two odd-looking silver coins with gold centres.

"Of course they are!" Dolly snapped. "It's the new coinage from 1987."

"You mean they've changed the money too!" Tim gasped, reaching into his back pocket for his own wallet.

"Stop!" the Janion ghost ordered sharply. "We have moved 70 years along in the history of this city. Now, if you can't handle the changes, I can take you back to 1935."

"Don't let her take us back yet Linda," Dorothy pleaded, "this is much more exciting than 1935!"

"If you like I can stay with you and explain things," Dolly offered.

"That would be helpful," Linda agreed with a sigh, looking over at her husband. "I agree with Dorothy, this is exciting; surely you think so too Tim?"

Tim just scowled back at her.

Disregarding the extravagance, they went inside Rogers' and each of them purchased a giant Victoria cream of a different flavour. Outside, they opened them and took their first bite, murmuring their delight as they nibbled at the tasty treat. As they walked, Dorothy tried to point out the changes to buildings she was familiar with, but it all seemed very confusing. When she pointed to the large, grey granite Federal Building on the corner of Government and Wharf, she commented that she knew this building as the Post Office, but the sign was missing and she had no idea where it had gone. Tim was gaping at the cars while Linda was goggle-eyed.

"Would you like me to take you back to 1935 now?" Dolly asked with a chuckle.

"I think I'm more than ready to go back," Linda sighed. "This is much too busy and confusing."

Dorothy finally agreed and, in the blink of an eye, everything was back to normal. Dorothy pointed excitedly to the Federal Building, with its large Post Office sign above the door.

"See," she laughed, "I told you it was the Post Office."

"You know what," Tim chuckled, "I'm not sure I want to see the future. If that woman comes back, we should get her to show us the past."

"If we go back to the past we could go back to Rogers' and buy lots of chocolates, they should be much cheaper in earlier days."

"I like that idea Dorothy," Tim grinned.

"Oh all right let's go back to 1914," Linda agreed, grasping the ring in her pocket. "My dad is always talking about the First World War. I wonder what Victoria looked like then."

"You have a request?" the Janion ghost whispered as she materialized beside Linda.

"Could you take us back to 1914 please," Linda whispered, still surprised when the lady appeared.

"Of course, would you like to be anywhere in particular?"

"No, right here will be fine."

She had no sooner said the words when the scene changed again. This time there were horse-drawn carts and old cars on the street.

"Oh my, this is before I was born. Let's go back and get some more chocolates," Dorothy suggested eagerly.

They began walking back up the street, but Tim suddenly stopped. "Looks like you're out of luck girls, they ain't there!"

"Well the building appears to be here," Linda said with a frown. "Maybe they hadn't started making their chocolates yet."

"Chocolates young lady?" A passing gentleman came to stand beside them. He had overheard their conversation and noticed their unusual attire. "You should try the green grocer across the street, they make the most delicious chocolates you ever tasted." They thanked him and he saluted and continued on his way, looking back again as he went.

Staring at the little shop across the street to which the man had pointed, Tim read the words written on the window. "Rogers' Fresh Vegetables, yep looks like this is an earlier Rogers' store.'"

Waiting while a troop of soldiers marched by, they crossed the street and gazed in the shop window. Half of the window space was taken by the display of big round chocolates and, true to Dorothy's prediction, the price tag was a mere 25 cents.

"Wow look at the price," Linda laughed, "let's buy a bagful Tim!"

Coming out of the store, it was Tim's turn to meet one of the locals when he was accosted by a man pointed his walking stick at him.

"Are you volunteering for the war young man?"

"No sir, we're here on holiday."

"Have you no sense of adventure lad?" the old man ranted. "If I were your age, I'd be off in a flash."

"But the war hasn't started yet," Dorothy piped up, remembering her history.

"When did it start Dorothy?" Tim asked.

"August 4th, 1914."

"Then ask that woman to show us August 4th," Tim suggested.

Linda's fingers had hardly touched the ring when the apparition appeared once again.

"Can you show us the day the war started," Linda whispered to Dolly.

"Which war, you'll have to be more specific."

"The one that started in 1914."

"Of course I can," Dolly sighed. "There you are."

Startled by the sudden and dramatic change, Tim reached out to grab the girls as pandemonium sounded all around them. People were rushing about in all directions shouting that they were at war. Soldiers marching down the street were urged on by encouraging calls from a flag-waving crowd, causing streetcars to stop until the crowd passed over the tracks. There was a feeling of euphoria in the air as ships in the harbour blew their foghorns in a noisy, continual blast.

"Holy hell, it's just like they said it was. Everyone has gone crazy," Tim shouted over the noise. "Linda, get us outa here!"

Pulled into the crowd Linda hung onto Tim who grabbed Dorothy's arm, but due to the press of people his wife was unable to reach the ring in her pocket. Buffeted and pushed toward the harbour, Tim scrambled to stay with the girls but young Dorothy slipped from his grasp. Twisting violently, he tried to grab her, clutching at air and watching in despair as her bobbing head disappeared into the crowd.

"Linda, we've lost Dorothy!" he yelled, then realizing his wife too had gone, both hopelessly lost in the sea of pushing bodies.

75

Dorothy fought like a demon, kicking and pushing at everyone around her, fighting to escape the suffocating crush of the crowd. Finally, she was squeezed out of the crowd into Humboldt Street where a haulier grabbed her and pulled her around the corner into Gordon Street.

"Where's yer folks lass?" he shouted above the noise.

"Somewhere in there," Dorothy snivelled pointing into the crowd.

Still in the thick of it, Tim caught sight of Linda's colourful tartan hat near the harbour wall and fought like a wildcat to reach her. Tears stained her face as he pulled her roughly into the safety of his arms and held her tight.

"We have to get out of here," he gasped.

Slowly, he was able to work them over to the wall and down to the harbour. They were standing on the dock among fishermen and burly dockworkers when a sleek blue boat nosed its way to the side of the dock, and an agile young man leapt onto the planking beside them.

"Where the devil have all these folk come from?" he asked with a grin. "I think they've all gone crazy. England goes to war so we're in it too … madness."

"Oh please can you get us out of here," Linda begged. "We're visitors and I'm terrified of being trampled to death." Fear and panic had driven all thoughts of the Janion ring from her mind but now she reached for her handkerchief in her pocket and her fingers touched the ring. Relief and excitement made her squeal as she brought it out and rubbed the surface.

"You called me," the Janion Lady asked appearing at their side.

"Hey lady, watch who yer pushing," a burly dockworker grumbled.

"Don't you dare speak to me in that tone of voice," Dolly retaliated, jabbing the man in the stomach with her walking stick.

Linda recoiled at the sudden confrontation, gripping tightly to her husband as the burly man slipped off the dock into the water, disappearing below the surface momentarily with a wild yell of alarm.

"Golly," Linda moaned, "I wish we were halfway up that mountain."

"The Malahat?" the Janion ghost clarified the request.

"Yes … yes!" Linda wasn't even sure what the Malahat was but before she could think about it, she and Tim gasped as they stared at their surroundings … trees of all sizes and rocky outcrops were all around them. In the distance was a large expanse of water and forested hills that seem to go on forever. The noise of people shouting had been replaced by total silence except for the wind whispering through the trees.

76

"Look at that old road!" Tim exclaimed, his displeasure easily recognized. "It's made of logs laid side by side with gravel on top ... how quaint, a 1914 highway! Now what do we do?"

"But where does it go?" Linda asked staring over the edge of the cliff. "That must be the sea away down there," she pointed over the tree tops and down past the rocky cliffs.

Suddenly, below them, they heard what sounded like the chugging of an old automobile engine, labouring as it struggled to climb the rough, winding incline.

"Someone's coming," she announced peering down the road.

"He'll never make it," Tim predicted. "I'll bet six pair of horses are needed to pull anything up here."

Finding a sheltered place to sit out of the wind, they were surprised to find that the sun had warmed the rocks. They gazed around in wonder at the awesome view and watched a dust cloud come closer. It was no doubt stirred up by an approaching automobile. Finally, a ridiculously old vehicle appeared, chugging laboriously as it came up the steep incline toward them. It had a top but no windows and the wheels had wooden rims.

Stopping beside them, the driver took off his goggles and stared at the couple in surprise. "How in heaven's name did you two get up here?"

"We're staying with friends in Victoria," Tim began to explain.

"But who brought you up here?" the man interrupted.

"Miss Dolly from the Janion Hotel ...," Tim continued.

"Dolly doesn't have an automobile, she hates them. I've never seen her in one."

Tim could see that there was no way they were ever going to convince this sporting gentleman that Dolly had brought them to the top of the Malahat Mountain, so he tried another course of action.

"How far are we from Victoria and where does this road go?"

"Twenty miles down the mountain is Victoria and that way is Mill Bay," the stranger explained, pointing in both directions. "They're still working on the track from Mill Bay to Duncan."

"And I suppose you think this is not a rough track," Tim mumbled sarcastically.

"Hell no son, you should have seen Government Street in 1904, now that was rough!"

"Will you take us back to Victoria with you?" Linda pleaded.

"Certainly my dear, but first I have to go to Mill Bay to fill my radiator at the spring."

There was an art to starting the Ford automobile and Tim watched with interest as the driver set his levers and switches before hand-cranking the engine from the area of the front bumper. When they climbed aboard, they found the leather-covered seats tightly upholstered and firm to sit on. Linda giggled, holding her hat in her lap as they bounced over the log road.

Rounding a bend that hugged the sheer rock face of the mountain, they were now grateful to find themselves on more level ground. Houses began to appear and, in about 10 minutes, the driver pointed out the little village of Mill Bay down in the hollow. The car picked up speed and Linda screamed. Seeing the driver grip the steering wheel with such grim determination, as he fought to control the bouncing vehicle, only added to her trepidation. Suddenly he jammed on the brakes and skidded to a stop beside a bubbling water pipe. His passengers breathed a heavy sigh of relief.

"I didn't scare you, did I?" he asked, attempting a little ill-timed half-hearted bravado.

It was late afternoon when Dorothy dragged her tired body toward home. She had spent the rest of the day unsuccessfully searching for the McCrays. Wandering past the noisy and boisterous crowds, then finding a higher perch on top of the Causeway wall, she hoped against hope she could see them, but it did not happen. A block from home, she stopped to rub her tired legs and dropped down onto the grass. *I just can't walk another step*, she thought. Across the street stood the prison that gave her the willies and suddenly a tear ran down her face as exhaustion and frustration surged through her body. How was she going to explain their disappearance to her mother? She'd lost their visitors on the first day of sight-seeing.

Leaving the car in a hurry, Linda glowered at the driver, unable to speak as the dread of riding in this automobile all the way back to Victoria welled up inside her. Taking her hand, Tim, although unnerved by the ride himself, made a valiant attempt to calm his wife, walking a short distance down the dust track to the waters of Saanich Inlet.

"I would rather try to swim back to Victoria!" she said angrily, staring across the short span of water. It was perhaps fortunate that she didn't have her fingers on the ring!

"We could ride with our eyes closed," Tim suggested.

"No, I have a better idea Mr. McCray," Linda declared, pulling the Janion ring from her pocket. "She got us into this mess, so she can get us out of it!"

Linda's touch was anything but gentle as she frantically rubbed the ring. Instantly the diminutive ghost materialized beside her.

"You have need of me ma'am?" Dolly asked with her usual smile.

"Yes I certainly have!" Linda snapped. "Can you take us back to Victoria?"

"Of course I can if that be your wish."

"Hold it a minute Linda," Tim intervened. "We need to find young Dorothy, she must be frantic by now. I just hope she's alright."

"Oh my goodness yes, poor Dorothy," Linda agreed. Taking a deep breath, she added succinctly, "Our friendly ghost should be able to accomplish that for us. Take us to Dorothy please."

Tapping her parasol on the ground, Dolly smiled. She loved to hear the determination in this country girl's voice—a woman who was discovering what she wanted and aimed to get it.

"Wait!" she yelped, interrupting Dolly's thoughts. "What is that place across the water?"

"That's Jennie Butchart's garden and the cement works. Over to the left is the Village of Brentwood."

"A cement works and a garden together?" Tim asked in a surprised tone. "That seems like an odd combination."

"Not really, Bob takes his limestone from the quarry, and Jennie turns what's left into a beautiful garden. You see, young man, the Butchart's have a pact with nature; instead of leaving an eyesore behind them, Jennie turns it into a wonderland of flowers."

"Can we go and see it?" asked Linda.

"Now?" the apparition inquired.

"No later dear, we really should find Dorothy," Tim reminded her.

"You must state your wishes clearly; I'm a little confused at the moment," said Dolly.

Glancing up the track, she saw the driver waving for them to come.

"I wish we were with Dorothy," Linda said quickly, chuckling.

Instantly, the couple found themselves sitting on the grass next to Dorothy. Wide-eyed, Dorothy let out a little scream and leapt to her feet.

"G-gosh darn, where did you come from?" she stammered, sitting back down beside them. "I searched everywhere for you. I was so worried; where have you been?"

Tim laughed self-consciously, anxiously glancing over his shoulder. He couldn't help but think of the automobile driver in Mill Bay who would certainly be wondering the same.

Soon the words were tumbling from Linda's lips as Tim helped her tell the story of their frustration with the crowd on the harbour and how the Janion Lady had transported them up to the top of the Malahat and where they had met the man in his automobile.

"I'll bet that driver wonders where you've gone," Dorothy giggled, then suddenly the smile went from her face. "Please don't tell ma about the ring, she's a bit funny about that sort of thing."

Over supper, they were all extra careful not to hint of their strange adventure, smiling when their hosts eagerly offered opinions on places to go or things to see. They readily agreed when Linda requested that Dorothy accompany them for the next few days.

Later that evening, in the privacy of their room, they finally relaxed, whispering together about the day's traumatic events and planning the next day's adventure.

Sunshine greeted the young couple as Dorothy led them to the streetcar stop on Tuesday morning. Boarding the noisy conveyance, she somehow managed to give them a new commentary as they passed. They also talked about their plans for the day and when they alighted near the bridge, Dorothy indicated the railway station across the street.

It was a short but hazardous journey to the corner of Store and Johnson Streets, darting between cars and delivery conveyances during the rush of early morning traffic. They watched for streetcars as they manoeuvred bravely across the myriad of criss-crossing tracks.

"It's great to see so many people working again or at least coming into town," said Dorothy. "Due to the depression it's been terribly quiet in Victoria with few people on the streets or using the trams. My brothers said this year is the best for a long time and they're finding more jobs. It's been really hard for my parents."

Tim and Linda exchanged glances.

"Your family is so light-hearted, you'd never suspect that the depression has affected you," Linda said thoughtfully.

"My ma says you have to carry on no matter what and they had the worst times when I was little and we followed the crops. The boys you met were quite young at the time but they still had to work. I don't remember it, but it must have been terrible for everyone."

"We really have no idea what lengths some people have had to go to in order to survive during these hard times, do we?" murmured Tim. "My

80

pa said hard times builds character. I guess that means your folks have plenty of it!".

Shaking off the sad thoughts, Linda turned her attention to the bustling E&N railway station. A twinkle of excitement came into her eyes as she realized it was really happening—at last she was going to ride the Island's famous mountain railway.

Acquiring tickets, they boarded and found seats together, watching as other passengers arrived. Soon most of the seats were filled. Finally, the conductor shouted 'All aboard' and the iron monster puffed out a great cloud of black smoke and jerked into motion.

"Oh, I do love these sounds," Linda squealed.

Whistles blew, hooters blared and iron wheels screamed as they crossed the bridge and were soon amongst trees and fields as they moved through Esquimalt toward Langford. On a bend, the engine thundered out a trail of steam and Linda watched both ends of the train from the window. Several tiny stations came and went, each with its own peculiarities, and they were soon climbing into the Malahat mountains. Linda and Dorothy moved from window to window, trying hard to catch each fleeting scene as they crossed enormous gorges on wooden trestles.

Trees lined the rail track restricting views of the magnificent scenery and only once did they get a glimpse of water when they passed Shawnigan Lake. From there it was downhill through Cobble Hill and a couple more short stops before bursting out of the forest into the Cowichan Valley and the little town of Duncan. A 10-minute stop allowed them time to buy some food and drinks at a store across the street from the town centre station. They all thoroughly enjoyed their scenic trip as they now crossed beautiful, fertile valley farmland and swampland with lazy rivers winding through the rolling hills. They knew they were close to the sea even though it was not visible.

The blackened coal port of Wellington and, Nanaimo, at the end of the line, each added memorable moments to the adventure increasing their knowledge and appreciation. Then, finally they saw the ocean. When Dorothy explained that this was only the southern tip of Vancouver Island and, the most populated areas they were seeing, they were amazed.

"This island is much bigger than I imagined," Tim commented.

"You saw what the road was like a few years back," Dorothy added as they left the train for a walk in Nanaimo. "It hasn't improved all that much yet and we have only driven it a couple of times. I suppose one day it will be paved like the roads in town."

Wandering through Nanaimo's hillside streets, Linda suddenly had a wonderful idea—a thought that would fulfil all her dreams of railways. Excitedly she turned to her companions.

"Why don't I get Dolly to whisk us back to Victoria, then show us all the other railways the island ever had."

"But they're gone now," said Dorothy.

"Go ahead and ask the ghost lady," Tim chuckled, "she seems to know everything about Victoria."

Eagerly producing the gold ring from her pocket, Linda gently rubbed its surface, smiling confidently when the Janion Lady appeared.

"Now you've got the right idea," Dolly complimented her. "I presume you have a request."

"How many railways have there been on this island?" Linda asked.

"Oh my," Dolly mused, raising her parasol to shield her from the sun, "this one is the E&N, but we used to have the V&S out of Victoria too. Shall I explain the initials as we go along?"

"Yes please!" they chorused.

"Well, the E&N is what you came here on, it's the Esquimalt and Nanaimo and the V&S is the Victoria to Sidney Railway."

"Where were the passenger stations?" Linda interrupted.

"Patience girl," Dolly snapped, "let me think for a moment. The E&N first ran only to Esquimalt, until the city built a bridge to bring it into Victoria. Now, the V&S first had a temporary passenger station at Tolmie and Douglas close to the tram route into the city. In those days, of course, Douglas Street only ran as far as Hillside Avenue. Beyond that, it was still known as Saanich Road. The station was between Herald and Fisgard on Blanshard Street."

"My gracious," exclaimed Linda, "you certainly know an awful lot about the railways."

"There's still more ... next came the BCER, the British Columbia Electric Railway, which also ran down the peninsula but on a different route that went along Burnside. It continued through West Saanich farmlands to Brentwood, terminating at its Deep Cove station. The fourth one was CPR, Canadian Pacific Railway, which ran along the wetlands of the Blenkinsop Valley and up the coast through Cordova Bay, cutting across the island to a terminus station at Deep Cove. We also had another line built by the CPR and affectionately named the Goose. It ran from a station on Bay Street out to Colwood, Metchosin, Sooke and the gold diggings at Leechtown, ending at Youbou. I think that makes five in all."

"Oh wouldn't it be fun to go for a ride on all of them," Dorothy said enthusiastically.

"That's just what we're going to do," Linda stated, "that is, if Miss Dolly can arrange it."

"You doubt my ability young lady!" the apparition snorted.

Over the next two days Dorothy and her Regina visitors rode on all the railways and hardly a moment passed when some thrilling new discovery was made. They also took the tram out to the Uplands and Oak Bay. It was a holiday of a lifetime for the McCrays and they amassed a host of memories that would bring them back to Victoria many times in the future. Three days later as they left the house in the morning, Linda reminded Dorothy and Tim that her three days of wishes had ended.

"I guess Miss Dolly will be coming to collect the ring now," she commented and was shocked when the Janion ghost appeared.

"I hope you've enjoyed your time travelling through history Linda," she stated, rather matter-of-factly.

Linda began to speak but the apparition had already disappeared. Feeling in her pocket, she realized Dolly had indeed retrieved her ring. "I guess we're on our own again, but what an amazing time we've had thanks to Dolly and to you Dorothy. What about it, Tim, do you feel like taking us girls on for a game of bowling?"

Dorothy looked startled, then grinned, smiling coyly at Tim. Before he could react, the girls linked arms with him in the middle and, despite his feeble protests, they pulled him along the street in the direction of Dorothy's bowling alley.

Motivated By Fear

The three Mhaovin boys sat quietly in the cramped attic space which had become their unwelcome playroom and hiding space from the world. Situated above their home on the top floor of a row of brick buildings, it was located on the edge of Berlin, Germany. Life had been difficult enough, even before the beginning of World War II, but recently it had become unbearable for many Jewish families. It was a horrific time as friends and neighbours were often forcibly removed from their homes and taken away by soldiers, never to be seen again.

On the afternoon of December 21st, 1939, this tiny top floor space, for it could not be described as a room, became the Mhaovin boys' sanctuary—it had begun only weeks before as a place which their parents silently hoped would save them from the soldiers of the Gestapo if they ever came to search the house. The boys spent hours here each day while their parents tried to live a normal life below, putting on a brave and seemingly normal face when anyone came to visit. The retractable ladder to their hideaway was pulled up after them, hidden from view, as instructed by their father. After many weeks of this unnerving and isolating routine, their father no longer needed to sternly warn them that the soldiers must not hear them. So, they patiently waited, often sleeping or reading, knowing many hours could pass before they were allowed to return downstairs.

At 3 o'clock this day, the sudden rumbling sound of heavy vehicles drew their attention to the road and the boys looked at each other fearfully. Frantz Walter, the eldest at almost 12-years-of-age, moved quickly to the single tiny window, covered by a thin curtain, which gave a view of the rooftops and part of the street below. Cautiously peering out, he was petrified by what he saw.

"Gestapo!" he hissed, moving back beside them and putting a protective arm around Yalta, nine, and Peter, five, not daring to tell them that the trucks had stopped right outside their building. "Stay very quiet."

This was not the first time this had happened in their neighbourhood. The soldiers, however, had never entered their building before. Frantz held his breath remembering the horror of seeing friends being loaded into a covered truck and taken away, never to return. He mouthed the word 'light' to Yalta and took Peter's tiny hand. He felt its urgent squeeze and he smiled down at the little boy he had sworn to protect. As Yalta reached for the string and turned out the light, fear suddenly gripped his throat. He moved back to his place and they silently huddled together hardly daring to breathe.

Suddenly, they heard a woman scream followed by a door banging loudly. They all looked at each other, their faces turning ashen. It was their mother's scream. Now, heavy, booted footsteps came running up the stairs toward them, but stopped at the first floor. Frantz let out his breath softly and held his brothers closer, trying to cover their ears. Gunshots and shouts followed and Frantz felt little Peter flinch. They knew that the Gestapo were moving from room-to-room. Were they searching for them, for other people or …? The thoughts were silently running through the older boys' heads.

Peter whimpered and wet himself as he squeezed tightly against his oldest brother. Terrified at what might have happened to their parents, they tried desperately to be quiet and still but it seemed forever until the sound of voices went quiet. Finally, the soldier's shouting stopped and the trucks rumbled off down the street again. Frantz moved quickly to the window, but it was too late … the street was empty and not a soul was to be seen.

84

Berlin was indeed a troubled city in 1939. Months of worry for the Mhaovin family had finally come to a crashing climax. Frantz, although unable to fully understand the severity of the situation, had listened to his father's warnings and knew that impending disaster could strike their lives at any time. Trying not to alarm his brothers, he had kept the secret to himself and watched as day-by-day his parents became more anxious.

Now, unable to hear any sound from downstairs, they all drifted off to sleep, as the hours passed and they waited, hoping their parents would come for them. Once or twice, they heard the sound of people moving about, but they couldn't tell if it was in their house or nearby. Frantz slept fitfully, each little sound alerting him to danger. He knew that soldiers could be guarding the house or street. Fearing they would be found, he let his brothers sleep as it was easier to keep them quiet that way as they huddled together in their hideaway.

There was silence for a long time and the room became dark. Frantz finally managed to sleep but at around four in the morning, Peter grew restless and asked to use the toilet. Yalta got the commode for him but Frantz remained silent. When Peter was finished, Yalta, knowing his older brother was awake, suggested they lower the ladder.

"We have to Frantz. We can't stay here forever," Yalta insisted. "We have to find out what has happened to mother and father." His voice choked as he said these last words.

Without a word, Frantz moved to the opening and slowly opened the door. Looking down into the darkness, he strained to hear any sound, but all was silent. He couldn't help it but the silence made him think of death and he shivered in the darkness. Yalta helped him lower the ladder as quietly as they could. Then, forbidding his siblings to move or make any noise, he ventured out warily, alone. Having practised this routine in the dark many times under the direction of his father, he checked for the flashlight he kept in his pocket and softly let out his breath. His stomach was beginning to feel as if it was tied in knots from the anticipation of what he might find in the rooms below.

Sounds from the street threatened to make him panic as, hardly daring to breathe, he slowly climbed down the ladder and felt his way along the upstairs passage. Silently wincing when his stocking-clad feet trod on something sharp, he realized it was a broken picture frame. He made his way to the narrow stairs and began moving toward the main floor. He suddenly had the urge to chance a moment of light and holding it inside his jacket, he flicked it on and quickly off again. He didn't have time to see much and nothing happened, so he breathed easier and continued down.

There was a moment of panic when he heard a vehicle turn into their street; he froze but it slowly passed by. Occasionally using the light, he moved from room to room, but found no sign of anyone. He did find several overturned chairs, a broken window and the main cause of the draft he now felt—the front door had been smashed in and lay broken on the floor. He went into the kitchen and his cold, groping hands found the food cooler and food still inside. Food was also on the sideboard where his mother had been preparing dinner. He stuffed some bread into his mouth and quickly filled his pockets. As he inched his way along the kitchen counter, he felt for his mother's shopping bag on a hook by the side of the sink, sighing in agitation when he found it was missing.

He heard someone cough and terror gripped him, forcing himself to suppress the urge to run. He soon realized the sound was coming from outside in the street and he suspected it was a soldier. He would have to hurry. Quickly, he stripped off his pullover and tied the arms together. Using it as a sack, he filled it with food and returned back upstairs.

"Is that you Frantz?" Yalta whispered from the hatch when he heard the ladder creaking.

"Shhh!" Frantz hissed as his head poked through the dark hole. "I think there's a guard out in the street."

Pulling the ladder up behind him, Frantz ordered them to get under the blanket with him and using the flashlight began pulling the food from the sleeves of his sweater. When his brothers saw the bread and cheese he had to warn them to keep their voices down and only eat a little bit. He'd also managed to collect some dried spicy sausage, strawberry jam, half a bottle of milk and a spoon.

"Did you find mother and father?" Yalta asked tentatively as they ate.

"No, I think the Gestapo took them," Frantz replied, with obvious hatred in his voice.

"I want mama," said Peter.

"Shh, little one," said Yalta, trying not to cry himself. "We'll look for mama soon. Go back to sleep." A few minutes later, they heard Peter's laboured breathing. Yalta whispered to Frantz. "Father said if anything happened to them we had to get away from here."

"Yes, when it gets light, I'll find the map and compass he gave us."

"Shouldn't we be going before they come back to look for us?"

"We can't go now, it's too close to daylight; we have to wait until tonight," Frantz muttered, trying not to display his own concern, "and only move about in the dark. We need to try and get some sleep. It will be light in a couple of hours. Then we'll make our plans. We'll be all right, I promise." Despite trying to sound reassuring, he was exhausted from the thoughts coursing through his own brain. He patted Yalta's leg and lay down on the blanket that was their bed. It was almost light when he finally fell asleep.

As soon as the sunlight came through the window, Peter awoke and again said he had to go to the toilet. The older boys looked at each other and silently knew what they had to do. Whispering, they planned their excursion downstairs, making it a team effort to first lower the ladder. Yalta took Peter to the toilet while Frantz stood on guard at the head of the stairs. It was a frightening experience and convinced them that it was time to begin their journey.

That day they took turns boldly moving through the house collecting every morsel of food they could eat or carry. They found the missing shopping bag and also their parents' supply of candles with which they had secretly been celebrating Hanukkah. Frantz felt a deep pang of sadness for his parents and was suddenly overcome with emotion. *How could this happen to such loving people, I just don't understand*, he thought, desperately trying to shake the picture, of them being taken forcibly away, from his mind.

He moved into the bedrooms and sorted through clothes for their warmest winter garments, adding some of his mother's socks to their bag. When he returned to the attic, he reminded Yalta to get the small battery-operated radio Peter had been given for his birthday. Then they waited for darkness. Frantz would have liked to stay in the house another day so they could get one more good sleep, but he knew it was far too dangerous to linger. He found the map and compass and he and Yalta studied it for a long time. On the map their father had written an address in Dover, England. Frantz remembered he had said it was his cousin's house. If they went there, they would be looked after. He sighed. *It's such a long journey*, he thought, *but we have no choice*. He folded the map and put the compass and the map safely into his deepest pocket.

As they packed their supplies, using some of the larger dark-coloured clothes as sacks to hold the food, they discovered that the flashlight had gone out. Frantz decided to pack it with the food anyway, just in case they found some new batteries. Emptying their piggy banks and their mother's hidden money box, which they weren't supposed to know about, they acquired a small amount of money. Frantz gave some of it to Yalta explaining that if they were separated he might need it and to carry it carefully. They put it safely in their trouser pockets.

Just after midnight, they lowered the ladder for the last time and left the only home they had ever known. Listening intently for outside sounds, Frantz patted Yalta on the shoulder and, with Peter on his back, they sneaked out of the back door and into the alley. A dog barked and Yalta almost screamed as they worked their way past their neighbours' dark houses by feeling along the fences. Thankfully, Frantz only had to remind Peter to keep quiet a couple of times as they avoided the night patrolling soldiers. Hiding in a broken-down garden shed about half a mile away on their first night, they huddled together in the cold and shared a little of their food. The desperation of their situation was now beginning to sink in.

It took them two days to reach the area their father had marked on the map as a good place to hide and perhaps find food before turning west toward the coast ... and safety in England. Finding an unlocked door to a wholesale vegetable supplier, Frantz refilled their food bag and they moved on quickly. Spending the daylight hours sleeping under a waterproof sheet that covered lumber at a building site, they took turns sleeping until darkness came again.

The next day, they encountered their first big problem—guards manning the bridge over the River Millow. Frantz soon realized they were going to have to find another way across. They trudged on through the dark until the moon finally poked out from behind the clouds and showed them some buildings in the distance. It had been raining and the ground was wet and muddy; they were very cold. Half an hour later, exhausted, they smelled the distinct odour of farm manure and heard sounds of cattle in a barn. Finding a ladder propped against a wall, they climbed into the hay loft, huddled together, and instantly fell asleep.

Frantz woke with a start, his heart pounding madly as he heard the truck arrive. It was daylight and he could see some farm workers moving amongst the milling cattle below. Waking his brothers, he pointed to a stack of hay bales a distance away, indicating they had to get behind them and hide. Hurrying, they pushed Peter up over the bales and just managed to join him as one of the men climbed into the loft and began throwing down bales of hay to a couple of workers below. They waited silently, not daring to peek, until they heard the truck drive away again and they all breathed a sigh of relief.

Afraid to be seen or move on while it was daylight, Frantz saw a small door above the rafters and realized it led to the roof. Climbing up, he managed to get the door open and with only his head poking through and using his father's binoculars, he surveyed the surrounding countryside. Taking note how far they had strayed from the river, he checked his compass. He was trying to find landmarks to sort out the direction they should take, when he suddenly heard a train whistle. Using the binoculars, he watched and couldn't believe it when the train slowed and finally stopped to take on water. Searching the length of the train through the glasses, he noted the lack of guards. Only one man showed himself as he climbed on top of the engine to fill the water tanks.

We could ride a train across the river! he told himself, eagerly scrambling down to tell his brothers.

Knowing this was the first time they had dared to move through countryside in daylight, they took every precaution but Frantz knew it could save their lives. Running along the hedgerows, they crossed a narrow lane and were soon close enough to see the watering stop. Lying silently in the soggy bushes, they waited for the next train and watched carefully to discover the railway men's system. Scanning the railway yard for guards and soldiers, Frantz planned how best they could get aboard one of the trains without being seen.

"There are only two enginemen in front and a man in the last coach," Yalta observed.

"We need to find a train with one of the empty boxcar doors open," Frantz pointed out. "Peter isn't tall enough to climb in by himself; if we watch both sides of the train maybe we'll find one open."

"I'll sneak across to the other side," Yalta bravely volunteered. "We can watch each other under the train and if I find one open I'll wave like this." He moved his hand in a quick circular motion and giggled.

Things moved quickly after that train left and they made up their minds to act, creeping as close as they dared. It was almost two hours before their patience was rewarded and a train with many cars came chugging laboriously toward the watering point.

"Success!" hissed Yalta, pointing to a group of cars with their doors wide open. He gave Frantz the sign and the two boys scrambled under one of the cars to meet Yalta. They pushed Peter inside then followed after him. They immediately knew why the doors had been left open as the over-powering smell of fish filled their nostrils.

"Yuck!" Frantz gasped. "I think we're safe for a while, nobody will come near these stinking carriages."

It wasn't long afterwards that the train began to move. Wheels squealed and the long line of carriages jerked and banged into motion, sending the youngsters bouncing against the walls and rolling on the floor.

"Hold onto Peter!" Frantz called in alarm, grabbing for his younger brother's coat as he rolled precariously close to the open doorway.

The moment of panic quickly passed as the train gathered motion, settling down to a steady clickety-clack as it sped on toward the river.

Wind, drawn in through the open doors, made the stink of fish more bearable and the boys chanced a peek out to check the line ahead. Darkness was closing in when they suddenly heard a change in the rattling of the rails as they crossed a bridge without slowing down.

Crawling into a corner, they huddled together again and aided by the gentle rocking motion, they soon fell into a fitful sleep. They were unaware that during the night they had travelled halfway across Germany, passing through Magdeburg in the darkest hours and, as dawn broke, they neared Hanover.

Yalta was the first to wake, urgently shaking his older brother.

"Where are we?" Frantz asked with a groan, crawling toward the open door and braving the cold wind as he peered out at the unfamiliar countryside rushing by.

Checking their father's hand-drawn map and using the compass to estimate the direction, they concluded they were travelling westward. Lying in the doorways at each side of the speeding train, they watched for any signs that would help identify their route.

Suddenly, the train began to lose speed, noticeably slowing as the land became more populated with first farms and then houses; country lanes were now roads with vehicles moving along them. One of those roads carried a convoy of German army trucks which stretched as far as the eye could see, reminding them that they were still in Germany. Danger was all around them and they must not be seen. Knowing they had to leave the train but afraid to jump while it was moving, especially with Peter, Frantz was hopeful when Yalta yelled that he had seen a sign telling them they were near the Hanover Marshalling Yard.

As their train chugged through the long lines of rail cars, it suddenly clanged to a halt with a violent jerk. Peeking out of the open door, Frantz saw the rail workers moving quickly down the row of carriages closing the doors. He motioned silently to Yalta to hide in the corner and he grabbed Peter and they squeezed into the opposite corner. Frantz felt sure they were about to be discovered and his mind searched frantically for a plan. The voices were coming closer and closer. Peter began to whimper as he felt his brother's tension and he clung tightly to Frantz. Suddenly the doors on both sides of their carriage clanged shut.

"Did you check those boxcars?" a harsh voice demanded.

"Yes sir!" a second voice lied.

Frantz and Yalta let out their breath and waited as the voices moved away. Yalta got up and paced back and forth inside the now dark container, spotting a light coming through a hole in the roof.

90

"Frantz look up ... there's light!" Yalta hissed. Frantz was examining the lock on the door with his fingers having already realized that they were locked in. He turned toward the sound of Yalta's voice and looked upwards. The light was coming from a broken ceiling board. A noise told him Yalta was trying to climb the wall. Pulling himself up by some ropes attached to hooks on the wall, Yalta thought he was succeeding until he slid back down the wet and slimy walls. He bumped his knees as he fell and Frantz came up behind him.

"Shh, we need to be quiet. Climb on my shoulders!" said Frantz.

The boy, suddenly remembering how tall Frantz was, did as he said. Using the top hook and rope, he was finally able to reach the hole. He wiggled the boards, making them creak and Frantz 'shushed' him again. Discovering he was able to move them, he peered outside, and then asked Frantz for help to get down.

"Well, what did you do? Can you get through?" Frantz asked, knowing the hole had gotten larger because he was seeing more light. He was very hopeful Yalta could get through. "Is it too high outside?"

"I can make the hole bigger but it's a long way to the ground. I'll have to get out and open the door," Yalta muttered nervously.

"If we tied our coats together, I could lower you down, but if you fell or the line broke, you could be hurt."

"I'm strong, I can do it. I will have to," he whispered, feeling Peter's hand in his. He hugged his little brother. "It's going to be all right little one, soon we will be safe. You're such a brave little boy."

"All right, let's get ready," Frantz interrupted. "We don't want to leave too early, it will be very cold and we don't know how far we'll have to go tonight. The train may leave in the morning and we could be in trouble if it went back the same way we came. We can't risk staying here. Let's have some food and a sleep."

The boys knew they shouldn't eat much so had a bite of bread with some jam before dropping into silence. Frantz soon heard the familiar sound of his brothers in sleep and sighed. He began to recite a prayer their family always said at Hanukkah, even though he realized it had ended the day they left home. Reciting the words in Hebrew helped to relieve his fear that someone would open the door and find them before they'd had a chance to escape. Before he had recited the second line of the prayer he too, fell into a fitful sleep.

A couple of hours later, they were awakened when they heard workmen calling to each other nearby. They sat with bated breath until the men had passed and all was quiet until it happened again soon after. Petrified, they again clung to each other and tried not to breathe. Peter seemed to be developing nerves of steel and was eager for the men to leave so he could get outside.

While they waited for the men to finish their shift and, hopefully, go home, they tied their pullovers and extra clothes together. When all the clothes were used Frantz estimated they almost had enough length so Yalta would be fairly close to the ground when he had to let go. For the next few hours, they kept a watch on the amount of daylight coming through the hole and, when it was almost gone, Frantz estimated it was 4 o'clock and time to get ready. He had noticed that he was beginning to feel more tired and his brothers had been less talkative making it better in one way but becoming a worry for him. He knew they had to find a new supply of food very soon.

They ate their small food ration and readied themselves for the evening's adventure going over what they were going to do after they got out ... if the door opened. Frantz was afraid to think of what would happen if it didn't open, so he put it right out of his mind.

At about 6:30, he put the plan into operation, helping Yalta, who was carrying the end of their makeshift rope as he climbed onto Frantz's back. They worked their way into position and Yalta easily climbed to the hole, poking his head outside. He whispered down to Frantz that the yard was quiet. Pushing the end of the rope out onto the roof, he called down again.

"Hold on tightly," he begged, moving the boards aside as far as he could. "I'm going out!" The jagged sides of the roof grabbed at his clothes but he managed to get onto the roof, thinking how glad he was that he had worn his heavy trousers.

Frantz braced himself against the expected tug, but when it came it still threw him against the wall, banging his head. He heard something tear and prayed that their rope would hold. Playing out the line, he had the last sleeve in his hands and, was reciting another prayer, when Yalta's weight suddenly released and he fell to his knees. When he heard a muffled exclamation, he visualized his brother falling to the ground. He held his breath until finally Yalta's voice came from near the door.

"I'm all right!"

Although he had landed on his feet, the gravel was sharp and cut into his already bleeding hands, but he knew he had no time to feel sorry for himself. He remembered the rope and reached up to pull it down, but he had trouble reaching it and then, it wouldn't move.

It must be caught on the boards, he sighed, knowing he'd have to get Frantz's help. Leaving it in the dim glow thrown by a small yard light, he explored the carriage's door lock. At that moment, he remembered seeing the men at the water tower and recalled how one of them had bent over before a door opened. *Somewhere down here there's a catch of some sort.*

As he felt around the darkness at the base of the door, he realized how sore his hands were. Finally, he found what he was looking for. Exploring the shape, he realized it was a hook. *A hook!* He thought elated that it sounded so easy. He pushed and pulled at the hook, but it was sharp and didn't want to move. He knew he was in trouble. He felt blood trickling down his fingers and wiped them on his trousers. Sinking to his knees, he fought off his frustration and pain. *I'm not strong enough, what am I going to do?* he thought, wanting to cry.

He shook himself knowing he had to figure it out somehow. First, he peered around to make sure no one was watching. He even looked under the carriages. He stood up and clenched his sore hands, kicking the catch. He suddenly stopped. *I know what to do!* he thought. *I can use my own weight!* He kicked at the catch again but stopped again realizing his heavy boot was making too much noise. He listened but no one seemed to have heard. He kicked again and again, hoping his boot would find its mark. He was finally rewarded by the sound of a click. The catch had opened. Frantz had heard it too and immediately pulled the door open.

"Is it clear?" he hissed into the darkness, barely able to see the outline of his brother.

"I think so," Yalta whispered, "but I couldn't reach the rope, it's caught on something."

In a few seconds, Yalta heard the sound of the clothes being pulled back through the hole and he breathed a sigh of relief.

Handing Peter down first, Frantz then threw down the rope of clothes and handed Yalta their meager food rations. He leaped down to join them, whispering to Yalta to help him close the door. They got the door shut but it squeaked loudly this time and they stopped abruptly. Checking the area for guards, they finally got the door closed and moved away from the building. Finding a little shack beside the track, they hid behind it and set about pulling the knots apart on their rope.

"I-I've hurt my hands, Frantz, c-can you help me?" Yalta whispered, noticeably shivering. The boys fumbled about in the dark and finally most of the knots were free and they got dressed.

"Are you all right?" Frantz asked in a concerned tone.

"Y-yes, I-I'm just c-cold," Yalta muttered, allowing Frantz to help him into his sleeves and give him a quick rubdown.

"We need to get out of here!" Frantz whispered.

Grasping each of them by the shoulder, he pushed them in the direction they had earlier planned and then he took the lead. It was very dark away from the lights as they got farther from the building. They moved stealthily between and under the carriages, bumping into and stumbling over obstructions. Finally, they crawled out from under the last rail car. Unable to see more than distant shadows, the boys kept looking around for workmen until they managed to get safely across the yard. Frantz stumbled into a ditch containing a trickle of water then realizing it would provide them with both water to drink and some safety. *Thankfully they haven't had much rain*, he thought, pulling the boys in after him. He tasted the water and told them it was clean enough to drink. They reached a fence but the culvert went under it leaving enough room for them and soon they were at a perimeter road.

The rumble of what sounded like a convoy of army trucks was heard and Frantz surmised they were close to a main road. *Their lights are off*, was the thought going through their minds as wet, cold and miserable, they waited until the convoy passed. It was about 10 minutes before they dared to move. Frantz left his brothers hidden in the culvert while he ventured out to check the area for soldiers. He could just make out the outline of a group of houses about a block away. He hid quickly when he saw some people moving around. Behind them, the rail yards blocked their escape, but in the distance he could see some church spires and thought it must be the city of Hanover.

We're trapped! he silently moaned.

"We were better off in the boxcar!" Yalta exclaimed in annoyance when Frantz gave them the news.

Frantz realized Yalta could be right and yet he knew they must go on. He had promised their parents. "We're going on, right now. We're going to get to England and we just have to keep telling ourselves that," he insisted, trying to sound like he believed it. He took Peter's hand and, with Yalta reluctantly following, led them out of the culvert. They moved from tree to bush to building stopping behind anything they could find to hide themselves.

Yalta was getting proficient in learning what Frantz wanted and which were the best places to hide. He knew his brother was right about moving on, there was nothing left for them in Berlin, or Germany. They came across another ditch, hoping it wasn't the same one. They slid gratefully into it taking a short rest and trying to get their bearings. Once on the move again, they were slow and cautious, breathing a sigh of relief when they found the houses now behind them.

Beginning to whimper, little Peter held tightly to his brother's hand, doing his best to keep his tired body moving until Frantz picked him up and carried him. About 10 minutes later, a truck came hurtling toward them and they dove into the grass. Yalta watched its headlights illuminate a sign just ahead of them. It said, *Brewery Entrance.*

Optimistic and, in desperation, Frantz led his brothers up the roadway. He stopped occasionally to listen to the night sounds, hoping he would hear any guards before they were detected.

"Something's burning," Yalta whispered, sniffing the air.

Dark, low buildings loomed out of the almost black air ahead of them though not a sound could be heard. Following the smell, Frantz cautiously led the way to the first building and, hugging the wall, they made their way around to the back. It soon became apparent what was burning, for not far away from the buildings a large patch of ground was glowing due to a smoldering fire. Staying in the shadows, they slowly approached the fire and the older boys wondered why the fire had been left unattended. Suddenly, Frantz became aware of a vaguely familiar hissing sound, and they were showered briefly with cold water.

"They're burning sawdust," he whispered. "We can dry our clothes but stay away from that sprinkler!"

Quickly removing as many of their outer clothes as they dared and laying them out on the warm ground close to the fire, they huddled together a short distance away sharing their warmth and the last of their food. They were now quite close to the building so Frantz left them and went to look around. A fleeting shaft of moonlight aided his search, exposing the open back of the building and, under the roof canopy, several large circular saws which he recognized as that of a barrel-makers. He found an unlocked door and, feeling his way, was hopeful when he located the workers' lunch room. He recognized it in the dark when his hand found the sink and drinking mugs. Searching along the wall, he located the fridge. Excitement gripped him as he opened the door a crack and saw that it contained some food. He shut the door quickly when the fridge light came on illuminating the room.

He found what felt like a tablecloth and, draping it over the fridge door, he was able to open it again, this time keeping the light to a minimum. He hurried to remove the food, piling it onto the floor. He closed the door again and spread the cloth out on the floor. In minutes, he was leaving the building with an armload of treasure. Cautiously, he made his way back to where Yalta nervously waited.

"Quiet now," Frantz hissed as Yalta tried to talk to him. "I have a surprise but you must not talk." He knew the boys would be excited about the food but he couldn't risk their conversation.

Peter woke up and he gathered them closer even though they were unable to see anything. He handed each of them something to eat, breaking off small pieces of cheese and bread, and stowing a few apples and some crackers in the sleeves of his sweater. Lastly, they shared a bottle of cider. He was careful to ration the food sensibly giving each only what he dared. He got their clothes and urged them to get dressed as dawn was breaking. Quickly bundling up the rest of their belongings, they were on their way again using a small wooded area as cover.

After two hours, they took a rest under a great evergreen tree. Frantz checked the compass stepping out from behind the tree as he tried to fix a landmark in his mind that would take them in the right direction. Snow was beginning to fall as he urged his brothers to start walking again. It was now full daylight and their footprints showed clearly in the fresh snow but there were no houses or movement in the vicinity.

"Shouldn't we stop somewhere and hide," Yalta inquired.

"No," his brother replied grimly, "we must continue. The snow will soon cover our tracks and I need to see where we're going."

"But Peter is so tired he's walking in his sleep," Yalta announced.

"I know, my legs feel like they won't go another step, but we have to. I'll carry him for a while."

Unknown to them, back at the building where Frantz had stolen the food, a search was already underway as local police and army recruits searched the surrounding area for the robbers who had raided the barrel-maker's refrigerator. Tracking them into the forest, they soon lost their trail and gave up the chase.

Almost a mile ahead, three shivering and snow-covered figures struggled on, hoping to find a safe refuge before their energy gave out. Hearing some trucks coming up behind them, they hid amongst the trees of what appeared to be an orchard. The convoy of army trucks slowed down as they passed and Frantz watched without breathing. One by one, the trucks turned off the road and stopped. Moving quickly, he urged the boys to follow him as he moved close enough to see what was happening. Realizing they had stopped at a small tavern, he listened to the soldiers' loud conversation as they got out of the trucks and went inside. Guards seemed to have been detailed to watch over the vehicles, but these men soon gravitated toward each other and the front group of trucks, standing with their backs against the warm radiators.

Almost invisible in his snow-covered coat, Frantz sneaked even closer. Lifting the corner of the canvas at the back of the last truck, he saw that their cargo only filled half the space. *They would never look for us in an army truck*, he thought. Detailing his plan to Yalta, who although afraid, had little energy left to argue, and quickly went along with his dangerous plan.

"Do you know where they're going?" Yalta asked.

"They mentioned a camp at Emden—said it was close to the coast but I have no idea."

Pulling Peter onto his feet, they climbed into the truck and made sure the canvas was pulled down. Hearts pounding, they could hardly breathe when they heard a harsh commanding voice telling the soldiers to return to their vehicles. Almost immediately, doors banged and engines burst into life. They were moving.

Frantz wasn't paying much attention to all this as he had suddenly realized there was a familiar smell in the truck. Thinking back to his mother's kitchen, he soon realized it was the smell of freshly baked bread! *We must have encountered a supply convoy!* He sighed gratefully. Moving on his hands and knees, he felt around at the wooden boxes and found one filled with loaves of bread. Without telling the boys, he took two of the loaves and hid them in the food bag. He was very careful to cover the boxes the way he had found them.

The boys didn't even ask him what he was doing, they were so well programmed to be quiet and, besides, they were exhausted. Peter complained that he was cold and cuddled up against him, soon falling asleep. In no time Frantz also heard Yalta's heavy breathing. Feeling relieved, as the army trucks tore on into the night, he soon dozed off himself. It was about four hours later when Yalta's eyes blinked open— the convoy had stopped and he could hear soldiers talking. Peeking out, he realized they were on a road and he could see a motorcycle stopped beside one of the trucks just up ahead. Several soldiers were standing in the light of the headlights talking while they puffed on cigarettes. Waking Frantz, Yalta told him what was happening and that it was now raining. Shouted orders startled them and Frantz stood up. They could hear the men scurrying back to their trucks, doors slamming and engines starting. The motorcycle roared into life and drove away.

"We have to get out of here!" Frantz urged his brothers, cautiously looking out the back of the truck to see if they were still the last vehicle. "Right now," he hissed.

Throwing their bags out into the darkness, and then pushing Yalta out as the truck began to move, Frantz clutched Peter to his chest and tumbled out into the wet snow. Winded, but safe, they collected their bags and dove into a nearby ditch. They soon realized how lucky their decision had been, for not far ahead they could see the floodlit gates of some sort of a camp ... and the convoy was driving right into it!

More trucks now roared past them, lighting the road with their headlights as they followed the others into the camp. As they waited for the trucks to pass, Frantz tore off three pieces of bread and gave them to the boys.

"Fresh bread, where did you get this from?" asked Yalta.

"It was in the truck." Frantz could tell Yalta was tired when he didn't press the question any further.

Soon the rain stopped and they were feeling much better as they got on their way again, following the ditch in the opposite direction to the camp. By the time dawn broke, they were two miles away and the compass showed they had not strayed far off their route. Finding shelter in a stand of trees, they settled down to rest and wait out the daylight hours. For the first time since leaving Berlin, Peter began to chatter.

"Where are we going? It's such a long way. Will it take much longer Frantz?" It was like the flood gates had opened.

"We're going to the coast little one, where there's a big sea of water. We'll find a boat that will take us to safety," Frantz quietly explained, trying to sound like he believed in what he was saying.

Yalta, who always used to make up stories, got in on the act and suggested they would find a big ocean liner that would take them to see the world. Peter hugged him and, as Frantz watched his happy brothers, laughing for the first time since they had left home, he realized how resilient they had all become. They were now seasoned night time travellers facing danger and discomfort without a moan or a whimper. He was so proud of them, but he knew their efforts to get to England would not be as easy as it sounded. Their troubles were far from over. Urging them to suck on a handful of snow, Frantz prepared them for the next stage of their flight.

Darkness was creeping over the nearby hills as the boys removed all signs of their stay and moved off into the night. Sometime later, as they walked across an open field, the familiar drone of aircraft was heard overhead. But tonight was different than all the other times they had heard the planes ... tonight the sound kept coming closer. Suddenly, the noise of anti-aircraft guns also filled the air. Startling them, the older boys realized they had strayed too close to a military base. Looking up, they saw lights in the sky and, for the first time, they actually saw a battle right in front of their eyes. The flack was beginning to light up the ground around them and Peter moved closer and clung to Frantz's leg. He was soon crying uncontrollably.

Yalta sat down and covered his ears. "They'll kill us!" he wailed.

Frantz sunk to the ground beside Yalta, pulling Peter into his arms and holding both of them close as they lay flat on the ground. It was impossible to talk but he tried his best to console them. Apparently this graphic and noisy battle in the sky and, their proximity to the guns, had finally brought home the full meaning of war. He knew they would be thinking of their parents and, as he was right now, this would turn their minds back to the scene in their home ... the home they had loved so much and knew they would never see again.

Frantz pulled his mind back to the present realizing he had to think of something fast or they could be discovered. As the shooting continued, he pulled the boys to their feet and dragged them across the field toward a small outbuilding he had thankfully noticed. He prayed that no one had seen them. As they ran, he considered that he should have anticipated their reaction. They had been under duress for so long; he was amazed it hadn't happened earlier. The shooting stopped and they hid in the building only long enough to have a rest and gather their wits.

They had lost track, but Frantz knew they had been on the run for nearly three weeks, moving ever westward as their father had instructed. Avoiding contact with people, so far they had survived undetected. Troop convoys with visible headlights were now more evident, moving quickly along the highways in the same direction they were going. Hearing the distant explosions of bombs, added even more fear to their already precarious situation. Would they be able to get to the coast? Frantz now sensed they had a new problem.

Snow fell often during the next week and Yalta pulled a tree branch behind him to wipe out their footprints. Food became scarce and several times they resorted to eating cattle food to satisfy their burning hunger. Frantz realized the situation was now desperate. They were all hungry, tired, and worse, he was losing his ability to concentrate. He had to carry Peter more often now and Yalta seemed to be always asking to stop. His patience was wearing thin as they saw the lights of what they thought was a small town. Yalta called his attention to a signpost that read, Vechta and they went in for a closer look. Wet, cold, and hungry, they moved expectantly, but cautiously. They saw two foot soldiers patrolling a very dark street and, at intervals, an army truck rumbled through. Moving like elusive animals, the boys entered the town, now highly experienced with melting into the shadows. Frantz again detected the odour of freshly baked bread drawing them like a magnet through an alleyway toward a bakery.

All of a sudden, they found themselves standing in front of an open door which seemed to shimmer as heat escaped. Inside, an amazing sight met their eyes, as racks of golden, crusted bread sat cooling on layers of shelves. The temptation was great, but the danger was enormous as they watched two white-suited workers move the bread from the shelves to a delivery truck. Once loaded it moved off and another took its place. Suddenly, a bell rang and the men stopped what they were doing. A soldier appeared and the driver of the truck joined them. The bakers took them over to a table where the bread was cooling. The driver and the soldier each picked up a loaf and they all went out another door.

"Now!" Frantz hissed.

Dashing into the glare of the lights, the boys grabbed what they could carry before dashing back into the dark. Gathering their breath outside, they hid the bread away while Frantz watched for the soldiers. He urged them to be quick and they made their way back to the main road and stopped to rest in some trees.

"Can we eat some bread Frantz?" Peter begged in a whisper.

"Yes, we can share a loaf but we're only having a little bit so we don't get sick. This will last us for a while."

While they ate, he tried to work out the direction they needed to go. A passing car's headlights illuminated the spire of a church not too far away and, without hesitation, he urged them to get ready to move. He told them where they were going.

"We can't go in there," Yalta whispered in horror.

"We can go anywhere!" Frantz replied fiercely. He set out with Peter in hand and Yalta followed reluctantly.

When they reached the door, Frantz found it unlocked as he had suspected. Pushing it open slightly, he took a look inside, then opened it enough for them to slip through. They found the interior lit by a single candle up at the front. Peter clutched tightly to Frantz's coat as they felt their way down the dark aisle toward the light. The little boy tripped on the altar step dropping his bag causing the loaves to roll out onto the floor. Outside, a whistle sounded and men shouted, then a truck engine.

"Get the bread!" Frantz hissed urgently in the dark, now regretting his decision. "They must be looking for us; we have to get out of here."

Dawn was creeping over the churchyard when the boys slipped out of the back door of the church. They heard more shouting, sounding closer, but couldn't see anyone or even the vehicle. A distant gunshot added speed to their flight through the churchyard tombstones, but suddenly Frantz disappeared and the other boys heard a thud.

"Where are you?" Yalta squealed.

"Careful, I'm here," Frantz groaned from below them. "It's a new grave—better jump in. Quickly ... before the soldiers see you!"

"I'm not getting into a grave," Yalta muttered. "There are dead people down there."

"Be still and get in here!" Frantz hissed, reaching up and grabbing their legs and pulling them in after him.

Motorcycles had now joined the search. They could hear footsteps running through the church and coming out the back door as it slammed too close for comfort. Strong lights now illuminated the churchyard moving back and forth above them. The boys clung tightly to the dark corners of their grave trying to stay clear of the light as soldiers scoured the graveyard right above them. Finally, the search party went back to the road and the boys got out of their hole. They hid behind the tallest monuments until it seemed clear to leave. Then they slowly worked their way back out of the area. They had been lucky once again, but Frantz wondered how long they could carry on like this. *At least we have some food to show for our close call*!

They walked a long way for the next two days before seeing any sign of a town and they decided to continue through the day as best they could. The next morning Peter pointed out a sign that read *Werlte*. It made them feel much better to know they weren't moving in a circle. By the time they saw the road sign for Lathen, Yalta jubilantly recognized it as one of the cities their father had noted on the map. If he remembered correctly, they were almost to the border, he told them. They stole two eggs from a chicken house at the next farm and ate them with a bit of their last loaf of bread. They also found some clean water and drank thirstily.

Country lanes made their flight a bit easier again as they could hide in ditches and behind the hedgerows when army trucks appeared. More often again, they heard the drone of aircraft overhead and watched the flash of exploding bombs. Frantz told them not to look up, but to watch where they were going and help him watch for people.

"I wonder where the planes are going?" Yalta asked. "Maybe they're bombing the ship we want to go on!"

"Don't you have anything better to think about?" Frantz snapped.

Two days later, their bread was gone and hunger was gnawing at their stomachs. Exhaustion and cold again caused Frantz to pray they would soon find some food. His prayer was answered the next night when they spotted a factory down a road with no buildings nearby. Desperate enough to break a window, they managed to get into a storage room. Finding the worker's lunchroom was easy despite internally locked doors. Peter had become adept at crawling through air vent pipes and opening doors for his brothers and by dawn they were more than a mile away. Hidden securely in the heart of some thick bushes in a roadside shrubbery, they ate until they were full.

They slept until the thunder of tanks travelling a road less than 20 feet away awoke them and soon soldiers were everywhere. Hardly daring to move, they watched through the thick bushes. For hours, the long columns of trucks, tanks and men moved past, travelling west. Walking became even more difficult now that the German army was moving toward the coast. Guards were everywhere, hunger was their constant companion and Frantz worried in silence, wondering what the next weeks would bring.

Signs of spring were showing on branches as buds got larger and began popping out on various trees and plants. It warmed Frantz's heart but did little for his body. They were skirting many small towns now and realized they had now crossed into The Netherlands. They had left Germany behind at last. Fields of partly-rotting vegetables became ready meals for the young fugitives and they ate them dirt and all! They had crossed Germany undetected in just over three months, a feat of almost impossible proportions. Now Frantz wondered how they were going to cross the English Channel. He was beginning to worry about the war being too close to their destination, but he didn't say anything; he just kept encouraging them to walk saying they were almost at their destination. They saw many large trucks carrying supplies toward the coast now and Frantz grew even more worried. Large building projects were obviously underway on the coast and now German army camps could be seen. As night fell, bombs rained down on the German defences. Frantz was aghast and unable to explain what was happening to his brothers. This was not what he had expected. Finding refuge in the basement of a bombed-out farmhouse, they were discovered by a boy of about ten, who stumbled into their hiding place.

"Who are you?" he asked suspiciously in Dutch.

Franz thought he understand some of the words and did his best to explain they were German Jewish fugitives and had travelled from Berlin in an effort to reach the safety of England. Clouse Van Biren shook his head in disbelief.

"Stay here and keep out of sight," he said in a mixture of German-Dutch and hand signals. "I'll bring you some bread and milk tonight."

True to his word, the boy returned after dark bringing two other boys with him. They had bread, milk and cheese for the hungry brothers.

"This house used to be my grandfather's place," one of the boys who spoke better German, sadly admitted. "He died when an English plane crashed into this house a couple of weeks ago. My father has farmed this land a long time with my grandfather, but it's now too risky. Sometimes the shooting or bombs kill our cattle so milk is getting scarce."

"Thank you even more for the milk then ... and the food. The Gestapo took our parents away and we've been on the run for a long time," Frantz informed the group. "What is the date?"

"It's the 15th of March. They took all the Jewish families away," the one named Hans said sadly. "I watched them loaded onto a train."

"Why did they do that? Where did they take them?"

"They took my father and uncles too," the third boy added sadly. "My mother was so afraid she threw herself under a train."

"How many are there ... like us?" Yalta asked, shivering with fear.

"Twenty-two, counting the girls," Hans replied, "and now you three. That makes us 25."

"But where do you all live and how do you feed yourselves?"

"Like you, we hide where we can and steal whatever we need from the Germans."

"And if they catch you?" Yalta whispered.

"They shoot us," Clouse snapped. "So don't get caught or make sure you shoot them first! We have guns too."

"You have guns?" Frantz said in amazement. "How did you get them or should I ask?" He was beginning to realize just how brave they all had to be to survive their different situations.

"We stole them off dead Germans after the English bombed this place. We have rifles too, but we give them to the Resistance men."

"We can't stay here," Yalta exclaimed. "We must go to England."

"There's no way to get to England!" Clouse hissed. "Germans are all along the coast; you're better off staying with us. You'd soon be dead if you keep wandering around out there."

With nowhere to go, the Mhaovin brothers realized the others were right. They would be safer here in Holland. As a result, they soon found themselves integrated into the resistance movement. They spent the next four years utilizing the skills they had learned on their own journey— avoiding the German occupation forces and the allied bombing raids.

In 1944, they emerged as heroes to greet the liberating army and soon discovered that their dream of getting to England was going to come true after all. The day they boarded the fishing boat that would take them to their father's cousins in Dover was the happiest day they could remember. They knew they were fulfilling their parents' wish. It was a wish born out of fear, but it became a tale of hope and survival like those of so many other families that year. The three boys had survived by keeping the memory of their parents alive.

Waving goodbye to their friends one last time as the boat moved out into the tide, Frantz felt the tears running down his cheeks. He put his arms over his brothers' shoulders and held his head high as he whispered, "Mama, Papa, we did as you told us. We're going to England … you may rest in peace now."

Say Goodbye To Tillie

Tillie Grant was celebrating her 65th birthday on the 3rd of September, 1939—the same day Britain declared war on Germany. This feisty old lady had lived all her life in London on the Thames and all its hubbub of activity.

"I'm a true cockney," she used to say to anyone who would listen. "Born within the sound of Bow Bells, I was, and proud as a winkle picker's daughter!"

Two years before, Tillie had buried her husband, Charlie, in a cheap wooden casket to save on the expense. Money was scarce in the Grant household; her sons Ronnie and Fred had long since emigrated to Australia. Alone, except for Nelson, her cat, in her tiny row house, she faced the world with a stubborn resolve.

When she heard the announcement on the BBC 6 o'clock news, she was sipping a pint in the local pub.

"Those Germans will never set one foot on English soil!" she proudly proclaimed.

"Are you joining up Tillie?" a barrow-boy yelled. "Take yer teeth out, you'll scare the poor buggers to death."

Tillie struggled to her feet, a half pint of beer sloshing wildly in her hand as she went on the attack shouting abuse at the lad. She swung her walking stick with murderous intent sending the barrow-boy racing for the door.

"Grab her, you fools, before she kills somebody!" the landlord screamed as the rampaging pensioner tottered toward the door sending several glasses crashing to the floor as she swept them from the tables.

"Tillie!" yelled Constable Jenkins of the London Constabulary. "Tillie, sit down and behave yerself."

Scowling fiercely, Tillie looked up at the huge frame of the policeman filling the doorway. She reluctantly made her way back to her seat as a drinker handed her the bright red tartan tam-o'-shanter she always wore but had lost from her head in her eagerness to get at the miscreant.

"Give the old bird another drink George," Jenkins shouted at the landlord, "and for God's sake keep her under control!"

Tillie was well-known in this part of London, born and raised close to the Thames and dockland, earning a meager living selling flowers from a basket on the old cobble streets. She was both friendly and helpful to neighbours and friends. Rationing had started in England, but every child in the area knew Tillie had a candy for them in her pocket—not one of her two-ounce candy allowance ever found its way into the old lady's mouth.

"Why do you do it?" her neighbours would ask.

"Damnit, I'm just trying to get rid of them," she replied irritably. "They just stick me false teeth together. Why, I had to spit them out one day in Cannon Street and then ask a stranger to help me pry them open again! No, no, I won't be eating them damned toffees again!"

Often, she would swap a rosebud to the sailors on the dock, insisting they pay her in butter, cigs, tea or some other rationed goods they could easily pinch from their ship. Then, she would quietly share the booty with her neighbours or a hard-up pensioner friend.

Even as bombs rained down on London, her shrill call, "Lights out!" could be heard echoing through the streets and alleys of London's East End. Steering people to shelters, she hurried them to safety, then turned back into the hell of exploding bombs and flying debris to help someone else.

Firemen and air raid wardens often saw her in the glow of burning buildings, searching through rubble for the plaintive cry she'd heard, with little or no thought for her own safety. Many times the row house she lived in had windows blown out, the door shattered, and the interior littered with dust and soot. Still Tillie battled on without a whimper.

Through those early years of the London Blitz, Tillie became a legend. Daylight hours would find her at Charing Cross railway station, perched on a pile of building rubble, cheekily selling her flowers to passing soldiers.

In November of 1940, she was at Kensington when the black cloud of German bombers arrived overhead and let loose their load of death. But Tillie ignored them, directing ambulances to the injured and trotting relentlessly back and forth to the Red Cross tea wagon, carrying welcome refreshments for hardworking firemen and police.

Her Tam O'Shanter became a symbol of stubborn hope to terrified citizens. Tireless and persistent, she recklessly roamed the streets of dockland in the worst of the blitz. Flying bombs, with their telltale noise and devastating explosions, roared into the city and whole streets disappeared in a single deafening bang.

They had almost seen the last of these wicked long-range missiles when Tillie tempted fate once too often. They found her in a doorway—she had used her body to protect three children and paid the ultimate price. Tillie's time had come.

Sunshine lit the graveyard when they laid Tillie to rest and weepy-eyed mourners crowded the street to say their last goodbye to the bravest of ladies.

The minister, choking with grief, fell to his knees. "Say goodbye to Tillie," he whispered.

Even today, on the darkest of nights, Tillie's ghost often roams the streets of dockland and some say they can still hear her urgent cry. "Put out those lights!"

Yesterday's Ghosts

Warming hands on grandpop's pipe
Walking side by side through day's last light,
These are the times I remember most
When I look back on yesterday's ghosts.

Memory plays tricks on all by the score
But leaves just a crack to yesterday's door.
No matter what we as mortals will do
Those thoughts will influence us all our life through.

We laugh on a whim or shed a short tear
It's something from long ago we can hear.
They will live on in your mind of that I am sure
For without yesterday's ghosts our life would be poor.

Revere them or fear them, I care not a jot
But remember them all the whole blessed lot,
For our mind is the host
Of those wonderful, yesterday's ghosts.

A Chance Meeting

Ben Grubard was a 20-year-old logger when the war started in 1914, a young man who dreamed of adventure like so many others of his age. Enlisting for service brought a chance to see the world, fight with glory and return home to Victoria with a chest full of medals and a hero's welcome.

His folks had done well in the pioneer environment of the fledgling Canadian province of British Columbia. Acquiring land on the shore of Shawnigan Lake on Vancouver Island, his father had built the log cabin where he was born. He sweated and toiled to clear the land and he and Ben's mother managed to establish a farm where they would raise all their family. Now, years later, with one younger brother and Ethel, an older unmarried sister still living at home, he felt free to follow the excitement and join the army.

Training had been rushed at Lansdowne army camp and they were shipped out two weeks later. Men were desperately needed at the Front and his gunnery training was completed in England on Salisbury Plain. Here he had met Dan Brown, another Victorian and a sergeant instructor—a genius with artillery weapons. Ben learned to kill with astounding efficiency under Sergeant Brown's tuition.

Fighting through the hell of Belgium, France and the Rhine, one day he sadly heard a rumour that his friend, mentor and countryman, Sgt. Brown had been killed in the fighting at Flanders. Solemnly, the gun crew said a silent prayer to a legend who had gone to his rest.

Fighting was furious in the days and weeks that passed and many young men lost their lives in the hell of battle. Ben too, had suffered—his left leg blown off above the knee—he was left fighting for his life amidst thousands of wounded. A meager pension, a second-class suit, and a cold goodbye were his medals.

Bitter, cold and lonely, he stood in the rain on Victoria's CPR dock in June of 1918 and watched numbly as ambulances were filled with the wounded and taken away, no doubt to hospital or a convalescence home. He wondered where he could spend the night before finding a way to get home to see his family. Darkness was falling when he looked up the street and wondered what life had in store for him now. It was a long way up Government Street but he slowly hobbled his way along Belleville Street. He was better off than many but right now he was tired and feeling sorry for himself. Intent upon finding a drink, when he reached the corner, he was startled by an unusual noise in the darkness.

"Who's there?" he barked, in his rasping voice—the result of a small piece of shrapnel still lodged in his throat.

Muffled sobs and the whining of a child were his only answer.

"Damnit, who are you?" his voice grated angrily.

Eyes straining into the darkness, Ben hobbled awkwardly toward the sound, his stick and wooden leg making the strangest of sounds on the newly-paved road. Raising his stick, he heard a rustling sound in the bushes and a figure stepped out. He stared in disbelief at a woman and a small child.

"What in heaven's name are you doing there woman?"

"Please sir," she whined, "is my Tom on that ship?"

"Everybody's off it now, did you not find him?"

"Oh dear," she sighed, pulling the child closer, "maybe daddy will come home tomorrow darling."

Forgetting his thirst, he offered to walk the lady home if they went slowly to accommodate his limp. She agreed and, with a silent nod, they moved off.

"Where do you live ma'am?" he asked, frowning as she vaguely waved her hand eastward. He hoped it wasn't too far. Ben could give himself no explanation why he felt the need to offer his protection and friendship. Could it be he'd found someone who would take his mind off his own troubles?

Walking in silence through the dark streets, Ben soon felt the pain in the stump of his leg and angry bitterness crept into his brain. Here he was at 24, a broken man who had given his all to the fight and now felt discarded.

Fleeting moonlight showed shadowy figures lurking amongst the trees. He could hear them moving and wondered if they were about to be attacked. He breathed a sigh of relief when the lady stopped in front of a cottage, he thought must be on Cook Street, and he heard the rattle of her key in the lock.

Turning to go, he heard her whispered plea, "Please stay sir."

Staring into the darkness of the doorway, he waited as first a match spluttered into life and then a candle flickered. He could finally see the woman's face and he moved painfully inside and closed it behind him.

"Do you have a lantern?" he asked.

"No."

"More candles and a fire we could light?"

"No," the voice whimpered.

"Do you mind if I sit down," he muttered, not waiting for her answer as he staggered toward an armchair. "I don't mind staying until morning

108

if you need the company." The next thing he remembers was opening his eyes as daylight crept into the room. He awoke with a start, then remembered where he was. The woman had put a thin blanket over him and he sat listening to the stillness. Then he heard a streetcar clanking in the distance.

"Yep, must be Cook Street," he mumbled.

Sitting up, he rubbed hard at the nagging pain in his leg, rolled up his trouser and checked the strapping that held the wooden pegleg in place. He was just about to stand when a tiny voice spoke at his elbow.

"Are you my daddy?"

A searing pain tore at his heart as he heard the child's plea which left him searching for answers to their plight. Words stuck in his throat but he instinctively folded the child into his arms, covered her with the blanket, and felt her relax as she drifted off to sleep. He must have drifted off as well because he felt cold when the woman came into the room and took the child.

"I'm sorry I can't offer you tea," she whispered apologetically, "but you're welcome to stay and sleep in that chair again."

She left as quietly as she had entered and he pulled the blanket around himself and fell asleep again. Daylight was streaming through the window the next time his eyes flickered open. Lying still, he realized that he was warmer than he had felt in months. He looked around the sparsely furnished room and noticed the blanket-draped figure of the woman watching him from the dark doorway.

"What is your name?" he asked.

"Dora Ryan and my daughter is Julia," she said shyly.

Slowly, over the next hour, Dora responded to his coaxing and haltingly told her story of heartbreak, worry and poverty. It had all begun when her husband Tom had answered the call and gallantly marched off to war, leaving behind his bride of less than a year expecting their first child. Dora told how she soon realized that army pay would barely pay the bills. Unable to work, she had soon become destitute as she waited for the monthly letter that often did not arrive. Unsympathetic government workers had driven the young mother to the brink of a mental collapse.

Ben realized that this thin, haggard face with tear-stained cheeks and a hopeless look in her sad eyes had once been a beautiful young woman who thought she was going to have a happy life with her new husband. His heart almost broke as he listened to her.

"Would you allow me to help you?" he whispered as little Julia came into the room and went over to him. He lifted her onto his knee and hugged her.

"B-but I-I can't impose," Dora stammered out her last vestige of pride without taking her eyes off her daughter. "You have your own life Ben."

"Dora, you need to think of Julia now. Let's go find some breakfast and we'll talk about it."

Julia clung to Ben's hand on the walk into the city. She was a delicate-looking child of almost four and, glancing down at her, his memory flashed back to his own happy childhood. He had never thought much about the fact that other children may not have the security of a loving home with carefree laughter and freedom to run and play.

Deeply affected by the war and very conscious of his own disability, Ben still felt a strange measure of responsibility toward these people. Allowing his angry thoughts toward the bureaucracy to churn silently through his head, he struggled with the long walk. Dora was talking more which helped pass the time, confiding in him more details of their predicament.

When they reached the 700 block of Fort Street, seeing soldiers standing on the sidewalk, brought Ben to a halt. They were outside the Army and Navy Tea Room and through the window he could see more uniformed men sitting at tables. He spoke to Dora and they went inside. Before they could find a table, however, a waitress stopped them.

"I'm sorry sir, but children are not allowed in here."

Julia buried her face in her mother's skirts and began to cry, but Ben wasn't being put off that easily. He raised his walking stick to get everyone's attention.

"We're very hungry, are you going to let them throw us out boys?"

Cutlery dropped with a clatter on half-eaten meals as all the soldiers rose to their feet as one, chanting, "Feed 'em! Feed 'em!"

The noise brought the owner rushing out from the kitchen, waving his arms in a nervous reaction to quiet the storm of protests.

"Boys, boys, please sit down," he pleaded. "We have rules I have to observe."

"Rules or no rules you'd better feed these folks," a soldier shouted from the corner, "or this place will look like a bomb dropped in it!" To emphasize his point, a coffee mug sailed through the air smashing on a wall.

Dora winced, instinctively turning her body toward Ben for protection.

"Stop, stop! I'll feed them," the owner cried.

Chairs and heavy-booted feet scraped on the bare wooden floor, as men moved to leave the centre table empty, an obvious invitation for Ben and his guests to join them.

"Thanks lads," Ben said gratefully, grinning at the soldiers and painfully swinging his pegleg under the table.

"Did ya leave yer leg in Europe matey?" someone quipped.

"Left it in Paris at the Follies," Ben chuckled to a roar of laughter.

Timidly Dora accepted a menu, looking around shyly at the men. "Toast would be fine," she whispered.

"I don't think so," Ben interrupted asking Julia if she liked eggs. When he saw Dora's eyes light up, he ordered three full breakfasts of bacon, eggs, and toast from the surly waitress.

The smell emanating from the food on the three heaping plates delivered to their table 10 minutes later, had a strange effect on Dora and her little daughter. Men turned their heads away as Julia asked her mother if she could eat. Dora whispered a tearful reassurance to the child before breaking the yolk of her egg with her toast and dabbing at an escaping tear with the back of her hand.

"Are they your family lad?" a bent old man at the next table asked.

"No, they're just two people who need a helping hand."

"But you know them?"

"Not really, I met them last night."

Dora blushed, lowering her eyes to her plate as some of the soldiers began to pay more attention, eager to hear the conversation.

"Only met them last night eh? Well, well, you seem to be making good time lad!" the voice cackled suggestively.

"Make another crack like that fella and you'll get a crack about the nose!" Ben retorted angrily. "They were waiting at the troop ship for the lady's husband to come home, a man who has been listed as missing in action for more than three years."

Everyone knew the connotation of Ben's statement and suddenly went quiet again. The waitress, with an audible sigh, swung on her heel and quickly made for the kitchen door.

"What regiment were you with mate?" an older soldier changed the subject abruptly.

"I joined right here. I'm from Shawnigan Lake. I trained with Dan Brown's artillery squad on Salisbury Plain."

"Me too," a young man near the window exclaimed. "Dan was a hell of a gunner."

"The best," Ben whispered reverently. "I shall never forget him."

"He's home now, lucky guy."

111

"He can't be, they took a direct hit in the frontline," Ben muttered glumly. "We didn't think anybody survived."

"I saw him yesterday over at the Wounded Soldier Restaurant opposite the hospital," another voice proffered. "They invalided him out but he's much better now, lost his memory for a while though I heard."

"Dan survived?" Ben repeated, unable to fathom it.

"He sure did lad. He owns a small shipping company down on the harbour and his wife's a partner in the Wounded Soldier."

"Maybe we should go Ben," Dora murmured, "you can visit better with your friends."

"Oh no you don't, we have things to do yet."

They finished up their meal and Ben nodded to the men as they left the restaurant. He couldn't get Dan off his mind as he led them to a streetcar stop and joined the line as the noisy tram came toward them. Julia giggled, holding tightly to his hand as they climbed aboard.

"Can you drop us off close to the Salvation Army offices?" he asked the conductor.

"We never ride the streetcars, do we mommy?" Julia asked, pressing her nose to the window.

"Hush darling," her mother muttered, "we can't afford such luxuries."

The conductor put them off at the corner of Government Street with instructions to the Fisgard Street Salvation Army office. Ben glanced at his companion and saw the look of defeat in her face and knew she had no great expectation of receiving help—there had been too many disappointments in the past.

Opening the big oak doors, he ushered his charges inside and made for the counter as a clerk suddenly appeared.

"How can we help you sir?" she asked with a smile.

"This woman has no food, no light, no fire and a child to raise," he explained, "and I think someone should be helping her."

"Yes I'm sure you do sir," the clerk continued to smile despite Ben's outburst, "but first could you tell me who you are?"

"I'm Ben Grubard, ma'am, recently invalided out of the army. She's Dora Ryan and that's her little girl Julia."

"And your relationship to them sir?"

"I haven't got no relationship," Ben responded in a slightly agitated tone as the outer door banged and he noticed an attractive, red-haired young woman who had quietly entered. Staying near the door, this woman gave the impression she didn't want to interrupt and stood quietly waiting. "I met them last night when my ship arrived. She was looking for her husband who was not on the ship."

112

"You were travelling sir?"

"No damnit, I was fighting for my country lady!"

"But you have no connection to these people?" The clerk struggled to comprehend. "So why are you here?"

"Perhaps I can help," the red-headed lady interrupted, coming toward them. "Sarah, please call Mrs. Coolridge and ask if she is able to see these people."

The receptionist scurried away to find her superior and Ben looked curiously at the young woman who had intervened. He felt the warmth of her smile, instantly switching his walking stick to his left hand and accepting the handshake she offered.

"Come in please," Sarah interrupted. "You too Nancy."

Limping after them, Ben noticed the woman named Nancy turn her attention to the obviously reluctant Dora, gently taking her arm and walking with her into the supervisor's office.

Following introductions, a smile crossed Nancy's face when Ben moved his chair closer to Dora, who had pulled Julia onto her lap. Sitting down awkwardly, he groaned softly.

"Now, how may I help you folks?" May Coolridge asked.

"Mrs. Ryan desperately needs some help Mrs. Coolridge," Ben blurted out. "Damnit, somebody has to care what happens to her."

Dora blushed, lowering her eyes to the floor and brushing a tear away. Nancy, who had remained standing, quickly moved in behind her to rest a comforting hand on her shoulder.

With gentle prodding from Ben, Dora slowly told her story. It was one of worry and hardship, hearing little of her husband and, meeting every troopship, praying Tom would be on board, and then, the hopeless feeling when he didn't arrive. She told of army pay that came irregularly and often didn't cover the rent forcing her to go hungry so she could feed her precious daughter.

As the whole story poured out, Ben's wooden leg began tapping on the floor with his growing agitation. Unable to contain himself, he struggled to his feet but found Nancy at his elbow.

"Please don't get angry Ben," she whispered. "I'm sure we can find a way to help Dora."

She was a calming influence and he reluctantly resumed his seat, then shook his head and murmured an apology.

"We can't bring your husband home Dora," May said quietly, "and the Salvation Army budget is stretched to the limit, however, there is one other avenue that we will pursue. Now that we are aware of your need, I'm sure we'll be able to find a way to help you."

"B-but she just said ...," Ben stammered turning to Nancy.

"Ben, you're going to have to stop worrying for a minute," May interrupted, "then we can do our job and find some help for Mrs. Ryan."

Nancy stifled a giggle at May's sharp rebuke and nodded her head as the supervisor's eyes locked on hers. May asked Dora her address and some other necessary details, writing it all down, raising an eyebrow briefly when Dora admitted her indebtedness to her landlord for rent. She jotted something down on a small piece of paper and handed it to Nancy who excused herself and left the room glancing at the note as she went. She found a chair in the waiting room, away from other people, and sat down. Reaching into her handbag, she extracted an envelope and counted out $12.50 before quickly returning the envelope to her bag. Going back to May's office, she placed the money on the desk in front of Mrs. Coolridge.

"Thank you Nancy, I thought you'd find some money somewhere," May sighed. "Would you please give it to Dora."

Nancy did so, receiving the brightest smile of gratitude.

"Thank you Mrs. ...?" she began.

"My name is Nancy Brown, Dora. I'm glad I was able to help. If you find yourself getting into this situation again, I want you to contact Mrs. Coolridge right away. Will you promise me that you will?"

"Y-yes, I will, but I'm sure my Tom will be home soon."

"Nancy ... Nancy Brown!" Ben muttered causing her to swing around and face the young soldier. "You've got red hair, too. You wouldn't know Dan Brown would ya?"

"Yes of course, he's my husband," she chuckled. "Do you know Danny?"

"He was my sergeant in the army," Ben whispered with a faraway look in his eyes. "I know you too. He never stopped talking about his red-haired angel waiting in Victoria for him. That was you, wasn't it?"

"Yes, I guess it was. He's home now you know."

"I'm so glad. I thought he was dead. I just heard today that he had come home. He probably won't remember me ma'am, but say hello for me. Tell him I've found a better job to do."

"Oh my, you have a job already?" Nancy asked.

"Yes ma'am, I have just decided to stay here in Victoria and fight for the people like Dora and Julia."

True to his word, in the months that followed, Ben became a force to be reckoned with—a regular figure prowling the corridors of power as he

114

attempted to right the wrongs of war. He also assisted Nancy in her local fundraising endeavours helping war-stricken widows and needy families.

Continuing his friendship with Dora and Julia, weeks after the war ended, to everyone's delight, Tom came home and Dora's family was complete once again. Soon afterwards, Ben won a seat in the Legislature where he continued to force veterans' family issues into the limelight. With the peculiar tap of his wooden leg and cane as his calling card, he ably proved he had earned his status as a local legend.

In Remembrance

They marched down the road
Eyes misty with tears
The hurt had always remained
Down through the years;
Of friends they had lost
In lands far away
But to hell with the cost,
We'll remember them today.

It's November and grey
Usually wet,
Their numbers are less
Some are dead you can bet.
Yet the few that are left
Will march straight and true
Because these were the people
Who gave freedom to you.

Part 3 – Lessons of Life

A Change of Attitude

Alice Ibordson screamed as she crashed to the kitchen floor, tears welling in her eyes as a numbing pain seared through her hip. At seventy-three and living alone in the tiny cottage her father had built in 1919, she had proudly refused to relinquish her independence. Feisty and abrasive, she had protected her domain from the new neighbours and their children, government agents, social workers and municipal men.

Pain had mercifully caused unconsciousness within moments of her fall but now she awoke and winced as she tried to move, struggling to clear her thoughts and make some sense on what had happened. Laying still on the cold hard floor she let her fingers wander slowly over the area of throbbing pain in her hip, squealing when she touched the sore area. The cold was beginning to make her shiver and she deliberately contemplated her options. With very few friends living locally she knew no one would be calling, reasoning her only hope of finding help was the phone.

Darkness now shrouded the kitchen as daylight turned quickly to dusk and she reached out slowly to explore the furniture around her—a table leg and an overturned chair. Her fingers found the salt cellar next to her head. *I have to get to the phone*, she thought squeezing the salt cellar tightly in her hand.

Gasping with pain, she pulled herself inch-by-inch under the table, stealing herself against the agony of movement and glad she had never carpeted the kitchen as her body slid over the highly polished linoleum.

Fighting nausea from the effort and pain, she was forced to rest and only became aware of the time when her clock chimed the midnight hour. She now became horribly aware of the goose bumps on her arms and the chilling cold of her back. It was the middle of September and Alice had no heat on in the house, her way of saving a few dollars on her heating bill.

"I will not die like this," she hissed into the darkness with dogged determination as she continued her inch-by-inch journey across the kitchen floor, aware that she could no longer feel the lower half of her body which was numb with cold and pain.

116

"You've got yourself into a hell of a pickle this time girl," she admonished herself with a groan.

Daylight was beginning to filter through the kitchen window when her hand felt the leg of the tiny table on which her phone sat. She mustered all her strength in an attempt to pull it over. Fainting from the painful effort, Alice was unaware the phone had smashed into pieces and now lay quiet and useless beside her.

Tears flooded down her face when her hand found the broken pieces and she knew her only hope of calling for help had gone and the stark reality of dying alone now tore through her mind.

Floating in and out of consciousness, she saw many faces from the past, as memories and delirium played tricks on her mind. Harry, her husband who had died 30 years before, appeared to her grinning foolishly as he whispered a word of encouragement.

"Come on, old girl, you can do it," his voice murmured.

The faces of two brothers lost in the war made a fleeting pass through her memory and she thought she heard their laughter in the garden.

Snapping back to reality she listened to the sounds outside and felt a twinge of anger when she heard her garden gate squeak as it opened and the subdued voices of the neighbour's children near the door. Then remembering her situation, she mustered all her strength and hurled the broken receiver of the phone at the door and fainted into oblivion.

As the broken phone came flying through the glass door panel, shock sent the two little boys in a mad dash for the garden gate, all thoughts of retrieving their ball disappearing in their effort to escape.

"What have you done now?" Their mother dashed toward them to investigate the sound of breaking glass. "Now Mrs. Ibordson will really have something to complain about."

"We didn't do anything mum," the boys whimpered, looking up at her.

"You must have," she snapped, brushing the boys aside. "I heard some glass break. Have you broken one of her windows?"

Mrs. Sarrah Pardu, Alice's Pakistani neighbour, nervously entered the garden expecting Alice in her usual abrasive manor to arrive at the door at any moment and begin her usual tirade of abuse. Glancing at the windows she sighed with relief when she saw they were whole, but her heart sank as her eyes fastened on the door and its broken pane of glass. Moving slowly toward it she gasped as panic clutched at her throat.

How could a broken phone get onto the steps? she wondered. Timidly peeking through the broken door panel she squealed as the still form of Alice lying on the kitchen floor took her attention.

"Oh my goodness," she repeated over and over as she stumbled out of the garden and dashed for home.

Police and ambulance sirens were soon wailing through the streets of old Esquimalt. Rushing to the road from Alice's garden gate, Sarrah waved frantically. A burly young policeman quickly opened the door and rushed to the old lady's side.

Alice's eyes flickered open and she managed a hoarse whisper. "Thank God you came," she murmured before floating off into oblivion again.

"I take it you're her neighbour ma'am," the policeman commented as the ambulance drove away, "you saved that poor woman's life by making that 911 call. Does she have family?"

Sarrah trembled a little as she shrugged her shoulders. She had long since stopped making overtures of friendship to Alice as nothing she did seemed to please the grumpy old lady, although her gentle nature had often felt sorry for the woman.

"You'll take care of the place until she gets back I assume," he said, moving toward his car. "We'll try to locate her relatives."

A look of astonishment spread across Sarrah's face, knowing Alice Ibordson resented any interference in her life. *Will she be grateful or angry?* she wondered.

Forgetting their differences, she quickly did what she could to cleanup the house, sweeping up the glass and putting the furniture back in place. When her husband came home from work, she persuaded him to put a new pane of glass in the door.

Two days went by before the policeman returned, informing her they had not been able to find any relatives and that Mrs. Ibordson was probably doomed to be sent to a home for the aged.

"No," Sarrah heard herself say, "she must come home; this place is all she has."

"But she can't," the constable frowned, "she'll need help and with no one to look after her it's an impossible situation."

"I'll help her," Sarrah found herself whispering. "The ambulance men said she had a broken hip. Tell me where she is and I'll go see her."

"She's in Royal Three at the Jubilee, are you sure you want to do this?"

"Yes," said Sarrah, nodding her head.

It was three o'clock the next day when Sarrah drove her little red car into the parking lot at the Jubilee Hospital. Somewhat unsure of herself as she had never been here before and always told herself she hated hospitals, she glanced up at the large modern building and adjusted her

118

silk scarf as she made her way nervously to the large front doors. Stopping at the Information Desk, she asked directions to Royal Three and was directed to an elevator. It was a long walk but she finally arrived and found the nurses' station. She shyly told the nurse she had come to visit Mrs. Ibordson.

"Are you a relative?" the nurse asked with a puzzled expression.

"No, I'm her neighbour."

"Oh, straight down the hall, third door on the right. She's in the first bed on the right, just inside the door. Don't stay too long, she's very weak."

Arriving at the third doorway, Sarrah paused, gathering her courage as she tried to decide how to confront Mrs. Ibordson and offer her help. She stepped through the door and stood at the foot of Alice's bed. Their eyes met as Sarrah gazed at the pale old lady, looking even more frail than she remembered.

"What do you want?" the old lady softly hissed, not recognizing her.

"I came to see how you were; it was me that called the ambulance."

"You did?" Alice's voice betrayed her surprise.

"Yes, I'm Sarrah from next door to you. Me and my boys cleaned up the broken glass and my husband repaired your door."

"Why did you do that?" Mrs. Ibordson asked in an emotionless tone.

"Because we're neighbours and you needed help."

Sighing, Alice closed her eyes to escape. Here was a neighbour she had shunned, now being supportive and helpful to her. She had never had an excuse for her behaviour, she simply couldn't bother. Now, being grateful was a new experience to the feisty old lady who desperately needed a friend. Tears filled her eyes as she reached out her hand to her brown-skinned visitor.

"Please forgive me my dear," Alice whispered.

From that poignant moment a new friendship was born, one that blossomed into mutual respect and affection. This friendship would last for many treasured years giving a lonely old lady the blessing of a new lease on life. In return, her adopted family gratefully accepted her into their home as a surrogate grandmother, a relationship which lasted to the end of her days.

Almost Too Late For Love

The string of mishaps that had plagued Jack Lewis for years continued as he crashed to the hard irregular surface of Fisherman's Wharf. Shocked, bruised, and with water soaking into his pants from the spring, rain-doused boards, he wondered if his clumsy feet really belonged to him.

"Are you hurt?" a friendly feminine voice murmured above him. "Can I help you up?"

Turning, Jack saw a small, grey-haired older woman smiling down at him. With a twinkle in her eyes, she extended her hand and he struggled to his feet, allowing his rescuer to guide him to a nearby bench.

"Sit for a while," she gently coaxed, "until you get your breath."

Jack's tall frame towered over the woman as he attempted to dust the dirt off his pants, grimacing when his hands touched his wet rear end.

"I don't think sitting would be a comfortable exercise right now my dear," he admitted, "but I'll buy you a coffee, if you don't mind me standing."

Nodding her acceptance, she adjusted her scarf and hat then followed as Jack led the way to the floating cafe and selected a table by the rail.

"Two coffees," he said to the young waitress, "don't mind if I just stand here do ya?"

"No sir, but don't fall overboard, we don't carry a life raft on this vessel!"

"I like that in a man," Jack's companion cocked her head and smiled at him. "A sense of humour even when you're in pain."

"I'm not in pain," Jack laughed.

"I would be if my backside were wet!"

The coffee arrived and they made their introductions.

"I'm Jack Lewis," he offered, holding out a massive work-gnarled hand.

"Pleased to meet you sir," she replied, extending her own much tinier one. "Molly O'Neil, an Irish girl who's never seen Ireland!"

"Glad to meet you Molly O'Neil," he muttered awkwardly.

Reaching for his coffee, he knocked over the cup, spilling the brown liquid across the table. Molly quickly shuffled her chair backward and chuckled silently at Jack's embarrassment. The waitress appeared with a towel and efficiently cleaned up the mess, bringing him a fresh cup.

"Sorry," Jack mumbled nervously. "I'm just naturally clumsy."

"Nonsense," Molly blurted, "you weren't always clumsy, I'll bet."

"All me life actually," Jack sighed. "If you could spill it, break it, or knock it over, then I'd manage it!"

Taking a sip of her coffee, Molly studied the big man leaning on the rail. He seemed a gentle soul and she suspected he was as lonely as she was—a man who had lost his confidence in living, with no special friends to share his thoughts or memories.

"I haven't seen you down here before," she murmured, "are you a tourist?"

"No, I live on Graham Street up near Hillside."

"That's a long walk."

"Not really, I like walking and I've got long legs," Jack chuckled.

"But you weren't born here were you?"

"Yes, I was born on Graham Street."

"Oh my, a native Victorian, lucky you."

"Where were you born?" he asked.

"In a little town near Edmonton."

"Never been there, I'm not too keen on snow."

"I live here now," she replied.

"Where?"

"At the Empress."

"That must cost you a pretty penny," he muttered in surprise, "how long have you been there?"

"Since April '94, almost 10 years now."

She must have a lot of money, Jack thought, as an attack of nervous embarrassment made his cup rattle on the saucer.

"Steady, why don't you come sit down, your pants must be dry by now," Molly said gently.

"I don't want to hold you up, you must have somewhere to go," he replied, a blush of crimson appearing on his cheeks.

"Sit down silly. I'm just like you, nowhere to go and all day to get there," she laughed. "You're a welcome interlude in my day."

"You must have seen all the sights," Jack muttered as he slowly eased himself onto a chair.

"Well," Molly giggled as she watched him, "are they dry?"

"Not yet," Jack replied with a grimace. "Did you say you'd seen all the sights?"

"I've seen all the tourist places," Molly sighed, "but I don't know anyone who could show me all the out-of-the-way places, unless," she smiled coyly, "you would volunteer to show me."

121

"M-m-me," Jack stammered, his coffee cup rattling again.

"Don't you dare spill that coffee again," she warned. "I've spent 10 years in this city waiting for someone to make friends with me and I think it's time I made the first move."

Jack's hair bristled on the back of his neck, at 70 years of age he'd never had a girlfriend, always being somewhat afraid of the fairer sex. Molly's proposition both scared and intrigued him.

Molly recognized his dilemma, smiling as she watched the colour again rise in his face. She liked this clumsy, gentle old man.

"I'm 72," she murmured, "how old are you?"

"70."

"Well, what do you say Jack?" she pressed him. "Shall we be friends?"

"Ah suppose it wouldn't hurt," Jack proffered nervously, "but what would you want to do?"

"You could start by asking me out to dinner tonight."

"Ah don't go out to dinner," he said meekly.

"But you do eat, don't you?" she countered, the twinkle coming back into her eyes.

"Yes, I usually get Chinese or fish and chips and take them home."

"Well, can I come and eat with you tonight?"

"My place ain't the Empress you know, it's just a little house my folks used to own."

"With a garden?" Molly asked, giggling excitedly.

"Yes, and a greenhouse."

"It sounds real homely."

"It was when the folks were alive," Jack reflected uneasily, "but now …," his voice tapered off as memories swept through his mind.

Molly could feel his pain. She reached out and briefly touched his hand. "Now it's just cold and lonely, isn't it?"

He sighed and put his head down. "Yes sometimes it is."

They talked awhile until the sun broke through the clouds and Jack relaxed a little taking sneaky little peeks at his newfound friend. He found they had a common interest in history, a passion he'd had all his life. Soon they were chattering enthusiastically on the topic of Victoria's past, giving him the opportunity to display his extensive knowledge on the subject.

"Show me something that's really old," Molly challenged.

"Right," Jack chuckled, "how are you at walking?" he asked as he climbed to his feet, promptly knocking over his coffee cup again.

"Never mind, it's empty anyway," Molly laughed. "I have my car in the parking lot at the Empress."

"We're only going to Wharf Street."

"Oh all right, I'm good for a mile or two if you don't walk too fast!"

He paid the bill and they left the restaurant, leaving behind a smiling waitress who had heard most of their conversation. Taking their time as they wandered past the Laurel Point Inn, he explained that a soap factory had once stood on this spot. Molly turned around looking at the nearby old houses with a newfound interest. Her guide's interest in local history was becoming infectious. Crossing the street at the entrance to the Ramada Inn, Jack pointed to the Gatsby Mansion set in the beautiful gardens of the modern hotel.

"That," he whispered reverently, "is the Pendray mansion, that's where the family lived that owned the soap factory I just told you about."

Continuing on, they crossed the street to the Wax Museum and Jack suggested a rest on one of the curbside seats.

"This wasn't always a wax museum, was it?" she asked at her companion, glancing over her shoulder at the substantial building.

"No, my dear," Jack grinned, "this was the CPR shipping office, built in 1929 as their passenger terminal."

"You mean passengers arrived right here?"

"Yes, thousands of them. Why lass, during the war, hospital ships came in here, even before this building was built, in a time when the CPR terminal was down on the water."

"Which war?"

"The first one, 1914-18."

"But you said it wasn't built until 1929."

"There were wooden docks and buildings back then, this old harbour has seen lots of changes since those days."

"I've read the history of the Empress Hotel," Molly murmured enthusiastically, "it was finished in 1908."

Jack cocked his eye at the lady beside him and smiled. "But did you know it's built on a swampy garbage heap and they had to drive piles into the mud to put the foundations on?" he chuckled.

"What are piles?" Molly asked innocently.

Suddenly Jack felt important, he knew these things and found a great sense of pleasure as he imparted that knowledge to his newfound friend.

"Molly, piles are like big straight trees that they hammer down into the mud."

"You're pulling my leg!" she giggled.

"No I'm not," he laughed, "that blinking hotel is built right on top of them."

"Oh my," his companion replied, shuddering noticeably. "I'm moving out of there. If it slips off those poles it'll sink out of sight!"

"It won't slip off Molly," he exclaimed, howling with laughter and absent-mindedly slipping his arm over her shoulder.

Molly playfully slapped his hand, enjoying the closeness. "I shall demand a guarantee from the manager immediately when I get back tonight," she muttered.

"He'll think you're off your rocker!" Jack chortled, his eyes suddenly following a seagull that had dropped a nasty deposit across the sidewalk nearby. "Come on girl, let's move on before that seagull craps on us!"

"Dirty beasts," Molly muttered.

Laughter had broken all the barriers between the old couple, each in their own way feeling more comfortable with the other as they walked. They reached the corner of Government and Wharf and stood for a moment to stare up at the old buildings.

"Tell me about those buildings Jack," Molly whispered, her eyes sparkling with interest.

Standing directly behind her, he rested a hand gently on her shoulder. "That building in front of you," he pointed at the big building on the southwest corner, "is the Federal Building; it used to be the post office during the early part of the century, built in the 1890s I think. It was one of the goodies Confederation brought to the city. The post office before that was at the southwest corner of Government and Yates."

"My goodness Mr. Lewis," Molly gasped in admiration, "what a fountain of knowledge you are! Now what about that one on the other corner?"

"Now that one is a very interesting building," Jack replied, trying hard to collect his thoughts. "That's the Belmont Building, it was built around 1900, but it had a very special feature."

"It was the first hotel?" his companion interrupted enthusiastically.

"No, it had the time ball on top of it!"

"Tell me, tell me," Molly insisted with eager interest, "don't keep me in suspense. Whatever is a time ball?"

Jack's ego bubbled. All those years he'd spent researching the past and here was the most attentive audience he'd ever had. Pointing up to the roof, he stretched his neck to see.

"Up there," he began, "was a pole that slowly lifted a ball, and on the stroke of one it fell back to the bottom and started all over again. People used to set their watches by it."

124

"It fell down into the street?" Molly asked with a frown, squinting as she tried to visualize the action.

"No, no, just to the bottom of the pole, still on the roof."

"That sounds a bit dangerous to me."

"Well it worked," Jack snorted, turning to look along Wharf Street.

"Not so fast Jack," Molly purred, "you missed one corner."

"You mean here where we're standing, in front of the Tourist Information Centre?"

"Yes."

"It was a gas station."

"A gas station in the middle of the city?" she murmured in doubt. "You're kidding me."

"No, Imperial Oil built it in 1931," Jack expounded, "with a beacon light on top of an 80-foot tower to guide aircraft into the harbour. Before that, it was part of the Black Ball Ferry system."

Satisfied with the explanation, Molly gazed around her trying to imagine the scene from the past.

"Close your eyes," Jack whispered, "and let the rumble of streetcars fill your ears and you'll be able to see it all right in front of you."

They stood for a few minutes in total silence, his hand still resting on her shoulder. Her eyes were closed tight as she filled her mind with the past and felt the wonderful caress of history.

"You should be a teacher Mr. Lewis," she whispered as her eyes flicked open.

"It's a bit late for that," he mumbled.

Moving off along Wharf Street, he stopped opposite the Custom House building, now occupied by a legal office.

"I think I know about this one," she said brightly, "it's the oldest Federal building in Victoria."

"Well done," he said with a smile, "and it was built in 1875."

"Is that the oldest thing still left here in Victoria?" she asked.

"No," Jack grinned, "it's only the oldest Federal building."

"You know something older than that?"

"Yes, lots of things," he said, winking at her.

They were making their way along the street when Jack suddenly stopped in front of a building with the large numbers ... 1125. Molly stepped back to the edge of the sidewalk and gazed up at the building, her eyes searching for something significant.

"This building?" she questioned blankly.

"No not the building, but it is 10 years older than the Custom House."

"Really?"

"Quiet now," he warned reaching for her hand.

Opening the big oak door, he led her inside and quietly closed it.

"Where are we going?" Molly whispered, gripping tight to Jack's hand.

"Hush," he ordered, leading her along the wide hall. "There you are," he pointed at the short brick wall at the end of the hall.

"My goodness," Molly squealed after reading the plaque, "it's the well from Fort Victoria!"

Standing back, Jack watched his friend with obvious enjoyment, as she touched a piece of long ago history. He could feel her excitement when her hand touched the old pump, gently caressing the handle with silent reverence.

"Come on Molly," he tugged on her arm, breaking the spell of her imagination as he moved toward the door, "we've more to see yet."

Quietly closing the big door behind them, they stepped onto the Wharf Street sidewalk. Waiting for a moment to allow people to pass, Jack pointed to the foot of the columns along the front of the building.

"Look," he chuckled, "they're cast iron, you can see the foundry mark."

Holding her hand while she bent over to take a closer look, she staggered a little with uncertain balance. Jack's face turned ashen white with sudden concern, reaching out to steady her. Grasping her in his arms he held onto her as she regained her balance.

"I'm sorry," she mumbled, holding onto him for a moment. "Can we find a seat? I'm just a little dizzy."

Holding tight to his arm, they moved slowly along the street and stubbornly made a cyclist dismount when Jack refused to hurry the lady at his side.

"There's a seat at the bottom of Bastion Square," he whispered. "Oh my look at that, I forgot the craft market is on at Bastion Square."

He led her slowly through the throng of tourists and shoppers to the alley by the side of the old Court House and the Blue Carrot Café. Settling her onto a seat under a colorful umbrella, he also sat down.

"Tea or coffee?" he inquired gently, as a waitress arrived.

"Peppermint tea would be lovely Jack."

The waitress left after Jack gave the order and they sat people-watching until she returned.

"Do you take anything in it?" he asked as the waitress set their tea cups and small teapots in front of them.

"No, it's not usually a problem," she replied, straightening her scarf. "I'm feeling better already. I'll be fine when I get a drop of tea into me and rest a while."

"My goodness, you had me worried," Jack whispered, releasing her hand. "Maybe I should walk you back to the Empress and call it a day."

"No, no!" Molly exclaimed showing her disappointment. "I'm really enjoying your company."

"We could meet tomorrow, when you're feeling better."

Molly slowly lowered the tea cup, adjusted her hat and asked pointedly, "Are you trying to get rid of me Jack Lewis?"

"No," he blushed, "but maybe I should take you home with me, you could sit in my garden and have supper at the picnic table."

"Now that sounds more like it," Molly chuckled. "Are you making a proposition, Mr. Lewis, or are you just thinking out loud?"

"It's probably too far to walk for you."

"Making excuses why you shouldn't ask, are you Jack?" Molly teased.

"I've never asked a lady out before," he admitted quietly. "I'm not sure how to say it."

"Try just asking me, I won't bite!"

Blushing, he stumbled over his words, "Would you like to come sit in my garden?" he asked.

"I'd be honoured," she replied.

"Does that mean yes?"

"It certainly does."

They took almost an hour to walk to Jack's Graham Street home. All along the way Jack talked of history and his childhood in the area, pointing out the streetcar route along Blanshard which he rode as a youngster. Resting at the building site of the new arena, Molly watched in wonder as concrete trucks pumped their liquid loads into preset formwork. Then she followed him down a side street behind the Island Dairy depot and offices, a shortcut to Bay Street and Quadra.

"Not too far now," Jack informed her as they crossed Hillside Avenue.

Tiring a little, Molly asked if she could hold onto his arm, sending Jack into a panic attack as he blamed himself for walking her so far.

Neighbours watched suspiciously from their gardens as they arrived at his own garden gate, never having seen Jack with a woman before.

"You'll be the talk of the neighbourhood," she giggled, "bringing a lady home with you."

"To hell with 'em," Jack growled defiantly. "I don't care what they think."

"Oh what a lovely garden," Molly gasped moving quickly to examine some of the blooms then gazing over the wonderful array of flowers.

"I'll put the umbrella up and get the chairs out," Jack muttered nervously fumbling with his basement door key, "or would you rather come inside?"

"I'd like to sit outside, but I would like a cup of tea."

"No problem," he grinned as his basement door flew open and he disappeared inside.

Smiling, she watched as he rushed back outside with two garden chairs in his hands, tripping on the edge of the lawn in his nervous urgency and almost falling flat onto the grass.

"Slow down," Molly laughed. "I won't run away."

Jack soon reappeared with the umbrella, putting it into the hole in the middle of the table. He said he'd get the tea and within 10 minutes was back with a loaded tray, his mother's best china teacups and a teapot under a fancy cozy. "Do you like it strong or weak?" he asked setting it down and turning back toward the house muttering, "I forgot the cookies."

"Oh stop your fussing," Molly chastised him with a smile.

Grinning as he re-emerged with two colorful tins under his arm, he placed one by his cup and pulled the tight lid off the other to reveal an interesting array of cookies.

"And what have you got there?" she pointed to the tin by his elbow.

"Me pipe," he blushed, adding quickly, "but I won't light it if it bothers you."

"Bothers me? Here, change seats with me. I used to enjoy the smell of a pipe and the breeze will waft it my way."

As he reached for the teapot Molly slapped his hand. "Oh no, you don't!" she chuckled. "I'll do the pouring if you're not superstitious. You sit down and light your pipe."

Stretching his long legs, Jack sipped on his tea and slowly worked on building his pipe. Watching curiously, Molly could see it was a ritual, shaped over a good many years. Those big hands and strong fingers worked with a delicate gentleness to produce the perfect smoke, his eyes never leaving his object of pleasure. Finally, he struck a wooden match and drew the first wisps of air up the stem, allowing the thick blue smoke to trickle slowly from the corners of his mouth.

"It's good," Molly murmured, smiling as she sniffed the air, "it smells wonderful."

"My grandfather smoked this pipe," Jack said absentmindedly, "he worked over there at the brickyard." He pointed the pipe stem at the 15 foot evergreen trees at the bottom of his garden.

"I didn't know there was a brickyard so close to town."

"It wasn't close to town in those days. We played there as kids. The kilns were down where the Mayfair Shopping Centre is now," he paused to puff on the pipe. "grandfather told me of the railway that used to run along Blanshard on its way to Sidney. I never saw it though; it had gone before I was born."

"A railway ran to Sidney?" his guest whispered in surprise.

Jack lapsed into silence as his mind wandered back to the days of his grandfather, the walks they took together through the brickyard or down past the prison at the corner of Hillside and Quadra.

Molly could see the faraway look in Jack's eyes and knew that memories were bubbling to the surface in the old man's mind. "Show me your greenhouse," she said suddenly, trying to shake Jack from his lonely journey down memory lane. "Are those tomatoes you have in there?"

"Yes they are, I like a nice tomato but I only grow a few now. Come on, I'll show you."

"My goodness I can smell them," Molly exclaimed as she followed Jack onto the wooden plank path up the middle of his greenhouse, and smiled as his oversized fingers gently nipped off a side shoot on one of the plants. "Golly," she whispered staring at two huge baskets of flowers hanging from the ceiling, "I've never seen fuchsias that big before."

"They were my mother's favourite," Jack whispered reverently, "they're called Texas Longhorns."

"Do you know what time it is?" she chuckled. "It's almost four o'clock, you must be getting hungry."

"Sorry, do you have to be back at the Empress at a certain time?"

"No it's a hotel not a nursing home, but it's time we thought about eating."

"We could walk down to the chip shop; it's just down on Hillside."

"I was under the impression, young man, that you had invited me to stay here for supper, but if you've changed your mind."

"No, no, I haven't," Jack spluttered nervously, his teeth losing a grip on his pipe allowing it to fall onto the grass.

"Good then, that's settled," Molly said with a glint in her eyes. "Just bring me one fish and I'll share a few of your chips. Now show me where your plates and cutlery are and I'll have everything ready when you get back."

Jack was speechless, everything was happening so fast. For the first time since his mother died, he was not eating alone. He led her through his basement workshop, past the old washer and dryer and on up the creaking basement stairs. The kitchen was neat, though sparsely furnished with a table, three chairs, a noisy fridge and an antique stove. On the countertop in the small pantry area lay a single plate, mug, and the necessary cutlery for one person to eat—stark evidence that Jack ate alone.

"Just show me where everything is before you go," Molly instructed.

Nervously Jack complied, sweating a little as he left by the front door. Glancing ahead, he smiled as his thoughts took him back to a time when streetcars rumbled noisily across the Hillside–Quadra Junction and his school friend, Stan Joyce, and his family lived on the corner.

"Hi Jack," Mike, the chip shop owner, greeted him. "You want your regular order?"

"No, I want an extra fish today."

"Cod or Halibut?"

"Halibut."

"Hungry or have you got company?" Mike inquired over his shoulder.

"Company," Jack admitted. Feeling a warmth creep up his neck, he turned quickly to stare out of the window.

Feeling the heat radiate through the newspaper wrapping as he hurried back home, Jack stumbled on the irregular sidewalk almost losing his package. He smiled when he saw Molly waiting at the gate.

"I found the salt and vinegar," she whispered. "You go wash up and we'll sit down and eat while they're nice and crisp."

By the time he returned to the picnic table, Molly had the food on the table. Jack stared at her realizing she was wearing a familiar-looking pretty red and white checkered apron.

"What's wrong?" she asked.

"That was mother's apron," he murmured almost incoherently.

"I guessed that, but I thought you wouldn't mind if I wore it. I found it in the tea towel drawer."

"No I don't mind at all, it just gave me a start seeing it worn again."

The smell of salt and malt vinegar on the hot fish and chips brought a smile to Molly's face as Jack, using his fingers, eagerly tasted the delicious golden brown, deep-fried potatoes.

"They always seem to taste better eaten with our fingers, don't they?" she laughed.

"It's the way I always eat 'em," Jack chuckled. "I don't even use a plate most times, saves on the washing up."

After supper, they forgot about the time as they swapped stories of their youth, causing Molly to laugh until tears ran down her face as Jack told humorous episodes of his clumsiness. Neither of them noticed the dark rain cloud that was sliding slowly over from the northwest. Rain spots fell onto the table, suddenly giving them notice.

"It probably won't last long," Jack laughed as they hurried to clear the table and put the chairs away.

She watched from the shelter of the basement door as he went out in the rain to close his greenhouse door, unhurriedly standing for a moment with the rain running down his face.

"It'll do my garden good," he chuckled as he stepped into the basement.

"Here, dry yourself," said Molly handing him a towel from on top of the washing machine.

"Sorry Molly, but it looks like you're staying awhile," Jack apologized with a twinkle in his eye as he nodded at the basement stairs. "Up you go, I could light a fire if you like."

"A real fire?" she asked pausing on the stairs.

"Yes, a real fire with sticks and a log."

Molly felt somehow at home here in this little house standing at the old kitchen sink, washing the cups and plates and letting the warm water run over her hands. She could hear Jack laying the fire in the tiny front room as her mind took her back to her farming childhood. She remembered the heartbreak she felt when her father sold to a developer, moving the family into a fine new house in Edmonton. Skipping on through the years, her thoughts dwelt for a moment on her marriage to a fine young man who died in a railway accident, leaving her alone and unblessed by children. And now, financially secure, but alone in the world, she longed to have a close friend.

"Are you trying to drown yourself?" Jack's voice cut into her thoughts.

"I think that would be difficult with just my hands in the water!" she giggled.

"Fire's lit," he announced. "Would you like a glass of my homemade plum wine?"

"I certainly would!"

The evening passed quickly as Jack showed her his family photo albums, causing bursts of laughter by adding his own little antidotal stories to each of the pictures.

"I should be going," she announced without enthusiasm about an hour later. "Is it still raining?"

"Yes, but it won't matter. We'll catch the bus."

"You don't need to go back downtown," Molly murmured. "If you put me on the bus and tell the conductor where to put me off, I'm sure I'll be fine."

"Hold on a minute girl." Jack's eyebrows rose. "You ain't been on a bus recently, have you?"

"I've never been on a city bus in Victoria," Molly admitted, "but I once rode on one of those funny English double-decker tourist buses."

"I'd better take you," Jack replied, shaking his head and grinning at the same time. "I wouldn't want you getting lost."

Searching through his closet, he found a lightweight raincoat that had been his mother's and coaxed Molly to try it on. He sighed when he saw it was almost a perfect fit. "There, that should keep you dry," he said.

"Was this your mother's too?" she asked, pleased with his concern.

"Yes," he brushed over the question reaching for his coat and an umbrella. "We'll go out the front door."

Walking close together under the umbrella, Molly linked her arm in his as they crossed the road to the bus stop. A car, travelling very quickly, splashed water onto the sidewalk in front of them.

"Bloody idiot!" Jack shouted after the car, and then stammered an apology when he heard his companion giggle.

The bus came and Jack fiddled with his coins before shepherding her up the stairs and dropping the coins in the money box. The bus was almost empty.

"My but this is thrilling," she exclaimed wriggling her arm back into his and pulling him closer. "What's that place," she asked, pointing across the street as the bus stopped near the Crystal Pool.

"Oh, that's the curling rink," he grinned. "Have you never been there?"

"No, when I was a girl, we used to curl on the farm pond."

"I'll take you there next week if you want," Jack chuckled. "It's been years since I was there. Curling is an interesting game."

"I'd like that," Molly smiled up at him, squeezing his arm again.

As the bus wound its way through the city streets, she watched the familiar shops go by and looked quite surprised when the bus pulled into the stop on Yates Street and Jack stood up.

"Oh dear, I thought it stopped behind the Empress, at the bus station," Molly murmured. "I may have gotten lost!"

It was after 8:30 as they went down Government Street. The rain had stopped and streaks of late sunshine found their way through the quickly departing storm clouds.

"Is it too late to ask you in for a night cap?" Molly asked.

"No it's not too late, but I hardly think I'm Empress material," Jack chuckled. "I ain't never been through those doors. It's a bit above my station in life."

Molly's eyes twinkled with mischief as she slipped off the borrowed raincoat, hung it over her arm, then took Jack's arm and led him toward the front door of the grand hotel.

"I'll leave you here," Jack said shyly as they neared the door, allowing his arm to slip out of her grasp.

"No, you will not!" Molly admonished him sternly. "You're going to accompany me to my suite."

Jack nervously backed away as courage deserted him, his mind conjuring up thoughts of his embarrassment if he was asked to leave.

Molly held out her hand and softly encouraged him. "Please Jack, you've made this day a wonderful adventure for me, don't spoil it now."

"But I don't belong in there."

"Yes you do. You're my guest, as I was yours this afternoon," she argued gently. "We're too old to be silly about this thing. You're my friend and I've enjoyed your company immensely, but we have to accept each other for who we are." She coaxed him inside the doors, watching him gaze around the foyer in wonder. She held his hand as they rode the elevator up to the third floor.

"See, that wasn't so bad, was it?" she whispered as she opened the door to her suite.

It seems needless to say that their first date was a total success and formed the beginning of a special friendship. If you keep a close watch, you may even see them sitting quietly on a Wharf Street bench watching the goings-on of the harbour or wandering arm-in-arm through Bastion Square. They are simply two lovely old people who found each other before life passed them by.

Confused Identity

Staggering forward, he clutched wildly for the support of his overloaded shopping cart. Groaning, he settled to his knees on the sidewalk as his face twisted with the pain. No one moved to help the old man in the dirty, torn coat tied with a string belt. His hat rolled into the street but people hurried on, after all he was only a street person. Empty bottles, plastic bags and mouldy bread spilled from his cart as it crashed to the ground.

An anonymous cellphone call brought a wailing police cruiser to the curb and a young policeman, pulling on latex gloves, went over to the fallen man. Turning the old man over with his foot, he grimaced when he saw the foaming vomit in the ragged beard, spewing out onto the sidewalk under him. He moved him slightly, unenthusiastically attempting to find a wallet or other ID. He pulled out his phone and called for assistance.

"Who saw what happened here?" the policeman shouted to the small group of people standing nearby. A few shook their heads, but no one offered any comment so he slipped his notepad back into his pocket.

Constable Raymond Abbot was a fairly new rookie with the Victoria Police Department and he was finding that his job often entailed dealing with issues relating to the city's street people. He had almost become accustomed to the squalor in which many of them lived and couldn't help but wonder why they refused help. He took a cursory look over the upset shopping cart and found a grimy-looking pillow. Handling it gingerly, he elevated the man's head as best he could then left him on his side so he wouldn't choke if he was sick again.

Minutes later, the urgent groan of an ambulance was heard as it passed through a nearby intersection, arriving seconds later. This brought more curiosity seekers, no doubt anxious to catch a glimpse of blood or a dead person. Medics performed their job with speedy efficiency and left the policeman and city workers to dispose of the man's possessions in a city garbage truck which then drove away.

When the disappointed crowd dispersed, Constable Abbot followed the ambulance to the hospital. Sometime later, he donned rubber gloves once again to check the pockets of the man's clothes for clues to his identity. Finding none, he frowned at the familiar emergency room nurse.

"Who is he?" she asked with concern.

"Damned if I know," Constable Abbot replied.

Two days later when his commanding officer called him into his office, he pointed sternly to the constable's report on his desk.

"He was a street person sergeant," Ray replied. "I followed procedure but found nothing to identify the man."

"Have you checked up on his condition?"

"No sir."

"Then I suggest you do it and find out who he is!"

Puzzling over his usually hard-nosed boss' concern, Ray was annoyed and racked his brains to find a way to verify the old man's identity. Dutifully he drove over to the Jubilee Hospital later that morning.

Parking his cruiser conspicuously in a no-parking zone, he marched through the main doors to the reception desk, ignoring the queue.

"Miss, miss, would you answer a question?" he called to a white-coated woman.

"Are you ill?" she snapped, but not waiting for an answer continued, "if you are, go through to emergency; otherwise take your turn behind these people."

"This is police business."

"Then go to the Main Desk and ask your question, I have sick people to attend to!"

Being sharply rebuked by the nurse added more frustration to Ray's already frayed temper. Holding his composure, in an effort to curb his bubbling abrasive reply, he turned away. Annoyed and realizing he was missing his lunch, he finally found someone who led him to a ward where the old man lay sleeping.

"Can we wake him?" Ray asked a passing nurse.

"I doubt it," she grinned, "he's been heavily sedated."

Staring down at the sleeping old man, Ray felt a touch of sympathy pass over him. *Who is the old fellow and why was he wandering the streets of Victoria alone and uncared for?* Checking the closet, he found no clothes and smiled wanly when he remembered the stinking, ragged attire the man had been wearing. The drawer did reveal a plastic bag stuffed with papers, however, and he slipped it into his coat pocket. He took note of the patient information hung at the end of the bed, took one last look at the man and left the room, turning back only to check the room number.

There was no time to examine the contents of the plastic bag during his shift that day, although his mind often wandered back to the sorry-looking man in the hospital bed. Stopping to eat in the station canteen, he was joined by Detective Tom Johnson, a man with many years on the city police force.

"You're quiet today Ray," Tom observed, "something bothering ya?"

"Yes and no," Ray muttered. "I need to find out the identity of an old fellow."

"Why don't you ask him?"

"Can't, he collapsed in View Street two days ago. They have him sedated in the Jubilee."

"Have you tried fingerprints?"

"I put in a request."

"Then wait and see what you get, your problem might be solved right there," the old detective proffered. He rose and moved slowly toward the door, stopping as he opened it. He turned and grinned at Ray. "Patience lad, use your imagination."

"Gee thanks for the help," Ray muttered sarcastically.

Calling at the hospital that night, he wandered into the old man's room and saw he was awake although the blank stare gave him little confidence of receiving any sensible answers. A nurse was attending to him.

"Don't stay too long, he's still quite confused," she whispered, turning to leave.

Ray sat down close to the man. "Hello. It's good to see you awake. Can you tell me your name?" A blank stare was all he received so Ray continued. "Can you remember anything about the last few days sir?" Waiting for any kind of a reply, Ray watched a trickle of spittle slowly drip from the old man's open mouth and run down his whiskered chin. Ray wiped it off with a nearby cloth. He could see the confusion and struggle taking place in the old man's eyes as he fought to grasp the situation.

"Don't you fret yourself pop," Ray continued sympathetically. "I'll find out who you are."

Instantly the old man's demeanor changed. He rose slightly and his boney hand reached out and gripped Ray's fingers.

"Tony?" he asked feebly, squinting at Ray.

"You think I'm Tony?" Ray asked. "Sorry, my name is Raymond."

Loosening his grip, the patient settled slowly back onto his pillow. As he closed his eyes, Ray watched in sad fascination as silent tears ran down the man's cheeks. Ray felt a sudden rush of heartfelt sympathy. He patted the old man's thin hand, told him he would be back again, and left.

Two days later, his pigeonhole held a message from the fingerprint boys. It coldly stated that no match to the old man's prints had been found. Ray breathed a sigh of relief. At least the old man was not in their criminal file.

By now, it had become a ritual that every night Ray would visit the hospital and spend 15 minutes talking quietly to the old man after he finished work. The patient had spoken very few words in reply to Ray's questions and certainly none which he could really call a clue. Today, when he entered the man's room, a nurse met him in the doorway.

"We're moving him over to the Eric Martin in the morning," she informed him. "He's improving but we're going to keep him for a while. You'll be able to visit him there tomorrow."

The frightened, helpless look in the old man's eyes caused Ray to instinctively reassure him that everything would be all right. Before he left, he assured the man that he would see him again tomorrow for their evening chat.

As Ray left the hospital, he remembered that he started his three days off tonight and he had almost forgotten the planned fishing trip to Campbell River. He looked forward to these trips and the friendly drinking company; he loved the smell of the ocean and the wild tales of the old fishermen. Nagging thoughts of the old man disturbed Ray's brain, however, and the next morning as he was loading the car, he remembered the old man's plastic bag with his papers. He didn't know how he had come to forget them for so long but he suddenly felt he was the only hope the old man had of recovery.

"We have to find out who you are old man," he muttered to himself, putting his fishing gear back into the cupboard in the garage. Going back into the house, he found his briefcase and removed the plastic bag, resolving silently to get to the bottom of this mystery.

He took the papers carefully out of the bag and set them on the kitchen table. Selecting each item, he turned it over, read it, then set it down until he had the small table covered with a mish mash of news articles, some even torn in half. The papers made no sense at all. He sighed and pushed his chair back with a squeal. Going to the fridge, he took out the bottle of orange juice and went to the counter to pour a glass. Turning, he looked across the room to the table. His eyes studied the curious collection of paper. Suddenly, even at this distance, he realized there was something odd going on and he carried his glass to the table and stood looking down at the papers. With the light shining directly on them, he saw something he hadn't noticed previously.

"What the …?" he exclaimed aloud, sitting down heavily. "Each page has these pencil marks crossing out some of the words!" Looking more closely, he realized that sometimes one or two words were crossed out and another time it could be several. "Now I wonder why you did that?" he mused, jotting down each of the cancelled words as he scoured the pieces of paper. Fifteen minutes later, he shook his head in surprise and stood up with the paper in hand. He realized he had filled a whole page with the odd assortment of words. "It's like a gigantic crossword puzzle," he exclaimed aloud, his brow wrinkling into a frown.

Then he had another idea. *Maybe the words were in groups collected on certain dates, making the smaller groups easier to decipher.* The idea was a good one except there were very few dates on the papers. Scowling fiercely now, Ray sat back in his chair in frustration. He knew there was a message in those words if he could just unlock the combination.

With nothing better to do and the puzzle now becoming an obsession, Ray wandered downtown, stopping to stare through the window of a second-hand bookstore. Going inside, he paused just inside the door and the clerk glanced up from her book with a bored expression, adjusting her glasses.

"Can I help you find something sir?" she asked in a lifeless voice.

"Yes, I'm looking for word games, crosswords or something similar."

Nodding, the clerk emerged from her counter space and sauntered between the overflowing shelves, stopping abruptly to point at a row of thin books.

"Take your time sir, there are lots to choose from," she commented.

Selecting several, Ray glanced at the faded covers and suddenly felt a rush of excitement as he turned the books over and looked at the cover of the bottom book. *Deciphering for the Genius*," it said in big bold letters and Ray knew he'd found the book he needed.

Selecting six books in all, in an effort to disguise his interest in the one book, he called out to the clerk.

"How much are these books? I can't seem to find a price."

Ray's voice brought an instant response from the clerk as she rushed to his side, snatching her glasses off as she snapped, "We do not raise our voices in a bookshop sir. Prices are clearly marked inside the back cover!"

"Back cover!" he whispered under his breath and blushing a little at the lady's outburst. Everything about this case seems to be unusual, he thought as he followed her to the front counter.

A few minutes later, glad to be back on the street, Ray breathed deeply trying to rid himself of the musty smell and taste of the bookstore and headed quickly for a nearby coffee shop to examine his purchases.

Taking a coffee and a muffin from the counter, he paid and glanced around for a seat. "May I share your table?" he asked a young lady scribbling on a notepad.

"Help yourself," she replied disinterestedly with a flick of her pencil.

Slowly nibbling on his muffin, Ray turned the pages over as he examined the cipher puzzles, shaking his head in amazement that anyone would put themselves through the mental torment of trying to solve them in the name of pleasure.

"Are you a crossword nut?" the young woman asked pointedly.

"No," he chuckled.

"Then why are you reading those books?"

"I'm trying to solve a puzzle."

"What kind of a puzzle?" she insisted. "Most puzzles work on a theme."

"A theme?" Ray repeated, now intrigued by the woman's chatter.

"Yes, all word puzzles are usually an extension of a single theme like sport or history or something quite common."

"Who are you?" Ray asked. "Would you take a look at a puzzle for me?"

"I'm a student at UVic studying English Lit. Show me."

Taking the paper with all the words on it from his pocket, Ray handed it across the table noticing the hardened palms of her hand and the strong fingers that quickly unfolded it and smoothed it flat. He was also aware that she had neglected to give her name. She frowned as she used the eraser end of her pencil to follow the words. She suddenly looked up and grinned.

"It's music!" she chuckled with a mischievous glint in her eyes.

"You mean the person who wrote this is a musician?"

"Yes."

"Could you decipher the whole message?"

"Probably, if I really wanted to."

"Then let me buy you a coffee and tell you the story. I'm a policeman with a problem."

Half an hour later, Ray knew he had a sympathetic ally when she gave her name as Joan Waddington and offered her help.

"Would you show me the papers you took these words from?" she asked. "I'd like to see if each word was crossed out in the same manner."

"Of course you can, I only live a short walk from here on Johnson Street."

Rising to leave, Ray felt the colour rising in his cheeks when he saw Joan struggle to her feet and grasp the two special crutches leaning on the empty chair next to her.

"Oh I'm sorry," he gasped in confusion, jumping up. "I'll call a cab."

"Yes, you can do that, but I don't need your sympathy. We're going to use our brains not run a four-minute mile!"

Ray's second-floor apartment proved to be the next problem. "I can't do stairs Ray, and if you've no elevator you might as well send me home," she informed him gently.

"I'm your elevator!" he grinned scooping her up into his arms and heading up the stairs, "and this isn't sympathy girl, it's because I need you, so quit your objections."

"You can put me down now," Joan whispered as they landed on the top stair, but Ray carried on to his apartment, setting her gently down at the door.

"I rather enjoyed that," he chuckled unlocking his door.

Standing silent for a moment she adjusted her crutches, blushing as she looked up at the policeman.

"That was a new experience for me Ray Abbott. I've never been in a man's arms before."

"Well, we'll be doing it again when you leave," he chuckled.

Showing Joan to the table, he produced the plastic bag of papers and busied himself with making coffee.

"Can I have a fresh piece of paper?" Joan asked. "There's something odd about the way he's crossed out these words."

Quickly marking the words on Ray's page with the same strokes of a pen as the writer had used, she smiled to herself as she rearranged the words on a clean sheet of paper.

"See," she murmured, "they're all capital letters."

"They spell Albert," Ray hissed excitedly, peering over her shoulder.

"Which leaves 'N-o-c-m-u-r-e' to probably form his last name."

"That helps a little but we need to positively identify his last name as well. You said he was a musician. How did you know that?"

"Actually it was just intuition, but now that I see the original papers, don't you see, they're all write-ups about music or reviews of orchestras and singers," Joan chuckled. "Is that coffee ready yet?"

Ray's blood raced as he poured the coffee. He finally had a clue to work on and he felt sure Joan's talent would soon unravel the rest of the hidden message.

"Cream and sugar?" he asked over his shoulder.

"Just sugar," she murmured as her eyes scanned the next set of words and whispered, "He's from Winnipeg."

"Show me how you found that out," Ray insisted as he set the coffee mugs on the table and peered at the jumble of words.

"Thanks," Joan giggled, "here let me show you. Take the first letter of all the words and they spell Winnipeg over and over again, and that can't be coincidence can it?"

"Amazing, now we should be able to find him."

"Tell me," she asked, looking at him strangely, "just what are you going to do with this information?"

"I'm going down to the police station and check the missing person's list."

"Can I come with you?"

140

"I don't see why not, you're part of my investigation. Drink your coffee first."

Outside his apartment door, Ray grinned foolishly as he picked Joan up again. She gently rested her head on his shoulder, clutching tight to the crutches as they descended the stairs. At the front door, he pressed the disabled door opener with his back and carried her out to the parking lot, setting her down beside his black, open-top Jeep.

"Can you get in on your own?" he asked.

"No," she whispered coyly, glancing up at him expectantly.

Ray grinned as he placed her crutches between the seats and lifted her onto the seat.

"Oh I like being with you!" she chuckled, drawing an instant blush to the policeman's cheeks.

"Behave yourself young lady and we might just do this again!"

They were quiet as Ray drove through the mid-day traffic to the police station. He quickly found a parking spot and went around to lift Joan out. A group of laughing policemen were leaving the building as they met at the door, but they suddenly went quiet and held the door open. Ray went inside and he put her down making sure she was balanced before letting her go.

"What are you doing here Raymond?" the sergeant's voice echoed along the corridor. "Isn't it your day off?"

"Yes sir, but we were working on the identity of the old man in the hospital and need to go through the list of missing persons."

It was then he noticed Joan standing behind Ray. "Come on in here," he said quickly, throwing his office door open. "Let's see what you two are up to."

Seated across the big desk from the sergeant, Ray could see the stress on Joan's face. Quickly moving his chair close beside her, he heard her sigh and she looked over at him and smiled.

"Okay, what's up? Is this your ...?" the sergeant's voice queried in a puzzled tone.

"My associate sir. May I introduce Joan Waddington. She's a whiz at word puzzles."

"You've lost me but continue, why a word puzzle expert?"

Ray stumbled a bit over his words as he tried to explain how the old man had marked his papers and how Joan was helping to decipher them. "She's already solved half of his message sir, and we think we may have a clue about his name."

"Alright, what do you need now?"

"It's rather involved sir, but we think he's a musician from Winnipeg," Joan proffered, "because all the papers were about music. We think he may be a missing person from that area."

Sergeant Beeson picked up his phone and made a quick call to another department. This call on an internal line brought instant action from the staff and it was only minutes before a constable appeared with some papers in his hand. He handed them to the sergeant and left.

"Here's a list of missing people from Manitoba and Winnipeg. Run your eyes over it," Beeson commanded with a frown, "and tell me if you want more information on any of them."

Ray peered over Joan's shoulder and they quickly scanned the list, simultaneously pointing to a name.

"That's him," Joan said excitedly. "Look at his last name Ray."

"Albert Moncure," Ray repeated. "That's him all right. Now all we need is his picture to positively identify him."

"Let me know if everything pans out Ray." The sergeant stood up dismissing them. "I'll call downstairs and tell them to get a package ready for you; it's been a pleasure to make your acquaintance miss."

"You can wait in the public area," Ray whispered. "I'll run downstairs and get the package." As he returned, he walked slowly scanning the pages as he returned to the public area. He was surprised to see that Joan was missing and waited in case she had gone to the washroom. When she still did not return, he walked over to the duty desk.

"Your girlfriend's waiting out at your truck," the constable said with a chuckle, not lifting his head.

"Thanks," Ray heard himself mutter through a sigh of relief as he dashed out of the door.

"You thought I'd left you, didn't you?" Joan commented.

"I wasn't sure what you were doing, why didn't you stay inside?"

"Do I have to do everything you tell me, to be your friend?"

"No, but it would save me having a panic attack thinking you'd wandered off on your own."

"Hey, just a minute!" Joan retorted. "I'm not your responsibility, I'm only here because I want to be. I go places by myself all the time."

"But I brought you here and I expected to look after you until we're finished."

"Are you suggesting I can't manage on my own? Are you feeling sorry for me again?"

"Oh for goodness' sakes Joan, relax. Let's go find somewhere to eat."

"I can't afford to eat out."

"You're still my guest and I'm not finished needing your help."

Over lunch, Ray opened the envelope again. "This isn't the man we have at the hospital," he told her.

"We could go to the hospital and see how he reacts to the picture," Joan suggested and Ray agreed.

On the way to the Eric Martin facility Ray asked why his companion walked with two crutches and why she was always so angry.

"You'd be angry if your life was ruined by a drunken driver, wouldn't you?" she snapped. "Anyway, it's really none of your business!"

"Well it is now. You're a gal with a brain who's great to be with, when you act normal. If I'm going to spend more time with you, we'd better come to an understanding."

"Who says you're going to spend more time with me?" she asked.

"I do," Ray grinned as he pulled the car into the Eric Martin parking lot and got his ticket, "but only if you agree to control your temper!"

"You want to control me—am I to smile and agree with everything you say sir?"

"No, but you can start by cutting out the crap and sarcasm!"

Getting out, he walked around the vehicle and opened Joan's door. She handed him her crutches and he propped them against the car. Then he leaned toward her and held out his arms. Joan blushed a little as she slipped her arms around his neck. This time she was more aware of the warmth of his body and the power in his arms as he lifted her out.

He stood for a moment looking down at her before he whispered, "I like the feeling of being needed by you."

"And I like being with you, Ray Abbott."

Recovering her crutches, she held them tightly as Ray carried her across the parking lot. Fortunately, a nurse was just coming out of the door and held it open for them, giving them directions up to the second floor.

"Hopefully he'll be feeling better," she whispered as they went up the elevator.

Ray noticed a marked improvement in the old man as they entered his room. Clean shaven and with his hair cut more neatly, he looked quite distinguished in spite of the ill-fitting hospital gown he was wearing.

"Is your name Albert Moncure?" Joan asked with a smile, but she watched him shake his head so she quickly posed another question. "You're Tony then, aren't you?"

Instantly a smile passed across the wrinkled face and he slowly nodded, never taking his eyes off Joan. Reaching for his hands, she noticed his long fingers and an idea flashed into her mind.

"Ask someone if there's a piano here," she murmured quietly to Ray.

"A piano?"

"Just do it, can't you see his hands, this man is a piano player."

Ray stared down at the old man's hands and realized that Joan's powers of observation had beaten him to the punch again. *I'm sure not much of a detective*, he thought to himself as he wandered around the hospital floor searching for a piano.

"What are you looking for?"

He turned to find an older nurse eyeing him with suspicion.

"Who are you here to see?"

"I'm looking for a piano," Ray admitted, adding quickly. "I'm Constable Abbott with the Victoria Police and I'm trying to ascertain the identity of the man in Room 410."

"And a piano is going to help you?" she asked doubtfully, continuing to frown as she watched him shrug his shoulders and blush. "There's a piano in the alcove by the window at the end of the corridor but we don't need any noise around here."

He thanked her and went back to the old man's room, telling Joan about his conversation with the nurse. He could tell she was thrilled with the news.

"Wonderful, you can wheel him over there," Joan encouraged. "Let's go find it." When they reached the alcove, sure enough, there was the piano and not a soul in sight.

Ray cleared the magazines off the bench and Joan told him she was going to sit on it and he could wheel the old man closer. He heard Joan mumbling and realized she was trying to negotiate her legs behind the piano stool. He quickly pulled the stool out, giving her room to sit down. She handed him her crutches and looked over at the old man.

"Watch him carefully Ray," she whispered as her fingers caressed the keyboard and a beautiful melody filled the room.

The old man's reaction was instantaneous as he pushed the blanket off his legs and tried to rise.

"Oh no sir you can't …!" Ray began, holding him into the chair.

"Help him onto the seat beside me," Joan insisted, continuing to play.

A newfound strength forced the old man to stand and, with Ray's support, he slid onto the stool beside the girl. There was a strange intensity on the old man's face as his fingers moved up to the keyboard. His back grew straighter and suddenly a smile crinkled his lips as his thin fingers placed themselves on the keys and began playing along with Joan. Ray was standing behind them and watched in stunned amazement. Joan stopped playing and reached up for his attention.

"Get my crutches," she mouthed almost silently.

Ray did as she asked, helping her to move out of the way but still keeping an eye on the old man. Together they stood beside the piano watching and listening to the amazing sounds that the old man's fingers were making as they danced over the ivory keyboard in effortless motion. Ray moved behind the old man and kissed Joan on the cheek. She grinned up at him and winked. They both somehow knew that the old man was going to be all right ... he had found his life again in the sound of his music.

Fate

Tom Colby sat on the rough-hewn stool staring hard at the dirt floor of his cell. His last day on earth had arrived and already he could hear the movement of jailers, no doubt readying the trappings of the hangman. All fear of the inevitable had left him as he sighed with a resigned sadness, knowing dawn would soon light his path to the gallows.

Life had been unkind to Tom, an unwanted child, he had been born into poverty in the slums of London's dockland. An instinct for survival and the pangs of hunger had taught him to lie, cheat, and steal at an early age. Thievery was a way of life in these litter-filled streets and Tom had learned his lessons well.

He smiled coldly to himself when he remembered the one act of kindness that had been his downfall. Killing a half-crazy hound to protect a child from injury, he had been accosted by the law and thrown into jail at the owner's insistence. On a minister's advice, he had pleaded guilty of destroying valuable property—a gentleman's dog. Now, his heart almost stopped beating when he heard the magistrate's sentence of two years naval service.

Those were the years Tom looked back on with sinister contemplation, remembering the evil captain and sadistic first mate that added to his torment. Scars on his back were testament to lashes and the deep, dark marks on his wrists and ankles were proof of the shackles. Hate had been born on board that vessel, a grudge Tom had satisfied when released, leaving two dead men in a dark alley behind a dockland tavern.

Free, yet once again a fugitive, he took to his old ways, stealing a horse at a livery stable to pursue a career as a highwayman, but fate was again to take its hand. His first attempt at highway robbery spelled disaster. Knocked unconscious when thrown hard by his skittish horse, he woke to the gentle administrations of an old lady, wielding a damp cloth across his aching head.

"Lay still awhile, lad," she whispered, "you'll soon feel better."

Tom glanced around in the dim light, his eyes searching for men folk, but saw none. "Are ye alone?" he moaned. "I saw a man driving that cart."

"T'were only me lad."

"Aren't ye scared?"

"Lordy me, no. Yer an amateur!"

"Who are ye?" he asked.

"Folks call me Wandering Lilla," she said softly.

Brushing her hand away, Tom rolled over onto his knees and struggled to his feet, staggering as a shooting pain exploded in his head.

"Ride with me," Lilla offered wobbling back to her wagon, "or stay here, suit yerself," she hissed over her shoulder. She scrambled up and onto the seat of the wagon, straightening her skirts and taking the reins without looking back.

Moaning and holding his head, Tom tied his horse behind the covered wagon and climbed with difficulty into the seat beside her. Darkness soon enveloped the countryside as the horse and wagon plodded slowly northward.

"Where are ye going?" Tom muttered.

"Longfella's Tavern."

The answer made no sense to the would-be highwayman but he was too tired to give it another thought. He closed his eyes and tried to sleep, groaning when the cart bounced through mud holes in the rough track. It was dawn when he became aware they had stopped. He opened his eyes to see that they were outside of a coaching inn and a group of men were milling around the wagon.

"How'd yer find this place?" a soldier snapped, grabbing him roughly by the arm.

"Lilla brought me," Tom muttered, glancing sideways for confirmation from his companion.

"Lilla brought him did she!" An eerie murmur ran through the group.

"Liar!" another voice shouted. "Lilla's been dead these last 10 years!"

"No!" Tom screamed, "she were here with me, she brought me."

"Do ye know what this place is?" snarled the soldier.

"Longfella's Tavern—Lilla told me," Tom replied as he slowly looked around at the men's miserable faces.

"Right lad, Longfella's Tavern is the hanging prison!"

Tom felt an icy coldness creep up his spine. Looking past the crowd, he could see the top of a scaffold above the dark walls of, what had to be, the prison. Feeling his body grow suddenly weak, he was powerless against the men as they led him toward those dark walls. His last thought before collapsing was that he was not going to see the sun set tomorrow.

Now that day had arrived and the deathly silence of the prison was interrupted by the sound of slow dragging footsteps stopped at his door. Keys rattled and the door creaked as it swung open. Tom stood up, kicking the stool away, and faced the sad-faced minister who without raising his eyes, made the sign of a cross and mumbled a few incoherent words. When finished, he silently beckoned for Tom to follow him.

Escorted by a number of guards, they made the slow walk outside into the sunshine. He realized that a crowd had gathered but somehow he managed to put one foot in front of the other and slowly follow the minister up the steps of the gallows. At the top, he saw the rope with the noose and shuddered. He turned to face the jeering crowd. His stomach was churning, yet he tried hard to show no weakness, offering his hands to be tied. The minister gently touched his hands shaking his head. They brought the hood which he refused, squaring his shoulders as the rope was slipped around his neck. Staring out at the crowd one last time, he could see the expectation in their eyes ... then oblivion.

As always, Tom awoke from his drunken nightmare at that crucial moment when his alarm clock shattered the stillness of dawn.

Janion Ring: The Politician

Kristina Cunningham stared into the water from the railing of the Johnson Street Bridge and took a deep breath, a headache gnawing painfully behind her eyes. She desperately needed a break from the constant arguing of political meetings, shaking hands with people she disliked and smiling tolerantly at their stupid suggestions.

Elected to the Provincial Legislature as an Independent, by the slimmest of margins at the recent provincial election, she was well aware of the constant effort it took to make her lone voice heard. Common sense seemed to have no bearing on arguments concerning the general public when party policies dictated each outcome irrespective of its value. Her voice was rarely allowed to be heard and she often felt that she was wasting her time. She felt useless, ineffective, and distressed that she was no longer a bubbling enthusiast of the system.

She had, however, become a realist through her struggle, and despite her frustration had become more determined than ever to represent the people who had given her their support. Pondering how she would do this was the burning problem that had raised her headache into a throbbing migraine before today's session broke for lunch.

Wandering aimlessly up Wharf Street to the Johnson Street Bridge, she tried to relax and enjoy the warm spring day. With no particular destination in mind, she began noticing the old buildings around her. She found a bench at the railway station and stopped to eat her sandwich. Soon, her glance moved across the tracks to the boarded-up windows of the once glorious Janion Hotel with its faded sign and rough dirt pathway leading down to the water's edge.

"We've got something in common you and I, old girl," she whispered aloud, frowning up at the old building. "We're both useless." Although she knew she should not be trespassing, she went across the street and peered through the cracks in the boards covering one of the windows. She was disappointed when it was too dark to see anything. On her way back to the sidewalk, she stumbled on the uneven path and fell to her knees. Looking down at her right knee she was surprised to see the hole in her nylons allowing a trickle of blood to escape.

"Blast!" she exclaimed, looking down at her other knee. The sun suddenly sparkled off something near her foot, taking her mind momentarily off her problems. Curious, Kristina bent to see what was causing the sparkle. Brushing away some loose dirt, she realized there was a small, golden ring caught in the pathway. She carefully tugged it from its resting place and examined the exquisite, old-fashioned setting. A stinging sensation in her knee jolted her back to the immediate and more pressing issue of her nylons. She stood up quickly, absent-mindedly dropping the ring into her pocket.

Hurrying back to the street, she crossed at the light, cut through Waddington Alley and then up Yates Street to Government. A few minutes later, she entered The Bay store and hurried to the Ladies' Wear Department. A sympathetic clerk listened to her story as Kristina paid for the pantyhose. Returning her credit card, the clerk opened a drawer and added two bandages to the bag. Kristina thanked her profusely and hurried toward the washroom.

It took only a few minutes to change her stockings and then she rushed outside. *I can't be late*, she warned herself as she went down Government Street toward the Legislature where the afternoon session was preparing to begin. Reaching her office with only minutes to spare, she picked up her briefcase and hurried back along the corridor.

A surly nod of recognition from a member of the ruling party was the only greeting as she took her seat in the farthest corner and opened her briefcase. The Speaker of the House entered, causing the members to rise, and Kristina to spill her papers as she struggled to her feet.

"Quiet in the house," the clerk hissed, glaring across the rows of empty seats at the Independent member.

Scrambling to quietly collect her notes, Kristina's glasses slipped from her nose bouncing off the back of the seat in front of her. To add insult to injury, when they landed on the floor, they slid out of her reach.

"Blast!" she hissed under her breath, motioning to a Page.

"Are you sure you're ready ma'am?" the Speaker quipped sarcastically, to the amusement of those nearby, as the Page handed her the wayward spectacles.

"I apologize for the disruption Mr. Speaker," Kristina replied, "as you should, for your intolerance!"

"The member is out of order," the Speaker's voice droned. "Any more outbursts will force me to eject you."

"Pompous ass!" Kristina muttered to herself, as the voice droned on with the first order of business.

His introduction of the Opposition Member's Bill was long and tedious, but he finally arrived at the real issue which was the installation of a heavily discounted ferry service to Vancouver for low-income Vancouver Island residents. Up went Kristina's arm. Of course, she had something to say on this subject, her constituents were mostly young families and retired people; they needed a break to help with travel costs. An hour went by as questions and insults flashed across the chamber— her presence completely ignored.

Tears formed in her eyes as frustrated reality set in. Reaching into her pocket for a tissue, she was surprised to grasp the ring and her mind turned back to her misadventure.

Suddenly, a figure appeared in the seat beside her. Dressed in a long black dress of the style of the late 19th century, the diminutive woman's outfit came complete with a tiny hat and a fancy parasol, which she tapped irritably on the floor.

"Who are you?" Kristina whispered suspiciously, sniffing the sudden scent of lavender in the air. "I wasn't aware we had any new members. We really can't talk here you know."

"It's quite all right deary. I'm Dolly Walker, the Manager of the Janion Hotel. It was you who summoned me and they can't hear us."

"What! Why can't they hear us? This is most confusing as I certainly did not summon you. Besides, the Janion Hotel is a derelict, you couldn't work there. I was there only today, it's all boarded up."

"Yes, you were, and you found my ring," Dolly continued, totally ignoring her questions.

"This is your ring?" Kristina whispered, taking it from her pocket again and staring at the tiny circle of sparkling gold.

"There *is* a reward for finding it, you know," the lady chuckled.

"A reward?" repeated Kristina.

"Yes, that's what I said. You can keep it for three days and I'll grant all your wishes," replied the little woman.

"Don't be silly, someone put you up to this. Do you take me for a fool?"

"Your time is rather short to argue young lady, so please let me demonstrate. You were trying to get the Speaker's attention, were you not? Well, if you would like to ask me to help you achieve that end, I believe you will be surprised with what I can do for you."

"That I would like to see; it would be a miracle in itself just to be heard," Kristina retorted.

"Then let's do better than that and make them understand how passionate you are about your responsibilities. Raise your arm girl and let's get at it!"

Still doubting this strange lady's words about wishes and helping her, Kristina looked at her slyly and whispered, "Would you please help me get the Speaker's attention?" Then she raised her arm again and waited, barely daring to breathe. Before any more doubts could come into her mind, the Speaker turned his head to look over the rows of sparsely filled seats and called for Kristina to speak.

"Sock it to 'em girl!" the Janion Lady chuckled as a shocked Kristina stood up to face the chamber for the first time.

"Thank you Mr. Speaker," Kristina responded, taking a deep breath, "for giving me the opportunity to tell the Honourable Members that you're a bunch of Wiffle-Wafflers and, in my opinion, you couldn't make an honest decision if your life depended on it! Here you have an opportunity to help the people who need it most and the cost is almost imperceptible. Look around you sir. Are the Honourable Members here to support this important Bill? No sir, their absence proves they shamefully have absolutely no interest in helping the aged or the poor."

News spread quickly through the corridors and offices of the Legislative Building and interest peaked as sleepy court reporters came to attention and furiously began taking notes. The chamber slowly filled with curious members, talking amongst themselves. Who was this Independent Member who dared to take other members to task so eloquently and now making a case for a fare reduction for the poor and aged which could hardly be denied by any reasonable-thinking member.

A standing ovation from the now almost full chamber came as quite a shock to Kristina who was so involved in her speech she hadn't noticed that so many members had returned. She looked around in surprise and quickly sat down. She could feel the heat moving from her neck to her face and she suddenly remembered the strange lady, but she was gone.

The Speaker had no alternative. He must, by parliamentary law, succumb to the request if a seconder to the motion was heard.

"Do I have a second to this motion?" his voice boomed through the legislative chamber breaking into Kristina's thoughts.

"I second this motion," a female member responded.

"Then so be it," the obviously agitated Speaker murmured. "All those in favour, raise your right hand."

Kristina gasped as a sea of hands shot into the air.

"Passed to second reading," the Speaker announced with a smile. "I now call a recess. We'll reconvene at 10 o'clock tomorrow morning. Would the Honourable Member who proposed the last bill spare me a moment in my office before she leaves?"

Sitting quite still as the chamber emptied, Kristina tried to gather her composure. *Why did the Speaker of the House suddenly want to see her?* Up to now, he had never even acknowledged her presence even in the corridors. Nervously rising from her seat, she inadvertently let her fingers touch the ring in her pocket and the Janion Lady appeared again.

"You were right," Kristina whispered, smelling lavender again.

"And were you satisfied with the result?"

"Oh yes thank you. They passed the Bill to second reading."

"Then why have you called me?"

"I didn't call you," Kristina declared.

"You rubbed my ring."

"Oh … are you a figment of my imagination or are you real then?" Kristina whispered. "If you accompanied me to the Speaker's office, would he be able to see you?"

"Of course," Dolly snapped, "but only if I allowed it."

"Then come with me, I want him to see you!"

Stares and whispered conversations followed their progress along the legislative corridors as they made their way to the Speaker's Office. His secretary jumped up in surprise when the Janion Lady used her parasol to rap on her desk. Kristina gave her name, saying she had an appointment.

Upon hearing he had two visitors, the Speaker went out to meet them. Seeing the two women, he smiled curiously, greeting them with a smile and indicating the two leather chairs in front of his large, highly-polished mahogany desk. He watched them both closely and, although he was very interested in the reason Kristina had chose to bring someone dressed in period costume, he knew he would not ask. He watched them seat themselves and went to his own chair behind the desk. They waited for him to speak.

"You structured a very convincing argument in the chamber today." He spoke from behind a deadpan expression looking directly to her. "Have you ever considered crossing the floor and becoming a Liberal?"

"Oh no sir, I was elected as an Independent."

"Who cares?" his face suddenly twisted into a strained smile. "Members have crossed the floor before."

"But isn't that a way of destroying my constituents faith in me?"

"Hell no girl! This is about you and the influence you could have if you joined the party in power."

"I would be able to speak on the subjects that affect my constituents?"

"Certainly, so long as you followed the party line."

"And if it was contrary to my electors' wishes?"

"Electors girl, they're merely ordinary people—fools who don't know what's best for them. If you intend to rise to a powerful position in government, you'd be well advised to listen to me."

Bristling with anger, Dolly Walker now leapt to her feet, crashing her parasol across the Speaker's desk with enough force to make a dreadful noise, leaving the parasol torn and wood splinters scattered on the desk and floor. Startled, he yelped and flew to his feet, fearfully pushing his chair back from the desk. Dolly wasn't finished and now swung the broken parasol at his head as he cowered behind upraised arms.

"You're an ungrateful excuse for a man!" she exclaimed. "You have no morality, loyalty or commitment in your body, but mark my words, you will have from this day on!"

Kristina picked up the wood splinters from the floor, trying to hide her embarrassment. She placed them on his desk, and glanced over her shoulder at the Janion Lady, but the chair was empty. Only the lingering smell of lavender perfume and the small splinters of wood remained as evidence that she had ever been there. Whimpering sounds drew her attention quickly back to Mr. Kelly who was now sitting down. She went around the desk to his assistance.

"Would you like a nice cup of tea sir?" she asked.

"Oh yes please," he replied meekly, looking around behind her. "Who was that woman and where has she gone?"

Ignoring his question, Kristina went toward the door, giving him time to recover his shattered composure. Then she stopped as an unusually evil thought entered her head. She turned around and keeping a straight face asked, "Would you like some cookies too sir?"

"Yes please Kristina, just ask my secretary if she could bring us a tray for two. You will stay for tea won't you?" he asked eagerly.

"He's invited you for tea?" the secretary whispered suspiciously. "Careful miss, he's a mean SOB and can ruin your career if you're not careful."

Kristina assured her she would be cautious. Going back into his office she found him smiling as he rifled through some papers on his desk. Tea was brought in and the secretary flashed Kristina a surprised expression. Staying for almost an hour, she learned much from the experienced politician and, true to Dolly's word, the harsh manner he'd portrayed was nowhere to be found. Even his dark frown was replaced by an easy-going smile and twinkling eyes. The substance of his conversation had also changed and he now advocated loyalty to her constituents. He really shocked her, however, when he admitted his admiration for her eloquence in the Legislative Chambers. He assured her that, from now on, she would be given ample opportunity to share her views.

It was lunchtime the next day before Kristina remembered Dolly had said she had three days to make wishes with the ring. *Quite an unusual situation*, she thought, going toward her favourite bench on the harbour where she planned to eat her lunch. *I wonder what I will wish for next.* She ate her chicken wrap and then took the ring out of her pocket and rubbed its shiny surface. When the Janion ghost appeared this time, Dolly was not at all surprised when Kristina immediately handed her back the ring, thanked her for her assistance and explained that her last wish would be for Dolly to be able to continue helping people.

"Thank you Kristina. There is no greater reward than when I'm given the opportunity to help someone as nice as you deary." She had no sooner finished speaking then she vanished.

Kristina stared at the spot where Dolly had been standing. "Well, I'll be darned!" she laughed aloud. Gathering up her belongings, she stood up and began walking back toward the Legislative Buildings. This time there was a skip in her step, something which had been missing for many years.

Part 4 - Novel

A Debt to Pay

Chapter 1

He had the appearance of a scrawny, rough-looking drifter when he rode his broken-winded old mare into the yard at the mighty Circle X Ranch that morning during spring roundup. It was hotter than usual for this time of year and, the group of cowboys waiting in the yard for the foreman's orders, jeered as they stood watching him ride in.

"Better climb off that bag of bones kid, before it collapses!" a red-bearded cowboy commented, causing a ripple of laughter to run through the group as they watched the young saddle bum.

Gilly Thompson sat perfectly still in the work-worn old saddle. Only his eyes moved, wandering slowly over the big-mouthed cowboy as he contemplated his next course of action. He squinted against the sun and slowly raised his hand to adjust his battered hat, before slipping to the ground. Almost imperceptibly, he flicked the tie down off the hammer of the big black, Colt forty-five on his hip but the action was obvious to the hard-nosed rangemen.

"Easy kid," one muttered, spitting a long stream of tobacco juice into the dust, "ain't no need for gunplay."

"Maybe you should tell that to hairy-lips over there," Gilly hissed.

"Why *did* you come here kid?" the old man insisted.

"Looking for a job."

"And you think this is the ideal way to make an application?"

"Mister, it ain't none of your damn business."

"Well it sure as hell looks to be *my* business," Jake Curry, the red beard, spoke up. "It was only a joke and I sure don't plan to kill over it."

Gilly pushed his hat back on his head and, without a backward glance, walked off toward the corral with his horse in tow.

The older man shook his head, breathing a sigh of relief, and then, at a safe distance, went after the stranger. A voice yelling orders quickly dispersed the rest of the crew.

"So you're looking for a job?" he shouted, letting his eyes wander first over the young man and then to his mount.

"Yes sir."

"How long since you ate kid?"

"Not for awhile sir." Gilly hated the reference to his age, but he had long ago learned to let it go by.

"Then get your arse into the cookhouse. After you've had some grub, cut yourself a horse out of the corral and head for that big white-topped mountain over there." He pointed to one of the highest peaks in the mountain range known as the Snowy Mountains. "You'll find us over that way and don't be all day."

Gilly nodded then went to find the cookhouse. He was hired and the man had asked him nothing of his past, not even his name.

"New man?" the cook grunted through his whiskers, cocking an eyebrow as Gilly entered his domain. "Better eat kid, ya look like you've missed a few meals, then scoot up to Panama Flats. Fred ain't got too much patience at roundup time."

"Is Fred the foreman?"

"Yup, are you Indian or Mex?"

"Neither, I'm a Canadian."

Cook's head swung around to stare sharply at Gilly, now tucking into his first meal in three days, frowning as he tried to grasp just what a Canadian was. He silently turned back to his task of cleaning up the breakfast dishes. Eating noisily, Gilly made short work of the meal barely noticing its palatability. Getting up to leave, he stopped and reached across the bare tabletop to scoop a leftover piece of steak between two thick wedges of dark bread. Then, without a word, he left the cookhouse. Grinning, Two Puffs, the long-time cook at Circle X, was well aware Gilly had taken the food and, he even approved, proving to the old cook the young man was no stranger to fending for himself.

Shaking the water from his hands, Two Puffs went over to the door and watched as the young man unsaddled his horse, fondly giving the animal a pat before turning it loose in an empty corral. Then, spotting a bucket of feed, he poked it through the rails and stood for a moment watching as his horse ate hungrily.

"Well I'll be damned, he's a farm kid," the cook muttered, going over to the fire and lighting a small stick. Returning to the doorway, he touched the light to his pipe.

Gilly removed a lariat from his saddle and holding it loosely in his right hand, stooped through the rails of the neighbouring corral, and slowly advanced toward the herd of range-broken horses. His eyes darted cunningly over their conformation before he made his selection. Suddenly, a blue-grey gelding went on the attack, head extended and mouth wide open as if intending to bite, he raced at the stranger. Gilly

155

stepped nimbly aside and swung his loop as the old cook grabbed for his pipe in alarm, but the rope settled smoothly over the pony's neck.

"That kid ain't no greenhorn," he muttered admiringly, taking a second puff on the pipe before stuffing it into his pocket and disappearing back into the cookhouse.

The fight was short and decisive between man and beast before Gilly pulled the gelding into the snubbing post and tied him tightly. Talking quietly, he saddled the angry, half-tamed bronco, slipping his Indian halter over its ears and nose. It bucked a little as he led it out of the corral but he prepared to mount. Glancing out of a window, cook shook his head when Gilly, with one hand on the saddlehorn, lifted his feet and the pony took off at full gallop. Bouncing about in the saddle like a rag doll, Gilly allowed the horse to run off its anger on the flatland. Gilly admired the horse's mile-eating long stride, its effortless precision of movement, and the way it avoided obstacles well in advance.

"I'm riding a thinking horse," he chuckled, galloping off toward the mountains.

As he approached the treeline, still some distance from the mountains, Gilly slowed the horse to a walk and reached into his saddlebag, pulling out an old army spyglass. He slowly scanned up into the hills for any sign of the Circle X riders. He scowled when his eyes settled on a mountain lion moving quickly down the rocky cliff face.

"That cat's got his mind on a meal," he said aloud before taking off after it at a gallop.

Passing cattle among the trees, he could hear voices and whip cracks of the cowboys as they flushed cattle from the base of the mountain. He veered off to one side setting the pony directly at the big cat. Like a mountain goat, the horse never wavered, courageously scrambling up the steep slope onto a ledge. Leaving his saddle in a single bound, Gilly clutched his Winchester and took off at a run across the rocky hillside.

Below, Jake Curry had stopped his horse for a breather. Wiping sweat from his eyes, he noticed Gilly and curiously watched his progress up the steep rock face.

"Where the hell are you going kid?" he called.

The mountain lion was now completely consumed with thoughts of his prey as he stood on a ledge looking below. Gilly could see the muscles quivering along the cat's back as it crouched and he knew it was now or never. He raised the rifle to his shoulder and fired two rapid shots. The lion had begun his leap when the first shot hit him, nicking his shoulder and setting him off balance. The second shot tore through its chest.

Jake Curry's horse leapt sideways as the first shot crashed through the stillness. Unseating his rider, Jake landed safely but barely able to hold onto the reins before the second shot reverberated against the rocks. The body of the mountain lion landed with a sickening thud less than 10 feet away.

"Holy hell!" Jake declared still struggling with his mount.

. Hidden in heavy timber Fred Long, the foreman, heard the gunshots and cursed fiercely. Turning his horse toward the sound, he moved quickly to investigate as Gilly made his way back to the gelding.

"So you don't want to bite me this time boy," Gilly chuckled as the horse waited, looking quizzically at him. Mounting, he turned the gelding's head down the rocky slope, holding on tight as they bounced and slid with wild abandon down the rock face and landed with a bone-jarring thud amongst the trees. Catching his breath, he rode toward the sound of Jake's voice, who was still cursing wildly as he stared at the large, dead cat. Fred also heard Curry's cursing and made haste toward him.

"I told you no shooting!" Fred ranted at the red-bearded cowboy.

"Weren't me boss, that new kid did the shooting," Jake muttered, mounting and riding away.

Bursting through the heavy undergrowth, Gilly ignored the foreman as he slipped from the saddle, Winchester in hand, to check the body of the mountain cat.

Staring at the cat, Fred muttered, "You must have sharp eyes son."

"I didn't think you wanted to lose a man so early in the drive," Gilly replied unsmiling. "He was stalking hairy-lips when I saw him."

A twinge of admiration brushed through the foreman's mind as he watched the kid mount and slip his rifle into its scabbard. The proof of his shooting ability was two neat holes in the animal's carcass. His awareness of danger and the action he had taken were impressive. It was at that moment Fred resolved to find out more about his new man.

All day Gilly skirted the mountainside pushing half-wild cattle, fat on the lush spring grass, down through the timber ever closer to the rolling prairie flatland. Twice more during the day, he saw mountain cat tracks causing him to keep a wary eye above.

As darkness crept over the rough rangeland, talk around the campfire centered on Gilly and the mountain lion as Jake told of the newcomer's prowess with a rifle.

"Where d'ya come from kid?" asked a voice from the shadows.

"From the north."

157

A short silence followed as the crew digested the young stranger's evasive reply. It was not rangeland custom to ask questions; men were usually taken or rejected on face value.

"You got a name kid?" another rider growled.

"Gilly Thompson."

"Don't stray too far away with your bedroll son, we're in Indian country," Fred advised, heaving his bedroll and saddle under the chuck wagon.

Grinning to himself, yet offering no conversation, Gilly moved away from the campfire and located a tree that would fit his requirements. He rolled out his blanket and went to locate a few rocks which he tucked underneath. Then he dropped his hat where his head would be. He reached up into the darkness and caught hold of a branch, pulling himself up. Sleeping wedged into a forked branch was hardly an inconvenience to Gilly and this simple precaution had saved his life on more than one occasion. Gilly was much more experienced than his skinny youthful-looking body portrayed; he'd been the only survivor when his family homestead was attacked and burned by a band of drunken cowboys. That night had been a nightmare for the nine-year-old boy, saved only by his enjoyment of sleeping in a tree. For three days, he cried over the remains of his parents and sister and when a lone rider appeared in the distance, Gilly returned to the safety of his tree.

Approaching slowly and smelling the burnt logs even before seeing them, mountain man Rube Caster had the eyes of a hawk. He'd seen the boy long before Gilly saw him. Rube was a mystery man, one of that strange breed who roamed the mountains and plains as he chose, a trapper, gold miner, and sometimes a ranchhand, fending for himself in a harsh, unforgiving land.

Remaining on his horse, he viewed the burned-out ranchhouse, patiently reading the signs of iron-shod hoofprints that told him this was white man's work. Sliding from his horse, he cranked the bucket in the well and drank the pure, cold water. Talking to himself, he built a campfire close to the tree where Gilly was hiding and unwrapped a recently skinned rabbit carcass.

"I got food kid, if you want to come down and share it with me," Rube growled into the flames, turning the meat on the end of a stick. "My guess is you ain't eaten for days. Come on down now, I ain't gonna hurt ya."

The old man's words, the kind tone of his voice, and the lure of food, finally conquered Gilly's fear. He was soon pouring his heart out as he chewed on the tender meat. Showing no emotion, the old plainsman listened patiently, puffing on a blackened pipe as the boy told his tale. It was then they heard the rapid beat of galloping horses and a terrified look appeared on Gilly's face as he jumped to his feet.

"Steady lad," Rube muttered slowly, "do yer know how to use a Winchester?"

"Yes sir."

"Then take my rifle and get back up in that tree."

Well hidden, Gilly trembled as he watched the riders' fast approach and recognized two of the men who had killed his family. He looked down and saw the old man reach into his saddlebag then quickly looked away.

"Who the hell are you?" one of the riders yelled, dismounting a short distance away in a shower of dust.

Gilly's rifle barked sudden death for the second rider, jerking him out of the saddle as the first cowboy went for his gun. When Rube's hand belched flames, the first rider went down with his pistol only half drawn.

"Well done lad," Rube muttered as he checked the two lifeless bodies. "I guess you recognized 'em."

Scrambling down from the tree, Gilly dropped the rifle as he ran over to kick the lifeless bodies of the men they had shot.

Those few moments of violent action endeared the boy to the old drifter. Riding double, they quickly left the scene and Rube Caster became his mentor and friend from that day forward. They were together for almost 10 years as the old drifter taught Gilly his own unique brand of self-preservation, roaming the mountains and range like father and son. Rube knew the boy had a mental image etched in his soul of those wild drunken cowboys who had murdered his folks. He knew the boy would someday be faced with a need for more vengeance.

Gilly had learned well under the old man's tuition, attaining knowledge far beyond his age or experience, but time had run out for Rube Caster in a cabin high in Canada's Rocky Mountains. He died in the young man's arms one spring day after coming down with a fever. There was no bitterness or tears as Gilly buried his surrogate father, then packed up his gear, saddled the horses, and worked his way down the mountain.

Trading Rube's horse and saddle for money and food at the livery stable of the first hicktown he entered, gave him the means to comfortably continue. Hiring on as a fence rider at the Big Valley Ranch gave him the time and seclusion to think out a plan. Now he was ready to search for the other men who had murdered his family.

Gilly's travels took many twists and turns over the years and time had seemingly erased the location of his family homestead—his memory blocking out everything except the image of their burning house and the faces of the murderers. He did remember, however, the hurt he felt as he buried the bodies of his loved ones and that memory hounded his dreams.

Moving from ranch to ranch, he slowly made his way south, sometimes panning a river, as Rube had taught him, or working for an army post tracking an Indian who had left the reservation. How or when he had crossed the line into Montana made not the slightest impression on him. He observed no boundary lines, moving when it pleased him or necessity pushed him on. Gilly, like Rube, was a law unto himself. Having no recollection of being this far south before, it was strange how he felt at home in this broken-hilled country.

Just days before, he had been following the winding foothills along the Bitterroot Range searching for strays when he lost his horse in a rock slide. Upon leaving that employment, the foreman sympathetically gave him a broken-winded mare, commenting they'd miss his strong back.

Curled up in the tree this moonless night, he was confident of his ability to sleep while remaining totally vigilant; several hours later he was awakened by the barely discernable movement of stealthy feet. He strained his ears against the silence and heard it again; someone was moving slowly toward him. Although the inky darkness made seeing impossible, he was very aware of a new smell in the air. *Indian*, he thought, taking a long silent sniff and smiling ruefully. This was the musty body odour of his enemy. Close enough to hear the native breathing, Gilly kept perfectly still. Whoever was below him was now standing over his bedroll. Then, as quietly as they came, the guarded footsteps moved away.

Slipping soundlessly from his perch, Gilly again sniffed the air. Still, a faint odour brushed his senses and he moved toward it. Then he heard it—horses' hooves moving about on the rocks near their picket line. *They're stealing the horses!* He knew he needed help, but to wake the crew quietly would take too long; he'd have to act on his own. Quickly finding his saddle in the dark, he retrieved his lariat and cautiously approached the picket line in a wide arc, sniffing the air repeatedly. He could hear the agitated horses now but still no sounds from the robbers. *These fellas are good, ya gotta give 'em credit*! he thought, stopping to set a trip rope between two trees.

Thoughts flashed through Gilly's mind—capturing the natives without help was going to be one of his greatest challenges. Suddenly he

160

grinned to himself as the obvious solution struck him. He had to work quickly before he was discovered. He made his way cautiously around and through the milling horses. Firing off two quick pistol shots sent the frightened riding stock charging through the makeshift fence and hopefully back on the robbers. Screams from several trampled men were the first indication that he'd been at least partially successful. *Will this alert the camp in time?* he wondered. Within seconds, the wild shouts of the drowsy crew told him the camp was indeed awake, but the ominous sounds of the half-crazed horses warned Gilly that his job wasn't finished.

Moving quickly, he caught hold of a mount and leapt onto its bare back clinging madly to its mane. Thankfully, dawn was now breaking as he followed the thundering noise of the frightened horses as they moved out onto the open grassland. It was then he got his first look at the three native riders. They had seen him too, and turned to meet him, realizing he was alone. Just in time, Gilly dropped flat on the horse's back as a rifle cracked out and a bullet whistled past his ear.

Now they'll aim for my horse, he thought, pulling the mount to a sliding halt. He leapt off its back, grabbed a front leg, and tipped it over onto its side. Flopping across its neck to keep it from rising, he tied a rein around one hind leg to hobble him and hid as best he could. From this position, he watched as three Indians approached slowly on horseback just out of gunfire range. He could see their painted faces and knew they meant business. He readied his revolver, putting some extra bullets in his vest pocket. The Indians now split up and his heart gave a little flutter with excitement. Old Rube had often said that patience was the best weapon a man could have in a desperate situation, and this appeared to be one of those occasions.

He clearly heard their jabbering argument as two of the three dismounted and, with rifles at the ready, advanced on him. Gilly flew into action, flinging himself away from his prostrate horse. He rolled over and over in the prairie grass shooting with deadly accuracy. Two Indians screamed as Gilly's bullets tore into their bodies and, seconds later, Gilly himself was surprised to feel a jolt as a single rifle shot tore the heel off his boot and the third Indian galloped toward him.

Leaping to his feet, Gilly sent three more shots screaming toward the out-of-range native rider who spun his horse and raced away. Quickly finding one of the dead Indians' rifles, Gilly raised it to his shoulder and took careful aim. He watched with a grunt of satisfaction as his bullet struck home, yanking his target from the horse's back.

"Job done!" Gilly hissed coldly.

Calming his struggling horse, he released the hobble, located the second Indian's rifle and mounted up. Riding toward the spot where the third Indian lay motionless in the grass, he cautiously stopped a good distance away and coldly sent two extra rifle shots into the still body. Moving closer, he searched the ground for the third rifle and found it in the grass about 10 feet away. He mounted again and, without a backward glance, headed toward camp, passing two of the crew on horseback. They silently watched him go.

Fred Long and Two Puffs stood watching the lone bareback rider lopping toward them.

"It's him," Two Puffs muttered, "and he's carrying two extra rifles."

"He didn't have a rifle with him and he's limping," Fred growled, as Gilly slipped from the horse's back and tied it to a tree. Approaching, he tossed one of the rifles at Fred and continued toward his tree.

"Are you hurt?" the foreman shouted after him.

"Where's he going?" cook asked.

"His saddle and blanket are under that tree."

"He slept over there? He's damned lucky they didn't kill him."

"I get the feeling that kid would take a lot of killing," Fred mumbled, stowing the extra rifle away before moving off to assemble the crew.

The morning's excitement had thrown the camp schedule into turmoil and breakfast was late as riders finally rounded up their horses and returned to camp. Grumbling and cursing, Fred tallied up the missing riding stock, then detailed two men to bury the four Indians who'd been trampled to death by the horses.

"We're about 10 horses short now," he shouted to the crew as they finished eating. "I might have to send one of you back to the ranch."

"No you ain't," Gilly stated flatly, "they're about two miles north of here. I'll go get 'em when I find my gelding."

"You left 'em out there?" the foreman growled in an accusatory tone. "The Indians will have them by now."

"No they won't; we got all the raiding party."

"How many were there?"

"Seven," Gilly replied.

The crew's attention had shifted from eating to being riveted on the young cowboy. His answer suggested he had killed three of them but you could see by their expressions they were doubtful. Two Puffs stopped rattling his pans as he waited for the discussion to continue. He knew it would have been almost suicide to chase men with rifles while only having a handgun, but Gilly was offering no further information.

"I'll send Jake with ya," the foreman rasped.

"No you won't; he goes or I go, but I ain't nursing no greenhorn out there!" Gilly replied.

Stung by the insult, Jake Curry leapt to his feet, hurling his tin mug across the campfire at Gilly as his hand swept down for his Colt. Almost simultaneously two shots rang out as the crew dove for cover and the tin mug leapt in mid-flight. Jake froze, his weapon only half-drawn from the holster as he stared in disbelief at the barrel of Gilly's smoking colt.

"Stop!" Fred Long shouted. "Put them damned guns away you idiots."

Holstering his gun, Gilly turned his back on the crew, moving quickly away from the campfire to locate a mount. Behind him, he could hear the chatter as the crew offered opinions on his lightning fast draw.

"Did you ever see anything so fast?" Two Puffs slobbered, drooling tobacco juice into his beard.

"He's trouble," Fred complained, "but he sure demonstrated how good he is with that gun."

"He did save us from the Indians but he won't find that half-broken gelding this side of hell's half acre after that ruckus," the old cook predicted, shuffling back to his camp stove.

"Won't have to find him, that damned pony is waiting by his bedroll," one of the riders chuckled, "they're two of a kind are them two!"

Fred Long mounted his horse taking one last glance over to where Gilly was saddling the blue-grey gelding. He cursed under his breath when he noticed there was no particular hurry in the cowboy's movement. Walking over to the hot bean pot, with the gelding following close behind, Gilly dipped a tin mug into the hot beans. He cleaned the rim with his tongue, winking at Two Puffs as he did so, and then mounted up, riding off slowly into the sun.

Two Puffs scratched his head in an obvious dilemma, wondering why Gilly had ridden east when he'd heard him say the horses were to the north. The Canadian cowboy's action was deliberate and, although the old cook didn't know why, he still sensed there was a good reason.

Moving along at an easy lope until he'd finished his beans, Gilly stopped to rinse the mug in a little stream. Filling his canteen with the pure, clean water, he stood tall and sniffed the air, patting his horse before he climbed back into the saddle. He turned downstream and within five minutes saw the hoofprints on the bank and easily followed the horses into a gully.

A head count, as he moved them out onto the range, brought a smile to his lips. There were twelve now in the tiny herd and this pleased him.

Assuming that two of the Indian ponies had joined the group, Gilly quickly set the ranch mounts moving toward the range camp. Experiencing little trouble and, with help from a wrangler, he had them corralled within the hour.

"Picked up a couple of strays did ya?" Two Puffs muttered handing Gilly a mug of thick black, steaming coffee.

"They're mine now!"

Three weeks later, when the roundup was complete, Gilly decided to move on. Making an easy deal with the foreman to swap the two Indian ponies for the blue-grey gelding, he tucked the 10-dollar bill Fred offered as roundup pay into his pocket. As he climbed into the saddle, Gilly noticed the old cook standing at the cookhouse door and waved. Two Puffs extended his hand in a brief salute.

Following the same stream from earlier, as it meandered southward, Gilly was in no hurry to get to anywhere in particular, always allowing his eyes to take in the scenery. He knew that one day he would recognize something that would ultimately lead him back to the family homestead. Staying hidden as best he could, he rode through the lowlands avoiding Indians whenever he saw signs of their presence.

Shots disturbed his thoughts as the sun rose on the morning of the 14th day. Saddled and ready to go, the blue-grey's ears stood up straight. Turning his head to the east, Gilly watched the crest of the hill.

"Thanks Blue," he exclaimed with a grin, "ah reckon we'll just have to go check out that noise."

Chapter 2

Riding hard across the valley, the pony seemed to recognize his rider's thoughts. Approaching the crest of a little hill, he slowed and then stopped abruptly. The scene in front of them caused Gilly to pull the horse back and out of sight from the crest. Scrambling from the saddle and grabbing his rifle at the same time, he flopped instantly onto his stomach just below the crest of the hill. Memories flooded back into his mind as he watched the horrific scene. Several cowboys were shooting and riding crazily around a small house while two cows and a pair of frightened mules ran around in a tiny corral attached to a small barn.

The decision was easy for Gilly and he hit his saddle at a run; urgently encouraging his pony over the hill while his rifle barked his presence. Suddenly, only the bellowing of scared stock broke the stillness and three cowboys lay gasping their last breath in the dust.

"Who's in there? Are you all right?" he yelled toward the little house, sitting in his saddle and waiting. "I won't hurt you, the others are dead."

Slowly the door opened and a black woolly head appeared, followed by a big awkward body dressed in patched coveralls. The man was tightly holding an old single-shot rifle and his white eyes displayed his fear even at that distance. This was the first black man Gilly had ever seen and he slowly moved closer.

"Are you black all over?" Gilly asked with a frown, climbing down and slowly walking closer. "I ain't never seen your tribe before."

"I ain't an Indian; I'm a negra. My folks were slaves for you white folk," he exclaimed, his voice showing his disdain.

"Are you homesteading?"

"Yes sar, can ah bring ma family out now?"

Keeping tight hold of his rifle, the black man moved slowly away from the door, turning his head as he spoke softly to someone inside. Then raising one hand, he reached inside the door and encouraged a coloured girl carrying a baby, to step outside with him.

"Who were those cowboys?" Gilly asked.

"Half Moon ranchhands trying to run us off."

"Where is this Half Moon Ranch?"

"Two or three days' ride east of here I reckon."

"Well these three won't be coming back to bother ya. I'll catch their horses and deliver 'em back to their ranch."

"They'll kill ya," the black man predicted.

"Not if I have anything to do with it friend, but I need to look these folks over."

"I'd better come with ya."

"No, but you can help me load the bodies onto their horses when I'm ready. I'll leave you a Winchester and a couple boxes of shells. You stay here and take care of this family of yours."

"Who are you sar? We wants to thank you, they meant to kill us. My name's Benji Jackson and this here's my wife Della and our baby."

"Gilly Thompson. I think you should try to forget about what happened here today. It won't happen again and I'm going to see to it as soon as I leave here!"

Gilly mounted up and went to round up the dead cowboys' horses. When he returned, he hitched their reins to the corral rails and Benji helped him load the three bodies across their saddles, tying them firmly. Reaching for his spare rifle and a box of shells from his saddlebag, he handed them to Benji.

Swinging into the saddle, he turned to the man and grunted quietly, "I wouldn't go wasting them shells mister."

Travelling slow and easy Gilly spent little time on eating or sleeping as he moved eastward as Benji had directed. It was the third day out when his sensitive nostrils picked up the smell of wood smoke, causing him to be more cautious. When the ranchhouse and buildings came into view, he whistled ... this had all the signs of a mighty successful outfit. Fences around the substantial house were painted, buildings were neat and tidy, and two large barns still held a surplus of winter hay. This was a spread that had taken many years to build.

Seeing there was no way to approach without being seen, he sat easy in the saddle and slowly walked in with his gruesome companions. He slipped the tie down off his gun when he saw two men move to intercept him. Stopping as he came even with them, he dropped the lead rope at their feet.

"Do these belong to you?" he asked casually. Slowly backing his mount away until the sun was at his back.

"They're our horses," the older man growled, stepping closer to examine the faces of the dead men before returning to stare questioningly at Gilly. "You a lawman? They belonged to a line crew working west of here."

"No, I ain't no lawman."

"Then where'd ya find 'em and how did ya know to bring 'em here?"

"Found 'em shooting up a black man's homestead, about two days west of here."

"He killed 'em?"

"No, I did."

"You've got nerve, fella," the younger man hissed. Stepping away from his companion, his fingers slipped the tie down from his sidearm.

"Hold it Jess," the older man snapped. "Can't you read the signs? He's just waiting to kill ya."

"He's a saddle bum," Jess muttered, his hand moving swiftly toward his holstered Colt.

Only one gun roared as Gilly's pony leapt violently sideways. Jess Ellis screamed in pain as he hit the ground clutching a bullet wound in his thigh. It bled profusely through his fingers.

"You want a part in this game mister?" Gilly coldly invited the older man.

"Damn you boy," Harvey roared, staring in disbelief at his wounded top hand. "There'll be hell to pay now."

166

"Who owns this spread?" Gilly asked calmly, sliding easily from the saddle and retrieving the wounded cowboy's handgun. "You can take me up to the house now."

"Like hell I will, this man needs some attention."

"He's had all the attention from me he's getting. Now are you taking me up to the house or are you gonna try to shoot me too?"

The gunshot brought men running from nearby buildings, guns drawn. Ignoring them, Gilly kept the pony between him and the ranchhands, allowing Blue to follow him as he walked with Harvey, whom he assumed was the foreman, toward the house. They were almost there when the door suddenly opened and a young woman rolled out onto the verandah in a wheelchair with a shotgun on her lap.

"Stop right there Harvey!" she yelled, turning the wheelchair until the shotgun's barrels faced the men. "Who the hell have you got there?"

"Don't know Miss Jenny, he ain't said."

"Well ask him you fool!"

"Why don't you ask him, Miss Jenny," Gilly shouted taking a few steps forward.

"I told you to stop mister!" she warned, turning the gun toward him.

"Hell lady, if you're going to shoot me, you'd better get on with it."

A rifle shot whizzed through the air coming from the direction of the farm buildings. The bullet buzzed harmlessly over Gilly's head. Unflinching, he continued walking, hissing a threat over his shoulder at the foreman.

"One more shot comes my way, Mr. Harvey, and you'll become my target."

Gilly's threat held a cold harshness that left the foreman in no doubt that he meant it. He raised his arm to signal his men. At the bottom step to the verandah, Gilly stopped and stared into the barrels of the girl's shotgun.

"They were your men," he stated quietly.

"Who were my men?"

"The three dead men laid across them ponies over yonder."

"You've got some nerve fella, now what else are you going to tell me about them ... that you shot them?"

"Something like that."

"Well then, how are you planning to get outa here alive?"

"Same way I came in lady, but I ain't leaving yet."

"If I pull this trigger you won't be leaving at all," she threatened.

"Lady you ain't no killer, if you were I'd already be dead!"

167

A look of shocked surprise appeared in the wheelchair-bound girl's eyes even though her face was calm and unmoving. When Gilly calmly lifted the gun barrels away from his belt buckle and sat down on the step with his back to the wheelchair, he heard Harvey and the girl sigh heavily.

"Why did you risk coming here?" she asked.

"I wanted to see the person who sends killers out to murder families."

"And you think that's me." Turning to Harvey, she waved him away. "You can go now Harvey, I'll call if I need you."

Reluctantly, the foreman slowly moved off toward the corral.

"I'm told those were your men," Gilly continued, keeping an eye on Harvey.

Jenny Louise Washington snorted in disgust, angrily sending her wheelchair rolling toward Gilly's back. He turned quickly, catching the wheel in his hand.

"Careful miss, if you fall down these steps you could get hurt."

Amazed at Gilly's brashness and alertness, she realized he was serious. Backing her chair away, she scowled fiercely. "You're not the law, so there must be something more that brings you to the Half Moon."

"Two things, ma'am," he began, standing up again. "I need to look your men over. I also have a warning for you. Stop harassing the coloured family homesteading about two days west of here."

"They're on my land."

"No ma'am, they're on government land, all legal and titled."

"Did they kill anyone?" Jenny asked with a catch in her voice. "I never ...," her voice trailed off.

"They tried, but I happened to disturb them. I brought them home so you'd be aware of the situation. I trust you won't allow your men to bother those folks again. Now that we understand each other, I'll check your men and be on my way."

"You're searching for someone?"

"Yes, a face from a long time ago."

"Wait," Jenny murmured, suddenly thinking there was more to this young cowboy under all the dust and bravado, than he was admitting to. "I want to know more about you." Then on impulse, she added, "I haven't always been in a wheelchair you know."

"Lady, I got enough troubles of my own!" he declared, taking a step down as if to leave.

"You had time for the black folks, how about listening to a cripple?"

"Seems like you ain't giving me much choice, ma'am. I'll just walk down to the stableyard and talk to your Mr. Harvey first."

Jenny suddenly felt an unusual sense of compassion for this brash young stranger and watched him with interest as he walked across the yard. She could feel his confidence when he tipped his hat against the glare of the sun. *He must have suffered some kind of violence in his life to react this way*, she thought, as her curiosity heightened. He was barely into manhood but she guessed him to be close to her age.

As he crossed the yard, his eyes darted in every direction, alert to any possible situation. Several cowboys near the corral shouted a warning to the foreman as he approached.

"Are you still looking for trouble boy?" Harvey demanded.

"Ain't never looked for trouble old man. Just looking to finish what's been started."

"Well you'd better cast your eyes toward the cookhouse mister, Whiskers has a shotgun trained on ya."

"I seen him," Gilly hissed coldly, staring hard at the group of men who now gathered a cautious distance away. His gaze landed on a tall cowboy standing by the fence, carrying a low holster. "You ain't from around here mister?"

Most of the men moved quickly away, suspecting a challenge. Just one older ranchhand stayed close, smiling coldly. Gilly's eyes carefully scrutinized him, noting the high-carried, swivel holster, deceitfully fast in the hands of a master. Many times in the past Rube had warned him of these specialist weapons.

"Are you in this game too mister?" Gilly asked ominously.

"Don't do it boy," Harvey warned.

Too late ... the die was cast as the evil smile again curled the man's lips and Gilly's mind flashed back to that fateful day he had watched his family die ... that smile was deeply ingrained in his brain.

Four shots roared in quick succession making Jenny Washington's wheelchair swing wildly around as she screamed for her foreman. Harvey Stubbs gasped in disbelief—two of his fastest guns were dead in the blink of an eye. Worriedly glancing over his shoulder, he hurried to answer his boss' summons.

"Who are you mister?" a young cowboy asked in obvious admiration. "Both of 'em came up from the Soda Springs country a few years back. Worked for the Star, I think."

"I'm only a boy in a tree," Gilly replied blankly, backing away and keeping a wary eye on the cookhouse window.

169

Moving slowly toward his mount, he casually threw the reins over the horse's neck. As he made his way toward the ranchhouse, he reloaded the three spent shells in his Colt.

"You're a bloody madman!" Jenny screamed. "I hope you're not planning on sticking around here."

"I'll be back if you touch that black man and his family."

"Who the hell is he talking about Harvey?"

"Squatters ma'am, I sent three of the boys to ask them to leave."

"That's how you asked my folks to leave too," Gilly muttered.

"Were your folks squatting on my land?"

"No ma'am, I figure it was farther south than here and it was before your time. What state is this?"

"Idaho, you're on the edge of the Snake River Plains country. Don't you know where you are?"

"Does it matter? I'll know when it's important."

Shaking her head in frustrated annoyance, Jenny turned her attention to Harvey, sharply ordering him to inform the cook she needed a coffee pot and sandwiches for two delivered to her on the verandah right away. "Then, please do something with those bodies!"

"I presume you won't object violently if we feed you before I send you packing," she snorted, as Harvey left them.

"That depends on the price ma'am."

"The price is I want to know who you are, where you're from, and what made you the way you are?"

"A rancher like you made me the way I am, when they sent some men to move my family on ...."

He heard her sudden intake of breath. "You were trespassing on rangeland?"

"We were homesteaders," he whispered, as if in a momentary daze.

Jenny now realized why the coloured family's situation was so important to him; she silently waited for him to continue. *What had happened, were they all right?* she wondered, fearing to hear more details. She now had a better picture of this man's hurtful past but he seemed unwilling to continue. Cook appeared carrying a large tray and she smiled briefly as he attempted to bow respectfully while nervously avoiding Gilly, before he hurried away.

"So your family had to move?" she asked, waving her hand toward the tray.

"No ma'am," Gilly's eyes dropped to the floor. "I buried them."

Looking at him with horrified eyes, she choked on her sandwich. "They murdered your family and left you alive?" she whispered.

170

"I was asleep in a tree when they came."

"How old were you?"

"Nine."

"And you've been on your own since then ... looking for these men?"

"No, not exactly. Rube found me; we killed two of the men and he took me with him."

"Rube?"

"Yes, Rube Caster, a range bum and mountain man. He became like a father to me and we lived in the Canadian Rockies."

"Did he teach you how to gunfight?"

"Yes, he said I'd need to know how when I found the men. This is his gun."

"You killed two of my men over by the cookhouse. Were they the men you were looking for?"

"One of them was. The other one just wanted a piece of the pie."

Sighing, Gilly took a sandwich and ate it silently, then reached for the mug of coffee Jenny had poured for him. At the same time, he watched the effect his story was having on the ranch owner as her eyes moved back and forth to her shotgun propped against the wall. He knew she was struggling with her thoughts and briefly wondered what she was thinking, yet he knew it really didn't matter. He remembered his horse and stood up suddenly.

"Maybe I could find some feed for my horse at the stable."

"Kerry's our stableman," she murmured, "just tell him I sent ya."

Gilly caught sight of the stableman watching him from the shadows as he ambled slowly across the yard toward him. Blue followed close behind.

"The lady says you might find a bucket of feed for my pony," he mumbled as the shadowy figure limped out into the open.

"I'll do better than that son. That pony needs a new set of shoes or yer going to lame the poor devil. Where ya heading?" Kerry Walker had been the Washington's stableman and farrier for almost as long as he could remember.

"Somewhere south of here I guess."

"You're a gunfighter."

"Hell no, just a man with a score to settle; how long have you worked here?"

"Upwards of 30 years, I came when Jenny Lou's pappy was a young man—even before he married."

"Why is Miss Washington in a wheelchair?"

171

"A runaway wagon ran over her when she was 16; she ain't never walked since then."

"An accident?"

"No lad, damned liquored up Indians on a rampage, they killed her pappy and left her for dead. We didn't find her for two days. Now get the hell outa here. Yer horse will be ready in an hour."

Dismissed so bluntly by the old farrier, Gilly could feel the man's loyalty to the ranch owner in the tone of his voice—a true pioneer with a heart of gold. Rube Castor would have shaken this man's hand.

Suddenly thinking of the black homesteading family, Gilly began to reassess the situation. Harvey had sent his men to move the family on without the owner's knowledge or permission. Did she ever leave the ranch or was he hiding her from the world? His eyes roamed over the now empty yard and he walked slowly toward the house knowing he would have to leave soon. Harvey Stubbs was standing on the verandah having a heated conversation with Jenny. As Gilly came closer, the conversation stopped.

"I thought you were leaving," the foreman snapped.

"Farrier's fixing Blue's feet."

"Is there anything else you want boy?"

"Yes sir," Gilly murmured adjusting his hat. "I'd like you to take the lady to see the coloured folks."

"We should do that Harvey," Jenny agreed.

"No ma'am that's at least a two-day buckboard ride. I don't have the time to spare and you ain't up to spending two nights out in the open."

"I'll take you," Gilly interceded.

"Like hell you will!" Harvey objected. "You ain't taking Miss Jenny nowhere."

"Harvey Stubbs," Jenny objected, raising her voice slightly. "I'm still quite able to make decisions about what I should or shouldn't do!"

"But Miss Jenny, he's a killer. He's killed five of your men and crippled our leading hand. I will not allow you to ride off with him."

"That's enough ... go and order my buckboard Harvey!" Jenny swung the wheelchair around and went back into the house.

Harvey stared fiercely at the Canadian cowboy, cursed under his breath, and walked away.

Helping himself to another sandwich, Gilly filled his mug with lukewarm coffee and studied the layout of the ranch. It was obvious to him that much thought had been put into the arrangement of interlocking corrals and barns in relation to the adjoining bunkhouse, cookhouse, and storage sheds, with the house set away from everything else. This was totally different from the mountainside log cabin Rube Caster had called home. He was deeply engrossed in his thoughts when a female voice chuckled behind him.

"All right mister, I think it's time we introduced ourselves. I'm Jenny Louise Washington, a relative of President George Washington. Just who are you?"

"Gilly Thompson, and I ain't got no kinfolk."

Jenny cocked an eye at him and was silent for a moment, and then she continued, "I packed a small trunk. Would you get it for me?"

"It's in the house?" Gilly asked guardedly.

"Yes, where else would it be?"

"But I ain't never been in a real house before."

"Well now's your chance to see how regular folk live. You'll find it in my bedroom, on the main floor naturally. Now off you go."

Carefully stepping into the house, he gazed up at the high-peaked ceiling, and then around the spacious room. It was littered with handsome furniture and the expanse of polished wood floor surprised him until he remembered the wheelchair. Moving on through the room to a passageway, he tried the first door. Sniffing the air first, he closed it quickly when he couldn't detect Jenny's scent. It was the third doorway that he confidently opened. He went into the room and, seeing a small trunk on the floor, picked it up and quickly returned to the verandah.

"How did you find my room?" she asked, watching him curiously as he came outside carrying the trunk.

"By smell," he replied, setting the trunk down and continuing down the steps.

It certainly was not the answer Jenny had expected. Frowning, she sniffed her own sleeve and watched him cross the yard. He was almost there when Harvey appeared leading the horse and buckboard. Gilly thanked the farrier for the service to his horse, mounted and followed the buckboard.

"Tie your pony behind," Harvey growled, "we can lift Jenny and the wheelchair in from the side."

"Don't need to, she's driving!"

"She's what?" Harvey exploded. "She's lame, haven't you noticed?"

Jenny Washington's blood raced with excitement. There was nothing wrong with her hearing and she liked what she heard. Here was a man who was not pandering to her affliction; he was treating her as a normal person. When they reached the steps, she expressed her own opinion.

"Of course I can drive myself Harvey. I'm lame not stupid! One of you lift me into the seat."

173

"This is crazy," the foreman objected, refusing to comply.

Moving forward, Gilly noticed the pile of blankets and large lunch basket in the rear. He pulled a couple of the blankets onto the seat, then went and scooped Jenny into his arms.

"Do you need me to strap you in?" he asked.

"No, I'll be fine. Shall we be going Mr. Gilly?"

"If she gets hurt," Harvey snapped, "I'll kill ya boy."

"You won't need to," Gilly stated coldly. "I'll already be dead. This lady's got the kind of courage I understand; now move out of my way old man."

Watching the rider and buckboard move out onto the grassland, Harvey Stubbs felt an immense resentment for this stranger. He knew in his heart that Jenny Lou was as safe with this man as any other, but he hated to admit it. The harsh voice of the old farrier, come up behind him, disturbed his thoughts.

"Stop yer worrying Harvey, that boy would die before he let anything harm that girl and some day I'll tell yer who Rube Caster was."

"Rube Caster," Harvey muttered over and over to himself as he went to close the door of the house. "That name ...."

Out on the prairie, the wagon moved along at a gentle trot, with Gilly taking up the rear and keeping a wary eye out for trouble. Two hours out, he rode up alongside.

"You tired yet?"

She noticed an unexpected note of concern in his voice. "Hell no!" she laughed. "You're the first one who's offered me a taste of freedom since I got into that blasted chair. I'm rather enjoying myself."

Gilly turned away so she couldn't see his smile. Nearly three hours later, they found themselves at a wide, shallow stream. The light was fading and Gilly moved them quickly across, calling a halt to the day's travel. Removing the harness from the buckboard horse and hobbling it, he turned it loose to graze. Next, he lifted the wheelchair out setting it firmly on the ground, carrying Jenny and placing her in the seat. He was beginning to get used to this ritual, although he found it mighty uncomfortable being so close to her. He asked if she was hungry and put the food basket where she could reach it while he prepared a fire.

"There's enough food here for both of us you know," she stated, holding out a paper-wrapped sandwich.

Keeping his distance, he accepted it, going to sit on the ground on the other side of the fire to eat. In a few minutes, he got up again.

"I'm going to find some real meat, I won't be far away."

Jenny controlled a quick pang of fear as she watched him go, rifle in hand, to disappear into the growing darkness. She was dozing when the single rifle shot reverberated in the silence and she shivered, hoping it was Gilly and he was all right. She strained to catch any further sound but only a coyote yipped in the distance.

Then, before she could really begin worrying, Gilly was back with something hung over his back. When he dropped it on the ground by the fire, she recognized it as a range deer and she watched silently as he skillfully butchered the beast. He added more wood to the fire and threaded thin strips of the blood-dripping meat onto a small spit produced from his saddlebag.

"Can you stand?" he asked, handing her a china plate and sitting down on the ground opposite her. She noticed his plate was tin from the cookhouse.

"Yes, but not for long," she replied, gingerly tasting the hot meat and raising her eyebrows.

"How about crutches?"

"I gave them up, they hurt my arms."

"Rube used to say sometimes we have to hurt a little to get rid of a bigger pain." He talked with his mouth full.

"Did Rube ever tell you to mind your own business?"

He went silent then and, when they finished eating, he took the dirty implements to the river and washed them. When he returned, he cut up the rest of the meat, put some more on the spit and dug a hole for the carcass. She watched his every move and decided that his Rube had taught him well. He was unlike any man she had ever met before.

"I want you to ah ... somehow get under the buckboard to sleep. Do you think you could do that?" His voice took her by surprise and she peered through the flame of the fire to see where he was, then she realized he was beside her.

"Yes," she said hesitantly, "but where are you going?"

"Up that big tree over there." He pushed her chair over to the wagon, bracing it while he helped her onto the ground. It was too dark to see how she was managing, so he added, "Don't worry I'm a light sleeper."

I'll bet you are, she thought, hearing him walk away. She was surprised how easily she was able to move into position. He had already made a bed for her and she pulled the blankets over her, going through her usual bedtime routine of stretches even in this restricted space.

Confiding in no one, Jenny had long ago grown restless with her restrictive life. She overheard the nasty comments and hated how the ranchhands talked about her. For many months ... almost a year no doubt, she had been secretly building up her strength, hoping that someday she'd be able to walk again. Working first on her upper body by lifting herself on the arms of the wheelchair, many times each day, she found she was able to get in and out of the chair even when there was no one around to help her. She had been very careful and, even Harvey was unaware of her actions behind private walls, but still her legs remained the frustrating problem. As the months passed, she had become even more determined to walk but it just wasn't happening.

As dawn broke, Jenny became aware of the crackle of a newly-stoked fire and saw the shadowy figure sitting on his haunches beside the flames as he reloaded his spit. The sun was already peering above the horizon and she knew it appeared quickly out here on the rangelands. Wriggling out from under the buckboard, she softly said 'good morning' and pulled herself painfully upright using first the wheel and then the side of the wagon. Awkwardly, she dropped into her chair, while he watched in amazement. When she tried to turn the wheels, however, they remained still in the sandy soil. He offered neither his help nor his encouragement.

"Damnit Gilly can't you do something; I'm in rather a hurry to get to those bushes!"

"Yes ma'am," he replied, moving quickly toward her and trying not to smile. He pushed her over to the bushes and stood watching.

"Could you look somewhere else for a minute or two!" she demanded.

Jerked out of his deep thoughts, Gilly went back to the fire and continued with his cooking. In a few minutes, he climbed to his feet and whistled for his pony. He was about to start packing when he heard the buckboard horse moving closer, hobbles still in place.

"Looks like that horse is eager to be on its way, as I am," she called from the wheelchair. "I'm ready to try that breakfast you're cooking."

He pushed her closer to the fire then handed her a plate.

"Hmm, scrambled eggs, toast and strange-looking beef," she murmured.

"Deer meat."

She smiled and started to say something, but he interrupted.

"We're ready to leave ... that is, the horses and me are. If you can eat fast we'll be leaving in a few minutes."

"Or I can juggle my plate as I drive, you're saying," she giggled, looking at him with a twinkle in her eye as she shovelled in another spoonful. He looked at her briefly then went to remove the horse's hobble.

176

By mid-morning, they made their first of several brief stops. Camping that second night was in a small stand of trees and when Gilly made no effort to light a fire, Jenny ventured a question.

"Is something wrong?" she asked nervously.

"Not yet, but we've crossed the tracks of Indian ponies twice today and we don't want to advertise where we are, do we?"

"Are you going into a tree?"

"No, I'm staying right here with you tonight."

"Do you think they'll find us?"

"Not until daylight and by that time we'll be out in the open."

Making sure she was wrapped up warmly under the buckboard, Gilly checked his rifle and sat with his back to the buckboard wheel. Twice in the night, he felt her hand touch his back, no doubt reassuring herself he was still there. He knew the feeling well—many times as a youngster, he had felt the need to be close to Rube when dreams had plagued his mind.

Dawn had just cast a ribbon of light across the eastern horizon when he heard the muffled sound of horses approaching. Moving quickly, he awakened and warned Jenny, loaded her wheelchair, and instructed her to get ready while he saddled the horse. He returned quickly to lift her onto the buckboard.

"Off you go," he hissed climbing into the saddle, "aim for that dip in the hills straight ahead."

Shaking the reins, Jenny gritted her teeth as she sent the buckboard moving quickly across the grassland. Glancing behind only after daylight flooded across the land, she saw Gilly sitting on his horse facing the oncoming riders. Urging more speed from her horse, she felt the rising ground and heard two rifle shots ring out behind her. Concentrating all her effort to guide the buckboard up the mountain pass, and, not daring to take her eyes off the boulder-strewn way ahead, she heard a rider coming fast behind her.

"Slow down!" Gilly yelled, coming alongside and passing her.

Waiting on the crest of the ridge, Gilly watched the buckboard toil up the incline. When a large male deer appeared at the edge of the tree line, he slipped from the saddle with his rifle. As the buckboard arrived at the ridge, he pointed to the deer before slowly raising his rifle. A single shot reverberated through the pass as the magnificent animal tumbled down the hillside. Gilly galloped off to secure his prize and Jenny watched him go before turning her attention to the other side of the hill. There below was a tiny shack, a ramshackle barn and a single pole corral. Smoke drifted lazily upward from a fieldstone chimney. This must be where they were headed, but how did people exist on so little, she wondered.

Arriving back with the gutted deer slung over his horse, Gilly waved her to follow. Galloping down the hill and across the grassland, he slowed abruptly to a walk as he came within shouting distance of the house.

"Hello Benji! I brought you a visitor."

Driving the buckboard up beside Gilly, Jenny watched with a stunned expression as Della appeared in the open doorway. She was the blackest person she had ever seen.

"You're the man who killed those bad ones," she murmured shyly. "Benji went into town for supplies."

"What town?"

"Fort Hall, it's just the other side of that hill," she pointed southward. "Ahs expecting him back later today."

"Can you take care of my woman if I go look for him?"

Jenny's head swung quickly to face Gilly, her eyes portraying surprise as he swung down from the saddle, releasing the deer.

"Do you have a place where I can hang this meat?"

The sound of a baby crying came from inside the house and Della turned back inside, returning quickly with a baby in her arms.

"If your lady would hold my baby sir, I'll show you where you can hang the meat."

"Sure she will," Gilly muttered, and Della took the baby over to the wagon and handed it to Jenny. He turned quickly away when he saw the horrified expression on Jenny's face.

Jenny cringed inwardly when Della placed the black baby in her arms, gurgling contentedly as it snuggled close. She gazed down at the big dark eyes and sighed as a myriad of thoughts coursed through her head. Slowly raising the warm bundle, she held it a bit tighter and buried her face in the covers, blinking away an escaping tear. She was unaware that Gilly and Della had returned and were watching.

"You can give it back now!" he said softly, startling her. As he lifted the wheelchair from the buckboard, he watched Della's surprised expression as she took the baby from Jenny. Lifting Jenny down, he must have held her too long because she squirmed fiercely.

"Put me down you fool!" she hissed.

Della had moved away but her eyes expressed her interest and surprise. Gilly released the buckboard horse, stripping the harness off before turning it into the corral, then quickly climbing into his saddle, he nodded to the women and urged Blue forward.

When he'd been riding for a little over an hour, he slowed to a walk and sniffed the air, picking up mixed smells that could indicate a town. Suddenly, two riders were coming fast toward him and he took the precaution of slipping the tie down from his Colt forty-five. The cowboys rode by with a friendly nod, showing little interest.

From the top of the next rise, he saw the town in a little valley just below. It was a small jumble of neat buildings gathered along one main street, that no doubt served the nearby ranches and farms. When he reached the valley floor and started down its dusty street, his eyes fastened quickly on a horse and wagon alongside a hitching rail. Glancing into the wagon as he dismounted and wound his reins loosely over the hitching rail, he noted the supplies in the wagon bed. He glanced up at the closest building—*Hardware and Feed* it said in big bold letters.

Stepping up onto the boardwalk, he stared through the window but saw no sign of Benji. Loud laughter from across the street, drew his attention to the saloon, and he moved quickly toward it. Pushing his way through the batwing doors, he slowly made his way toward the bar.

"Beer?" the barman asked, as Gilly cast his eyes around the room.

"No … milk, and some information—who owns the rig outside the hardware store?"

"Milk!" the barman roared. "We ain't no cow barn mister and we don't give out information to strangers."

Laughter erupted amongst the patrons at the barman's reply, several commenting loudly as he moved to the end of the bar. Conversation stopped abruptly when he turned to face them with his hand hanging loosely over his Colt.

"I'll take that milk now," his voice hissed menacingly, "and somebody had better remember where that black man went."

The challenge was evident, causing the barman to stumble hurriedly toward the kitchen and return with a jug.

"Mister, is you lookin' for me?" said the deep, melodious voice that belonged to the head of curly black hair peering over the batwing doors.

"I sure am, come in and have a drink with these friendly folk, Benji."

"No sar, ah drinks no liquor."

"It's milk," Gilly hissed, "you look like you need it."

"Blacks ain't allowed in here mister," the barman ventured somewhat nervously.

"This one is. He just happens to be my friend." Gilly turned his ice-cold eyes on the barman. "Now you can pour two glasses."

Shaking, the rotund man nervously filled two glasses with milk, spilling a little on the bar and grabbing his cloth hurriedly to wipe it up.

"Come on, drink yer milk," Gilly encouraged him as Benji stayed by the door. "We don't have all day to hang around here."

Hesitantly Benji pushed open the door and strode over to the bar, glancing with wide fear-laden eyes at Gilly. Who drank his glass of milk in a single gulp.

"Thanks," Gilly murmured pitching a quarter onto the bar and moving toward the door. He watched out of the corner of his eye while Benji downed his drink and hurriedly followed him. "Where the hell were you when I came in?" he demanded when they were out of hearing range.

"At the outhouse, is there a hurry?" he asked gathering the reins and climbing onto his rig. "I wasn't expecting to see you again mister."

Gilly stopped in mid-stride and went over to the buckboard. "I was out to your farm before I came to find you." Seeing the sudden look of concern in Benji's eyes, Gilly hurriedly added, "Your wife is teaching a friend of mine all about babies! The friend is a she and, don't fret, they'll be right good friends by the time we get back!"

Chapter 3

Della made Jenny comfortable, pushing the wheelchair into the shade and asking her to hold the baby while she made them a cup of mint tea. Jenny was more comfortable with the baby now and quite enjoying the new experience. When Della returned, it was as if they could not begin to get to know each other quickly enough. They talked of life's hard trials and the difficulties of living so far from neighbours. Jenny found herself needing to suppress a feeling of shame and embarrassment when Della shared her hopes and aspirations for her family's future.

"Benji wanted to come West. He thought we could find a corner of this great land where freedom was truly every man's right and coloured folks could live in peace. We never expected to be shot at," Della whispered. "If Master Gilly hadn't come along, we might be dead now."

"Tell me what happened," Jenny gently insisted. "Those were my men who shot at you, but I promise you I never sent them. In fact I didn't even know you were homesteading on my grazing land."

"They just rode in here shooting at us, Miss Jenny. My Benji tried to protect us but we only had one old rifle and he ain't much of a fighting man."

"But all three of them were killed."

"Yes ma'am, my man never fired a shot. Mister Gilly rode straight in here shooting at those men. He didn't seem to care about the danger. Then he left us a better rifle and bullets, and went to find you."

"He told you that's what he was going to do?"

"Yes ma'am and he took the dead men with him."

Jenny went quiet as all the questions she'd been thinking about Gilly surfaced again and she tried to understand how he could be such a caring man and yet so unafraid of violence. Who was that man who had raised him and taught him to be so confident? She'd had a great deal of time to think about this as they travelled, but Gilly's quiet and rather aloof manner prevented her from asking questions. She was confused by his actions, yet she trusted him implicitly. She looked toward the distant hills hoping he'd soon return.

Shadows lengthened as Benji allowed his horse to slow for the walk the last hill. Up ahead, he could see Gilly sitting his mount on the crest. The only sound was the rattle of his wagon and the clanking of the iron-rimmed wheels, until he picked up the sound of hoofbeats behind him. Glancing nervously over his shoulder, he realized the rider was gaining fast. He whistled with relief when he saw Gilly thundering toward him.

Sheriff Charley Tripp slowed as he closed in on the wagon and saw the rider approaching. He was an old-time pioneer and recognized a guard on duty when he saw one. As Gilly reined in, he did also.

"Rest easy son, I ain't here looking for blood," Sheriff Tripp announced. "I just want to know who you are?"

"Why?" Gilly growled evasively, noting the sheriff's badge.

"Because you scared the hell out of Rolly and the boys at the saloon."

"And that's a crime in your town, sheriff?"

"No son it ain't, but when a gunfighter comes to town, I like to know about it."

"I ain't no gunfighter."

"Are you working at the Half Moon spread?"

"No."

"Well you sure as hell ain't working for the coloured folk."

"No, but I should be, three Half Moon cowboys raided him a few nights ago."

"Are you sure of that?"

"Yes, are you going to do something about it?"

"I could ride over there and hear what they have to say."

"They won't say nothing, they're dead!"

"The black fella killed 'em?" the sheriff asked staring hard at Benji.

181

"No I did," Gilly stated, looking the sheriff in the eye.

"I'll ride in with you. I should collect the bodies. Harvey won't like this mister."

Believing the conversation was over, Benji shook the reins, stirring his horse into motion and continued up the hill. He was well aware that Gilly hadn't told the sheriff he'd already delivered the bodies back to the ranch. *Why would he want the lawman to follow them to the homestead*, he thought. Straining his eyes as the wagon crested the hill, Benji could see the faint spiral of smoke from his chimney. *One more hour and I'll be home*, he thought. He was never comfortable leaving his family alone and even less so after what had happened the week before.

Darkness had enveloped the valley when Jenny watched Della hang a lantern out on the well, returning to the porch to thoughtfully wrap a blanket around her shoulders. She listened again for the sound of the wagon before going inside.

"They're coming," Jenny called only minutes later.

Gilly was the first to ride in, quickly stripping his saddle and bridle from his mount. He turned Blue loose and then caught the bridle of the wagon horse. Jenny turned as another rider walked his horse into the lantern light and she realized she recognized him.

"Charley Tripp," Jenny exclaimed in surprise as the Fort Hall sheriff slid out of his saddle in front of the house. "What brings you out here?"

"Murder ma"am, I believe you lost three men."

"No five, but who said anything about murder?"

"Are you the town sheriff or a US Marshall mister?" Gilly's voice asked from the darkness.

"I'm the law son."

"Like hell you are old man. Outside the town limits you're a nobody."

"He's kept the peace around here for as long as I can remember," Jenny interrupted softly.

"What peace—helping the Half Moon spread kill off the homesteaders?" Gilly added sarcastically.

"No homesteaders have ever been killed on my property," Jenny retorted.

"How would you know? You didn't even know your men had attacked these coloured folks!" Gilly pointed out.

"If Harvey had asked me I would never have authorized such brutality and those cowboys would still be alive."

"Yes ma'am, those cowboys would still be alive but Benji, Della and the baby would be dead and you'd be saying how sorry you are," Gilly replied.

"Damn you Gilly Thompson, who made you judge and jury of our lives?"

"You forget something ma'am." Even in the low light, Gilly's eyes flashed icily. "I'm also the executioner!"

"Stop it, please stop!" Della interceded nervously. "I have a meal of venison stew and fresh vegetables ready for eating, if you folks can stop arguing long enough."

"Best news I've heard all day," Jenny replied trying to turn her wheelchair on the small porch, "and please let me apologize for my bad-tempered friend."

Moving quickly to her aid, Gilly lifted her into his arms, grinning as he called over his shoulder, "Benji, would you bring madam's wheelchair into the house." Slipping her arm around his neck, she tweaked the short hair at the base of his neck. When he whispered, "I'll drop you if you don't behave!" … she punched his chest.

As they waited for Benji to set the wheelchair down, the sheriff stepped inside and pulled his gun, aiming it at Gilly. "I never thought you'd make it so easy boy."

Still holding Jenny in his arms, the Canadian turned to meet the challenge. She could feel the steady, strong rhythm of his heart through the closeness of their bodies.

"What the hell are you doing Charlie?" she snapped, wriggling in Gilly's arms so she could extract her arm. Hidden from view, she slipped it down between their bodies to his holster and slowly pulled his Colt up between them. Gilly didn't stop her.

"He killed five of your men, Jenny Louise. I'm going to take him in and send for a US Marshal."

"No sir, you ain't," Benji growled.

"Well for God's sake, let him put me down," Jenny moaned, "or are you going to shoot us both?"

"Put her down boy!" the sheriff snapped, waving his gun toward the wheelchair. He kept it pointing at Gilly as he set Jenny into her chair and stepped away.

"How quickly do you want to die Charlie," Jenny asked, pointing Gilly's Colt at the sheriff's middle, "because if you don't drop your gun and leave in five seconds, I'm going to kill ya! One …!"

Taken totally aback by Jenny's actions, the sheriff set his gun down on the chair and strode through the door. Benji followed him onto the porch, watching as he galloped off into the night.

"Would you have shot him?" Gilly asked her, picking up his gun.

"Yes I would have, but now I want to forget about it. Tomorrow we're taking these folks back to the ranch; they can stay with me."

"Let's eat," Gilly muttered, "and maybe food will help you see this differently. That ain't what these folks want."

Over the meal of venison stew, Della gently made it plain to the ranch owner how much they needed a place of their own—a home to raise their children in—where fear would be a thing of the past. They had had enough of fighting and turmoil.

The moon had risen high in the sky when Della suggested she could build a bed in the corner for Jenny, and Gilly could sleep out in the barn. Jenny's face swung instantly around to Gilly.

"I'd like to be outside, under the buckboard," she said in a determined tone.

"You'd be better in here tonight," he muttered, moving toward the door, "but suit yourself."

"Well, are you going to take me out there?" she asked, pouting.

"Certainly, if that's what you want. I'll go get it ready."

Standing for a moment on the porch, he heard a quiet snort of greeting and knew Blue was on watch duty. Sniffing the air, Gilly moved silently around the yard, stopping suddenly when a faint but disturbing aroma touched his nostrils. Automatically letting his hand fall onto his Colt, he moved cautiously in the dark going toward the smell. He soon recognized the aroma and stooped to pick up a rock. He hurled it in that direction and heard the instant retreat of tiny feet. "Coyote," he grunted under his breath, "and I'll bet that's the chicken house over there." Retrieving his saddle from the fence rail, a flash of moonlight broke through the clouds to light the yard. It gave him enough light to easily organize Jenny's bed.

"Ready lady?" was all the conversation Gilly offered as he returned to the house. Picking up Jenny from the wheelchair, he stepped out into the darkness, kicking the door shut with his heel. He could feel Jenny's heart beating against his chest and heard her quick breathing as he walked down the steps to the buckboard.

"Can you see in the dark?" she murmured into his ear.

"No," he hissed, turning and walking backwards until his back bumped the buckboard. "Can you stand for a moment?"

"Yes, if I hang onto something."

184

"Hang onto the side of the wagon."

"I would rather hang onto you," she whispered as Gilly lowered her feet to the ground.

"No, you wouldn't. I'm a killer and you don't want to think what you're thinking. I'll be gone right after I take you home."

He heard her sudden intake of breath. "And if I don't want you to go … oh, help me Gilly," she begged as her body began to sag. "I told you I can't stand for long!" Her voice displayed her legitimate panic and he grasped her around her tiny waist. Jenny sighed and leaned into his body.

"I've never known what it felt like to be held in a man's arms. Nobody has ever treated me like you do," she whispered.

"I don't treat you any different from anybody else," he declared.

"That's exactly what I mean. You treat me as a normal woman."

"You are normal and someday you'll walk again," he said without emotion. "I know an Indian up in the mountains that would help you."

"Then take me there and give up trying to revenge your family."

"No ma'am, I have to find those graves and the men who put my family in them, maybe then I'll take you to see the Indian. Now it's time you crawled under that wagon and left me in peace."

"Just hold me for another minute Gilly, then I promise to go quietly."

Inside the house, Benji and Della were already in bed sharing their thoughts on the day's events.

"I don't think Miss Jenny sent those men to kill us," Della said softly, "and Mister Gilly has done nothing but help us. He was most concerned when I told him you'd gone into town."

"He came looking for me all right; I recognized his horse at the hitching rail."

"Do you think the sheriff will come back?"

"No, Mister Gilly scared the locals to death in the saloon. I don't think nobody will come looking for him!"

Back in Fort Hall, Sheriff Tripp entered the saloon and went up to the bar, desperate for a drink.

An older ranchhand noticed his missing sidearm and called out, "Has somebody stolen your Colt Charley?"

"I left it in my saddlebag," Charley lied nervously, gulping down his drink and indicating to the hovering barman to pour him another.

"I thought you'd maybe loaned it to the gunfighter you chased out of here."

"How'd you know about that?"

"Two of the Box Y riders told me on the trail. Who was he?"

"Don't know, but I think he rides for Jenny Washington."

"Another gunslicker on Harvey Stubbs' crew. That wouldn't surprise me. I wonder if that crippled woman knows what Harvey's up to?"

"And what exactly do you think Harvey is up to Mac?" the barman asked.

"It's obvious," the ranchhand named Mac grinned. "He's filling the crew with gun hands and one day that woman will just disappear."

"She's a cripple," the sheriff muttered in alarm, "and Harvey would kill you if he heard you say that."

"Well, you just tell him, and I'll bet you my last dollar he sends Jess Ellis to find me."

"Jess is nursing a shot hip and five of Harvey's men are dead," offered another man.

"Five, holy hell what happened Davie?" asked the sheriff.

"They tangled with that new man."

"He don't sound like no ordinary gunhand; I'd stay well away from him sheriff, if I were you," Mac advised.

It was well before dawn when Gilly climbed out of his tree and sniffed the air. He moved silently toward the Jackson house and sat down against the wheel of the buckboard. He felt Jenny's fingers touch his back and heard the groan of reassurance as she sleepily whispered his name.

Fingers of sunshine soon appeared in the eastern sky creeping higher and higher as the black of night burst into the grey of dawn. A bucket clanged not far away and hogs screamed for food as Benji began his morning ritual. The noise of hungry stock sent Gilly's mind flashing back to his childhood and he could hear his father's voice yelling to him in the crisp morning air.

"What's wrong?" Jenny asked, a concerned note in her sleepy voice as she pulled on his coat. "What are you groaning for?"

"Just memories tormenting me," Gilly muttered, climbing to his feet.

"I need you to take me to the outhouse."

Clearing his mind, Gilly waited for Jenny to crawl out from under the buckboard. Seeing her painful expression, he moved to help her then scooped her into his arms. Walking quickly over to the outhouse door, he set her gently onto her feet as she clung to the door frame.

"Go take a little walk and clear that nightmare away," she said, smiling sweetly as he opened the door. "I'll yell when I need you."

A few minutes later, Jenny called again for assistance. "Don't come all the way," Jenny ordered, "I want to try three steps."

"Start with two," Gilly hissed.

"I did that yesterday, now do as you're told Gilly Thompson."

Obeying the order, Gilly stopped three strides away from the door and held out his arms, watching in admiration as Jenny painfully moved her feet, biting her lip in determination as she forced her feet to take the three strides. Finally, standing in front of him, she smiled and lightly touched his arms.

"I did it Gilly, I did it!" she squealed.

"Yes you did, yes you did," he replied sweeping her up into his arms again. "Now I'm sure the Indian can help you."

"Benji's waving."

"Well wave back to him, I ain't got a hand to spare right now!"

They were met at the door by Della. Through the air wafted the smell of frying bacon and, in the background, the cooing of the baby.

"Breakfast's ready," Della announced.

"We need to eat quickly," Gilly ordered Jenny, "we're leaving right away."

Nodding her agreement, Jenny picked at the food with her attention riveted on Della who was breast-feeding the baby. Benji arrived soon afterwards, just as Gilly was leaving to prepare the horses. He stopped and they spoke briefly then Benji went into the house. When Gilly had the horses ready, he brought the buckboard to the house, groaning when Jenny didn't show. He went up the steps and opened the door. Benji was standing nearby, his arm around his wife, as they both watched Jenny cooing at their baby.

"I want them to go with us," Jenny stated glancing up at Gilly.

"No!" Gilly shook his head. "I told you yesterday it's not what they want."

"But they'd be safe with me," she argued, looking down at the child in her arms.

"And how safe do you think you really are fastened in that wheelchair?"

"I own the ranch and Harvey Stubbs follows my orders," she replied. There was a trace of anger in Jenny Washington's voice as she handed the baby back to its mother and turned her wheelchair to face her tormenter.

"He works to your orders?" Gilly continued.

"Yes, of course he does, I make the decisions for the Half Moon Ranch."

"So you sent those men to kill these folks?"

"I did no such thing!" she snapped in frustration.

187

"Then who made that decision Miss Washington?" he goaded her.

"Harvey did and he'll pay dearly for it when I get back to the ranch."

"We'll see," Gilly sighed. "Have you finished eating because I want to get going."

"I'm staying here," Jenny snapped defiantly. "You can go where the hell you want. I'm tired of hearing your mountain-man wisdom."

"Benji, put her wheelchair in the buckboard, she's going home."

Swinging a punch at him as he bent to pick her up, she cursed him as he walked out into the yard and heaved her up onto the seat. Nervously, the coloured man followed, placing the wheelchair in the back and tying it securely in place.

"I won't drive," she pouted, keeping her hands in her lap.

Sweeping his floppy hat off, Benji moved cautiously to the side of the buckboard. When he spoke he was tentative and obviously nervous.

"Please Miss Jenny do as Mister Gilly says, it's best for all of us; you can come visit anytime you like."

They were interrupted by the sound of riders approaching quickly and their conversation stopped abruptly.

Gilly snapped an order at the homesteader. "Back to the house now, Benji!"

Reaching for the reins of her horse, Jenny turned the rig to face the oncoming riders. Glancing over at Gilly, she noted his hand move slowly taking the tie down from his holstered Colt, as he walked toward them.

"They're Half Moon men," he growled over his shoulder, as the horses slowed and attempted to go around him. "Hold it boys!" Gilly's voice stopped the riders' manoeuvre. "Stop and state your business where I can see you both."

"Harvey sent us to check on Miss Washington, we're Half Moon riders, mister," the older cowboy muttered, folding his hands over the saddlehorn. "He said we had to bring her back."

"And what are you supposed to do if she decides to stay here awhile?"

"Harvey said to bring her home mister," the second rider hissed, "and Harvey's word is law around the Half Moon spread."

"You ain't on the Half Moon boy, and keep that damned horse still. Miss Washington's got a mind of her own; why don't you ask her?"

"She's a cripple and, when Harvey says to bring her home, she's going home!"

Gilly tipped his hat against the sun and moved to block their path. "Well, I think you had better ask her first boy!" he hissed with icy menace

"I'm going home with Mister Gilly when I'm ready," Jenny stated firmly, before they could say another word. "You can go back to work."

"But miss, Harvey said ...."

"Hell boy," Gilly snapped, "She don't walk as good as you do but she's the one who owns the ranch and you work for her. It's her legs that are damaged not her brain; you don't want to die for being stupid do you?"

"Mister, I'm paid to follow orders," the cowboy argued, but he quickly jerked his head around when he heard Jenny snap a shell into the breach of the Winchester she was pointing at him.

Finally, convinced they were not about to complete their orders, the men resignedly turned and galloped away. Watching them for a moment, Gilly adjusted his hat then walked casually over to his horse and climbed into the saddle. He waved to Benji and Della standing in the doorway and rode out of the yard with Jenny following. It was almost noon when he stopped in a stand of trees and waited for the buckboard to catch up. He lifted Jenny from the seat and set her down on the grass.

"We'll rest for an hour," he said flatly, producing water and salted meat from his saddlebag. "I'm going to ride ahead and check out the land."

"Why, are you expecting trouble?"

"I always expect trouble."

"You were prepared to fight for me back there at the Jackson's, weren't you?"

"Would you have shot that cowboy if he'd gone for his gun?"

She looked him squarely in the eye. "Yes, I would have."

She continued to watch his face as their conversation bantered back and forth, but he showed no trace of emotion. Walking over to the buckboard, he retrieved the Winchester, laying it on the grass beside her.

"One shot will bring me back in a hurry," he muttered, turning back to his horse.

Mounting quickly, he cut back to the trail allowing the pony to lope along comfortably as he watched for signs of riders. It was a little more than a mile along when the hoofprints divided in the dust, one set heading into the hills and the other heading back. Spinning the pony around, he rode wildly back through the brush to where he'd left Jenny. A single rifle shot in the distance made him cringe, adding additional urgency. Jenny would be an easy target to a competent rifleman.

Chapter 4

Leaving his mount in the trees, he moved cautiously toward the buckboard already feeling panic when he couldn't see her. He found her lying in the grass, unmoving and silent. Now crawling closer, he spotted the red patch of blood as it stained the grass. He found his rifle and, assuming the shooter was still nearby, he deliberately stood up, exposing himself briefly before moving behind a tree.

He saw the flash even before the bullet tore into the bark, too close for comfort. He sent two shots screaming in the bushwacker's direction. Then taking another chance, he dashed over to Jenny and picked her up, moving to the cover of the buckboard. He could tell she was still breathing but the bottom of her dress was soaked in blood and he knew he had to do something fast. He pulled her dress aside and found the source of the blood—the bullet had gone into her upper leg, exiting through the fatty tissue of her behind. He knew instinctively that she had a burn line joining the two wounds—the sure cause of much of the bleeding. Opening her eyes, about 10 minutes later, he was tying the last strip of her petticoat in place when her eyes flicked open.

"What are you doing?" she asked weakly. "Ow, that hurts!"

"I'm bandaging a bullet wound on your arse; is there a doctor nearby?"

"Yes, Doc Forbes in Fort Hall," she replied, groaning as she moved.

"We're going to have to go back to the Jackson's and it won't be an easy ride for you. Do you hurt anywhere else—you must have fallen out of the wagon."

"That could explain my headache but I think I'm all right on the upper part of my body! Thanks for your help Gilly."

A spot of red touched his cheeks and he turned to finish what he was doing. He assumed the gunman had taken flight by now or he would have caused more trouble for them already, so he got busy preparing a bed in the buckboard using blankets and his saddle.

When he picked her up to move her, she groaned sharply and clung to him. He knew she was in a lot of pain but trying her best not to show it. He got her into the buckboard and then had to move her into position—a difficult manoeuvre, but he did it as gently as he could. When he finished, he realized she had lost consciousness. He whistled for the gelding, tying it on behind, leapt onto the seat of the buckboard and they were off at a gallop back the way they had come. Three hours later, he pulled into the Jackson's yard with the horse covered in sweat and gasping for breath.

"Jenny's been shot," Gilly shouted when Benji appeared on the porch. He immediately dropped his rifle and ran toward them. "It ain't life threatening and the bullet came out through her back, but she's going to be hellish sore for a few days and she won't be able to sit! Can I leave her here while I go get the doctor?"

"You go Mister Gilly, we take good care of her," Benji assured him as his wife came outside to join them. Picking up Jenny's limp form, he took her inside the little house with Della fussing around them.

Grim-faced, Gilly wasted no time re-saddling and leaving the yard at a fast gallop in the direction of Fort Hall. Allowing his mount to pick his own pace on the trail, his eyes moved across the landscape, ever watchful. He made quick time into town, reining in his horse at the blacksmith's shop. Gilly inquired of the doctor's whereabouts from the knurled old smithy working in the doorway.

"He'll be at the saloon lad," the blacksmith growled, hardly glancing up from his work.

Riding slowly up the wide street toward the building with the large sign that said *Saloon*, Gilly pulled up to the hitching rail and dismounted. He noted the two Half Moon horses tied at the rail and cautiously approached the mounts. Quickly loosening the saddle girths, he ducked under the rail onto the rickety boardwalk. He slipped the tie down from the hammer on the Colt at his hip before approaching the saloon's batwing doors. He was well aware there could be a heap of trouble waiting for him through those doors, but there was no way to avoid it. He needed the doctor urgently for Jenny.

Pushing the doors quietly aside and stepping through, he stood and looked around. Two old men playing checkers glanced up uninterestedly and quickly focused their attention back to the game; a lone cowboy stood at the end of the bar fidgeting nervously with half a glass of beer.

He quickly recognized the two Half Moon riders standing at the bar with their backs to the door. A dusty-suited man with a medical bag on the table in front of him, drank alone in the corner. *That will be Doc Forbes*, Gilly thought. He was about to approach the doctor when one of the Half Moon riders called to the cowboy at the end of the bar.

"Who the hell do you ride for boy?"

"Sam Burgers, Box T," was the reply.

"This is Half Moon range and Harvey Stubbs don't take kindly to strangers sneaking around our stock."

"I ain't sneaking, I'm checking fenceline stock," he retorted, sizing the man up more carefully.

"Driving a few extra cows south of the fenceline are you boy?"

The accusation had struck home and range law demanded he respond. Pursing his lips, the Box T rider pushed his beer away and stepped out from the end of the bar.

"Mister, I ain't no rustler and I don't want to fight, but I will if you don't take that back," he hissed.

The cowboy pushed himself away from the bar and stood up. Gilly instantly recognized the Half Moon rider as the man at the Jackson farm who had insisted he was taking Jenny back home. Gilly watched as, almost imperceptivity, the cowboy eased the tie down from his sidearm.

Doc Forbes suddenly sat up straight in his chair. "Frank, stop this nonsense, you don't even know this man!" he said sternly.

"Sit down old man and be quiet, I'm protecting the range I work for."

"Yeah, by bushwhacking the owner!" Gilly grunted from near the door.

Turning to answer the accusation, Frank Barlow's face contorted in anger. "Mister, you've butted into my business twice today, but you don't have a woman to save you this time."

"No, I guess ya took care of that when you shot her!"

Moving out of the line of fire, the other Half Moon rider, an older man, looked shocked at Gilly's revelation, obviously unaware that Jenny Washington had been shot. Keeping his hands well away from his Colt, he eagerly displayed that he had no intention to interfere.

The situation quickly changed as Frank Barlow's hand flashed down to his holster and Gilly's Colt thundered its own lethal message. Barlow crashed against the bar before falling to the floor motionless.

"Hell, you're fast!" the Box T rider muttered. "Who are you?"

Doctor Forbes leapt from his seat muttering incoherently to himself as he hurried toward the fallen man. Turning him over, his fingers reached for a pulse. "He's dead."

Showing no emotion, Gilly holstered his gun. Alerted by the sound of the batwing doors being opened, he turned to see the back of the other Half Moon rider as he disappeared outside. Moving quickly to the door, Gilly was just in time to hear the squeal of a horse and the crash of a rider hitting the dirt. Stepping back inside, he could still hear the fallen rider cursing his loosened saddle.

"There'll be hell to pay for this when Harvey Stubbs hears of it, I hope you're moving on son," Doc addressed Gilly.

"Yes sir, you and I are leaving straight away."

"You're going to force me to go with you?"

"Jenny Washington's been shot, she's at the Jackson place."

192

"Why the hell didn't you say so? I'll get my buggy at once."

"No sir, you'll be riding, it's faster. You can use his horse," Gilly pointed to the body on the floor. "It's a Half Moon horse and he won't be needing it anymore."

After fixing the saddle on the dead man's horse Gilly helped the doctor mount, leading the way out of town at a steady mile-eating gallop. Glancing up at the sky, Gilly was aware they would be hard-pressed to get to the Jackson farm before dark. Slowing down to give the horses a breather after pushing on for more than an hour, Gilly was surprised at the amiable conversation Doc Forbes offered.

"You ain't the kind of ranchhand Harvey employs at the Half Moon," Doc chuckled. "There will be hell to pay when he finds out you killed one of your own."

"I don't work for Harvey," Gilly replied.

"Do you know who that young Box T rider was?"

"No, but I suspect you're going to tell me, ain't yer?"

"He's the son of Luke Burgers, owner of the Box T."

"Come on, let's stir some dust up, we're only an hour away from the Jackson place," was Gilly's response.

Darkness was creeping slowly over the range by the time Gilly and Doc galloped into the Jackson's yard.

"Go straight in Doc," Gilly ordered, jumping to the ground and holding the horses, "but better be quiet, they have a baby in the house."

A noise from the barn drew his attention as he stripped the saddles off the horses and turned them into the roughly built corral.

"It's me Mister Gilly," Benji called, stepping out of the darkness into the half-light with a Winchester in his hand.

"You expecting trouble Benji?"

"No sah, Miss Jenny said I should be prepared."

"Prepared for what?"

"Oh, I don't rightly know, Mister Gilly, she just said you were always prepared for trouble. Why don't you go in and see her? She's been anxious for you to come back. I'll feed the horses."

Nodding gratefully, Gilly left, going straight to the house. He opened the door and stuck his head around the door frame. Jenny was lying on a makeshift cot with her head facing the door. Doc Forbes was bending over her bare backside and she let out a scream as he prodded her wound. Gilly was shocked to see the large red bruise covering her lower back.

"Shut that door!" Doc snapped. "Half an inch and this lady would not have been as lucky!"

"It don't look like she'll be sitting for a while though!" Gilly grunted.

"Oww!" Jenny squealed again as the doctor continued his prodding. "That hurt!"

"But where did the hurt go girl?" insisted the doctor.

"Down my leg to just above my knee."

"Well I can't do much more for you girl," Harry Forbes chuckled, "except to advise that you sit on some cushions for a while. And now if Mrs. Jackson will feed me, your man can escort me back to town."

"Gilly isn't my man," Jenny replied, her eyes locking onto the Canadian's. "He's my friend."

"Well, he's going to need your friendship when Harvey finds out he killed Frank Barlow."

"He didn't kill Frank Barlow, he chased him away from here when he wanted to take me back to the ranch," she replied.

"Yes I did," Gilly stated emotionlessly, "but he was also the one that bushwhacked you."

"You knew that when you went for help?"

"Only suspicious, I found the tracks when one of them doubled back on us."

"And you just had to hunt him down even though I needed a doctor."

"You think what you like, it don't matter to me," Gilly hissed, turning abruptly and leaving the house.

"He didn't go looking for Frank Barlow, Miss Washington, he came looking for me. I was in the saloon and Frank Barlow was trying to goad young Tom Burgers into a gunfight."

"You think he was right don't ya?"

"If he hadn't intervened, Tom Burgers would be dead, and that's the truth of it."

Della was looking uncomfortable with the conversation as she produced a steaming plate of food and slid it onto the table in front of the doc. "Mister Gilly is a good man, sah," she murmured, placing a knife and fork in his outstretched hand.

"Call him in to eat; we have a long ride back to town," said Doc.

"I'll do it," Benji volunteered.

Stepping outside into the darkness, he walked a few paces into the yard. "Ah knows yer here, Mister Gilly. Della is wanting to feed ya."

"I'm here," Gilly's voice whispered from behind him. "Let's go eat."

Avoiding Jenny's eyes, he ate in silence, grunting or nodding in answer to the doctor's attempt at conversation until he finished. Jenny's voice quickly demanded his attention as Della cleared his plate away.

194

"Well swear at me you heathen, I know you're angry and, I'm sorry for doubting you, but for God's sake say something!"

"Don't tempt me woman, you're my responsibility until I get you back home. Rube said a man should never break his word and I gave you my word on it. Now why don't you stay quiet and get well. You're with the first real friends you've ever had."

"Yes sir I will," Jenny said thoughtfully, closing her eyes.

It was almost midnight when Gilly and Doc Forbes walked their horses out of the Jackson's yard, allowing the range bred mounts to follow the trail with little direction. Aided by fleeting moments of moonlight, they moved up to a mile-eating canter, slowing to a walk when the moon hid in the clouds. Taking advantage, Harry Forbes directed a few questions at his companion.

"You're a stranger in these parts son," he began, "can I ask where you're from?"

"Alberta," Gilly muttered in the darkness.

"That's up in Canada, ain't it lad."

"Yes sir, Rube and me lived in the mountains, trapping in winter and wandering the range in summer."

"Rube was your father?"

"No sir, Rube Caster was my friend." Pushing on a little faster, Gilly destroyed the chance of further conversation.

Could this young man's mentor be the same Rubin Caster he'd known as the Sheriff of Placerville in California. Several things Gilly had done reminded Doc of the former Placerville lawman. His quiet, unassuming, yet confident manner, the way he accepted his self-imposed responsibility to Jenny Louise, and how he thought his word was a cast-iron bond that should never be broken. Yes, Harry Forbes was sure this young man's mentor was indeed the Rubin Caster he had once known.

Only two oil lamps glowed over the doorway to Fort Hall's run-down boarding house, as the two riders walked their mounts along the town's dark, deserted street. Stopping at a darkened shopfront with a sign in the window that said, *Doctor*, Doc Forbes groaned with pain as he slowly dismounted and limped toward the door.

"Are you going to rest awhile?" he asked opening the door.

"No, just tell me what I owe you and I'll be on my way."

"You don't owe me one damned thing son. I brought that girl into the world and watched her mother die. I treated her after her father got killed and I know how hard she's tried to keep that ranch running. She needs a friend, lad, a friend like Rubin Caster was to you!"

195

The speech had drained the tired old doctor; baring his innermost feelings to a stranger had been hard but necessary. Jenny needed this Canadian cowboy as a friend, needed him more than she realized.

Collecting the reins of the spare horse, Gilly watched the doctor disappear inside his office before moving off again. He eased the horses into a slow canter as they passed the blacksmith's shop and left the town behind. Grey streaks of dawn pushed at the black of night as they crested the hill and moved toward the flatlands. Knowing the horses were almost too tired to move, he urged them slowly onward clucking words of encouragement. Morning sunshine was heating the air as they rode into the Jackson's yard and Benji rushed out of the barn to meet him.

"How is she?" Gilly asked.

"Miss Jenny's fine, sah. Let me help you into the house. You need sleep and food."

"No, I just need a tree," he said slowly, obviously having trouble keeping his eyes open. Using his last reserve of energy, Gilly dropped his saddle on the ground and returned to the tree he had slept in the night before. Wedging himself in the natural fork of the trunk, he covered his face with his hat, and appeared to have immediately fallen asleep.

Benji Jackson stared in amazement, shaking his head as he went to report Gilly's return to the women.

"Where is he?" Jenny asked as he entered.

"He's asleep out there in a tree!" said the coloured man, rolling his eyes. "He so tired he could hardly walk, Miss Jenny."

Waking in the early afternoon, Gilly slowly unwound, sniffing the air and cautiously letting his eyes roam over the Jackson's yard before stretching his cramped muscles. Dropping out of the tree, he went over to the well. Removing his hat and shirt, he poured a bucket of cold water over his head, shivering as he did so.

"Are you ready to eat now Mister Gilly," Della called from the doorway. "I got a nice venison stew that just be waiting to jump onto yo plate!"

Waving his acceptance, Gilly lightly wiped himself down with his blanket and struggled into his shirt. He stuck his hat back on his head, tossed the blanket into the buckboard as he passed, and followed Della into the house.

Jenny was still lying face down on the cot, but she propped her head up on her hands as he walked in, beside her lay the Jackson's baby. Reaching down, he ruffled her hair as he passed and went to sit down at the table.

"Have you told him yet?" Della asked with a chuckle as she filled a bowl with hot stew.

"Tell me what?" Gilly asked, his spoon hovering over the bowl.

"I can feel my toes, Gilly!"

"You've had no feeling in your feet since you were hurt; can you wiggle your toes, too?" he asked.

"Yes, with an effort I can wiggle them, but it hurts all the way up my legs."

"That means something's working again, maybe that bullet shook something loose."

"Will you stay and help me walk again Gilly?"

"You know why I'm here, I promised on my family's graves that I would avenge their deaths."

"Let him eat," Della coaxed gently. "I'm sure Mister Gilly knows what he has to do."

Disturbed by the noise of the conversation, the baby whimpered at Jenny's side. She held it closer until Della was ready to relieve her. As Gilly finished eating, he noisily scraped the bowl with his spoon but stopped suddenly, raising his head.

"Two riders coming!" he exclaimed, getting up and going outside.

Raising her head, Jenny listened but heard nothing. *He must have ears like a cat*, she thought, finally picking up the sound of rapidly approaching hoofs.

"Ah's here Mister Gilly," Benji's voice growled from the doorway of the barn as the Canadian stepped out into the yard to meet the riders.

Relaxing a little when he recognized the young Box T rider from the Fort Hall saloon, Gilly calmly waited. The younger man tipped his hat in acknowledgement as he reined in his horse.

"Doc Forbes gave us direction to this place sir," he began. "I'm Tom Burgers and this is my father. He owns the Box T about 10 miles south of Fort Hall. I heard you say the owner of the Half Moon spread had been bushwhacked and was here at the Jackson's place. My father would like to have a few words with her.

"This ain't a good time friend," Gilly replied, "maybe you should wait until she goes home."

"I came out here to talk to Jenny Washington boy," the older man snapped as he prepared to dismount, "and that's what I'm going to do!"

"Better just sit where you are mister," Gilly's voice held an undisguised menace. "I ain't invited you to step down yet!"

Settling back into his saddle, he stared hard at the younger man and suddenly broke into a chuckle. "Tom tells me you're another of Harvey Stubbs' gunslicks waiting for the war to begin."

"I never said that dad. I said he was fast with a gun."

"Same thing boy, nothing moves on the Half Moon spread unless Harvey condones it."

"Dad, Frank Barlow was a Half Moon hand," a now agitated Tom Burgers shouted at his father, "but this man accused him of shooting Jenny Washington. Doc Forbes heard it all, ask him yourself."

"Why don't you ask me?" Gilly stated coldly. "It might save us a lot of time."

"I've wasted enough time on this already boy. My son said we could talk some sense to the Washington girl and now we have another fool to deal with; we're leaving."

A gunshot rang out, lifting the old man's hat from his head. Cursing, Tom Burger's father fought to control his startled mount, and Benji Jackson's voice cut through the noise.

"Mister, you'd better cut out the high-and-mighty jabber, 'cos you ain't going anywhere until Mister Gilly says you can. Now suppose we start all over again. We want your name and your business with Miss Jenny or I'll drop you out of that saddle right now!"

"All right, all right!" the older man shouted. "I'm Luke Burgers and I own the Box T Ranch. My grazing land butts up to the Washington range. I want to talk about the trouble we've been having along the fenceline. Now put that damned rifle down before you kill somebody."

Inside the house, Della was watching through the window eagerly relating to Jenny what was happening in the yard. "I think Mister Gilly's coming to talk to you miss."

"What's happening out there?" Jenny demanded when Gilly met Della at the open door.

"Do you want to talk to one of your neighbours?" he asked.

"Like this?" Jenny sneered sarcastically punching the pillow in frustration. "Who are they?"

"Says he's Luke Burgers from the ranch on your south fenceline."

"Harvey says they're rustlers and fence jumpers, he's always having trouble with their riders. Yes, I'd like to give that man a piece of my mind."

"Can you stand up?"

"I don't know, I've been on this cot since you put me here."

"I think she could stand sir," Della interrupted, "but sitting would be very painful."

"Help me get her up," Gilly murmured moving to Jenny's side. "You can hold her up in the doorway."

Moving the injured ranch owner proved to be quite a task but despite her squeals of pain they eased her slowly onto her feet. Gripping tightly to their arms, she walked with surprising ease toward the door.

Jenny suddenly gasped. "My feet don't feel like lead anymore Gilly."

"Tell me later, for now just concentrate on standing up. Hold onto the doorpost and Della, I don't want you falling over."

"Any more orders sir?"

Ignoring Jenny's sarcasm, Gilly left the women standing in the doorway as he walked toward the still-mounted riders. Adjusting his hat against the sun, he finally invited the Burgers to step down.

Jenny smiled when she heard Gilly hiss at Luke Burgers, "Don't raise your voice and be disrespectful mister or you'll regret it!"

"Miss Washington," Luke Burgers began, sweeping off his hat. "It's a pleasure to see you again," he sneered.

"Well now we've got over the formalities, what is it you really want to talk about Mr. Burgers?" Jenny asked coldly, trying not to show her pain.

"Your men are cutting the fenceline, shooting my riders and running my stock onto your range."

"Harvey says the same about you and your men."

"Harvey Stubbs is a liar, he's planning to cause trouble then pick up the pieces for himself." Luke Burgers' face contorted in frustrated anger. Jamming his hat on his head, he stepped toward the door and snapped, "Damnit girl, you're a cripple, how the hell do you know what's going on out on the range?"

"Meeting's over Mr. Burgers," Gilly stated menacingly lifting his Colt from the holster. "I warned you, and if you say one more word I'll make you into a cripple. Now get out of here while you can."

Della squealed, automatically covering Jenny's body with her own as they slowly moved back into the house. Still shaking, she gently lowered her onto the cot.

"He won't shoot him Della, stop worrying. Gilly's just let the Burgers know I'm not on my own anymore."

"But he said he's leaving when he gets you back home miss, I heard him say it."

The sound of fading hoofbeats brought a smile to Jenny's face but then she winced. "Get me back onto my bed quickly Della."

Watching the riders, Gilly waited for Benji to join him and they returned to the house.

"I think you made an enemy today Benji," Gilly said flatly.

"Yes sah, but I also made a friend."

A slight nod of the head as they reached the door, told the coloured homesteader that Gilly agreed.

"I think Luke Burgers just threatened me with a range war," Jenny said as the men entered. "Do you think he was serious?"

"He was mighty angry miss," Benji offered his opinion, taking a chair and rolling his eyes.

Taking little notice, Gilly accepted a mug of coffee from Della and seemed to be lost in thought for a minute. Then he suddenly turned to Jenny and asked, "How much did it hurt?"

"What a stupid question?" Jenny snapped. "Who in their right mind would want to be at war with their neighbour?"

"Did you move your legs or shuffle?" he insisted.

"Damnit Gilly, I'm talking about a range war."

"Then don't, we'll deal with that back at the ranch. I want to know about your walking."

"It hurt a little but my legs moved." She stopped to adjust her position and a look of pleasure moved across her face. "Gilly, I'm going to walk again, I'm sure of it!"

Chapter 5

On the trail back into Fort Hall, Luke Burgers could hardly stop thinking of Gilly Thompson. Who was he, where had he come from and why was he here on the Snake River range? *Doc Forbes has been out at the Jackson homestead*, he thought, *maybe he knows more than he's admitting*. Pushing the horses harder, it was almost dark when the Burgers arrived at Fort Hall. Dismounting outside the doctor's office, Luke left his son to deal with their sweat-caked mounts. When he saw the note on the door, he cursed aloud.

Walking over to the saloon, he waited outside until his son returned from the stable. "Doc's gone out to the Box T and won't be back 'till Friday. We'll eat at the saloon and get fresh horses. I'll go order some grub; you better see to the horses."

"Are you here to eat or drink Luke?" the barman called to the rancher as he entered the almost empty room.

"Both Rolly, put two steaks on and bring us two beer."

"Have you been out to the black fella's place?" the barman asked, when he brought two pint mugs to Burger's table. "Where's Tom?"

"At the livery stable changing horses. Tell me more about that young rider who works for the Half Moon."

"You mean the one who killed Frank Barlow. He don't work for the Half Moon."

"Then who is he, you fool!"

"Doc says he's the kid who rode with Rube Caster for years."

"Rube Caster, the Placerville lawman?"

"The same and he's faster than lightning with that Colt of his. We saw him draw on Frank Barlow."

"Does he have a name?"

"Doc said he's Gilly Thompson, from up in Canada." Rolly frowned. "You should thank him Luke, Frank was just setting Tom up to kill him."

"Tom can take care of himself."

"Not against Frank Barlow he wouldn't. He was fast."

Dismissing the barman, Burgers took a long thirsty drink of his beer, thinking hard on the last few days' events. He downed the beer, but the name of Gilly Thompson kept rolling over and over in his mind, sounding familiar. He was unable to attach any significance to it. Calling for another beer as his son entered, Luke stared off into space, offering no conversation until the meal arrived.

"Why were you going to fight Frank Barlow?" he suddenly asked his son, turning to look hard at him.

"He called you a rustler."

"That's when the stranger walked in?"

"Yes sir, he sized up the situation in an instant, then drew Frank's attention off me by accusing him of bushwhacking Jenny Washington."

"I bet that got his attention."

201

"Doc tried to stop it but it all happened so fast. I just got the hell out of there."

"Do you know anyone called Thompson son?"

Tom looked thoughtful for a brief moment before he answered his father. "I know the name but I can't think who it belongs to. Why?"

"That's the stranger's name."

Riding south out of Fort Hall, despite the near darkness, they had little difficulty following the trail onto the Box T range. Both father and son had been born in these parts and knew virtually every inch of the Snake River Plains. For years they had lived in harmony with Edward Washington and his family as two pioneer families who fiercely guarded their holdings. Things had begun to go wrong, however, soon after Edward's untimely death, when his only heir, Jenny Louise was hurt.

Luke surmised that the girl would now need to sell the lease of the Half Moon range so she could go live with relatives and seek medical attention. He found out very quickly that this was not the situation and he was left trying to negotiate with the strong-willed girl. Adding to his misery, Harvey Stubbs, her father's foreman, decided to remain and help her manage the property. Jenny Louise, now supported by Harvey and her eastern relatives, beat Luke's application to have her lease revoked by the court and, sometime later, he decided to purchase the property adjoining their southern borders, at last leaving Jenny alone.

It was almost midnight when father and son rode tiredly into the Box T yard, attending to their horses before going up to the house, a stately, impressive-looking home. The first thing Luke noticed was Harry Forbes' medical bag sitting on the hall stand. Shaking his head in slight annoyance, he strode toward the living room and stood in the doorway.

"Hello Harry, what brings you out this way?"

A different scene was being played out at the Jackson homestead. Gilly suggested that Jenny try to walk a little, explaining that exercise would assist in her healing. Della offered to make a cushion from grain sacks stuffed with hay and chicken feathers so that sitting would be more comfortable. Eager to try, Jenny asked for help to stand up.

Gilly shook his head and whispered grimly, "No girl, you're going to have to sort it out for yourself, you ain't no cripple anymore."

"I can't do it on my own," Jenny whined. "You'll have to help me."

"No, I won't," Gilly snapped. "You can help yourself now. You've played on folks' sympathy long enough."

Della gasped at Gilly's harshness and moved in to help.

"Don't touch her!" his voice barked, stopping Della in mid-stride. "She can do it."

"You animal!" Jenny hissed, but she grit her teeth and grimaced as she slid her leg slowly over the side of the cot, screaming as it reached the earth floor. She raised her tear-stained face and shouted, "Someday I'm going to kill you Gilly Thompson!"

"All right, I'll help you Miss Cripple." Gilly stood up and moved toward her, his jaw set.

"Don't you dare touch me, you … you fiend. I'll manage without *your* help!"

Della turned away, unable to watch, as tears welled in her eyes and, at that moment, Benji entered, looking puzzled by the scene. He tried to console Della as Jenny got herself painfully into position, groaning softly as she eased her first leg over the side of the cot by holding onto it. They could all see that the pain was excruciating for her as her cheeks got red and tears streamed down her face, but she barely uttered a sound. Her second leg flopped down to meet the first and, as it did so, she lost her balance and toppled out of the cot onto the floor screaming pitifully, yet only briefly.

As the others watched spellbound, she pushed herself up onto her knees and crawled inch-by-inch until she was within reach of the doorway. Reaching out toward the door frame, she cursed under her breath and stretched even farther, clawing at the frame with her fingernails. Then, with one determined effort, she grasped the frame with one hand and then the other. Groaning with effort, she pulled herself forward and upright, screaming as she pulled each leg in line until they held her weight.

Gilly moved quickly to her side and held her.

"I did it, Gilly. I did it!" she whispered, beginning to cry as she turned to face him. She wrapped her arms around his waist and he felt her body sag against his.

Scooping her up in his arms, he called over his shoulder, "Bring some blankets and a lantern, Della."

Striding across the yard with Della hurrying behind him, Gilly stopped at the buckboard and ordered her to spread out the blankets under the wagon. "Can you crawl under there?" he whispered in Jenny's ear. "You can hang onto me until you get in the right position."

Offering no resistance when he lowered her feet to the ground, she clutched the side of the buckboard, slowly settling onto her knees and then crawled onto the blankets.

"You can leave the lantern Della," Gilly murmured. "We'll be in for breakfast in the morning before we leave."

"That was cruel!" Della complained to her husband when she returned to the house. "Why didn't you help her?"

"Mister Gilly was trying to prove a point ... to Miss Jenny," he replied. "He was acting like he didn't care but he cares a lot. He needed to prove to her she could move on her own. Some day she'll thank him for that."

"There had to be a better way," Della muttered, going to the sink.

Outside, Gilly sat with his back to the buckboard wheel, his rifle resting across his outstretched legs, as he listened to Jenny's breathing.

Feeling her hand on his back, she whispered tiredly, "Gilly Thompson, I don't know if I should love or hate you!"

Gilly made no effort to answer, patiently waiting until her rhythmic breathing told him she was asleep and he moved off to climb his tree.

Light rain, pushed by a gentle breeze, swept across the Snake River Plains just as dawn was breaking, partially waking Jenny when a drip of cold water found its way through the buckboard's floor to splash on her face. Without opening her eyes, her hand felt through the wheel for the reassuring touch of Gilly's back, and was instantly awake when she realized he wasn't there. Raising her head, she sleepily searched the yard, seeing only Benji busy at his morning chores.

"Now where have you gone?" she said aloud, easing her body away from the dripping water.

"I'm here girl," Gilly's voice spoke softly behind her. "Do you need the outhouse?"

"Yes."

"Then crawl out, I'll help you stand up and we can walk over there together."

Offering no argument, Jenny grit her teeth and raised herself awkwardly onto her knees, crawling painfully out from under the buckboard.

"Oh that rain feels good," she gasped, accepting Gilly's hand and willing herself into a standing position.

"Can you feel your legs?" he asked.

"Yes, they're tingling and, I can move them, but my back is very sore."

"And so it should be. That's a bullet burn you've got back there. It's only luck that stopped you from being killed."

"But why would a Half Moon rider want to kill me?"

204

"The only reason I can think of is Harvey told him to do it. I thought you wanted to go to the outhouse."

"I do."

"Then shut up jabbering and concentrate on your legs, we don't have all day."

Watching from the tiny window of the house as she held the baby, Della's pulse quickened when she realized Jenny was actually walking. *Has Gilly been right forcing her to make the effort?* she wondered. Continuing to watch with fascinated interest, she caught her breath when she saw the girl stumble and watched as Gilly's arm flashed around her waist. Suddenly she realized Benji was right—the cowboy's show of uncaring cruelty had only been a ploy to make Jenny angry enough to prove she could walk.

"It's going to be painful sitting," Gilly muttered as they arrived at the outhouse door.

"I know, but I have to find a way."

Walking a few feet away from the door, he stared across the yard until Jenny let out a shriek, cursing fluently. Unsure of how to react, he returned close to the door and kicked at the dust as he waited. In a few minutes, he heard Jenny chuckle behind him.

"What's the matter Gilly? You didn't offer to help me!"

"Save yer breath for walking!" he snapped.

The smell of breakfast cooking and Della's off-key singing took them back to the house. "I made you a cushion, Miss Jenny," the coloured woman giggled, pointing to a chair with a big fat grain sack on top. "Ah recon you might be able to sit, if you're careful."

Benji arrived with some fresh eggs in his hat and smiled as he took his place at the table, motioning impatiently for Gilly to sit. Sighing, Jenny cautiously negotiated her behind onto the cushion, settling slowly as everyone waited for her reaction.

"Not bad Della, at least I feel more normal," she chuckled nervously, glancing at the men. "I dare say I could drive the buckboard if you let me take it with me."

"Glory be, Miss Jenny. You can have it with my blessing," Della beamed. "Now eat your breakfast while it's warm."

There was a mood of success in the Jackson home that morning as the rain stopped and the sun seemed to chase the dark clouds away.

Twelve miles to the south, an argument was raging at the Box T ranchhouse. Tom Burgers was telling his mother about Jenny Washington and Gilly Thompson, when his father rose angrily to his feet.

"That's ranch business," his father roared across the table. "Your mother doesn't want to know."

"Yes I do, Luke Burgers, and stop shouting at the breakfast table." Tom's mother replied sternly. "I want to know more about Jenny. Is she still in a wheelchair son?"

"Yes she is, but it's the man she's with that's upsetting father."

"You mean Harvey Stubbs?"

"No, he's a young man and very protective of her."

"He's a gunman and a killer," Luke interrupted fiercely. "He shot a Half Moon rider in the Fort Hall saloon."

"I told you why dad," Tom argued. "Gilly Thompson accused Frank Barlow of bushwhacking Jenny Washington."

"Has Jenny been hurt again?" Mabel Burgers gasped in horror.

"Yes, mother, but not by this fella. She's all right," Tom assured her. "We rode over to the Jackson's place on the Half Moon range, where she's staying, and dad tried to bully her."

"Now I understand why your father is so angry this morning," Mabel murmured. "Mr. Thompson must have put a stop to your father's natural instincts."

"Yes, he chased us off the property," Tom admitted, looking over at his father.

"Nobody chases me anywhere!" Luke bellowed crashing his coffee mug onto the table.

"Oh for goodness' sake, stop it Luke. Did you find out who this young man is, because the only Thompsons I know are in that little graveyard at the burned-out homesteaders' place—on that land you bought when our southern neighbours moved away."

"That's the place you take flowers to, ain't it Mom?"

"Yes, and I had the markers replaced last year as well."

"How did you know who they were Mabel?" Luke asked, frowning.

"County records show a family named Thompson had a homesteaders' title to the place, but never proved it."

"When I bought it from Simpson, there was no homesteaders' title on any of that land; they must have moved on long before I bought the range lease."

"No Luke, I think they're still there. That place was burnt to the ground and three wooden crosses marked three graves."

"You think old man Simpson did it, mom?"

"Most likely his foreman and some of his ranchhands went to move them off the land and things got out of hand. Would you fight son, if someone came to put us out?"

"Well mom, let me tell you the real story of what happened in the Fort Hall saloon," Tom murmured quietly. "It was me Frank Barlow was intending to kill that day. He accused us of rustling Half Moon cattle and breaking down their fences, so I called him a liar."

"And you stupidly let him draw you into a gunfight son?" his father snorted.

"It was you he was insulting Dad and, I couldn't stand for that, could I?"

"But you could have gotten yourself killed son," his mother gasped.

"I know," Tom sighed, "but Gilly Thompson walked into the saloon and pulled Frank's attention away from me. He butted into the conversation by accusing Frank of bushwhacking Jenny Washington."

"You think he did it to save you?"

"I think he was ready to kill Frank for shooting Jenny, but he seemed to have heard what was happening and decided I was no match for Frank."

"He's a gunfighter and a killer," Luke snorted. "I wouldn't be surprised is he was one of Harvey's crew."

"Don't be absurd Dad," Tom argued. "Even Harvey Stubbs wouldn't start a fight between his own men."

"I'd like to meet this man," Mabel remarked with a sigh. "Ride over to the coloured folks' place Tom, and ask Gilly Thompson to bring Jenny to see me. It's high time we contacted that girl. After all, she is our neighbour."

"You will not invite that man onto my land!" Luke shouted.

Tom agreed with his father by nodding vigorously. "She's just as bad as he is mom. We want nothing to do with the Half Moon spread."

Mabel Burgers smiled at her son, motioning for him to leave and follow her request. Luke scowled angrily as he watched their son leave. He was well used to his wife's steadying and common-sense attitude, a true contrast to his own rough, range-bred persona. As an educated lady from an old southern family, she had fallen in love with him when he was an exciting young rancher. For 25 years, she had endured the boredom of range life, with only distant neighbours for company and an occasional visit to the city.

"You were once proud to be the Washington's friend Luke."

"That was a long time ago Mabel, that daughter of his was mighty strong-willed and we never could see eye-to-eye."

"We neglected our duty when Edward died and Jenny Louise was hurt. Why didn't we go to her assistance?" Mabel asked with concern. "We were their closest neighbours."

"Harvey Stubbs was her foreman. That girl inherited everything and he ran the ranch for her. It was months before Doc Forbes told us she'd always be a cripple. Now leave it alone woman, you've done enough damage already sending Tom back there."

Tom made his preparations at the cookhouse, packing food into his saddlebags for the three-day trip. Using the horses from the Fort Hall livery stable, he intended to return them as he passed through town. Tom was born to the range and, at home in the saddle more than any other place; he loved the open space of the plains. It was almost two hours later when he saw a buggy approaching and recognized the hunched-over shape of the Fort Hall doctor.

"Are you going out to our place Doc?" he asked as they came abreast.

"Not today son," Harry Forbes replied. "I thought I'd ride down to the old Spencer place. Your dad still has a crew working from there, doesn't he?"

"Yes sir, 10 men and a foreman in the bunkhouse. Old Pokey York's in the cookhouse, he'll be glad to see you."

"If he is, it'll be a first," Harry chuckled, "he's never been glad to see anybody I ever knew."

Riding away, Tom wondered why doc found it necessary to go to the old Spencer ranch. There was nothing of interest out there. Hunger touched his stomach as he rode into town. It was very quiet as he rode down the muddy main street of Fort Hall, making straight for the livery stable. He paid his bill, switched the saddle to his own mount and led both horses across the street to the hitching rail in front of the saloon. Glancing along the boardwalk, he noted two sweat-stained mounts with star brands on their shoulders at the rail.

Remembering quickly that Frank Barlow had once ridden for the Morgan Brothers at the Star Ranch near Soda Springs, Tom forgot his hunger and quietly left, walking the horses to the edge of town before mounting. As he did so, he looked around to make sure he hadn't been followed, then galloped off at a mile-eating speed. Urgency spurred him on and he changed horses along the trail to save time.

"Rider coming fast," Benji yelled from the barn.

"You stay inside," Gilly ordered the women, "until we see who it is." He went outside and observed the obvious cloud of dust coming quickly over the hill toward them. He adjusted his hat, slipped the tie down from the hammer of his Colt and went to retrieve the rifle he'd left propped against the wall. As he moved out into the yard to meet the rider, Jenny showed her own concern and determination by easing herself onto her feet and slowly walking to the open door using furniture and walls for support. Grasping the door frame, as soon as she gained her balance, she reached for the spare rifle.

"Don't do it, Miss Jenny!" Della pleaded.

Tom slowed the horses to a walk, making sure his hands were visible to Gilly as he pulled up and waited for an invitation to step down. His trained eye had already noticed the coloured man at the barn but Jenny was hidden in the shadows.

"Can I talk to Miss Washington sir?" he asked as Gilly approached. "My mother has sent me with a personal invitation to visit her."

"Your father can't be too pleased with that request," Gilly commented. "Why don't you step down and go ask her? She's stood right there at the door. I ain't her keeper!"

Tying both horses to the corral rail, Tom moved cautiously toward the little house, removing his hat in surprise when he saw Jenny holding the rifle.

"I-I thought you were a cripple!" he stammered. "I-I wondered when we were here earlier but the lady was holding you up and I didn't want to aggravate my father any further. Folks said you were bound to a wheelchair, ma'am."

"What is it you want Mr. Burgers?" Jenny snapped, increasing his nervousness when she slowly raised the rifle barrel to point directly at his belly.

"I came to invite you to visit with my mother. She would very much like to see you again and feels badly that she hasn't done this sooner."

"Hell boy, your father accuses me of being a rustler and your mother wants to have tea with me! What am I supposed to think?" she asked.

"Well ma'am, I know you'd like my mother; you won't remember her but she's certainly a lady even if my father does tend to be a bully at times."

"Your invitation includes Gilly I assume?"

"Yes, it certainly does ma'am."

"Supper's ready miss," Della's voice came from inside the house. "Call Benji and Gilly, Miss Jenny, and bring that young man inside. I'm sure he can do with a meal too."

Gilly and Benji were standing near the porch by now and heard Della's announcement. While Tom waited to be directed to a chair, he watched Della with undisguised interest as she took two pillows from one of the chairs, banging them together to fluff up the contents. Jenny took Gilly's arm and he helped her walk to that chair before Della handed her the baby so she could serve up the meal.

"Can we visit the Box T, Gilly, before you take me home?" Jenny asked later, as Benji cleared the dishes away.

Nodding silently, Gilly turned his attention to Tom Burgers and asked, "How many men ride for your father?"

"Fourteen, I think, 10 at the ranch and four on the fenceline. Why?"

"I'll need to look them over."

"Gilly Thompson," Jenny interrupted sharply, "this is a social visit, not a killing mission!"

Rising from his chair, Gilly sent her an icy stare and reached for his hat. "We leave at dawn, and remember my promise," he hissed, going outside.

"Where's he going?" Tom asked.

"To find a tree and, if you need to know, he promised to take care of me until he takes me back to the Half Moon."

"Ain't you scared of him, Miss Jenny?"

"No Mr. Burgers, I ain't. He's the only man I'd trust with my life. He's a man who lives by his word and he's also a man with a mission. Now, I'm sure the Jacksons won't mind if you bed down in their barn for the night."

Daylight was already fading as they went out onto the porch, while Gilly, who was ahead of them, stood still to sniff the cooling air before he crossed the yard. He stopped suddenly, slowly turning his head to face an alarming smell which his sensitive nose had detected ... he knew it well, it was a bear! Automatically feeling for his Colt, he cautiously moved toward it. Following the odour through two paddocks of young, growing crops, he frowned as he now detected a second distinct scent—that of Jenny Washington.

Puzzled and, exceedingly concerned, even though he knew Jenny was on the porch, instinct now told him that the bear was very close. Leaping forward, he began to yelp like an Indian on the warpath, succeeding to startle the animal that crashed through the small stand of timber and escaped. Now, sniffing the darkness again, he followed Jenny's scent to a blanket lying on the ground. Feeling the heavy, woven material in his hand, he sighed and swung it over his shoulder, carefully making his way back the way he had come, until he reached the house.

"What's going on out there?" Benji called from the lighted doorway. "Is you all right Mister Gilly?"

"Yes, but you two make perfect targets standing with the light behind you. Damnit Tom, you should know better than that, get away from the door. Your horses are gone. There was a bear checking the

210

place out. He's gone now too, but not before he picked up Jennie's scent on the blanket under the buckboard."

"Oh my word!" exclaimed Jenny, coming to the doorway. "He's torn it almost to shreds! I'm not sleeping outside tonight."

"That bear was here a month ago. Ah thought ah'd scared him off," Benji moaned. "Ah didn't have the heart to kill the little fella. I'm awful glad no one were hurt."

"Dad's going to be as mad as a tick on a dog's back when the horses come home on their own," Tom muttered. "I don't seem to be having much luck these days."

"Too late to worry about that," Gilly replied, "you can ride with Jenny on the buckboard. I'll track the horses as we go in the morning."

Jenny again said she didn't want to sleep outside so Della offered to make her a bed on the floor, if she could get up.

"I'll do anything but sleep outside with the bears!" she declared.

It was not long before dawn when Gilly entered the house and woke Jenny. Groaning softly as she stretched the cramped muscles of her legs, she allowed Gilly to pull her to her feet and walk her to the outhouse while Della tended to the baby. Smells from the kitchen told them that breakfast was already cooking and things were moving along toward Gilly's desired early start.

The first rays of sunshine were spreading their warming rays across the plains as Gilly lifted Jenny onto Della's pillowed seat, handed her the reins and glanced over at Tom, climbing up beside her. Gilly's eyes gave their unspoken warning for Tom to take good care of her.

"I'll be right behind you," he muttered stepping up into the saddle of his eager mount.

Riding out past the paddocks where he had tracked the bear, Gilly soon picked up the signs of the animal's headlong flight through the heavy undergrowth. He followed for another 15 minutes until the gelding snorted loudly and slowed to a walk. Slipping from the saddle, he sniffed the air before cautiously moving ahead. The bear was close by, he could smell it. Peering ahead, he spied the dark mound under a tree about 150 feet away. Watching suspiciously for the slightest movement, he wasn't ready to assume the animal was dead so he cautiously approached.

As he neared the animal, its stillness gave him a slight pang of regret and, seeing no blood or obvious wound, he briefly wondered what had happened. Approaching only close enough to be sure, he retreated by widening the circle, until he picked up the Box T horses' tracks and followed them into the foothills. Within minutes, he reached the top of the ridge and had Tom's horses in sight. Skittish but easily caught, he fastened them on a lead line and took off after the buckboard. Cutting across country, he made good time over the next ridge and into the hills. Following a deer track through a boulder-filled pass, he emerged on the trail to Fort Hall. As he neared town, he searched the road for fresh buckboard tracks until he was sure Tom and Jenny were still behind him.

Leaving the horses at the livery stable with instructions to groom and feed them, Gilly made his way up the street to the saloon.

"How come you got Luke Burgers' horse and a spare at the livery stable mister?" the barman asked.

"Are you nosey by habit or choice?" Gilly hissed. "Order me a steak and trimmings, and I'll have a beer."

"I'd like to hear you answer that question, mister!" a young cowboy asked from the end of the bar. "Luke thinks that gelding's pretty special."

As the barman put Gilly's beer onto the table a noise outside suggested someone was arriving and the barman nervously hurried away. Heavy footsteps sounded outside and the batwing doors burst inwards as Tom entered carrying Jenny. Putting her down near one of the back tables, he absorbed the scene while she got her balance yet chose to remain standing. Tom turned to face the cowboy at the end of the bar.

"You think this is a good day to die Billy?" Tom asked angrily as the boy eased away from the bar. "What the hell are ya doing? Isn't my father keeping you busy enough or has he sent you to spy on me now?"

"He's got your dad's gelding down at the livery on a lead rope Tom," Billy retorted by way of defending himself.

"How the hell did you know that?"

"The kid from the livery ran up to tell Rolly," Billy said quickly.

Watching Tom vent his anger on his father's own employee, Jenny glanced down the room at Gilly who was calmly drinking his beer. He showed no indication he was either interested or involved in the altercation until the beer was finished, and then, he suddenly pushed the mug away from him.

"That's enough Tom!" his voice shot through the room with an icy blast. "He was trying to defend his employer's interests. Let him be."

Leaving Tom shouting his last angry words at the young cowboy, Jenny walked slowly down the room calling to the barman as she approached Gilly's table. "Bring us two coffees, barman."

"Are you going to sit down?" Gilly asked her as Tom joined them.

"We're going to have something to eat, Mr. Thompson, and I'm going to perch delicately on one corner of my arse, if that answers your question."

"You would have killed him," Tom moaned as he joined them.

"No," said Gilly.

"Billy was set to brace you."

"Tom, it was just talk; he still had the tie down on his Colt."

The barman brought Gilly's steak and took Jenny and Tom's order. Eating hungrily, Gilly finished first and left the others walking slowly down the street to the livery stable. He recovered the Box T horses and waited patiently at the hitching rail until his companions left the saloon. Mounted again, Tom rode off, leaving Gilly to accompany Jenny and the buckboard the rest of the way to the Box T.

Chapter 6

The day dragged on as they passed many fine cattle grazing on the plains. They stopped once to rest the horses and allow Jenny to stretch her aching legs. It was late in the afternoon when Gilly pointed out the buildings in the distance and Jenny suddenly felt a moment of indecision and slowed the buckboard. Gilly quickly turned Blue alongside.

"Don't you go getting scared of meeting these folks now," he ordered gently. "You're as normal as they are. It's just a visit to your neighbours."

"You won't leave me alone with them will you Gilly?"

"Courage lady, Tom will be there. He won't let 'em hurt ya."

"You said I was your responsibility and I'm going to hold you to that."

"You don't have to; I gave you my word. Now shake some speed into that nag, they're waiting for us!"

Galloping ahead, Gilly dismounted in front of the four people waiting on the porch, acknowledging no one as he turned his back on them and went to meet the buckboard.

"Did I ask you to step down mister?" Luke Burgers' voice snapped

Ignoring the ranchman's unfriendly gesture, Gilly caught the bridle of the buckboard horse and led it to the fence. He fastened the lead rope as he watched Jenny push her unruly hair under her hat. Only then did he turn to face the Box T Ranch owner.

"We're here at the invitation of your wife and son sir, and if that gripes your innards, you can take it up with them or me. The choice is yours." The Canadian cowboy's voice was flat and even, and not a trace of emotion showed on his face. He slipped the tie down from his Colt and levelled his eyes on the senior Burgers.

"Luke Burgers you still have the manners of a bucking horse!" his wife snapped. "These people are invited guests."

213

Gilly helped to release the tension when he turned away to lift Jenny down from the buckboard. Pushing his arms away when she reached the ground, she struggled shakily to keep her balance.

"Mr. Burgers, there ain't one cent of difference between you and Harvey Stubbs," she shouted angrily at the Box T owner. "You both think I'm a cripple of body and mind. But you'd better take note sir, there's a new man on the Snake River rangeland and he's looking out for me!"

"Are you threatening me young lady?" Luke replied.

"No Dad, she's not," Tom intervened. "I think she's warning you sir, because Gilly Thompson won't put up with your pompous crap!"

"Enough of this nonsense," Mabel interrupted, raising her voice. "I don't want to hear another word out of either of you. Jenny Washington is my guest and Doc Forbes would like to talk to Mr. Thompson. Now go away and spend your bad tempers somewhere else. Miss Washington, please come inside out of the heat and join me for a little refreshment."

A smile creased Harry Forbes' face as he listened to Luke being berated by his wife. In the many years he'd known Luke and Mabel, he had never heard her raise her voice in anger at Luke, or to even disagree with him in public. *Why has she chosen this moment to make a stand?* he wondered, then a myriad of thoughts coursed through his head. *Tom finally found some backbone when confronting his father. Was it the sight of Jenny without her wheelchair or the threat of Gilly Thompson's reputation that had caused the sudden revolt in Luke Burgers' family?*

"Could I take your arm please sir," Jenny asked, beaming up at the Canadian.

Feeling betrayed by his family's reaction, Luke brushed his son aside and stormed off the porch. Gilly offered his arm, and he and Jenny walked slowly up the path to the house. She painfully climbed the steps trying very hard not to lean obviously on him.

Leading the way into the house, Mabel showed them into a room that Jenny thought must be the most beautiful parlour in all of Montana. She offered Jenny a seat in a comfortable-looking upholstered armchair but the girl panicked a little as she began to sit down, glancing quickly up at Gilly as she gripped his arm. Tom came to the rescue with an armful of cushions and she relaxed, letting go of Gilly. Looking inquiringly at the strange procedure, Mabel's eyes begged an explanation.

"She was shot by Frank Barlow," Tom whispered to his mother. "Sitting is rather painful."

"Does your father know about this Tom?"

"He knows Gilly killed Frank in the Fort Hall saloon," Tom replied.

"I was there Mabel," Doc Forbes interrupted from the doorway. "If Gilly hadn't arrived when he did, your son would be dead!"

"Tom, go tell the cook we're ready for the sandwiches and coffee." Mabel appeared a bit shaken by the doctor's statement and, after a brief hesitation, she looked up at the men with shining eyes. "Gentlemen, I kindly ask you to please leave us now as we ladies have much to talk about."

After a cup of coffee in another room with Tom and Doc Forbes, Gilly became bored with their chatter and wandered outside. He sat on the porch rail, letting his eyes roam over the well-kept buildings and checking out any Box T rider who passed close by. He was joined a little later by the doctor who pointed out the distant landmarks with his pipe stem; the Smoky Mountains in the west and hot springs to the south, carefully watching Gilly's facial expression for any sign of recognition.

"You said you were a Canadian son," Harry coughed through his pipe smoke. "How'd ya know that?"

"Rube told me."

"I knew Rubin Caster many years before you did lad."

"Careful Doc, Rube was special to me."

"Oh I ain't about to bad mouth him son. All I'm doing is trying to tell you I think you're an American not a Canadian."

This time he saw Gilly's eyes show a glimmer of interest and he slipped off the porch rail and turned his full attention on the doctor, waiting for him to continue.

"Would you tell me all you can remember before Rube got ya? How old you were, where you lived—anything that would pinpoint the place."

"Why the hell are you so interested Doc?"

"Because you intrigue me, and I think I know who you are. Rube found you after your farm was raided and burned, didn't he? A long time ago, we found two dead cowboys and three new graves out at one of the homesteads southwest of here, but no one seemed able or willing to explain what had happened. Neither Jake Simpson nor his riders would talk about it."

"Jake Simpson," Gilly whispered.

"Yes, Simpson had the Broken Star Ranch. Luke Burgers owns it now. It's all part of the Box T range."

"You have proof of all this?"

"I have my diary and Tom's mother went and checked the county records to find out who they were. She's had headstones erected and has been taking flowers out there for the last 10 years."

215

"Frank, Lydia and Cassy Thompson," Gilly whispered. "They were my parents and my sister. It happened almost 14 years ago. Will you take me there in the morning sir?"

"Yes I will son."

There was a dampness in Gilly's eyes as he turned and left the porch, walking quickly toward the outbuildings as doc watched.

I might be an old country doctor but it all makes sense now, doc reasoned. *Gilly's on a mission of vengeance and it all started right here on the Snake River Plains.*

"Where's Gilly?" Jenny asked when the doctor came into the parlour. "We have some news for him."

"I told her about the burned-out farm and the Thompson gravesite on the old Simpson property," Mabel murmured emotionally.

"I just told him as well," Harry muttered. "We're going out there in the morning, but I think he needs to be alone for a while. He's walked down toward the bunkhouse."

"Oh no, you must stop him," Jenny gasped in alarm. "He's going to check out your riders for the last man who he knows killed his family."

"I can't stop him but it's going to be all right Jenny." Tom now joined them on the porch and tried to reassure her. "You don't have to worry. There are none of old man Simpson's crew in our bunkhouse."

"How does he know who he's searching for?" Mabel asked.

"Their faces are burned in his memory. He was there and watched it all as a nine-year-old," said Jenny.

"Oh my, I'm not surprised he's out for revenge," Mabel declared. "I think I would be too."

A single tear rolled down Gilly's cheek as he walked toward the barn. His conversation with Doc Forbes had stirred up the old terror-filled memories that had haunted him for so many years. He wiped the tear away nonchalantly. It now brought back in vivid detail the faces he had been searching for so long. Now, the realization that he had found the location of his family's graves was almost more than he could bear.

Clenching his fists, he checked the barn and found Blue and the Half Moon horse, clean, brushed and standing contentedly munching on hay. He relaxed slightly until a gruff voice came out of the dim light.

"That horse is carrying a brand I'm not familiar with mister."

"Circle X, a long way north of here," Gilly replied amiably. "Are all your riders in?"

"Yep they're in the cookhouse ah reckon," the old stableman replied, grinning an almost toothless grin as he limped out of the stall and into the light. "Why don't ya come for a coffee with the boys?"

216

It was an invitation Gilly could hardly refuse, a chance to look the whole bunkhouse crew over with only the fenceline riders missing. Walking slowly to keep pace with the old stableman, Gilly could hear the laughter from the cookhouse as they approached.

"Are you the only one left from the old days?" he asked the old man.

"What old days?"

"Oh, the days when ranchhands set fire to homesteaders' farms."

"Hey, you hold it one minute sonny," Walt Horn snapped. "This spread ain't never been part of anything like that."

Knowing he'd hit a nerve, Gilly continued, "Were you around when Simpson ran the Broken Star, south of here?"

"I been here over 20 years son and I knew every rider Simpson ever had on his payroll."

"How long since you busted that leg?"

"Almost 15 years, ah think," Walt growled, turning to face the Canadian as he opened the cookhouse door. "Is there something you're trying to get at lad?" he demanded loudly.

"Yes sir, why don't you step inside?"

Silence settled over the cookhouse even before they entered. The last piece of their conversation had been overheard, just as Walt intended, and the boys eagerly waited for the young stranger's answer. Closing the door behind them, Gilly stood for a moment allowing his eyes to become accustomed to the low light as he silently scanned the room.

"Do you remember the fire at the Thompson place about 14 years ago?" Gilly asked, again directing his question at old Walt. "I believe it was on the Simpson range."

"Yes I do, it was some months after I broke this leg. Luke went mad and damn near got into a gunfight with Jacob Simpson. They were never friends again after that."

Dismissing the conversation, Walt called for two coffees from the cook before introducing Gilly to the crew.

"Hey, ain't you the dude that rode in with the crippled Washington girl?" called one of the men from the next table. "It must be fun travelling with a girl who can't run away!"

Walt and some of the others laughed but Gilly raised his eyes coldly to fasten on the speaker. The laughter slowly subsided into a poignant silence and they watched the Canadian stand up and slip the tie down from the Colt on his hip. The cook's nervousness added to the tension when he dropped two of the tin mugs he was collecting.

"Mister," Gilly's voice hissed, "being a cripple ain't funny, and if you ever talk about Miss Washington like that again, you'd better have a gun strapped on and be prepared to use it." Backing up, he left the cookhouse, closing the door behind him and returning to the barn, relieved that so far he hadn't seen any of the faces he searched for.

"He's coming back," Tom whispered to Jenny and his mother about 10 minutes later, seeing the shadowy shape of Gilly coming up the road toward them, his horse following behind him.

"Are we leaving?" Jenny asked in surprise.

"You ain't. You're sleeping here tonight."

"I'm coming with you."

"No you ain't. This is one place I'm going alone."

"You're going out to Thompson Flats aren't ya?" Tom murmured. "It's not easy to find, maybe I should go with you."

"No you shouldn't son," Mabel whispered, "and you're staying here too Jenny. I think Mr. Thompson needs to be alone for a while and we can only hope that he will be sensible when he is."

"Oh please don't go Gilly," Jenny begged, trying to stand.

Gilly moved to her side and sat her back down. His gesture was firm and gentle but his emotionless expression frightened her and she looked helplessly at Mabel and Tom as Gilly turned back toward the door. The Burgers began to follow him outside but Mabel silently put her hand on her son's arm and he returned to stay with Jenny.

"Thanks for understanding Mrs. Burgers," Gilly mumbled as they reached the door then, without a backward glance, he mounted and rode away into the failing light.

Tom had helped Jenny walk across the room and now listened to the hoofbeats as they raced away. Jenny could keep her emotion in check no longer and burst into tears. Mabel went to console her and they finally persuaded her to sit down again.

"Don't cry my dear, he'll be back," Mabel predicted. "He's fonder of you than he's able to admit right now. His mind is simply too far away."

Riding southwest, Gilly felt the freedom of the open rangeland allowing Blue to pick his own way. After an hour or so, he topped a ridge, the moon broke free of the clouds, and he saw the dark shapes of sleeping cattle below. He sensed he was close to his destination and urged the gelding forward, slowly making their way off the ridge and onto the flatland.

The sound of running water brought him to a halt, as a memory crashed through his mind and the pain of that fateful night twisted his heart into knots. He found the well still intact and let his hands explore the now-frayed rope. He found an old bucket tied to the end and began to sob, knowing it was the one he'd used as a boy. Jerking himself away, he

218

walked slowly to the tree that had been his refuge, the place where Rube had found him. He fell against it and took his first action of revenge, silently kicking it time after time as he sobbed his family's names and begged them to forgive him.

When he was able to calm down, he looked around and found three small dark mounds marked by fancy stone grave markers. Mabel Burgers had looked after them just as Tom had said. Dropping to his knees, he pulled off his hat and twisted it violently in his hands. For the first time in a long time, he felt the searing pain of remembrance—the happy voice of his younger sister at play, the harsh grumbling of his tired, overworked father, and his mother's soft patient voice and gentle touch. Standing up, Gilly squared his shoulders and stared at the three graves.

"I came home ...," he whispered, crumpling to the ground.

It was almost dawn when Jenny heard the hoofbeats and knew he was back. "Gilly," she murmured aloud, rolling to the edge of the bed and struggling to a sitting position. She stood up and, holding onto anything she could find, she made her way to the window. Darkness restricted a clear view of the stable and barn, but a single lantern swung over the stable doorway and its light illuminated the dim shapes of cowboys preparing their mounts for the day. Opening the window, she sniffed the air like she had often seen Gilly do. She grimaced when the strong aroma of fresh horse droppings filled her nostrils.

Lighting a lamp, she reached for her clothes then stopped and momentarily let her fingers explore the drying crust where the bushwhacker's bullet had burned a track across her back. She sighed and carefully stepped into her skirt, pulling it up over her sore backside. She sat down again on the bed and began pulling on her boots, threading her foot first into one boot and then the other, groaning each time she moved. Once the boots were on, excitement gripped her as she finished dressing and made her way quietly out to the hallway and ever so slowly down the wide stairway.

Reaching the main floor, she listened for any sound of people moving about. Hearing none, she took her coat from the hallway closet, blew out the lamp leaving it inside the door and went outside. It was growing lighter now but she stumbled in her hurry, stopping to silently reprimand herself before stepping off the porch. *Can I walk that far?* she wondered, glancing down the yard toward the bunkhouse and the cookhouse. Shivering a little in the cool morning air, she gathered her coat about her and pressed on, a burning desire and sheer determination keeping her moving toward her destination.

219

The cowboys she had seen earlier were long gone but there were still several horses tied to the railing outside the cookhouse door. Wiping the sweat from her brow, she took a deep breath, pushed the door open and stepped inside.

"Holy hell, a woman!" the cook wailed, high-tailing it back to the stove.

Gilly dropped his loaded fork onto his plate with a clatter and leapt to her assistance. Without a word, he helped her over to the chair next to his, folding his coat and laying it on the seat before she sat down.

"Coffee for the lady," he demanded calmly.

"Yes sir," the cook replied, hurrying to comply now that he had regained his composure. He quickly returned with a scruffy, but clean, tin mug filled with black steaming coffee. "Sorry miss, we ain't got no china here!" he said nervously.

Realizing that he would have no idea who she was, she merely smiled sweetly at the man before turning back to Gilly. "Did you find the place you were looking for?" As she waited for his reply, she glanced around the room as several cowboys hurried to leave with coats and gunbelts in their hands.

"I found it."

"Would you like a plate of breakfast miss?" cook asked from across the room. Seeing her nod, he quickly served up a plate, not as full as he gave the men, and took it over to the table, rounding up some cutlery at the same time. He put them down in front of Jenny.

Gilly silently watched her eat and the thought passed his mind that he enjoyed watching her. She was half-finished when he finally spoke again. "How did you know I was back?"

"I sniffed the air like you do and smelt ya," she said flippantly, keeping her voice down. "Didn't you know you smell just like fresh horse droppings ... from a distance that is!" She put her hand over her mouth and giggled.

It was the first time she'd seen Gilly's expression change so spontaneously. The stern cold eyes of the previously angry man now lost their icy glare and his lips slowly twisted into an amazing smile.

"My goodness, I think you might be human after all!" Jenny laughed, unable to take her eyes off his face.

It was at that moment Tom burst into the cookhouse.

"Thank goodness I've found you!" he gasped. "Mother's going frantic. She said Jenny was gone and is worrying that you're out looking for you ... I mean him!"

"I was," the girl laughed. "Now please go tell her I found him Tom!"

Nodding, Tom hurried off to set his mother's mind at rest. Jenny ate a bit more of her breakfast, washing it down with some coffee. She stood up and Gilly moved quickly to help her. She linked his arm and they went outside, slowly walking up to the house. They reached the porch to find Mabel waiting for them, looking none too pleased.

Their hostess glared in annoyance and told them she had searched the house and garden after taking tea up to Jenny's room and finding her guest missing. "I sent Tom out to look for you worried that you had somehow gone out after him. I'm so glad Gilly came back before you did something rash."

"Don't you know better than to wander around in the dark young lady?" asked Tom.

"I woke early and heard Gilly ride in, it wasn't dark."

"You could have waited until breakfast to talk to him."

"No ma'am, I needed to be with him."

"Why?" she asked, looking at the girl curiously, totally aware she was putting her guest on the spot.

"Damned if I know," Jenny muttered, surprised with herself for her spoken revelation. "I-I just feel safe when he's around."

"Leave 'em be woman, yer fussing like a broody hen!" her husband's voice barked from the doorway. "Cook's had breakfast ready for over an hour but the rest of you have eaten in the cookhouse it seems," he chuckled. "I'll come sit with you my dear, and the boys can go get the horses ready. Doc got called back to town so Tom and his mother will be taking you out to the old Thompson place Gilly. Jenny would you like to sit and have a cup of tea …."

The boys went outside and Gilly looked curiously over at Tom who merely raised his eyebrows and smiled as they went down the steps. He was obviously used to his father's changing moods. Tom slapped Gilly on the back and they headed for the barn.

Chapter 7

The sun was already warming the Snake River Plains by the time the buckboard pulled away from the Box T Ranch. Mabel was on the seat beside Jenny and Tom rode close by, while Gilly let the frisky gelding blow the sleep from its lungs in a joyful gallop across the grassland. Gilly did not relax his usual caution, however, letting his eyes wander warily over the terrain as the morning progressed. Two hours from the ranch, he suddenly turned and rode off toward a low ridgeline, moving out of sight of the others.

221

"Is he always this cautious?" Mabel asked, glancing nervously behind them to make sure Tom was still nearby.

"Yes, more or less. Don't worry Mrs. Burgers, we might not see him but he's out there watching us."

Just below the ridgeline, Gilly settled into a watchful position from a small stand of trees. The focus of his attention was a rider moving quickly in the same direction they were going, though oddly, he was making every attempt to keep out of sight. Gilly had been aware of him for some time, but why was he trying to pass the buckboard undetected?

Unobserved, Gilly crossed the ridge and raced along the hillside, crossing back over when he was sure he was well in front of Tom and the buckboard. Easing his Winchester out from its scabbard, he deliberately walked his mount into the oncoming rider's view and carefully observed his reaction. Slowing, the rider prepared for the meeting, cautiously releasing his rifle and laying it across his lap. It was then Gilly recognized the rider as Luke Burgers.

"Are you planning some mischief Mr. Burgers?" he asked in a cold, emotionless voice.

"No boy, I wanted to make sure no one was at the Thompson place waiting for you."

"No one knows I'm going there, except you."

"Yes they do. I told all the riders at the old Simpson bunkhouse last night. You got me so damned angry in front of my wife and son that I rode over to the Simpson ranch to cool off."

"You told them to bushwhack me?" Gilly's eyes were now blazing.

"No I did not, but after thinking about it on the way home, I remembered one of the old Simpson riders asking a lot of questions about you. Then I thought about Mabel and Tommy being with you. He's a Mexican, I think—dark eyes and skin—always in trouble with the boys."

"He could be Indian," Gilly hissed, as a vision of the last face he was searching for flashed across his mind with startling reality.

"Now out of my way boy!" Burgers demanded. "I have a job to do and I don't want Mabel to know about it."

"Sorry mister, this is my job," the Canadian's voice was hardly audible, but the underlying threat sent shivers down Luke's back.

"I'm going with you," he insisted, hesitantly.

"You're going to look after Jenny and your wife sir. Leave the killing to a fool like me who has no ties to a family. And if you decide to follow me I'll shoot that high-bred mare out from under you!"

Once again Gilly saw the signs that Luke's temper was rising as he forced his decision on the rancher. Luke, on the other hand, was fully aware that this young man with the hard, cold eyes would follow through on his threat. Cursing violently, Luke watched the blue roan race away and felt a fleeting moment of admiration for this stranger who was so intent on revenge. Using his intimate knowledge of the countryside, Luke quickly joined the little-used trail and spotted his son riding toward him.

"Where's Gilly and what are you doing out here?" Tom called as his mount stopped beside his father.

"He's gone ahead to make sure nobody's waiting for us."

"Is that why you're here Dad?" Tom snapped. "To warn us because you know somebody's there waiting. I'm going in to help him. You stay with Jenny and mother." Leaving no room for argument, Tom put the spurs to his horse and tore off up the trail. Luke's shoulders sagged as he waited for the buckboard to catch up.

"Luke!" Mabel called as they came up beside him. "What the devil are you doing here?"

"This is my rangeland, I go where I please."

"And what did Gilly have to say about that, Mr. Burgers?" Jenny asked in a slow accusing tone. "You couldn't have got near us without him knowing."

"Oh, he's out there some ...." Luke's comment was interrupted by the sound of two distant shots which cracked through the morning air. It was loud enough to cause the horses to fidget nervously and their heads and ears pointed at the crest of the hill. Grabbing the reins, Jenny screamed at the Box T Ranch owner as the buckboard took off.

"If you've sent my man into a trap, Luke Burgers, I'll kill you myself!"

Shocked by Jenny's statement and, the sudden turn of events, Mabel hung onto the buckboard seat with terrified strength as the wildly pitching wagon raced over the rough ground toward the hill. Minutes later, Jenny hauled back on the reins when she saw the broken fences outlining the burned out Thompson farm. Tom's riderless horse was standing amongst some trees. Luke saw it too, and he galloped past them veering toward it.

"Oh no, not Tommy!" Mabel moaned, trying to scramble out of the moving buckboard as Jenny moved it toward Tom's horse.

"Sit down, Mrs. Burgers!" Jenny screamed.

Luke leapt from his horse as he reined it in, stumbling briefly as he searched frantically for a sign of his son.

"Get down!" Tom's voice ordered sharply from above. "There's a rifleman out there."

Luke looked over at the wagon and was horrified to see his wife standing beside the wagon sobbing. Jenny, lying across the seat, was begging her to get under the buckboard. Luke also yelled for her to get under the wagon, but she continued to stand there repeating Tom's name and sobbing. Luke hurried over to his wife.

"He's coming!" Jenny yelled, slapping the reins on the horse's rump. She swung the buckboard around and galloped toward the rider. They met in front of the shell of the burned-out house. Jenny pulled her horse to a stop in a shower of dust and gazed at Gilly. Sitting on his mount with his hat in his hand, staring at the ashes, she could feel the hurt that touched his soul in the sparkle of tears which ran silently down his face.

"Help me down please Gilly," she softly pleaded.

Replacing his hat, he slid from the saddle and helped her. "Don't you go soft on me girl, this job ain't done yet," he whispered against her neck as her feet touched the ground.

"You didn't find the shooter?" she asked, looking at him carefully.

"No, but he left me a memento ...."

Conversation stopped abruptly when they were joined by Tom and his parents. Mabel was still in a state of shock clinging protectively to her husband's arm.

"Did ya get him?" Tom asked.

"No, but I will," Gilly stated adamantly.

Moving away while Gilly answered Tom's questions, Jenny saw the three modern grave markers standing in what once appeared to be the family garden plot. Wilted flowers drooped wearily near each headstone.

"Did you bring those flowers, Mabel?" Jenny asked.

"Yes, but that was almost a week ago," Mabel replied, drying her eyes as she joined Jenny in front of the graves. She seemed to have forgotten her fright. "I've been taking care of these folks ever since Luke took over the property."

"And you knew this was Gilly's family?" Jenny murmured in astonishment.

"No, no, not right away. Doc Forbes and I decided to do a little research and found them in the homestead records at the county office."

"I put markers on them," Gilly's voice crackled with emotion from behind them.

"Yes you did, but to us, there was no way of knowing who they were," Mabel replied, moving closer to the markers and kneeling at the side of one of the graves. "They're still here," she whispered, as her hands disturbed the thin layer of crusty soil and revealed rough sticks in the shape of a cross.

Gasping, Gilly turned quickly and walked away across the space that had once been the yard where he had played with his sister. He stopped beneath a tree and kicked the ground. Jenny followed him, weeping softly as she awkwardly moved across the uneven ground.

"Stand tall Gilly Thompson," she murmured, resting her hand on his arm. "It ain't over yet."

"No, it ain't girl," he sighed. "Rube once told me peace wouldn't be easy to find. Now let's start thinking of getting you home, and then I can get on my way."

"Why don't you go now? Tom will see I get home and I know you're itching to go after that shooter."

"It ain't up for discussion. I gave you my word."

Glancing up into the branches of the tree, Gilly patted the trunk reverently with the palm of his hand, before turning away and walking back to the gravesite. Ignoring the Burgers, he removed his hat, bent down and whispered a few words at each grave.

"Are you going to reclaim the homestead Mr. Thompson?" Luke asked.

"Not if you give me unrestricted access to these graves sir."

"You have my word on it."

"Mine too," Tom agreed loudly as Gilly walked toward them.

"And you, Mrs. Burgers," Gilly spoke softly, "have my total respect and gratitude."

As they left the burned-out homestead, the sun was high overhead but Gilly insisted they move quickly and stay close to the buckboard. By the time they arrived back at the Box T Ranch, Jenny had already accepted Mabel's invitation for them to stay another night, informing Gilly of their obligation as he lifted her down from the buckboard.

"You shouldn't have," Gilly hissed. "I ain't got no fancy table manners."

"Don't be silly, we couldn't leave again at this time of day. We should be thanking the Burgers for their kindness, but then I'm sure they'll forgive that you're happier acting like a wild animal!" she muttered sarcastically. "I suppose you'll have to rely on me to keep you from making a fool of yourself."

"Words can hurt too Jenny."

Shocked into silence by Gilly's solemn reply, Jenny watched him walk away toward the blacksmith's shack, unsure if he would even return to eat with them. Mabel quietly took her arm and led her into the house.

Standing at the blacksmith's open door, Gilly watched the old stableman at work on the foot of a horse, cursing quietly to himself as he grunted and wheezed with effort.

"Hot horse?" Gilly inquired sniffing the air.

"Yep, a stupid linerider, damn near killed it."

Gilly's interest rose. *Could this horse have been ridden hard from the Simpson range?* he wondered, as he fingered the two rifle shells in his pocket and decided to investigate further. "How long's he been here?"

"About half an hour. What the hell's biting yer arse now lad?"

"He's in the cookhouse?" Gilly hissed the question menacingly, sliding his gun hand down to release his tie down.

"Wait boy!" Walt Horn shouted in alarm. "That's Derby in there!"

Ignoring the stableman's concern, Gilly was already moving quickly toward the cookhouse door as Walt lurched awkwardly along behind him.

"What the devil is old Walt yelling about?" Luke muttered as he walked to the porch rail and stared across the yard.

"Gilly!" Jenny squealed, falling as she hurried to get out of the chair.

Tom leapt to Jenny's side, but his mother waved him away and he raced past his father, telling him he would handle it.

Stepping into the cookhouse, Gilly's eyes fastened immediately on the stranger eating at the table, but he was unable to see the man's face behind the black derby hat he wore. Slowly raising his head to check the new arrival through dark eyes set deep in a furrowed brow, the cowboy named Derby smirked as he set his fork down and reached for the rifle laid across the table in front of him.

"Don't touch it mister!" Gilly's voice stopped his movement. "I need to see that gun."

Rising and kicking the chair away, Derby stood glowering at the Canadian, his hand hovering over the well-polished butt of his sidearm. Recognizing the inevitable outcome of the confrontation, Box T riders scrambled out of the line of fire as Tom Burgers burst into the room.

"Hold it boys!" he snarled with angry authority. "We don't allow gunplay on the Box T."

"I want to see that Sharps rifle he has," Gilly hissed. "Fire a shell and show me the empty case Tom."

"Oh no you don't!" Derby threatened. "Ain't nobody touching that rifle!"

"Don't be stupid, Derby!" Tom snapped. "A look at yer rifle ain't worth dying for."

"Go to hell!" the linerider snarled as his hand streaked for his Colt and Gilly's weapon barked its deathly message, flinging Derby onto his back in front of the cook stove with a big red stain spreading across his shirt front.

"Now I'll take a look at that Sharps," Gilly growled.

Reaching for the rifle, he fired a shot into the floor and ejected the empty shell onto the table as the bunkhouse boys crowded around Derby's body. Coldly comparing the firing pin marks on the shell cases in his pocket, he dropped them in Tom's hand. "There's the man who shot at you this morning."

"Two shots," Luke muttered, pacing the porch when the second shot rang out from the Box T bunkhouse. "I'm going down there."

"No, you're not," Mabel snapped. "Tom can handle it."

"Somebody's coming out," Jenny announced hopefully, as she hugged the verandah post for support.

"Where's Tom?" Luke snapped as Gilly stopped at the bottom of the steps.

"In the cookhouse cleaning up the mess you left us," Gilly replied.

"I left no mess in the cookhouse."

"You told the bushwhacker we were going to my folks' graves and damned near got your son killed when he mistook Tom for me."

"Did you do that Luke?" Mabel moaned.

"I told the riders in the Simpson bunkhouse to stay away from that place while we were there today."

"Was that the man in the cookhouse Gilly?" Jenny murmured as he climbed the steps and offered her his arm. "You killed him, didn't ya?"

"Yes ma'am."

The house door creaked and a tiny, nervous voice asked, "Me eat for you now, missus?" Conversation abruptly changed to food.

"Yes," Mabel replied, firmly in control of her emotions again. "You may set out lunch now Mr. Fong, Tom will be here in a moment."

"Who was that?" Jenny asked in surprise.

"Our Chinese cook, he's been with us for years and still talks back to front."

"I've never seen a Chinaman," Jenny admitted as they moved into the ranchhouse, "and this is the first time I've been off the ranch since my father died."

"It's a shame it's been spoiled by your injury. Doc Forbes treated you, did he?" Mabel inquired gently, as her son joined them at the table. "I noticed you had a wheelchair in the buckboard."

"Oh, I won't need that again," Jenny replied. "Gilly says that bullet did something to my back and now I can walk again. I just ain't so good at sitting yet!"

"At least one good thing came from Frank Barlow ...," Tom began, but he was interrupted as the Chinese cook brought a tray of sandwiches and fruit to the table.

Conversation ceased while Jenny's eyes followed the Chinese cook as he hurried around the table placing a napkin on each of their laps. Gilly looked uncomfortable and nervous every time the little man came close to him, snatching his coffee mug from the table as the Chinese cook reached for it, then bashfully handing it back to the grinning little man when he pointed to the coffee pot he was holding.

"Yes, I remember Tom telling me about Frank Barlow," Mabel murmured as yesterday's conversation returned to her memory. "Where were you when it happened? How did you reach Doc Forbes so quickly?"

"Actually we were out on the flatland, two days from the ranch and a day and a half from Benji Jackson's place. Gilly treated my wound and took me to the Jackson's before going for the doctor; the bullet burned a track across my back and went through the cheek of my arse. Pardon me ... my behind!"

Mabel almost chocked on her sandwich and Tom chuckled, but Gilly kept his eyes down on the table while Luke smiled at the raw frankness of their young neighbour's description.

"Oh my," Mabel chuckled. "I would say you two are well and truly acquainted!"

Drinks were offered and immediately rejected by Gilly who fidgeted uncomfortably when Mabel suggested the group retire to the drawing room. Making a feeble excuse to leave and check on his mount, he started for the door.

"We leave soon after dawn Jenny," he called over his shoulder.

Walking slowly toward the stables, Gilly contemplated the kindness of Mabel Burgers and Harry Forbes in respecting his family graves. He sighed as his mind went through a jumble of thoughts—the power Harvey Stubbs seemed to have over the events at the Half Moon Ranch, Luke Burgers' accusation of rustling cattle, and the gunfighters on the Half Moon payroll. It had all the ingredients of a range war waiting to happen. He was still brooding as he saddled Blue.

"Is Rube Caster still alive boy?" It was the gruff voice of the stableman.

"No sir, he died in the Canadian Rocky Mountains last spring."

"You were there?"

"Yes sir."

"It was him who taught you about the marks a firing pin makes on a cartridge case, weren't it?"

"Yes."

"I knew him when he was sheriff of Placerville. Kerry and me sided him when he fought the Carson gang."

"Kerry who?" Gilly turned to face the dark shadow.

"Kerry Walker. He's worked over at the Washington ranch for many years, a real magician with horses and guns."

"You worked for Simpson when they burned the Thompson place?"

"I told ya, my leg got broke awhile before that," Walt sighed. "That's the last time I saw old Rube, never saw him again."

"We went to Canada and never came back. Why don't you tell me about Luke Burgers."

"Straight as a die is Luke; crotchety as hell these days but a real old pioneer. He'd never do a man wrong. Young Tommy's not half the man his father used to be but he'll learn with experience. His mother's a first-class lady. What more do yer want to know?"

"Is there a range war coming?"

"Looks like Harvey wants it that way and old Luke won't back away, he'll fight," Walt growled adding, "unless Rube puts a stop to it."

"Rube's gone."

"No lad, Rube's still here ... in you. I saw how fast you were with that hog leg, how you proved where those shells came from, and the way you protect Miss Washington. You're every bit as good as Rube was. Ah'll bet a silver dollar you even live by Rube's code of honour."

Stepping into his saddle, Gilly looked down on the dark shape of the old stableman and whispered emotionally, "I'll never be half the man Rube Caster was."

It was midnight before Jenny relaxed her vigil of staring through the bedroom window in the hope of spotting a lone horse standing near a tree where Gilly would be perched watching the house. Rising and dressing well before dawn, she was standing on the porch when Gilly rode up.

"Are you coming for breakfast or just going to stand there?" he asked swinging himself to the ground.

"Can I take your arm?"

"Sure, if you stop jawing and get moving."

Grinning to herself, Jenny hooked her arm through his, knowing he was well aware she no longer needed the help. Her wound had healed and the soreness was merely an annoyance now. Her hips and legs were

229

moving almost without aching and she was beginning to feel more like a normal person with each passing day. She had been trying to read his mood since Derby's killing, he seemed to have relaxed somewhat. Maybe the faces had gone away, she hoped so.

There was not a single sassy comment passed between them as they walked toward the cookhouse. Space was quickly made for them as cowboys changed places, glancing furtively at Gilly. Walt Horn arrived saying the buckboard was ready, then he stayed just long enough to shake Gilly's hand and ask that Jenny say hello to Kerry Walker for him.

Disappointment showed on Mabel Burgers' face when they returned to the ranchhouse and Jenny informed her they had eaten and were leaving immediately. She ordered the cook to fill a basket of food for the journey and take it out to the buckboard. Luke offered his hand to Gilly and stumbled over his attempt at apologizing for his behavior at the Jackson place, assuring him he would leave the coloured family in peace. Tom surprised them all by shaking Gilly's hand firmly, then moved in to hug a startled Jenny, who squealed and hugged him back.

Waving to the Burgers on the porch, Gilly led the way out onto the rolling grassland, letting the horses run as they followed the well-worn trail north to Fort Hall. Eating as they travelled and, wasting little time, they were entering Fort Hall's main street as the sun set. Driving straight to the livery stable, Gilly arranged feed for the horses and ordered their feet to be checked before lifting Jenny down.

"I think I can manage on my own," she said brushing his arms away.

"Not this time you can't," Gilly muttered, lifting her out of the seat and holding her tight.

"Are you intending to stay like this for awhile, Mr. Thompson?" Jenny giggled as she tightened her arms around his neck and rested her head on his shoulder.

"No, I'm thinking of dropping you in the horse trough for that little display back at the Burgers."

"You're jealous," Jenny chuckled impishly, "but you don't need to be because nobody ever treated me as bad as you do. Now put me down, I'm hungry."

Ignoring her, he carried her over to the trough and held her over the water. As he did so, he noticed the horses tied up at the saloon.

"Ain't them your horses?" he asked, setting her down.

"Lineriders maybe, in for a night on the town."

Offering no reply, Gilly adjusted his gunbelt then led her along the rickety boardwalk toward the saloon. Doc Forbes looked up from his evening drink and smiled tiredly as he motioned to them to join him.

230

"Are you on your way home?" he asked, watching Jenny walk unaided to the table. He drained his drink and called for service. Jenny and Gilly gave their food and drink orders to the barman.

"Hey kid, have you shot any big cats lately?" a familiar red-bearded cowboy yelled as he stepped away from the bar and turned to face them.

"Howdy Jake." Gilly rose to shake hands with the cowboy. "What the hell are you doing way down here in Snake River country?"

"Roaming boy, but I just signed on for a drive with the Half Moon Ranch. They needed an extra rider for a small herd going south."

Introductions were made, then their meal arrived and Doc dismissed the listening barman with an angry wave. "Heard enough yet, Rolly?"

"How many are you driving?" Gilly asked innocently as the barman walked moodily away.

"A hundred prime head all the way to Carson City."

"Where the hell's that?" Gilly asked.

"South on the Nevada-California border," Doc informed them with a suspicious tone in his voice.

Called by his friends as they left, Jake shook Gilly's hand and went to join them.

Jenny frowned obviously waiting for the men to leave as she picked at her food. "I didn't authorize any sale of cattle," she murmured, "and I don't know any of those riders. They don't work for me."

"Eat your food," Harry growled. "I think we just met the Snake River rustlers. What do you think Mr. Thompson?"

"First things first Doc. I need to find out where they're holding them beeves and see what they've got. My guess is they'll have some of the Box T steers too."

"But it's too dark to track them," Jenny moaned, "and what could we do on our own?"

"Lady, you ain't going nowhere," Gilly hissed. "I'll do it alone. You're staying here with Doc until I come back."

"You can't force me to stay here!"

"I can tie you to a wagon wheel quick enough, if that's what you want!"

Harry Forbes chuckled as the argument raged quietly between the two strong-willed combatants. Finally, he interrupted, "If you'll both shut up for a minute, I'll tell you how to find out where the herd is." He pushed his chair back and stood up.

Gilly and Jenny stopped talking and watched as Doc strode over to the bar.

"Where did you say those boys were holding their cattle Rolly?"

231

"South of here Harry, along the river just before it enters the canyon."

Doc nodded and grinned at Gilly as he returned to the table. "Rolly not only listens, he also likes to tell all he knows. Now what do we do?"

"We could get the sheriff to raise a posse and go after them," Jenny suggested hopefully.

"Charley's not up to that sort of thing," Harry frowned, "and raising a posse in this town would be like looking for a chicken with teeth."

"Could you take Jenny back to the Box T Doc?" Gilly asked, watching Harry nod. "The Burgers have a bunkhouse full of men. That's the easiest way and Luke will be eager to get at the rustlers too. I'll go slow them up for a while!"

Using Doc Forbes' intimate knowledge of the trail, a fresh horse, and his comfortable buggy, he and Jenny had soon left the few lights of Fort Hall far behind them. The cool night wind on the plain caused Harry to produce blankets and whisky-laced cold coffee that took Jenny's breath away when she drank it.

"I hope he's not going to do anything foolish Doc," she moaned after they had travelled little more than an hour.

"Stop worrying," Harry muttered. "He's Rube's boy."

"Who is this Rube he keeps talking about? It seems he lives on every word that man ever said."

All night as they travelled, doc took great delight in relating the stories and times of Rubin Caster, a lawman who left a legend behind him as a man who fought with a lightning fast gun for the honest men of the West. "He finally tired of greed and corruption and took to wandering far and wide, going missing for years at a time into untamed territory. He must have rescued Gilly and just disappeared into the Canadian mountains."

"You seem to have known him well," Jenny commented.

"Yes, very well. So did your blacksmith Kerry Walker, and the Box T stableman Walt Horn. They were in Placerville in the wild days too. They backed Rube when he fought the Carson gang."

"But why would a man like that saddle himself with a kid?"

"Rube wouldn't think twice about it girl. He saw a desperate need and would have wanted to help."

"So you believe everything Gilly says about this man?"

"I don't have to believe anything, Gilly is Rube Caster all over again. Haven't you seen him tip his hat against the sun? Where do you think he learned to sniff the air and read the smells ... and the way he thinks ...? Yep, he's Rube Caster's boy all right."

It was still two hours before dawn when the buggy arrived in the Box T yard; Walt Horn challenged them with a loaded shotgun from the dark stable doorway. He listened intently when the doc explained their mission.

"Go wake the bunkhouse crew," Harry urged. "We'll go wake Luke and Tom. Hurry Walt, there ain't no time to lose. Gilly's trying to hold 'em up until we get there."

Wild excitement filled the darkness in the Box T yard when Walt woke the range crew with a blast from his double-barrelled shotgun. Men hurriedly dressed as the cook plied them with black steaming coffee, grabbing for their guns as they raced to saddle their mounts. Luke and his son listened to Harry's directions and led the charge out into the darkness.

Mabel took the news in stoic pioneer fashion, masking her worry as she offered hot drinks, food and a bed to the weary messengers. She smiled tolerantly when doc promptly drifted off into a noisy, snoring sleep, in his favourite chair. She urged him awake and, as she took them upstairs, she assured Jenny she would wake them in three hours.

Chapter 8

Gilly rode south from Fort Hall using the sound of the river as a guide to lead him to the cattle, allowing Blue to pick his own way in the dark. Slowing to a walk when the sound of the river changed, he sniffed the air to pick up the familiar aroma of cattle. Swinging wide, he moved around the rustler's night camp and listened intently for sounds of a nightrider, hearing the low, off-key notes of a cowboy mumbling the words of a song. A familiar grunting cough mixed in with the song helped him pinpoint the rider's position and when the glow of a match illuminated the red beard of Jake Curry, his suspicion was confirmed.

When he detected the scorched smell of their campfire, Gilly silently dismounted and led the pony cautiously around the nightrider. His plan was to steal their mounts which would effectively hold them until help arrived. It was still an hour before dawn when he located the horses and led them away from camp; stopping some distance away, he tied them nose to tail and keeping an eye on the fast disappearing stars, headed due north. He was more than a mile away before the first grey streaks of dawn appeared from behind the mountains.

A shot twanged against his water bottle and he looked up to see the outline of a lone horseman. Another shot whizzed by his head and Gilly thundered after him. The rider disappeared behind some rocks and Gilly sought protection among the low-hanging tree branches. He securely tied the horses and reached for his rifle. Dropping on one knee, he waited. The instant the rider appeared, Gilly let a single shot crash from his rifle barrel. The shot was true, flipping the rider from the saddle to lay still in the grass, while his horse moved some distance away.

Unhurriedly Gilly returned his rifle to its scabbard cover, and mounting, rode cautiously over to the moaning figure of Jake Curry crumpled in the grass. He tied him hand and foot before examining the bright red furrow left by the bullet that had brushed his scull and torn part of his ear away. Glancing around, he saw Jake's mount watching suspiciously but it put little resistance into being caught and left tied with the others.

Jake recovered enough to groan and curse incoherently as he tried to focus his eyes on his captor. A short while later when hoofbeats sounded from the north, Gilly knew his help had arrived. Mounting, he rode out to meet the Burgers and the Box T crew, quickly explaining what had happened and that the suspected rustlers were on foot a mile or so away. Gilly felt a little awkward as he warned the men he wanted no shooting unless it was absolutely necessary and unavoidable, explaining there was no proof that the men were rustlers.

"You sound like a lawman," Luke growled, "but don't get in the way if we find they've got my cattle."

"Mister," Gilly replied icily, "we shall be doing this Rube's way, or you'll find yourself fighting me on the difference."

"Boy!" Luke Burgers exploded. "You ain't in charge of the Box T riders!"

"No sir, you are. That's why I'll be holding you responsible."

"Dad," Tom interrupted, "he's right. We have to prove they're rustlers first. That should be easy, they're on foot. So for once in your life, listen to somebody!" Tom's outburst surprised his father to such a degree that it seemed to calm him—at least enough to be quiet while Gilly gave Tom and his men their orders.

"Tom, ride a wide loop to the south, one of your men needs to swing in from the north. It shouldn't be hard to find that herd, I suspect there's a canyon through those rocks and we'll be able to hear the cattle. I'm going in on the point. I've given one of them a head wound and he'll cause no trouble now. There are three more still out there, so be careful. If you see any one of them, fire one shot for help and dismount. The rest of you stay with Luke and be prepared to come in fast if you hear shooting."

Gilly signalled the outriders away, then turned the pony and rode straight at the herders' camp. Luke and the Box T riders watched with admiration, knowing Gilly had taken the most dangerous position for himself. Riding slowly and, using every instinct Rube had taught him, Gilly found the cattle and realized his suspicions had been correct about the canyon. Three riders with rifles stood spaced out near the canyon entrance and watched him ride in. *If they're going to shoot it'll be when I dismount, but they won't want to risk spooking the herd,* he reasoned, turning toward some rocks.

The two Box T outriders were now in his sight, moving cautiously and drawing some attention as Gilly rode behind the rocks and dismounted, gun in hand. Looking back, he saw Luke and his six riders sitting on their horses in a menacing show of strength.

"Lay the rifles down boys," Gilly yelled. "You ain't got nowhere to run!"

Apparently realizing the futility of resistance, all three of the rustlers dropped their rifles and Gilly stepped out of the rocks as Tom rode off to check the herd brands.

"They're all legal stock mister," one of the herders shouted after him. "We ride for the Washington ranch."

"You ain't their regular riders," Gilly yelled.

"We're drovers; we move small herds down south to the markets."

"You have papers for the drive?"

"Yes sir."

"Thieves!" Tom Burgers yelled as he rode quickly back toward them. "These are all Box T beeves."

Things happened fast now as all three herders went for their side arms. Tom's disclosure distracted his outrider's attention momentarily but Gilly was wide awake. The Canadian's gun cleared its holster and was belching flames before anyone could blink an eye. Justice had been served with the speed of a striking snake and three rustlers were dead.

"You just saved the hangman a job," Luke muttered. "Now we've only one to deal with."

After detailing his riders to drive the cattle back home, Luke and Tom caught up with Gilly as he walked his mount back to the tree where Jake Curry, now fully awake, was sitting.

"Why do I get the feeling we ain't done with you yet boy?" Luke grumbled.

"Because you ain't hanging anyone Luke. Red's going home to Montana where he belongs."

"I want justice, it didn't take you long to cut down those other three."

"You know better than that, you old goat. I killed them to stop them shooting us, not for being rustlers. Rube always said to be careful when rats are cornered."

"Oh, to hell with Rube Caster! We have enough Box T riders here to do what I want."

Tom was shocked with his father's attitude, but it was Gilly's answer that really stunned him.

"Mr. Burgers, you ain't got enough men to ensure you'll see Red hang and it would be stupid to risk your life because you'd be the first one I'd shoot!"

Luke cursed, and kicking his horse, rode after his men. Tom stayed back to help Gilly load the bodies onto their horses, then he watched with interest as his friend pulled a shirt from his saddlebag and tore it into strips to bandage the Montana cowboy's injuries. All morning the two men kept a steady pace and the odd-looking cavalcade entered the main street of Fort Hall by mid-afternoon. Leaving the horses at the livery stable, they drew a small crowd that excitedly whispered their assumptions as the two cowboys escorted Jake Curry over to the sheriff's office.

Glancing through the window, Sheriff Charley Tripp watched the stern-faced trio approach and noticed the injured man. He hoped they were heading for the doctor's office two doors away but when he realized they were coming to his door, he scooted quickly behind his desk and nervously waited.

"Are you boys looking for me?" he asked haltingly.

"We brought three bodies in Charley ... rustlers ... caught them down near the falls with Box T cattle," Tom explained.

"D-d-did ya hang 'em?"

"No, but Dad wanted to," Tom chuckled. "They tried to throw down on Gilly and me."

"You killed 'em, Tom?"

"No Charley, Gilly was too fast!"

"And this fella, is he one of your men, Tom?"

"I think you'd better talk to Gilly about that one," Tom grinned. "He's one of the rustlers."

"Do you need my services?" Doc stuck his head through the open door. "That man looks like he's been hurt. Has something bitten his ear?"

"Yes sir, I shot him, you can fix him up. Where's Jenny?"

"I'm right here," Jenny called from behind the doctor, "and I ain't coming in there."

"Come on Tom, let's go eat," Gilly muttered. "Doc and the Sheriff can take care of the prisoner."

"No! You don't leave him in here," the sheriff bleated. "He's dangerous."

"Doc, look at his wound would you, then send him over to the saloon to eat with us," said Gilly.

Harry Forbes smiled then nodded at the Canadian before leading the prisoner over to a chair. He unwound the makeshift bandage and stared at the raw furrow down the side of his head. "I'm afraid you've lost part of your ear son," Harry sighed. "You're either very lucky or somebody's a hell of a good shooter!"

Outside the sheriff's office, Jenny joined them; clinging to Gilly's arm, they walked up the boardwalk to the saloon.

"You don't seriously expect that rustler to eat with us do you?" Jenny asked sharply.

"He's eating with me lady, you don't need to come if it bothers you."

Gilly's statement left no room for argument; the tone of his voice told her it was unlikely he would alter his decision.

"Ooh you're the most frustrating man I ever met," Jenny snapped, still holding onto his arm. "There are times I wish I'd never met you."

"Wish for whatever you like girl, but for goodness' sake, be quiet!"

Tears sprung into Jenny's eyes as she followed Gilly to the table, but Tom went to her defense, resting his hands on the back of her chair. "If you two don't stop arguing I ain't eating with either of you," he hissed. "And you, Mr. Thompson, ain't got the manners of a mountain goat. I think you need to apologize to Miss Washington."

The situation was unexpectedly interrupted when Doc Forbes and the prisoner arrived, the latter looking mighty nervous as he was led to their table. Tom pulled up an extra chair and stood waiting for his answer.

"You're right, Tom," Gilly sighed. "I should apologize for speaking the truth. She ain't used to hearing it, so ... I'm sorry. Now could you please ask her to be quiet until we get outa here."

Jenny burst into tears, resting her head in her hands as Tom shook his head in amusement. She quickly calmed down as intermittent conversation passed around the table. As they ate, Jake Curry told of his involvement with the rustlers, unaware that Jenny was the owner of the Half Moon Ranch.

"Where was the herd when you joined the drive?" Gilly asked as Jenny listened carefully for the cowboy's reply.

"A few miles back from where you found us."

"Hey, just wait a minute," Harry Forbes spluttered. "This cowboy wasn't in on the rustling; he was employed as a drover."

"How do we know he's telling the truth?" Tom growled.

"Because he told me and Doc right here in this bar," Gilly replied.

"That's right," Doc muttered. "I remember him shouting something about shooting a big cat."

"Yep, Gilly saved my life that day," Jake admitted soberly. "He put two bullets into that mountain cat. Shot him clean out of mid-air in the middle of his leap. He's good with a gun."

The comment caused Harry to burst into laughter as he pointed at Jake's bandaged head. "I ain't sure if you should thank him or hate him for helping you this time, but you won't be likely to forget him!"

"Damn you, Gilly Thompson," Jenny muttered. "You knew he wasn't no rustler, you had no intention of letting him hang."

"That's right missy," said Gilly, turning to the girl, "but as old Rube would say, there's a deeper meaning to all this and I think you missed it."

"You hypocrite!" Tom snapped at the Canadian. "Jenny's been worried sick about you and all you do is try to make her look stupid, but I'm just about ready to put a stop to it. What he's trying to say Jenny, is they were your men who were stealing Box T cattle. Jake's the only one not on the regular Half Moon payroll. It looks like dad was right and Harvey Stubbs is at the bottom of all this."

It wasn't long to sundown when they left the saloon and headed over to the livery stable. Extracting a solemn promise from Jake that he would return to the border country, Gilly gave him back his horse, rifle, and handgun, and set him free.

"I like your kind of justice," Tom said, shaking Gilly's hand and mounting up, "but I'm not sure how Dad's going to react to us turning Jake Curry loose."

"You just keep him away from the Half Moon for a while."

"Are we leaving now?" Jenny asked quietly.

"No, straight after breakfast in the morning. Tomorrow night we'll stay over at the Jackson's place and you can visit with their baby."

Gilly was surprised to find it was both windy and rainy as he saddled his horse and prepared the buckboard for their trip to the Jackson homestead the next morning. When he was ready, he made his way up the deserted street to the saloon where he found Jenny with Doc Forbes seated behind two steaming mugs of coffee. Jenny grinned at Gilly's look of surprise.

"We need a raincoat Doc," Gilly muttered, accepting the coffee Jenny pushed in front of him.

"I took the liberty of searching the bodies of the rustlers last night before sending them off to be buried," Harry informed them as they ate breakfast. "You'll find the guns and saddles in the buckboard. Boots, hats and coats go to Widow Jenkins for her boys and I came across this interesting piece of paper."

"What is it?" Jenny asked reaching across the table.

"Read it," said Doc.

Quickly unfolding the paper, she stared at the handwritten note in astonishment then exclaimed, "Good grief, Harvey's incriminated himself!"

"Not quite," Doc said with a broad grin. "It's a Bill of Sale for 100 cattle all right, but it don't say whose."

"Keep it," Gilly ordered, "it might just baffle the writer more than the reader."

"Is that another of Rube's puzzles?" Jenny muttered sarcastically, "or are you going to explain it to me?"

"You thought it was damning evidence, Harvey might think so too."

Doc watched them from the boardwalk outside the saloon, a funny sight as Gilly led Jenny, dressed in Doc's ill-fitting rain gear, through the rain trying to miss the puddles in the rutted road. Gilly recovered the rustlers' Half Moon horses from the stableman and they were soon on their way out of town. Turning, Jenny waved to Doc before focusing her attention on the road. In the hours ahead, thoughts often ran through Jenny Louise's head of how her world had expanded since Gilly came along. Her wheelchair was now a thing of the past and only an occasional feeling of pain in her butt came back to remind her of being bushwhacked. She felt completely secure with this Canadian cowboy despite his strange code of conduct.

Progress was slow as the rain continued and the trail turned to mud. Riding close to the buckboard as the noon hour approached, Gilly offered her a thrilling suggestion of trading places for a while to ease her aching legs. Rainwater spilled from Jenny's hat as she nodded enthusiastically, pulling the buckboard to a halt.

"Don't go too far away," he ordered, handing her Blue's reins and watching as she happily settled herself into the saddle.

Unable to contain her enthusiasm, she urged the range pony into a gallop, feeling the rain beating on her face and the freedom of riding the open range again. Never in her wildest dreams had she thought this could ever happen. It was more than an hour later when she saw Gilly wave her back to the buckboard and she reluctantly surrendered the pony.

"We're not too far away from the Jackson place," he explained. "I need to do a little riding before we get too close. You keep that rifle handy."

She experienced a moment of apprehension when Gilly and the pony disappeared into the hills. Staring through the rain, she followed the muddy trail through the pass until the Jackson farm came into view and she remembered Gilly's advice. Reaching under the seat for the rifle and standing it between her legs, she felt more prepared to face any unknown danger, but where was Gilly she wondered, as her eyes frantically searched for a sign of her companion.

They were still half a mile out from the farm when, to Jenny's surprise, Gilly stepped into the buckboard, having ridden up behind her unnoticed. He tied on the pony and strode over the seat to sit beside her, making no effort to take the reins as his eyes searched the farm buildings.

"It looks deserted," Jenny observed.

"No it ain't," he muttered. "He's working on his forge."

"I don't see him."

"Use your ears."

Lapsing into silence, Jenny strained to catch any different sound above the groaning of the wagon. Gilly's curt reply meant he had no time for conversation; for some reason, he was concentrating to pick up clues as to what lay ahead.

"He's got company," he finally muttered.

"I don't see anybody."

"There are two extra mules in the corral."

Going quiet, Jenny felt a knot of apprehension in her stomach as they trotted on into the Jackson's yard. Gilly's observations caused her to be nervously aware of the surroundings. Following her companion's whispered directions, she drove the buckboard to the corral and waited for Gilly to help her down. There was no obvious urgency in his movements as he lifted Jenny from the seat. Holding her close, he murmured, "Stay here, and for God's sake keep the buckboard between you and that barn door."

Reaching for the Winchester, he placed it where she could easily reach it against the front wheel. Then he moved off to untie the three horses fastened to the rear of the buckboard, turning them loose into the corral with the mules. She could almost see his mind turning as he banged the water from his hat using the corral post then slipped smoothly out of his rain slicker and flicked the tie down from his Colt as he took the reins of his horse and started toward the barn.

Using the pony as a shield, Gilly moved unhurriedly as Jenny watched, barely daring to breathe. She kept behind the buckboard and levered a shell into the Winchester. Her heart was beating hard against her chest. Looking up again, she saw the pony standing alone and realized Gilly must have gone through the open side door of the barn. The yard was enveloped in an eerie silence broken only by the moo of a cow and her heart began to race. The hair on her neck suddenly bristled when Gilly reappeared carrying a small bundle in his arms.

Squealing, Jenny threw her Winchester into the buckboard and hurried to join him. "Where's Della and Benji?" she asked, taking the baby from him.

"They're helping a cow with a difficult calving."

"Where? Can I see it?"

"Ain't you got enough to do with the baby?"

Oblivious to everything except the baby in her arms, Jenny sheltered the tiny bundle inside her rain slicker, moving slowly toward the house. Turning back to the barn, Gilly joined the Jacksons who were now tending the newborn calf and encouraging it to find food suckling eagerly from its mother's overfull udder. It was then he saw the broken harness and puzzled at its condition.

"You've had company Benji?" Gilly inquired as Della rushed away to the house. "Looks like you bought two extra mules."

"No sah, dem mules ain't mine."

"They're in your corral."

"They were lost Mister Gilly. Harness all broke. I expect somebody will come lookin' for 'em."

"How long have they been here?"

"Two days. There were here in my yard two mornings ago when I wakes up. Ah don't know where they came from."

"Did you try to find out where they came from?"

"No sah, I wouldn't know where to start."

"I'd better take a look out there," Gilly muttered, walking over to his mount and pulling his rain slicker over his head again. Riding out into the rain once more, he stared at the ground as he eased the pony into an easy canter leaving Benji to explain his whereabouts to Jenny. It took more than an hour before he found the barely discernable tracks of two mules walking side by side under some trees. The tracks led him westward away from the Half Moon lands. He could see mountains and rolling hills in the distance and he kept going. Sitting his horse on the crest of a hill, he heard a rifle bark in the distance then silence again. Trying to locate the single shot, he rode hard in the general direction.

Searching a hilltop, he found the mule tracks again and down below, a rain-swollen river charging along its course. Following the mules across the hillside, he saw the wagon half in and half out of the water. Shaking his reins, Gilly sent his mount thundering down the hillside.

Chapter 9

"Hey there," he yelled at the wagon. "Is anybody in there?"

The barrel of a rifle and a small head poked out of the front flap, staring wide-eyed at Gilly. "Ma's hurt," the young boy of about 9 or 10 gasped, stepping through the opening. "Can you help us sir?"

"Who's in there?"

"Ma, Vicky, and Tommy," the boy replied, as a smaller head appeared.

"It's a cowboy Ma," the older boy called into the wagon.

Riding into the water, Gilly slipped out of the saddle onto the wagon seat and scooped open the flap. The woman lying inside stared vacantly back at him, her face as pale as death as she held a Colt revolver in her thin, shaking hands.

"You won't need that ma'am," he said gently. "We're gonna get you outa this mess."

"Please take care of my children," she deplored, speaking so softly Gilly had trouble hearing her.

He took the gun from her hand and then realized she seemed to have lost consciousness. The older boy, who said his name was William and that he was 10-years-old, found Gilly a tarp and together they rigged a shelter in nearby trees. They got the younger kids, Vicky 6, and Tommy 4, out of the wagon and kept them busy by telling them to find dry leaves and branches to light the fire. He and William moved his mother with great difficulty out of the wagon using some of the broken wood from the wagon—she obviously had broken bones and a fever, and Gilly feared much worse. The children found some canned meat, a can of beans and some flour in their meager supplies and followed Gilly's instructions in making a meal. William was most concerned about his mother and gently persuaded her to take a little food but the move had obviously exhausted her.

"You'll have to leave me here," she whispered to Gilly, "one horse won't carry us all."

"I won't leave my ma sir," William announced defiantly. "You can take the little ones and come back for us."

Gilly took their axe and silently set out into the trees where he cut two long saplings. He brought them back to the camp and using a long piece of rope they had, he wove in some cross members, telling the children it was a bed for their mother. He and William covered the whole thing with blankets and pillows, just like he and Rube had done in the mountains when they helped an injured Indian. It was well into the afternoon when they had another bite to eat and were ready to leave. The pony worked hard to pull the travois out of the valley up onto the plain but with the children helping they were on their way. Estimating they were about five miles away from the Jackson farm, Gilly knew they had little chance of making it before dark. Having used his rain slicker to cover the woman, Gilly was just as wet as the others. He had done his best to explain the situation to the children telling them that every step took them closer to the Jackson farm.

Jenny had been pacing the Jackson's porch and house all afternoon. She knew from experience that Gilly must have found trouble somewhere out on the plain and, as darkness fell, she helped Benji light the lanterns and hang them where they could be seen from a long way off. It was almost midnight when Benji yelled from the yard that Gilly was back and he had people with him. Della and Jenny were shocked to see the children and set about feeding and comforting their tired little bodies as William talked incessantly about what Gilly had done. Jenny cried when she saw the state their mother was in, incoherently muttering in the grip of fever. They tried to make her comfortable, but with multiple injuries, it was obvious a doctor was needed urgently.

"I'll ride into Fort Hall," Jenny offered. "We could have Doc Forbes here by morning."

"No," Gilly said firmly. "Della will need you here. I'll take your horse."

"But you're tired out," she argued. "You're going to kill yourself."

"I'd do the same for you," he growled, gulping down the remainder of his hot meal and coffee. Then he donned his rain gear and left.

Jenny followed him outside. Waiting on the porch, a few minutes later, she heard the sound of a moving horse coming out of the barn. Although she couldn't see them, she stood in the rain and listened until she could hear the hoofbeats no longer. With tears streaming down her face, she whispered through her sobs, "Gilly Thompson, please come back to me. I need you."

Benji came upon her on his way to the barn and tried to console her, assuring her Gilly would be fine and urging her to go inside and get warm. Sleeping arrangements inside the house were somewhat restricted now and Della told her Benji was sleeping in the barn. The woman was sleeping in their bed and Della planned to sleep in a chair with the baby. William and his siblings were already in a corner on the floor near the fire wrapped in an odd assortment of clothes, towels and blankets. Jenny offered to watch over them and keep the fire going.

Out on the rain-soaked range, Gilly was again soaked to the skin as the wind had come up again. He slipped from Jenny's horse at two in the morning and banged on Doc Forbes' door. Well used to frontier town emergencies, Harry Forbes struggled from sleep, dressed hurriedly and opened his door.

"What is it?" he asked staring at Gilly's bedraggled figure.

"They need you at the Jackson place Doc," Gilly mumbled through his tiredness. "There's been a wagon accident and a lady is hurt bad."

Harry was now awake. "Go get my buggy, I'll pack a bag."

With the help of a small oil lamp in the livery stable, Gilly found the doctor's harness and his buggy horse. Tying his horse behind the buggy, he could see the good doctor pulling a rain slicker around his shoulders as he hurried toward them. Helping doc into his seat, Gilly soon had them moving up the muddy track away from town.

"How the hell can you see?" Harry grumbled nervously in the dark. "I can't see a damned thing!"

Thankfully, the rain stopped before they reached the hills and Gilly soon spotted the first glimmer of a lantern light in the distance; he knew it was the Jackson place. Dog tired and almost to the point of exhaustion, he shook the reins to push the horse along a little faster.

Hearing the buggy, Jenny went out onto the porch, lighting an extra lamp. Doc Forbes staggered out of the buggy, groaning from stiff limbs and followed her into the little house.

"You'd best bed down, Mister Gilly," suggested the deep melodious sound of Benji's voice as he stood just inside the barn's doorway. "I'll take care of the horses sah."

Collapsing onto the hay, Gilly fell asleep almost instantly and Benji covered him with some of the hay. Across the yard, the house was alive with the noise of children, almost covering their mother's screams as Harry set the woman's broken leg. Della cooked up a big pot of porridge, fed the children, and sent them back to bed while Jenny acted as nurse helping Harry and trying to get the exhausted woman to eat.

"Who are these folks?" Doc inquired.

"I don't know," Jenny admitted. "Gilly brought them in late last night and rode straight into town for you."

"It's a good job he did, that woman in there wouldn't have lasted much longer without attention. Is there no man with them? Didn't Gilly say anything?"

"He was trying to find out where the mules came from," Benji muttered from the kitchen table.

"What mules?"

"Two mules that arrived here with broken harnesses a few days ago."

William, who had been listening to the conversation, came to join them at the table. "Our last name is Hepple. Our Pa drowned while we were crossing one of the rivers about a month ago and it's been real hard for Ma without him. Those mules broke free when we got stuck in the river."

"Could you find that place again? Is it close by son?" Harry asked.

"I don't think so sir, it's a very long way and it was dark when Mr. Gilly brought us out of there. I'm sure Mr. Gilly could find the wagon again, he sure knows how to do things."

Waking in time for lunch, Gilly found William and Jenny quietly watching him as he opened his eyes. "What are you two doing?" he muttered hoarsely.

"We thought you were dead," Jenny whispered, "but you snore too loud!"

"No he doesn't," William laughed. "She's funning you sir."

"How's your mother?" Gilly asked as he got to his feet. "Gee, I could eat a horse unless there's something better to eat."

"My ma's still real sick sir, but the doctor'll help her, won't he?"

Jenny watched as the youngster turned his eyes onto the cowboy who had rescued them and waited for an answer. He had that trusting look that anything Gilly said would be the truth.

"Yes, I'm sure he will," he assured the boy, "but you're going to have to help by looking after your brother and sister."

"Come on William, let's go get Gilly a bowl of stew. He can eat it out here. We don't want him smelling up the house, do we?"

Sunshine finally broke through the clouds in mid-afternoon as William followed Gilly around the farm, watching with interest as the cowboy repaired the broken harness and Benji forged new shoes for the mules. They could see the excitement in the boy's eyes when Gilly asked if he wanted to try them out. Benji led the way over to a corner of the barn and pulled back an old, holey piece of canvas to reveal an odd-looking wagon.

"What is this thing?" William asked as he scrambled over the side.

245

"It's a wagon without wheels called a sledge; see it has runners on the bottom," Gilly tried to explain, offering the reins to the boy. "Do you want to drive? Let's get the mules attached."

Squealing their objection, the mules pulled the dead weight outside into the yard and the noise attracted the attention of everyone in the house.

"What are you doing?" Jenny called as the children shouted their encouragement and ran toward the barn.

"I'm trying out the mules, we're going to get a load of logs," William called pointing over to the trees.

"Can we come along too?" Jenny asked Gilly. "It would be fun for the little ones."

"Sure they can, can't they Mr. Gilly?" William glanced over at Gilly for his assurance, grinning at his siblings when he saw the Canadian nod.

Gilly helped Jenny climb over the side of the sledge, then he handed over the two children. "All right William, head the mules straight for those trees. I'm going to saddle up and follow you."

They were almost at the trees when Gilly rode past, sitting his pony as he waited near a pile of cut cordwood. Helping Jenny and the youngsters out of the sledge, Gilly detailed William to hold the mules' heads while he loaded the logs. Meanwhile, Jenny took the younger children exploring. Gilly was almost finished when Tommy started screaming and ran back trying to tell them something. When Gilly went to investigate he found a bees' nest in a tree with angry bees buzzing all around. He explained what they were to the children, cautioning them not to go near them unless they wanted to get stung.

Finished loading the wood, Gilly helped William get the mules moving and this time the children ran alongside. Gilly smiled as he watched them, also assuring himself that Jenny was managing all right on the uneven terrain. It took longer to get back to the barn but Benji showed them where to unload and this time they all helped. Gilly told Benji about the bees' nest and they lit a torch and went off to inspect it. What they found surprised them as a pair of young raccoons were sitting on the branch happily tearing the nest apart to get at the honey.

"Weren't you afraid?" William asked, after Gilly told them what had happened.

"Yes I was, but I knew that smoke makes them sleepy. So if you ever need to escape from bees, build a smoky fire and stand in the smoke. The bees won't come near you."

"Is that what you did?"

"No lad, there was no need, it weren't us that were annoying them. There were two young raccoons eating their honey."

"I suppose Rube taught you that?" Jenny murmured.

"Yes ma'am. Would you like to ride Blue and take Tommy and Vicki back to the house?" Gilly murmured. "I'm sure William will take care of me and you can just send Blue back and he'll find us."

"I sure will, Miss Jenny," William volunteered eagerly.

Mounted with Vicky clinging tightly behind her and Tommy in front, Jenny smiled down at the cowboy, realizing how easily he had made William feel important. "Did Rube teach you how to deal with children?"

"No, I once had a sister!"

Regretting her comment, Jenny moved off at a slow canter leaving the boys to put the sledge away. On the porch of the house, she could see Doc Forbes with Benji who was holding Della in his arms. *Oh no, what's happened now*, she thought, instinctively pulling the children close.

Walking to meet her, Doc had misery etched on his face as he lifted the children down and held tightly to their hands as he led them back toward the barn. Slipping awkwardly from the saddle, with Benji's help, Jenny asked worriedly, "What's happened?"

"Mrs. Hepple just died," Della sobbed. "Doctor Forbes tried so hard to save her."

Shocked, Jenny covered her mouth with her hand. "But how? I thought she was recovering."

"She was too badly Miss Jenny, and she knowed it," Benji growled.

"With her last bit of strength she asked for you and Gilly to take care of the children," Della added sadly. "Then she just closed her eyes and died. We thought you might like to leave the children here with us."

"That's mighty generous of you, but you folks have enough responsibility right now." Jenny wiped her eyes and sighed, turning to look over at the barn. "Somebody's going to have to tell those poor children." She turned and slowly walked back the way she had come.

Bubbling with enthusiasm, William was chattering about his driving abilities to Doc Forbes but Gilly stopped what he was doing to watch her approach. Doc also saw her coming and led the two children away toward the corral.

"I need to talk to both of you men," she said, flicking a tear off her cheek, knowing that Gilly was watching her. "Can we sit down?" She told herself she had to be strong for these children and that they would work it all out together. Taking a deep breath, she began the most heartbreaking statement she had ever had to make. "I really don't know

247

any other way to tell you this William, but your mother has died. I'm so sorry."

"No ma'am, she can't have. Mr. Gilly said she was going to get better." William bounced onto his feet standing in front of Gilly and staring at him with pleading eyes. Gilly looked at Jenny with questioning eyes then he turned back to William and shook his head. The boy burst into tears and Gilly took the boy into his arms, restraining him from running to the house.

"We have no one now," he sobbed hysterically against Gilly's chest. "Let me go sir, I have to go tell my brother and sister."

"We'll go tell them together William," said Jenny putting her arm around the boy and kneeling beside them.

"You have us William," Gilly murmured, staring at Jenny, "and we know how you feel, we once lost our parents too."

A heavy sadness hung over the Jackson farm as the children said their last goodbyes to their mother and buried her under the trees out beyond the woodlot. William dried his tears and was trying hard to shoulder his responsibilities by agreeing to go with Gilly to recover the wagon and their belongings.

Sharing Gilly's horse and leading the two mules, they headed out across the grazing land. Following close behind, Benji drove his own mules attached to his own wagon loaded with tools, rope, and an extra wheel. Water was still running high when they arrived at the river and, the tracks from the travois poles, which had cut deep into the mud, were still evident.

"Are you going to swim out to the wagon William?" Gilly asked.

"No sir," the boy replied adamantly. "I can't swim."

Ropes were attached and all four mules combined their effort to drag the bogged-down wagon up onto the riverbank, revealing that its front axle, wheels and some of the wagon's floor were missing. Scrambling into the jumble of boards that was once their home, William was soon heard yelling frantically.

"What is wrong William?" Benji yelled, looking at Gilly. "We're taking it all with us."

"You can't, our wagon has no front wheels!"

It was a statement that brought a wisp of a smile to Gilly's normally serious expression. He and Benji prepared the dray to lift the Hepple's wagon out of the water. William's eyes opened wide with excited interest as he climbed out and saw what the two men and mules were doing. They finished the job, had a meal of dried meat and water, and began the long slow trek back to the Jackson farm.

Thankfully the day was warm and the mud no longer a problem. By late afternoon they were pulling their precious cargo into Benji's yard and William dashed off to tell his siblings, alerting the women that they were back.

Repairs on the wagon began at once and they soon had a list of what was needed in addition to the new axle and wheels—tomorrow Gilly would be making a trip into Fort Hall. Far into the evening, after the children were asleep, a discussion took place and Jenny brought some much-needed reality to the situation. There was hardly room for all of them to sleep inside the Jackson house and waiting for the covered wagon to be repaired would only cause more hardship for their very caring but overworked friends. Jenny watched Gilly's face as she spoke of her plan.

"I think we should turn my buckboard into a covered wagon. It should be quite easy," she added with a grin, "we're only three days away from the Half Moon Ranch. It would ease the burden for Benji and Della, give Benji and Gilly time to repair the Hepple wagon and be a great adventure for our children."

"Our children?" Gilly growled.

"Yes, *our children* Mr. Thompson. Their mother asked us to take care of them and I think it's a perfect solution."

"I know you have room for them at the ranch, but what does that have to do with me? We can't look after them ourselves," Gilly stated, somewhat defensively the others thought.

"We certainly can. You do what you like, but I've grown to love these poor little kids and I have the house, the money and the space. What more do they need ... except a father, that would be perfect. We could try to find relatives, but I would have thought their mother would have mentioned that if there were any. As far as I'm concerned they're mine. I'm their mother and ... well, I guess you're going to have to be their father!"

Benji's eyes followed the conversation as Della dabbed at an escaping tear and reached out to touch Jenny's hand as they waited for Gilly's reaction.

"That boy idolizes you, Mister Gilly," Della whispered when Gilly failed to comment.

Shuffling his chair away from the table, Gilly avoided Jenny's eyes and moved toward the door, "Are you sleeping inside tonight?" he murmured without turning around.

"No, it's dry outside, so I'm sleeping under the buckboard, unless you've forgotten your promise to take care of me too!" Jenny said softly, rising stiffly and moving to follow him.

Sniffing the air outside, Gilly heard Jenny say goodnight to the Jacksons and then he felt her hand gently touch his arm.

"Are you hurting?" he asked with a new note of concern in his voice as they walked to the buckboard.

"Yes, but it's not my butt! I realize it won't be easy taking care of three children ... and arguing with a man as stubborn as you!"

"I never intended to get so involved, Jenny. I'm a drifter; I haven't had a real home in almost 15 years!"

"I know, but you've found most of those men you were looking for, and now, me and the children are a bonus. We would like you to stay with us, in any capacity that you feel comfortable. I will accept your decision. It's a good reason for you to stay at the Half Moon."

"Actually Jenny, there ain't no more faces," he said softly, stopping at the wagon but continuing to hold her arm. He felt her catch her breath.

"I'm glad," she replied softly, desperately wanting to turn to him, yet knowing now wasn't the time. She released his arm, grasping the side of the wagon as the sliver of the moon slipped out from behind a wispy cloud. She knew he had to get the blankets from the barn so she waited as he sniffed the air and moved away. She could see his silhouette and smiled as his head swung left and right. Suddenly it was dark again and a familiar faint aroma touched her nostrils. Trying hard to identify the smell, she sat down with her back to the wagon wheel. Listening intently to the prairie night sounds, she tried to hear Gilly's movements, and then suddenly she heard him whisper from nearby and she almost screamed.

"Shh, don't make a sound!"

The mules were moving restlessly around the corral and somewhere out on the grassland a coyote called to its mate. Jenny shivered in the silence and then his whispered voice startled her again when he spoke from close range.

"Rest easy, girl. We had visitors but they were just passing by."

"Who?" Jenny whispered back, reaching to locate him as he crawled closer and finding his arm.

"Indians, now be still. I'll get the saddle and blankets."

Slipping from her grasp and making no sound, he faded away into the darkness again. Straining to hear, it took five minutes but she finally heard the familiar creak of his leather saddle.

"Can you see in the dark?" she asked. "You must be part Indian; don't you ever fall over things?"

"Shh!" he warned and she knew he was anxious.

Settling Jenny into her bedroll under the buckboard, Gilly sat with his back to the wheel listening and occasionally sniffing the air. It was almost dawn when she felt him move, alerted by her hand slipping from his coat which she must have held all night.

Streaks of daylight showed from behind the mountains as Jenny struggled out of her hiding place and gazed around the yard searching for him. Noises from the barn drew her attention and Gilly's shadowy figure appeared leading the pony by its reins.

"Are you going somewhere?" she asked when he arrived and collected his saddle and blankets from under the buckboard.

"I need to find the visitor we had last night," he announced as he threw the saddle on Blue. "Benji doesn't need any more surprise visitors."

"You said he was an Indian, he could be miles away by now."

"He was on foot, I'll find him."

"I need to help Della with breakfast and get the children ready for travelling. Are we leaving today?"

"No, we'll leave after breakfast tomorrow. You and William can sort out what we're taking, and remember, space is limited. It's a buckboard, not a full-size wagon."

Offering his arm, she declined and took his hand and wrapped it around her waist. Smiling up at him, she said softly, "I think that will give me a little more support."

They were met at the door by Della and the young children who were obviously excited.

"Good morning Mister Gilly, Miss Jenny," Benji greeted them, pushing past the women and children and blocking the doorway.

Squeezing in beside them, William looked alarmed when he noticed that Gilly's pony was saddled.

"Are you leaving sir?" he asked in a voice that portrayed his dismay.

"No boy, only going for a short ride," Gilly replied, kneeling down and taking the boy by the shoulders. "I'll be back around noon. I'm leaving you in charge of helping Miss Jenny with the little ones and getting the buggy packed for our trip tomorrow. Can you do that for me?"

"Yes sir!" exclaimed William, his frown changing to a broad grin.

Watching quietly, Benji shook his head in amazement. Gilly's new sensitive manner had completely won the boy over. He had no idea where the Canadian was going or why, but was sure Jenny would inform them over breakfast.

As suspected, Gilly had no trouble picking up the trail of the Indian. Following the faint tracks out onto the grassland, he saw where the lone walker had joined more Indians, smaller by their footprints, with an unshod horse and travois. *I'm following a family*, he thought, speeding up and following the easy-to-read trail.

Within an hour he had his quarry in sight and knew he'd also been seen when the taller Indian turned back to face him, rifle in hand. Slowing to a walk and keeping well out of rifle range, he opened his saddlebag and pulled out his torn white shirt, tying the arms around the barrel of his Winchester and raising it over his head. He slowly continued walking but breathed a sigh of relief when the Indian lowered his gun. Gilly was even more relieved to see he was an older man.

"Who are you?" Gilly asked augmenting his words with sign language. He was surprised when the native replied in good English.

"I Big Bear from Ute tribe ... take daughter and her children home."

"I'm Gilly, you passed the place where I stayed last night."

"We no steal anything," the old Indian's dark eyes flashed a warning. "You stay with black man."

"So you know the Jacksons?"

"No, I see them."

"Do you have food?"

"A little, we can't give you much."

"No, I don't need food. I want to give *you* food."

"We need," Big Bear growled, setting his rifle butt on the ground and sitting down on his heels.

"You go back to your family, I'll bring you some meat."

Swinging Blue toward the eastern hills, Gilly left at a gallop knowing that somewhere amongst the hills and hollows he was sure to find a deer. Racing toward the sloping timberline, he quickly spotted movement amongst the trees and using his years of training with Rube, soon had a deer in his rifle sights. Bringing it down with a single, well-placed shot, he took little time to load it over his saddle and headed back to locate the Indians.

Two riders were ahead of him as he came out of the timber. Half Moon ranchhands, he guessed, and they too were heading for the Indians, unaware Gilly was behind them. Slowing, Gilly eased his rifle out and kept careful watch on them. He could see they had drawn their handguns and when his rifle barked two rapid shots, they swung away.

Calmly dismounting, Gilly pulled the deer from his horse leaving it at Big Bear's feet as he reached out to shake the Indian's hand. "You ain't got any shells for that rifle have you, old man?" he said sharply.

"Used the last one 10 days ago."

"How do you expect to feed these folks, or defend 'em?" Gilly asked, turning back to unbuckle his saddlebag and reach inside. "I've got a few spare. There's only ten, I hope they'll get you where you're going."

He helped them load the deer meat onto the travois, then watched as they moved slowly off toward the mountains. He silently wished them well. Taking his spyglass out of his saddlebag, he scoured the plain for some sign of the cowboys. Finding none, he shrugged his shoulders in a gesture of unconcerned resignation, knowing they would have left a trail that would be easy to follow.

Thankfully, the cowboy's trail led him north back toward the Half Moon Ranch. Assuming they would not be bothering Big Bear and his daughter again, Gilly left their trail and rode hard for the Jackson's. A surprise awaited him as he rode into the yard and saw the buckboard now draped with the hoops and cover from the Hepple wagon. Boxes, trunks and bags littered the surrounding area and children's laughter emanated from under the wagon cover.

"Mr. Gilly's back," he heard William yell and saw four heads suddenly appear out of the back of the wagon, squealing a greeting. Tommy, in his eagerness, tipped over the backboard, landing in the dust at Gilly's feet.

"Did you find what you went looking for?" Jenny asked, smiling when Gilly nodded but offered no details as he scooped the four-year-old into his arms.

All afternoon they worked at turning the buckboard into a travelling home, sorting out clothes and necessities rescued from their own covered wagon. Unneeded supplies were left behind with a grateful Benji and Della. Benji had managed to finish repairing the broken harness and, by the fading light, the two men completed the preparations by attaching a small water barrel on the side of the wagon. Fatigue finally assisted the children to sleep after they had eaten supper and even Jenny expressed her desire to get an early night. As Gilly walked her outside, she told him about their day with the children, then asked him about his search for the Indian. She listened with interest when he told her what had happened.

"Did you see anyone else out there?" Jenny yawned, squeezing close to him as they sat with their backs to the buggy wheel.

"Just two cowboys some way out."

The answer seemed to satisfy the tired girl, who suddenly kissed him on the cheek and crawled underneath the buggy. She sighed a little as she rolled into her blankets, whispered 'good night' and immediately fell asleep. Making sure she was covered, Gilly climbed to his feet and sniffed the air.

Chapter 10

Dawn brought bedlam to the Jackson farm as Jenny tried to keep the children under control, making sure they were all washed, dressed and adequately fed before they left. They were almost ready when Gilly insisted they should go to visit their mother's grave and say their goodbyes, surprising everyone when he led the children in prayer, promising faithfully never to forget the heroic effort their mother had made to keep them together.

Warm sunshine bathed the Snake River Plains as Gilly led the buggy out of the Jackson's yard and onto the grasslands. The two mules made it easier than a horse to handle and Jenny was able to give William a turn with the reins. Riding out ahead, Gilly made sure the way was clear, finding places to camp while resting the mules. After five long days of travel, they saw their destination in the distance and Gilly assured them they would be at their new home early the following afternoon.

That evening, when the children had settled into bed and Jenny reluctantly agreed to stand watch, Gilly rode off to check out the ranch. They had seen no one and things seemed suspiciously quiet.

Kerry Walker, the blacksmith, had worked until dark and was now sitting in a patched-up rocking chair outside the stable doors, sipping on his daily glass of Red Eye Whisky and puffing contentedly on his pipe. When Gilly spoke close behind him, his heart skipped a beat.

"Where is everybody, Mr. Walker?"

"Damn you boy, didn't Rube teach you any manners?" the old horseman spluttered.

"Rube taught me self-preservation sir. Are you going to answer my question?"

"Harvey and most of the riders are gone, lad, rode out almost a week ago. He left Jess Ellis in charge."

"Jenny and the kids are camped half a day south of here. We should be back sometime tomorrow."

"What did you say?" the blacksmith gasped, grabbing his pipe before it slipped from his mouth. Jenny Louise is a cripple stuck forever in that blasted wheelchair and she ain't got no kids."

"She has now."

Noiselessly Gilly slipped away from the stables, leaving the old blacksmith talking to himself as he tried to make sense of Gilly's information. He made his way back to the camp, arriving long before daybreak and climbed into a nearby tree. A while later, he woke to see Jenny busy organizing the children as she yawned and hugged herself in the cold morning air. He smiled as he watched her gentle dedication to the young orphans and climbed down from the tree to light the fire.

Great excitement governed both Jenny's and the children's actions that morning as they were as eager to see Jenny's ranch as she was to be home. Only William could remember when they lived in a house like city folk. He had only brief memories of a father who worked long shifts on the docks before seeking a better life out West. Joining a large wagon train that spring, his dreams would only cause more heartbreak when he drowned crossing a river in Montana, and now another river had taken their mother.

Warm sunshine flooded the Snake River Plains as Gilly pointed out the house and the other buildings to his charges then he rode out ahead of the little, odd-looking, covered buggy.

"Who's driving that contraption?" Kerry Walker snorted when he came out of the stableblock to investigate the visitors.

"Jenny Louise Washington sir. Better hold onto that pipe, I think you're in for a shock."

"Shock, lad, what shock?" the stableman grumbled walking toward the buggy to watch. He stood speechless when first young William jumped over the side and helped Jenny climb down and stand upright; then he blinked in disbelief when Tommy and Vicky joined them, each taking one of Jenny's hands.

"Shall we eat in the cookhouse Gilly?" she asked with a grin. "Why don't you come too, Mr. Walker? I'm sure you have questions galore that you're dying to ask!"

"Goll dang it missy, yer walkin!" her stableman spluttered, "and who do these kids belong to?"

"They're ours, Mr. Walker," she exclaimed. "Gilly's and mine."

Whiskers, the cook, dropped an empty cooking pot on the floor with a crash when Gilly opened the door allowing the three youngsters to race into his domain. Jenny followed, shouting orders for the youngsters to sit quietly at the table. Gaping, Whiskers spluttered tobacco juice into his beard, shook his shaggy head and went to work producing plates with generous portions of apple pie and his own special sweet sauce. He grinned from ear-to-ear when he brought out a second pie, asking as he set it down on the table, "Where did ye find the yunguns?"

Jenny laughed at the old cook until tears ran down her face. She had never seen such confused expressions as her two old employees displayed.

"Where's Jess Ellis, Mr. Walters?"

"Out on the range; he left before dawn with two of the men."

"How many men have we left?" Gilly growled.

"Six old boys who won't go on a drive, a busted-up wrangler, and Jess."

"Hey, you're forgetting the red-bearded rider who came looking for a meal and Jess talked him into staying," Whiskers chuckled.

"Yeh," the stableman agreed. "I got the feeling this cowboy knew Gilly."

Jenny glanced up at Gilly and smiled, catching his sly wink.

"Why don't you take the youngsters over to the house while I try to explain what's happening and how we came to suddenly have three children," Gilly suggested.

All three children looked at Jenny expectantly and, when she nodded, they leapt from their seats and raced for the door. Letting his siblings run ahead, William turned back at the door and offered his arm to Jenny as he'd seen Gilly do.

Replenishing the coffee with a new steaming pot, Whiskers sat down at the table with Kerry and waited for Gilly to begin.

"We were only two days on the trail when a bushwhacker shot her. I think he was after me but didn't take the time to make sure of his target."

"How could he mistake a woman in a wheelchair for you?" the old stableman snorted. "It's more likely he were sent to kill you both."

"He got away?" Whiskers asked, dribbling coffee into his beard as he spoke.

"Yes, I had to take care of Jenny first and she needed a doctor."

"Well I heard you promise to look after her when you were arguing with Harvey before you left here, but I never thought they'd try to kill you."

"I never saw any bullet wounds in her," Whiskers mumbled. "Where the hell did they shoot her?"

"Across her back and down through her backside and leg."

"And you dressed the wound?" Kerry asked raising his eyebrows.

"Sure, there was no one else to do it at the moment!" Gilly replied, cocking a challenging eye at the oldtimer.

Questions were asked and answered as the two men struggled to comprehend all that had happened since Gilly first rode into their yard, showing surprise when he told them Frank Barlow was the bushwhacker and he'd killed him in the saloon at Fort Hall. He also told them of the rustlers driving Box T and Half Moon cattle with a Bill of Sale signed by Harvey Stubbs. Lastly, he described how he found the Hepple children and their mother in the river, mentioning how Jenny had agreed to honour the dying woman's wish and take care of the children. Climbing to his feet he asked his own pointed question.

"How many of the men left here are loyal to the Half Moon spread?"

"I know that Jess Ellis is one of Harvey's men, left here to keep an eye on things. He don't walk too good since you hip shot him," Kerry replied. "The rest are a bit long in the tooth but all good men. Redbeard's new so we don't know him yet."

"Are you planning to go after Harvey and the cattle drive?" Whiskers asked.

"I have no idea what she'll want to do. Jenny Louise Washington will be the one to make that decision," exclaimed Gilly.

Leaving the cookhouse, Gilly could hear the excited squealing of the children across the yard as they explored their new home. There was no sign of Jenny as he mounted the steps onto the wide verandah. Cautiously approaching the open door, he stared suspiciously into the huge living room and listened intently to the sudden silence. Suspecting an ambush, he sniffed the air, moving on down the passage as the faint aroma of Jenny and the children led him to his quarry. Knocking confidently on the door, he quickly stepped back into the room on the opposite side of the hallway.

"Nobody here!" Tommy shouted to the others

"Oh he's there Tommy," Jenny called. "You go find him son."

Gilly watched the little boy through the partly open door as he raised his head and sniffed the air before confidently pushing the door open where Gilly was hiding and then shouting over his shoulder as he took Gilly's hand.

"I found him Ma."

"Now that was smart," Jenny complimented the boy as he tugged on Gilly's hand, pulling him into the room. "How'd you find him so quick?"

"I sniffed him out!"

When the others stopped laughing, Gilly told the children to go play as he needed to talk to Jenny. "Harvey's taken most of the crew," he informed her. "Sounds like they're stealing the rest of your cattle and driving them north."

Sighing, Jenny glanced at the children. "Well I don't suppose we can do much about it; we don't have the riders to chase 'em down and I have the children to consider."

"What do ya want me to do about it?"

"Don't be silly, what can one man do against ten?"

"I can help," William volunteered, stepping back into the room.

"Oh no you can't!" Jenny countered, pulling him close. "You don't need to be concerned about Gilly, you have enough to look after with Vicki, Tommy and me!"

"We'll talk about it later," Gilly muttered, "but for now William can go for a ride with me. He might as well start learning."

Turning, he strode for the door, hearing Jenny whisper behind him, "Go on William, and don't let him out of your sight."

After talking to the old stableman, who saddled a quiet black mare for the boy, Gilly and William rode out of the yard. Swinging east across the open rangeland, they let the horses run for a while slowing to a walk when they spotted two of the ranchhands herding a small group of stock toward the ranch. "Stay behind me," Gilly instructed the boy as they rode toward the men.

"Where's the rest of the crew?" he asked as he studied the older men.

"Jess and Red are picking up strays on the Box T fenceline; Wilf and Dan are north of here doing the same. Are you working here now?" the older cowboy replied before spitting a stream of tobacco juice onto the ground.

"So you two must be Monty and Len?"

"Yeh, I'm Monty, he's Len and you're a gunslick she brought in."

"No mister, I ain't no gunhand but I sure know how and when to use one. Now you can just tell me where Harvey held the herd before he took off."

"About a mile over yonder." Monty pointed his hand to the north then shook his reins and moved off.

Leading the way, Gilly let Blue stretch his legs leaving William and his mount behind. He slowed to a walk when he saw the fresh hoof tracks in the dirt. Slipping out of the saddle, he was following the tracks as William rode up beside him.

"What are you looking at Mr. Gilly?"

"Come down here and take a look son," Gilly chuckled as the boy eagerly joined him. "See, this horse is walking."

"How do you know that?"

"Look how clear the print is. That foot was laid slowly onto the floor and picked up cleanly."

"Would it look different if he was running?" the boy asked intelligently.

"Yes, go look at my tracks. I rode up at a fast gallop, then you'll see the difference."

Staring at the ground, William walked back to where Gilly had ridden up to the ranchhands. He checked the tracks with a serious intensity then, reaching down, he traced the outline with his fingers.

"We could follow the men who took the cattle," the boy stated, glancing up at Gilly for confirmation.

"Yep we could, but what would we do when we found them?"

"Tell them we want the cattle back!" William snapped.

"And what if they wanted to keep 'em?"

The question puzzled the youngster as he struggled to climb back into the saddle.

"Can you find your way home from here?" Gilly asked.

"Yes sir. Do you want me to lead the way?"

Gilly nodded and the boy moved quickly ahead at a gallop then slowed to watch the ground as he followed the tracks back the way they had come. They caught up to Monty and Len and it was late in the afternoon when Jenny heard the horses arrive. William called to his sister and brother as he passed the house.

Daylight was fading fast when Jess Ellis and the other three riders rode into the yard, leaving their horses at the stable before heading noisily for the cookhouse as Gilly finished his meal in the house with Jenny and the children. Pushing his chair away from the table, Gilly rose shaking his head as William hopped off his chair intending to accompany him.

"Not this time Will," Gilly murmured gently. "I need you to stay here and take care of these three."

"What are you going to do?" Jenny asked nervously.

"Just talk woman. I'm going after those cattle tonight and I want to know who to leave here."

"And if I don't want you to go?"

"Won't make any difference; you know me better than that."

Leaving the ranchhouse with his gunbelt swinging in his hand, Gilly strolled unhurriedly toward the cookhouse, stopping for a moment to follow his habit of sniffing the air and to buckle his gun around his hips. Skirting the building, he moved toward the open back door and stopped to listen to the loud conversation coming from inside before stepping through the door.

"Are you afraid to use the front door, mister?" Jess Ellis commented sarcastically letting his right hand slip below the tabletop as Gilly appeared in the cookhouse's kitchen doorway.

"We've done this once before, ain't we mister?" Gilly commented. "And if you don't bring that hand back onto the table empty, you won't see another sunrise."

The Canadian's hand hovered menacingly over the butt of his Colt as he delivered his ultimatum with a cold, hard edge to his voice. The other men moved quickly out of the line of fire. Jake Curry's eyes held no hint of recognition for Gilly as he slowly pushed his chair away from the table. Tension was building when a huge butcher's knife thumped into the tabletop in front of Jess, causing his hidden hand to suddenly spring into sight.

"We've buried enough men from this outfit lad. If yer don't want to stay here, then saddle up and go 'cos I sure as hell don't want to dig another hole!" Whiskers' voice rasped from near the stove before shuffling over to the table to retrieve his knife.

"He doesn't have to go," Gilly hissed, "but I have to be sure he's a Half Moon rider."

"Some day you and me are going to tangle again mister," Jess snapped as he eased his stiff hip from the chair and stood facing Gilly. "You gave me this limp and I don't suppose Harvey will ever come back, so now I owe you both. I'll get my things and be gone within the hour if I get my pay."

"How much are you owed?"

"Ten dollars'll square me off."

Producing a billfold, Gilly dropped 10 dollars on the table and added, "That sets you free boy, be careful to take only what's yours."

Anger showed in Ellis's face as he rose, slamming his chair over as he limped out of the cookhouse and in the direction of the bunkhouse.

"What now?" the old blacksmith snapped. "You sure know how to get rid of men in a hurry kid."

"Now I want some dynamite, Mr. Walker."

"Yer going after Harvey, ain't yer?"

"Yes, Mr. Walker, we're going into battle."

"You can't do it on yer own. He's got at least 10 men with him, it's madness."

"Can you get me that dynamite?"

"How soon do yer want it?"

"Now, I'm leaving right after we settle things here."

Leaving the table, muttering to himself, Kerry followed Jess Ellis out of the door and headed across the yard to his stable area, intent on seeing that the ex-foreman took his own beat-up saddle and the horse he had rode in with. Using a lame horse as cover, he watched as Jess stormed

260

into the barn and threw his blanket and saddle on a good-looking bay gelding.

"Hey there, boy," Kerry revealed himself as he shuffled out of the stall. "That ain't yer pony."

"Stay out of my way, old man," the ranchhand hissed menacingly.

The old stableman blocked his way reaching for the bridle as the rider mounted, but he quickly felt the barrel of his Colt revolver across his head, falling in a heap on the floor as blood rushed down his face. Rapid hoofbeats leaving the yard caused the cookhouse conversation to pause.

"He seems to be in one hell of a hurry," Whiskers commented.

Hearing the hoofbeats, Jenny thought the same thing and quickly moved to a window in an effort to identify the rider, puzzling in her mind why someone would be leaving so late in the day.

William went out onto the verandah, looking toward the stableblock just as Kerry stumbled through the big doors. "Somebody's hurt Ma," he yelled through the open door before running out into the yard.

"William, come back here!" she screamed hurrying onto the verandah with Vicky and Tommy close behind.

Bursting into the cookhouse, the boy gasped out his message at Gilly then spun on his heel to race back to the house. Bounding after William, the men were quickly assisting Kerry into the lighted building.

"He'll live," Whiskers muttered as he took a quick look at the open wound, shuffling off to the kitchen to find his medical kit.

Following William back to the house, Gilly felt the full force of Jenny's anger as he walked into the room. "I know you're going after Harvey and the cattle," she snapped. "All we have for men are a broken-down bunch of old ranchhands, but you'll go anyway, won't you?"

"Yes ma'am and we'll bring the cattle back."

"Sit down, you mule head. We're a family now and with you out there chasing Harvey, who's going to protect me and the children?"

"I'll leave you two men."

"And what if none of them old coots want to go get killed with you?"

"Then you'll have lots of protection."

"You're stubborn as hell but just you remember mister, that there are four people waiting for you to come home—people you promised to take care of and who want you back." She angrily stifled the sob that welled up in her throat.

Walking back to the cookhouse, Gilly thought hard on Jenny's words. He knew little of the old ranchhand's capabilities except that Harvey had declined to take them along. Getting closer to the cookhouse, he could hear the fluent cursing of Kerry Walker and saw his bandaged head when he stepped through the door.

"Did you find the dynamite?" Gilly asked.

"Didn't have time before that mongrel belted me," the stableman muttered. "He stole one of our best geldings."

"Well, who wants to go after the cattle with me?"

Every head in the room nodded vigorously in agreement.

"Somebody will need to go after Jess Ellis, he might be out there just waiting to take pot shots at any of us," suggested Whiskers.

"I'll take care of him," Gilly hissed. "I need four men to follow the herd and three to stay here. Whiskers, Kerry and Jake can stay. The rest of you follow the herd and get ready to drive them back here where they belong."

"And you're going to fight Harvey's crew single-handed and bring the herd back to us?" the blacksmith snorted. "Don't be stupid kid, one man can't do that."

"Oh I won't be alone," Gilly said coldly, "Captain Dynamite's going to help me."

"That could work," Jake Curry chuckled. "That's the same thing you did at the Circle X when the Indians raided the horses."

"Almost," Gilly admitted, "but this time I can pick the place."

"You two know each other?" Kerry asked suspiciously cocking an eyebrow at the Canadian.

"We rode for an outfit on the Bitterroot Range," Gilly admitted sourly.

Darkness had settled over the Snake River rangelands when Gilly saddled Blue and gathered a bulging saddlebag of dynamite, tying it securely behind him. Walking his mount over to the house, he saw the single light and knew Jenny was waiting for him.

She was glad that the darkness hid her tears when she met him in the doorway and slipped into his arms. "Be careful, Gilly," she whispered, kissing him quickly. She felt his fingers squeeze her back and suddenly he was gone.

As dawn broke and the first rays of sunshine touched the distant mountaintops, Gilly sat on the edge of the holding ground where Harvey and his crew had held the Half Moon cattle. Hundreds of milling cattle had cut the grassland to dust and recent rain had left the surface ready to accept fresh imprints. Certain that Jess Ellis would follow the herd, now all he had to do was find fresh tracks.

Gilly's experienced eyes soon had him on the riders' trail and he moved more quickly, searching the land ahead. Somewhere out there he

262

guessed, there was a railhead and cattle buyers. By the end of the first day, he could see the dustball Jess was leaving behind him as he pushed his mount hard to catch the herd. It was now Gilly who left the trail riding a wide loop. He wanted to get ahead of Jess but remain undetected; surprise was the only ally he had.

On the second day he saw the dust against the rising sun. He was now riding level with the herd. That night Gilly could easily have killed the nightriders; the cattle were tired from being on the trail all day and were only too pleased to eat fresh grass and sleep. He rode all night until he was sure the herd was far behind him and he could openly ride for whatever town lay ahead. It was another day's ride when he spotted the railway line and heard the train whistle. There, for the first time, he saw the huge steam monster thundering along the ribbon of steel and knew it was time to turn the herd for home—time the battle began. Selecting a well hidden spot, he watched through his spyglass. The pointman had selected a good resting ground and he nodded his head when he saw the campfire burst into life, blocking the cattle from returning the way they had come. Clouds shrouded the moon and Gilly decided to move into action.

Leaving Blue ground-hitched and, taking a few sticks of dynamite tucked into his belt, he made his way silently around the perimeter of the herd. Lying in the grass, he heard the slow plod of the nightriders' mounts as they circled the herd, coming closer and closer. Hunched over in the saddle, this told him the rider was dozing and Gilly sprang into action. Using the butt of his rifle, he knocked the rider to the ground and caught the reins of his horse. Not a sound had left the rider's lips.

Gilly mounted and moved on, stopping often to listen; he could hear the cattle grinding their teeth in sleep. He went behind some trees and dismounted, ground-hitching the extra horse and removing the lariat. He fastened the loop around its saddlehorn and tied one stick of dynamite to the end of the rope. He removed two more sticks of explosive from his saddlebag and sat down on the ground to wait.

Light, misty rain began to wet the ground as the inky blackness slowly turned into dawn. Gilly was ready. He struck a match and lit the fuse on the dynamite tied to the lariat and slapped the horse's rump. The horse ran off with the lit dynamite stick bouncing erratically a distance behind. Next, he lit the fuse of the explosive lying at his feet and ran for his horse. The first blast was a resounding crash which brought the sleeping cattle to their feet, bellowing in alarm. The second explosion set them charging madly back toward the herders' night camp. Leaping onto

Blue, he followed the cattle, lighting another stick and hurling it into the air in front of him.

Two miles away on the back trail, Dan, Wilf, Monty and Len heard the explosions. Waking with startled expressions, they climbed out of their bedrolls and saddled quickly; they knew Gilly would need help.

Caught by surprise, Harvey Stubbs and his crew of rustlers woke to the deafening noise of a stampeding herd bearing down on them. Screams of trampled men shattered the morning air as Gilly urged the cattle on with more explosions. Dust and noise filled the air as Gilly sent Blue swinging far out from the herd. He pulled to a halt, jumped from the saddle with his rifle in one hand and spyglass in the other. Finding the herders' camp, he watched two mounted riders fighting their way out of the herd. Gilly's rifle barked and one of the riders disappeared under the pounding hoofs. Gilly lost sight of the second rider in the dust.

The sun came out in full force as the Half Moon riders saw the herd thundering toward them. Quickly taking cover, they waited, expecting a fight with some of Harvey's riders, but no one showed. The cattle had run all their energy off and were almost at a stop when Len yelled at his companions.

"Ain't that Gilly up there on the ridge?"

"Sure it is," Monty assured him. "He said all he wanted was for us to drive the cattle home. It looks like he's coming this way."

The old cowhands whooped with jubilation when Gilly arrived. "How did ya manage to run them off?" Wilf asked.

"Oh, they had an inconvenient stampede," Gilly muttered. "I want you all to ride back a couple of miles with me. We'll pick up the strays and check who's left at the camp. I want to know who got away."

Gathering strays all day, the cowboys worked hard pushing them into a sizable herd and, by late afternoon, they were back at the grizzly site of the night camp. The sight of human bodies trampled to death by a thousand stampeding hooves was not for the faint-hearted. Each one was identified and buried with the minimum of fuss and ceremony.

"That means two of them got away," Gilly hissed. "Can you boys take care of the cattle if I go after them?"

"There's three of 'em missing lad," Wilf growled.

"No, two," Gilly insisted. "I got the nightrider before I started the stampede."

"Well, I ain't seen Harvey or Billy amongst them bodies. They must have got away," Wilf muttered. "Are you going after them?"

"Sure, you wouldn't want me to disappoint Harvey, would ya?"

"I think Miss Jenny would rather yer didn't," Dan commented.

"I'm sure you're right oldtimer, but some things just have to be done. Maybe I'll catch up before you get back to the ranch."

Leaving the old ranchhands to work out their own schedule, Gilly rode away from the stampede area toward the northwest, his eyes alert for the tracks of two fast-running ponies. An hour later, luck was with him when the tracks swung back to the south and Gilly felt a chill run up his spine. The tracks were leading back toward the Half Moon range. Quickening his pace, but staying with the tracks, Gilly pushed on abandoning the tracking as darkness began to fall. He knew he'd have to ride all night and hope that somewhere out in the dark, he would pass Harvey and Billy undetected. The night mist, common on the plains, helped to refresh both horse and rider as they pushed on relentlessly.

Having crossed to the south side of the ranch during the night and, once more quickening his pace as dawn broke, Gilly asked for every ounce of strength in Blue's tired body. Neither of them had slept or eaten for two days when he saw the ranch buildings in the distance and whispered to his mount, "Ain't got far to go now Blue."

Shaking away the pain of tiredness as they approached from the south, he heard a shot come from the north side of the buildings. Mustering Blue's last ounce of energy, Gilly charged, then dropped out of the saddle clutching his rifle as he came level with the house. He was snake crawling his way around the perimeter as Whiskers came running out of the cookhouse waving a shotgun, then ducked across the yard into the horse barn.

"That's Gilly's pony," he growled at the stableman, as Blue staggered into the barn and made his way to an empty stall. "Is he back?"

"How the hell do I know?" Kerry snapped. "I don't even know who's shooting at us yet."

Gilly could hear Jenny shouting at the children and saw a rifle barrel poking through the kitchen window. A noise near the water barrel at the corner of the cookhouse drew his attention. Rolling over into a better position, he drew a bead on the barrel and waited. Suddenly two shots rang out, one from the intruder behind the barrel and one from the cookhouse window. Gilly's rifle barked twice and a scream from behind the water barrel told him the man had been hit.

Moving to a better position, Gilly focused his attention on the cookhouse, waiting for some slight indication of the shooter. Jenny's rifle boomed from behind him, sending splinters of wood leaping from the cookhouse window. Suddenly a horse and rider raced away from behind the building and the cowboy behind the barrel leapt into view in an obvious attempt to follow. Two shotguns roared from the barn doorway and, almost instantly, the cowboy behind the barrel flew into the air caught between the two shells.

Easing onto his feet, Gilly moved quickly to catch sight of the fleeing rider, and yelled down to the stableman, "Saddle me a good horse, Mr. Walker!" before hurrying toward the house.

He heard Jenny's voice echo down the hallway as he stepped cautiously through the back door. "Don't come any closer mister, or I'll blow your innards out!"

"I thought you wanted me to come home," Gilly shouted back, standing quite still.

"It's Gilly!" William's excited voice squealed as his footsteps came running down the hall and leapt into the cowboy's outstretched arms.

"We were scared to death," Jenny murmured, trying to wipe the tears that had began to stream down her face. "I didn't know you were home."

"I just got here as the shooting started," Gilly admitted, looking at her with sorry eyes as he set William on the floor and lifted Vicky, gently hugging her before also setting her back on the floor. Then dropping on one knee, he held his arms out to Tommy. The little boy held tightly to Jenny's hand and stated through quivering lips, "I won't let you hurt my ma!"

"He won't hurt us honey," Jenny whispered, picking up Tommy and moving toward Gilly.

He wrapped his arms around them both and sighed. "The herd's on its way back. They should be here in four or five days," he murmured. "Harvey Stubbs was the man shooting at you and he got away. I have to go after him; you know that. We don't need him planning any more devilment for the Half Moon."

There was no objection as she lowered Tommy onto the floor to join his siblings, then again wrapped her arms around Gilly. Burying her head in his chest, her body began to shake as she wept. Gilly hugged her quickly, kissing the top of her head.

"Jenny Louise Washington, you're the only person I would ever consider spending the rest of my life with. We have a family to raise, so dry your tears and get ready to put this ranch in order when I return."

She wiped her tears on his shirt and, trying hard to smile, gasped, "Don't you dare forget to come back Mr. Thompson!" Then trying not to cry again as she watched him go, she whispered, "I love you Gilly."

Walking quickly across the yard, he saw Whiskers standing over the dead cowboy as Kerry came out of the barn leading a good-looking bay pony carrying his own scruffy saddle.

"Where did ya leave the boys?" the old stableman asked him suspiciously.

"They're bringing the herd in. They should be home in four or five days. Where's Red?" Gilly walked over to the water trough and filled his bottle from the tap.

"They caught him in the open. Harvey plugged him with a rifle shot. That's how Whiskers and me knew they were here. I only knew you were back when that blue pony of yours ran into the barn."

Gilly swung into the saddle and turned to face the two trusted old ranchhands. "Take care of things for me boys. That girl and those kids are very special to me."

As he passed the house, he waved his hat to Jenny and the youngsters on the verandah, then swinging into a canter, he headed for the last place he'd seen Harvey Stubbs. Harvey's fresh tracks were easy to follow, though Gilly knew he had to be alert. Leading straight out onto the grassland, he surmised that Harvey would wait until after dark before making any change in direction.

Fading light brought Gilly to a halt. Sliding from his saddle, he sat in the dark watching around him for the flicker of light from a campfire as he ate some dried deer meat and washed it down with water. *Maybe you ain't as smart as you think you are Harvey*, he thought as a plan formed in his brain.

Fumbling in the dark, he gathered enough dry material to light a fire, carrying it well away from his mount before lighting it. Then he ran quickly out of the fire's glow, mounted and moved farther away, sitting like a statue in the dark.

Almost a mile away, Harvey Stubbs was watching over his back trail when he saw the fire erupt on the flatland and guessed that Gilly was attempting to lay a trap for him. Suddenly, a noise in the darkness caused an instant nervous reaction and he jerked his horse around.

Gilly grinned silently to himself as he lay with his ear to the ground. He had heard the horse's hooves from nearly a mile away and now pinpointed the general direction in the dark.

All night long Gilly walked slowly toward that last sound despite knowing his quarry would have also been on the move. A slight breeze from the west now rustled the trees and scrub and, not to be fooled by the silence of the grasslands, Gilly selected a tree for his night's sleep and took the horse some distance away where he ground-hitched him. The grove of trees was up against some rocks and close enough to whistle for him if needed.

Gilly went back to where he'd selected a tree and climbed into it. Sniffing the air, he hunkered down and prepared to wait for the dawn

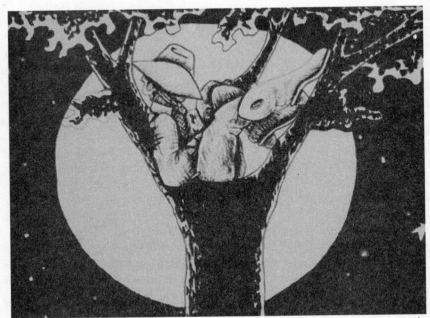

ever-aware that the moon was rising and he needed to be even more alert. A while later, a coyote howled and some prairie birds lifted noisily into the dark sky. Gilly's eyes warily opened; he knew that something was nearby, moving silently closer. Dropping silently to the ground, he crawled back toward his horse and climbed another tree listening for the direction of the birds until dawn.

From his elevated position, he watched the sun's rays inch upward until he could see far out onto the grassland. A distant movement caught his eye as a jack rabbit raised his head out of the grass. Grinning to himself, Gilly climbed out of the branches and pressed his ear to the ground, jerking suddenly upright when he heard the sound of a fast-running horse coming closer. Going over to his horse, he grasped the reins, picked up his Winchester and mounted, to silently wait.

Suddenly a shot crashed through the morning stillness and Gilly's head swung around as a riderless pony tore past. Making no attempt to stop the runaway mount, he watched for the shooter to reveal himself. Fifteen minutes he waited, sitting alert in the saddle for the slightest sound or movement. Then, moving slowly out from the cover of the trees, he bent low in the saddle following the route of the riderless pony back the way it had come. He was almost sure the shooter had gone but he remained alert. Five minutes later he saw the crumpled form lying in the grass and shook some urgency into his mount.

Using caution, Gilly dismounted. He could hear the words of Rube in his head as he approached the man's back. *Make sure they know you're a friend before disturbing someone.* It was good advice. He had dropped onto his knees ready to examine the rider when the body rolled over and Gilly found himself staring down the barrel of a cocked 45. The man's arm and face was covered with blood.

"Easy mister," Gilly hissed, "how bad are you hurt?"

"Why the hell did ya shoot me?" he groaned angrily.

"I didn't, I think that bullet was meant for me. We need to get you to a doctor."

Groaning again, the cowboy let the revolver slip from his hand as he clutched his wounded chest and slipped into unconsciousness. Cursing under his breath, Gilly removed the gun and turned the wounded cowboy over, scowling fiercely when he saw the gaping wound oozing blood through the cowboy's fingers.

"Who are you?" Gilly asked but received no reply.

Sadly shaking his head as he mounted, Gilly raced after the cowboy's mount. He was following at speed when he suddenly saw a mounted rider up ahead with a rope on the runaway pony.

"Is this your hoss, mister?" the young rider asked suspiciously as Gilly rode up to him.

"No it ain't, but the rider's been bushwhacked and I need to get him to a doctor, if he's still alive."

"Do ya know him?"

"No, but the brand on that pony might tell us where he's from."

"It's the Two River brand, I'll go with you."

Riding together, the two young men were quickly back to the cowboy. Realizing he had died, they loaded his body on the pony.

"Where is this Two River spread?" Gilly asked.

"Five miles north of here, but who are you? That's a Half Moon brand pony you're riding from the Washington ranch on Snake River Plateau."

"Gilly Thompson from the Half Moon, and you?"

"George Arthur, we're neighbours to the Johnson's Two River Ranch, and no, I don't know the dead guy."

"Did you come from home today?"

"No, I've been out here for a week."

"Have you seen anybody else?"

"No, I heard a few shots but you're the only one I've seen. Are you chasing somebody?"

"Yes, Harvey Stubbs."

"Harvey runs the Washington ranch for the crippled girl."

"He tried to kill her."

"Are you the law?"

"Judge, jury and executioner when I catch up with him!" Gilly retorted.

It was long after dark when the two cowboys rode openly into the yard of Ben Johnson's Two River Ranch, tying the horses at the cookhouse hitching rail and easing their cramped limbs beneath the dim light of an oil lamp before entering.

"Go right on in, boys," a deep voice chuckled in the darkness. "I've got a loaded shotgun pointing right at yer backs."

"Go to hell, Sammy," George Arthur snapped. "We're hungry so why don't you feed us." He stood for a moment to adjust his eyes to the light and allow the occupants to recognize him.

"What the hell are you doing here, George?" the grizzled old cook hissed as he heaped food on two large plates. "You're a long way from home."

"We brought one of your riders in. He was bushwhacked on the southern range this morning."

"Must be Rolly," piped up one of the other cowboys, moving quickly toward the door and disappearing outside to check the body.

"You found him George?" someone else asked.

"No Gilly found him. I just happened to be in the area and caught his runaway horse."

"You're Gilly," the cook murmured staring hard at him. "Who you riding for?"

"Jenny Washington on the Half Moon spread."

"Your boss was through here earlier today," said the cook, moving closer and watching Gilly's reaction.

"Did he say where he was heading?" Gilly asked, locking his eyes on the cook.

"Canada, but he lied. Can I see that gun you're carrying boy?"

"Why?"

"Because I think you're carrying Rube Caster's gun and that can only mean you're Rube's boy. Are you?"

"Yes I am and I'll be moving on at dawn. Can you tell me what Harvey's riding now?"

"I can," the man who had challenged them outside hissed. "He's riding a black gelding with a half-white face."

"Are you the stableman?"

The man nodded.

"Are all your Two River horses shoed with a bar across the shoe?" asked Gilly.

"Every one of them. You should have no trouble tracking that horse, but why are you chasing your ranch boss?"

"He shot Jenny Washington ... at least, he ordered it."

"She's dead?"

"No, and she ain't in a wheelchair no more either and she's got three kids."

"Now that's impossible. I've known that girl all her life and she was in a wheelchair two years ago. She couldn't have three children, there hasn't been time and we would have heard if she were married."

"I didn't say she were married," Gilly grinned. "I said she had three children. Now tell me, cooky, how did you know Rube?"

"I was a barman in Placerville when he was sheriff. I'd know that black Colt anywhere."

George pushed his empty plate away and rolled himself a smoke. "Would you like some company tomorrow Gilly?" he asked quietly. "I know this country and now we have a score to settle with Mr. Stubbs."

"No George, I'd rather you stayed here. If you got hurt, I'd feel right responsible."

"He's right," cook commented. "You're a cowboy, not a gunfighter George. You should leave it to an expert like I suspect Gilly here is."

"I'm going," George insisted stubbornly. "Where was he when you last saw him, Sammy?"

"He was riding out north from here, waved his hat as he passed the big rock next to the stand of trees."

"Anything else you can tell us about that horse?" Gilly asked. "Has he got a peculiar gait or anything that would point us to his tracks."

Scratching his head, Sam looked puzzled and muttered something unintelligible before admitting, "Well, now you mention it son, that gelding turns his near front foot when he stops and starts. It's not a fault, just a bad habit ... and you can sleep in the stable tonight."

"Thanks Sam," Gilly nodded, noting that George was still watching him intently.

Leaving the cookhouse, the cowboys now moved slowly toward their bunkhouse, talking quietly about the news Gilly had brought to their attention. Finally, Gilly, Sam and the cook stood alone.

"You ain't taking George are yer?" cook muttered, lighting his pipe, then coughing. "Rube always worked alone."

"How well did you know the old man?" Gilly asked.

"Well enough to know ya act just like him. You've met me before son, but you were just a skinny kid then."

"I'm still a skinny kid."

"Is he still alive?"

"No I buried him in the Canadian mountains at the start of spring."

"Then how come you're at the Washington ranch?"

"Searching for a shadow."

"I bet them shadows wore guns too."

Turning away, Gilly went back into the cookhouse. Pouring another cup of coffee, he waited for the cook and requested a bag of jerky beef.

"You're planning to leave early, ain't yer son?"

Taking his bag of dried food, he turned on his heel and left another of cook's questions unanswered as he headed for the door, striding unhurriedly toward the stable. The smell of Sam's pipe told him the old stableman was nearby, no doubt watching him. Quickly saddling his mount and stowing his food away, he stepped into the saddle and walked across the yard. Minutes later, he reached the stand of trees, where Sam had last seen Harvey.

Chapter 11

Dawn was just breaking when Gilly slipped down from his tree and began his slow methodical examination of the rain-soaked soil. Quickly finding the sought after hoofprints, he examined the direction of the tracks. Climbing into the saddle, he followed them at an easy clip until about a mile away the tracks turned due west, cutting along the base of the mountains and through a fast-running creek. He guessed Harvey had stopped for a drink here, leaving his footprints at the soft muddy edge. He wasn't being very cautious and Gilly wondered why, growing suspicious.

Late in the afternoon, he stopped to sniff the air and his sensitive nose picked up the smell of people and smoke. Continuing cautiously as the smells grew stronger, he saw smoke rising and realized there was a town ahead. Swinging wide, Gilly let his horse run hard until he had circled around the town, then turning, he rode down main street. He examined the buildings, noting the position of the livery stable, rooming house, several stores and the two saloons. It was then that several of the horses at a saloon hitching rail turned to look his way and he saw the half-white face of the Two River Ranch mount. He also became aware that the rifleman on the verandah had moved inside.

A lookout, Gilly thought, ducking quickly down an alley and dismounting. Standing for a moment, he began walking back to the corner of the alley. He needed to get across the street but the rifle-toting lookout was back. Returning to the alley, he looked along the back lane and grinned when he saw the cow in a tiny corral. It took him only minutes to release the docile animal, driving it up the alley and out into the main street.

"There you are," he growled quietly to himself, "that should keep your attention for a few minutes."

Mounting again, Gilly completed his manoeuvre by riding slowly down the back lane, past the back door of the saloon and crossing the street unnoticed from an alley. Tying the horse out of sight, he slipped his rifle from its scabbard and began a slow walk along the rickety boardwalk. A storekeeper watching the cow wandering in the street, nodded amiably as he passed. Suddenly the lookout dashed into the street, shading his eyes as he stared off to the south.

Gilly watched with growing interest. *Maybe I'm not the object of his attention.* Standing still with his back to the wall, he waited as a fast-approaching rider entered town. Almost immediately a shot echoed along the street. He saw the rider jerk to one side, slipping from the saddle as the horse came to a stop. Gilly raised his rifle, lining up on the shooter above. His shot startled the storekeeper, sending him hurrying back to his store as the man on the balcony screamed in pain and disappeared inside.

What the devil's going on here?" Gilly wondered keeping his eyes on the saloon.

Hearing a horse move, he realized that the injured rider had mounted again and was slowly continuing into town. The way he sagged in the saddle told Gilly he'd been shot, but them he suddenly realized there was something strangely familiar about this rider. Gilly let his eyes wander over the dusty figure, noting the cork bottle stoppers dangling from his hat on strings. Searching deep into his memory, he could hear Rube talking of a hermit that wore such a hat—a man who wore moccasins and homemade buckskins. Gilly moved to the edge of the boardwalk to show himself as the rider came closer. He noted the dark, tanned face and dirty, grey beard beneath the odd-looking hat and suddenly a name jumped into his mind.

"Corky Turner!" he whispered.

"They burned me cabin," the old man muttered hoarsely as his eyes met Gilly's searching gaze.

"You've been hit," Gilly observed, watching the dark stain soaking through the buckskin shirt. "Who are you after with that old rifle, Mr. Turner?"

Gilly's use of his name made the old man's head swing to take a closer look at the young cowboy.

"You know me, boy?" he hissed menacingly, tilting his rifle barrel onto Gilly.

"Rube told me about you years ago. I recognized your hat first."

"Is Rube here?"

"No sir, I buried him in the Rocky Mountains last spring."

"You're Gilly."

"Yes sir."

"You can bury me in the mountains too boy, when this is over."

"Wait, you don't stand a chance with that old rifle and I've got a little business in there with the man who rode in on the white-faced pony, so maybe we should do this together."

"The men on them other four ponies are mine," Corky hissed. "They thought I was in the cabin when they burnt it down. I been following ther tracks for a week."

"I think there's only three of 'em left. I wounded the one who shot you. If you stay here, I'll go in the back way. When you think I'm ready, just send a couple of shots through the front door. That'll get their attention."

"Steady lad, I hope yer as good as Rube was with that gun 'cos ther might be others in ther."

"Well, if anybody comes out this way, you can shoot 'em!"

A few minutes later, Gilly stood outside the back door of the saloon waiting to hear Corky's warning shots. Suddenly the old man began blasting away, creating pandemonium inside the bar. Two men, obviously not cowboys, came tearing through the back door, almost bowling Gilly over as they ran up the back alley. Gilly stepped inside, unnoticed, and saw Harvey standing with his back to the bar. He was calmly holding a drink in one hand and his Colt in the other—the barman was kneeling behind the bar, shotgun at the ready.

All hell broke loose when someone noticed Gilly and threw a quick shot his way and Rube Caster's gun began belching flames and death. Harvey Stubbs collapsed against the bar as he turned to face the danger and died without hearing the barman's shotgun roar. Gilly felt the sting of shotgun lead before he downed the barman and turned his attention to two other cowboys firing his way. Suddenly all was quiet as gunsmoke haze filled the room and a voice cut nervously into the silence.

"We ain't no part of this, mister."

"Then go," Gilly replied flatly, "but use the front door. There's an old man out there that wants to look you over."

"Oh no, I ain't going out there," one of the gamblers whined.

"Yes, you are," Gilly's voice murmured threateningly, as he slipped fresh bullets into the chamber of his handgun and fired a shot toward him. "You're all walking out into the street or you're going to die right here; the choice is yours mister."

Nervously pushing the doors open, the first of the men walked slowly out into the street, slowing only for a moment as Corky Turner scrutinized them before waving them toward the watching townspeople. Suddenly the old mountain man's rifle boomed and a man trying to sneak off toward the crowd staggered sideways and fell with his sidearm only half drawn. Two other men tried to turn back into the saloon, stopping short when Gilly blocked their way. Desperation showed on the men's faces as they went for their guns and Gilly calmly cut them down.

"Thank yer lad," Old Corky muttered, settling slowly across his horse's neck as Gilly quickly walked over to him.

"We need a doctor," he said loudly, going to help the old man off his horse.

"I'm as good as you'll get in this town son. Bring him over to the forge," the blacksmith growled.

With little choice, Gilly helped Corky back onto his feet, following the blacksmith. A knife removed the blood-soaked shirt as the blacksmith heated an iron.

"Hold him, boy," the smithy growled.

"Get on with it," Gilly snapped, "he won't move."

The stink of searing flesh suddenly filled the air and Corky lapsed into unconsciousness. Gilly used Corky's shirt to wipe the blood away from the roughly cauterized wound.

"If he survives my doctoring he'll live," the blacksmith chuckled coldly, "but now what you going to do with him?"

"Take him home with me."

"Where's that?"

"The Half Moon Ranch."

"Ain't that a fair way south of here? Hell boy, that old man wouldn't last a mile on horseback."

"He'll get there," Gilly mumbled, stubbornly adjusting the blanket covering the old man. "I'm going to eat; you'll watch him for me?"

"Oh, he ain't about to go nowhere!"

Smiling ruefully, Gilly moved off into the street and headed toward a sign that said, *Two Pistol Saloon*, easing the tie down from his Colt before stepping through the doors. Men and range workers glanced nervously his way as he found an empty table and settled into a seat, giving his order before letting his eyes wander slowly over the occupants. No conversation was offered or any expected. These men would be glad when he left their town.

Returning to the blacksmith's after eating, he inquired if there was any chance of buying a buggy in town.

"Are you really going to take that old man with you?" the blacksmith growled, glancing at Gilly over his anvil.

"Ain't got no choice mister," Gilly replied flatly. "Who else gives a damn about him?"

"Why do you care?"

"Because he needs help."

"It's pretty simple in your eyes, ain't it son, and damnit I believe you. You can take my buggy."

"Thanks, I'll make sure you get it back sir, I'll be leaving in the morning after I scare up some grub for the trail."

It was two weeks later when Jenny was alerted by a ranchhand that a buggy and rider were only a day away and moving directly toward them. There had been no news of Gilly since he'd left and the ranch was still in a state of tension. They had no idea that Harvey Stubbs was dead.

Corky Turner had shown an amazing aptitude for healing and was now sitting on the floor of the buckboard. Grumbling constantly, he peered out at the surrounding landscape.

"You promised to take me back to the mountains," he muttered.

"No I didn't," Gilly growled. "You told me to bury you there."

"Well this ain't the mountains kid, or hadn't ya noticed?" Corky replied.

"Yep I know, and you ain't dead yet, are ya old man? So why don't you stop grumbling."

Back at the ranchhouse, William had coaxed Kerry Walker to saddle his pony and was riding toward the house when Jenny saw him.

"What do you think you're going to do young man?" Jenny shouted at the 10-year-old.

"I'm going to check on who's coming in," the boy said confidently. "I think it's Gilly."

"And if it ain't?"

"Then I'll come back and tell you."

"Just that simple, is it Will, but what will you do if they won't let you come back?"

Jenny watched as the boy pondered the question and slowly slid from his pony's saddle, hanging his head as he tied the reins to the hitching rail and walked dejectedly up the steps to the verandah.

"We need you here son," Jenny murmured, reaching out to pull him closer. "Who's going to protect us if you go riding off?"

Kerry Walker, keeping an eye on the boy, arrived at the verandah and heard the end of their conversation. "You think that's Gilly out there don't you boy? Well, let me show you a way to check it out." He looked up at Jenny and she nodded.

Limping back to the stable, he led Blue outside and walked him back to the house. Jenny and the children patiently waited until the old man returned and suddenly turned the blue-grey loose.

"Go find Gilly boy!" he shouted, whacking him gently on the rump.

They watched spellbound as Blue turned to face north, raised its head to smell the air and screaming savagely tore out onto the grassland.

"Ah reckon the boy can go meet that buggy now, Miss Washington. That horse knows it's Gilly."

"Go on Will, go bring him home son; you two children," Jenny said emotionally, giving them all a little push.

Covering her mouth with her hands, she held back her tears and stood watching as first William and then Tommy and Vicki ran off the verandah screaming. She smiled joyously as the little ones chased after Blue yelling Gilly's name. William ran to his pony and could not mount fast enough. He turned it around to face the oncoming buggy and galloped wildly out of the yard.

THE END

For more books by these authors, visit:

JRobertWhittle.com